BEL-AMI

GUY DE MAUPASSANT was born of upper-middle-class parents in Normandy in 1850. After the failure of his parents' marriage he lived with his mother at Étretat, a newly fashionable seaside resort. Having enrolled as a law student in 1869, he was called up after the outbreak of the Franco-Prussian War in 1870 and served as a quartermaster's clerk in Rouen. Following the war he left the army and eventually secured a post as a minor civil servant. His favourite pastimes included boating, especially at Argenteuil on the Seine, which was also a favourite haunt of the Impressionists. Flaubert, whom he knew through his mother, encouraged his literary activities and shaped both his style and his pessimistic outlook on life. Through Flaubert he came to know the leading figures in Parisian cultural life, notably Émile Zola, who recruited him to his new 'Naturalist' school of writing. 'Boule de Suif', his short story about a prostitute during the Franco-Prussian War, was hailed as a masterpiece by both Flaubert and the reading public. A leading figure in fashionable society and artistic circles, Maupassant wrote prolifically and was soon the bestselling author in France after Zola. During the following decade he wrote nearly 300 stories, 200 newspaper articles, six novels, and three travel books. He earned substantial sums of money, which he spent on yachts, women, travel, and houses, and on his mother, and his younger brother Hervé, who eventually died insane in an asylum in Lyons in 1889. Despite his enthusiasm for outdoor pursuits, Maupassant's own health had never been good. A nervous disorder possibly inherited from his mother was compounded by syphilis, contracted in 1876, and he consulted numerous doctors in the course of his short life. On New Year's Day 1892 he attempted suicide with a paper-knife and was removed to the clinic of Dr Blanche at Passy, suffering from the syphilitic paresis, or general paralysis, which had driven him mad. He died on 6 July 1893 at the age of 42.

MARGARET MAULDON has worked as a translator since 1987. For Oxford World's Classics she has translated Zola's *L'Assommoir*, Stendhal's *The Charterhouse of Parma*, Huysmans's *Against Nature* (winner of the Scott Moncrieff Prize for translation, 1999), Constant's *Adolphe*, Flaubert's *Madame Bovary*, and Diderot's *Rameau's Nephew*.

ROBERT LETHBRIDGE is Master of Fitzwilliam College, Cambridge and Emeritus Professor of French Language and Literature at the University of London. He is the author of *Maupassant: 'Pierre et Jean'* (Grant & Cutler, 1984) and co-editor of *Zola and the Craft of Fiction* (Leicester, 1994), *Maupassant conteur et romancier* (Durham, 1994), and *Artistic Relations. Literature and the Visual Arts in Nineteenth-Century France* (New Haven, 1994). For Oxford World's Classics he has edited Zola's *L'Assommoir* (1995) and *La Débâcle* (2000), and Maupassant's *Pierre et Jean* (2001).

OXFORD WORLD'S CLASSICS

For over 100 years Oxford World's Classics have brought readers closer to the world's great literature. Now with over 700 titles—from the 4,000-year-old myths of Mesopotamia to the twentieth century's greatest novels—the series makes available lesser-known as well as celebrated writing.

The pocket-sized hardbacks of the early years contained introductions by Virginia Woolf, T. S. Eliot, Graham Greene, and other literary figures which enriched the experience of reading. Today the series is recognized for its fine scholarship and reliability in texts that span world literature, drama and poetry, religion, philosophy and politics. Each edition includes perceptive commentary and essential background information to meet the changing needs of readers.

OXFORD WORLD'S CLASSICS

GUY DE MAUPASSANT

Bel-Ami

Translated by
MARGARET MAULDON
With an Introduction and Notes by
ROBERT LETHBRIDGE

OXFORD
UNIVERSITY PRESS

OXFORD
UNIVERSITY PRESS

Great Clarendon Street, Oxford OX2 6DP

Oxford University Press is a department of the University of Oxford.
It furthers the University's objective of excellence in research, scholarship,
and education by publishing worldwide in

Oxford New York

Athens Auckland Bangkok Bogotá Buenos Aires Calcutta
Cape Town Chennai Dar es Salaam Delhi Florence Hong Kong Istanbul
Karachi Kuala Lumpur Madrid Melbourne Mexico City Mumbai
Nairobi Paris São Paulo Shanghai Singapore Taipei Tokyo Toronto Warsaw

with associated companies in Berlin Ibadan

Oxford is a registered trade mark of Oxford University Press
in the UK and in certain other countries

Published in the United States
by Oxford University Press Inc., New York

Translation © Margaret Mauldon 2001
Editorial matter © Robert Lethbridge 2001

British Library Cataloguing in Publication Data

Data available

Library of Congress Cataloging in Publication Data

Data available

ISBN 978-0-19-955393-8

5

Typeset in Ehrhardt
by RefineCatch Limited, Bungay, Suffolk
Printed in Great Britain by
Clays Ltd, St Ives plc

CONTENTS

INTRODUCTION

Bel-Ami is a novel about money, sex and power. As such, one dimension of its modernity is the sense in which the reader feels that it explores the dynamics of an urban society uncomfortably close to our own. For Maupassant depicts the relationship between politics and the press not as the mere backdrop to an individual's fictional biography; instead, that context is integral to both personal destinies and an entire social world dominated by ferocious self-interest and prostituted values. It is almost jolting to note that *Bel-Ami* was published as long ago as 1885. For only the novel's specific historical references and its evocation of a Paris of horse-drawn carriages, gas lights, and the contemporary sites immortalized by the Impressionists remind us that *Bel-Ami* is in fact firmly located in the early 1880s. Indeed, the text also enjoys the status of an authentic record of the apotheosis of bourgeois capitalism under the Third Republic. So rigorously has Maupassant adhered to the imperatives of verisimilitude that 'rarely', wrote Ferdinand Brunetière (1849–1906), the leading critic of the day, 'has a novel so closely mirrored reality'. Such a creative tension between its analysis of modern behaviour and its identifiably late-nineteenth-century fabric is one of the reasons why *Bel-Ami* remains one of the finest French novels of its time as well as being recognized as Maupassant's greatest achievement as a novelist.

Maupassant the novelist

Maupassant has a formidable reputation as a short-story writer, not least for an Anglo-Saxon public always more receptive than the French to that genre. To some readers, it comes as a considerable surprise to learn that Maupassant wrote novels at all, let alone that Tolstoy hailed his first extended fiction, *Une vie* (1883) as the greatest French novel since Hugo's *Les Misérables* (1862). Yet Maupassant himself was anxious to demonstrate the importance of his work as a novelist. Not long before his death in 1893, at the age of 42, he calculated that the sales of his novels in fact outnumbered those of his *contes* and *nouvelles*; and he could claim, with some justification, that, second only to Zola, he was the most commercially successful novelist of his generation. What is more, the decade 1880–90, which is the most productive period of Maupassant's career, saw him gradually moving away from the short-story form, particularly after the success of *Bel-Ami* itself. The appearance, in rapid succession thereafter, of *Mont-Oriol* (1887), *Pierre et Jean* (1888), *Fort comme la mort* (1889), and *Notre cœur* (1890), together with the steadily decreasing number of published short stories, makes it clear that the genre in which Maupassant had originally established his reputation with 'Boule de suif' (1880) was being relegated to a secondary activity.

Paradoxically, this change of direction was partly inspired by the very admiration his stories had provoked, and can be seen as a challenge to the implications of the disparity between the talent of the author and the inherent limitations of an essentially journalistic medium. Growing critical impatience to see him undertake substantial projects merely confirmed Maupassant's awareness that the novel was the privileged contemporary form. For example, while the nine volumes of short stories Maupassant published between 1884 and 1886 were hardly noticed, the discussion generated by Zola's *L'Assommoir* in 1877 provided the spectacular proof that the novel was the genre in which the serious writer could make his fame and fortune. And that same year saw the difficult beginnings of Maupassant the novelist, an ambition so deeply held that, by 1891, he could confide to a colleague that he intended never again to write a short story, reserving all his creative energies for his mature fiction. With its extended genesis (1877–83), its stitching together of earlier texts, its Norman setting during a thirty-year span beginning in 1819 and its story of private failure, that first novel, *Une vie*, could not be more different from *Bel-Ami*. Maupassant wrote the latter in the space of nine months, starting it in the summer of 1884 and finishing it by the end of February 1885, thereby testifying to a new-found fluency and confidence. This was repaid in the shape of an instant as well as durable commercial success: 13,000 copies of the book were snapped up when it appeared in volume form on 22 May 1885; within two years, it had reached its fifty-first edition (i.e. sales of over 50,000).[1] In spite of many differences, *Bel-Ami* also bears witness, of course, to

---

[1] Its continuing popularity has not been harmed by cinematic versions of the novel, notably Albert Lewin's stylish *The Private Affairs of Bel-Ami* (1947); nor by the equally stylish Hotel Bel-Ami, recently opened on the Left Bank (*The Times*, 12 May 2000).

the same pessimistic vision we find in *Une vie*. But what really distinguishes his second novel is its altogether broader canvas and its evocation of a specific period. It accounts for Maupassant's claim to a significant place in the French literary tradition which brings both fictional characters and aspiring authors to Paris. While it is inevitably situated in the shadow of that tradition, the originality of *Bel-Ami* lies in its reconfiguration of the themes and structures of the classic nineteenth-century realist novel.

The historical context

Bel-Ami supposedly opens in June 1880 and ends in the autumn of 1883, a time-frame so immediately adjacent to its own composition that the novel has to negotiate the risks, as well as the advantages, of topicality. He certainly did not need to do any research for it: Maupassant's familiarity with its context, simultaneously writing as a Parisian journalist for the *Gil Blas*, *Le Figaro*, and *Le Gaulois*, undoubtedly partly explains the speed with which he was able to produce the 436 manuscript pages of *Bel-Ami*. On the other hand, a novel based on current affairs may be less interesting to posterity once it has overcome charges of being a *roman-à-clef*. In respect of the latter, Maupassant was forced to publish (in the shape of an open letter to the *Gil Blas* on 1 June 1885) a long defence against the accusations of slander levelled by contemporary critics who unsurprisingly objected to the devastating portrayal, in *Bel-Ami*, of the newspapers for which they themselves worked.

The more transparent indexation of current affairs lies in his allusions to the very political situation which helps us reconstruct the novel's fictional chronology. In particular, *Bel-Ami* transposes the stage of French colonial expansion between 1880 and 1885 which generated a debate to which Maupassant himself contributed. The government of Jules Ferry (1832–93) which, for economic and military reasons (as well as those of national prestige) had advocated an enhanced French presence in the Gulf of Tonkin, Madagascar, the Congo and North Africa, was bitterly contested by those who argued that such an investment of resources would divert France from its priority of reclaiming the provinces of Alsace and Lorraine lost as a result of the Franco-Prussian War of 1870–1. The parliamentary manifestations of that debate are echoed in Part Two, Chapter 5 of

Bel-Ami (p. 213). The novel includes, indirectly in conversations and asides, a number of the political and military figures involved; and its topicality was underlined by the fact that, only a few days before its serial publication in the *Gil Blas* (6 April–30 May 1885), Ferry lost a vote of confidence generated by opponents to his Tunisian policy.

It is that French colonization of Tunisia that Maupassant barely disguises in his references to Morocco throughout the text. That country, too, by virtue of its proximity to Algeria, found itself within France's sphere of influence. In reality, however, it was not until 1905–12 that French intervention in its affairs led to the establishment of a protectorate. The substitution of names in *Bel-Ami* in no way constrained Maupassant from integrating into its texture both a personal experience of North Africa and the politics of its colonization. He had spent two months there during the summer of 1881, reporting for *Le Gaulois* on native insurrections in the Algerian province of Oran. His familiarity with its landscape and customs is reflected in Duroy's evocations of them under the heading of his 'Recollections of an African Cavalryman' (p. 24), the substance of which draws on some of Maupassant's own articles in the press between 1881 and 1884. And the fictional character, no less than his creator, displays an incisive understanding of the moral, financial, and strategic issues at stake in the French appropriation of territory on the other side of the Mediterranean.

Ever since its conquest of Algiers in 1830, France's incremental expansion of its rule into the interior had gradually turned its attention to Tunisia, the country to the east of Algeria. Not only was the instability of this kingdom a potential threat to French hegemony on its borders, but the competing claims of Italy (which had, by 1884, 10, 000 of its citizens there compared to a mere 900 French) lent an added urgency to relieving the hereditary Bey of Tunisia of his unserviced debts, referred to in *Bel-Ami* as 'the Moroccan loan' (p. 223). On the pretext of driving back tribal incursions across the Algerian frontier which had supposedly resulted in the deaths of five French soldiers at the end of March 1881, France invaded Tunisia and (by the May 1881 treaty of the Bardo) established a protectorate before proceeding, in subsequent military expeditions until the end of 1881, to suppress local opposition to its self-declared mandate. The government was less successful in securing formal ratification of the latter, faced as it was by a virulent press campaign focused on the speculative gains made by those 'prescient' enough to foresee that the French underwriting of the Tunisian national debt would result in the doubling of a bond-price which had been depressed by official denials of planned intervention. This is exactly the machination related in *Bel-Ami* (pp. 222–4). And, as in the novel itself, the principal target of the polemical campaign was those Jewish financiers, later also held responsible for the 1882 stock exchange crash, who were accused of manipulating the government and the press in order to make enormous profits from the Tunisian affair.

But while the above provides Maupassant with a key moment in his narrative, his more general analysis of the political and financial role of the press is also grounded in the particularities of its development in the years immediately prior to his writing of *Bel-Ami*. For a law of 29 July 1881 had liberated French journalism from a panoply of state controls, leading to a proliferation of papers exploiting a new-found editorial freedom and the financial opportunities afforded by the technical advances underpinning mass-circulation (notably the rolling presses which meant that, by 1882, *Le Petit Journal* had a daily print-run of 700,000 copies). One consequence of that freedom was the licence to engage in scurrilous gossip-mongering of the kind in *Bel-Ami* which leads to Duroy having to fight a duel with the journalist from *La Plume* (pp. 113 ff). Another was the widened scope of a newspaper's conception of the 'public interest', retailing the private lives, domestic interiors, and fashionable entertainment of high-profile figures. Alongside serialized literary texts, genuine facts, and serious political comment, the modern newspaper now also offered its readers, within its broadsheet-formatted four pages, a virtually unregulated concoction of anecdotes, trivia, rumour, and advice. And its own existence as a speculative capitalist venture, backed by powerful commercial interests, meant that its involvement in monetary affairs extended well beyond reporting on movements on the stock exchange. As we are told of M. Walter's paper in *Bel-Ami*, '*La Vie française* was above all a financial paper' (p. 94), 'only founded to further his dealings on the stock market and all his various other enterprises' (p. 49). For, in the climate of stupendous economic growth which characterizes the *fin-de-siècle*, the press becomes a lever of astonishing influence in the financial domain. Given, however, the imbrication of politics and economics, it also assumes (as it arguably does today) such a role in shaping opinion that governments and ministers are in its thrall and at its mercy. Maupassant's invention of *La Vie française* (in which the politicians Firmin and Laroche-Mathieu are its 'unacknowledged editors', p. 99) perfectly captures the tactical inventiveness, brazen energy and bankrupt integrity of a certain kind of French newspaper in the early 1880s.

It has been shown that *La Vie française*, without corresponding precisely to any of them, is in fact modelled on a number of papers: the proximately titled *La République française*, which orchestrated the campaign against the colonization of Tunisia; *Le Gaulois*, with its own 'Un domino' not unlike the pseudonym of 'Domino Rose' (p. 96); and, above all, the *Gil Blas*, whose licentious tone did not preclude its also publishing the work of creative writers such as Maupassant himself. Similarly, the staff of *La Vie française* are verifiably composite portraits of journalists Maupassant knew at first hand. The most sustained literary detective-work has been devoted to finding the real-life model for M. Walter, its founder. The obvious suspect is Arthur Meyer (1844–1924), the director of *Le Gaulois* who shared with his fictional counterpart his race, competitive rapacity, business cunning, reputed avarice, and paradoxically luxurious ostentation. It was even rumoured that, to be employed by Meyer, his editorial staff had to be as good at cup-and-ball as are the journalists in *Bel-Ami* (p. 41). But M. Walter also has something in common with other press barons of the period: the wealthy Auguste Dumont (1816–85), of the *Gil Blas*; or Edmond Magnier (born 1841), of *L'Événement*, equally as adept at exploiting the gossip column for his own ends and bribing colleagues and rivals alike.

Far more problematic, and yet itself exemplary of Maupassant's handling of his historical sources, is the case of Georges Duroy. He borrows traits from Catulle Mendès (1841–1909) only to the extent that the latter too, like Duroy in the novel (p. 256) was physically likened by contemporaries, not least by Maupassant himself, to Jesus Christ. Another journalist and friend of Maupassant's, René-Jean Toussaint (1856–1918), with his military background, lifestyle, and lack of moral scruples recounted in his *Amours de garnison* (published under his pseudonym of René Maizeroy in 1886), also bears an uncanny resemblance to Duroy. But however many names suggest themselves, we are finally forced to subscribe to Maupassant's denial that his protagonist is based on the personality or career of an identifiable individual. In his response to his critics, he was at pains to stress that Duroy was less a professional journalist than a contemporary type for whom journalism was merely a convenient stepping-stone: 'I simply wanted to recount the life of a careerist of the kind we bump into in Paris every day of the week, and whom we come across in every profession'. In that sense, Duroy has both numerous models and none. The historical context in which *Bel-Ami* is set provides countless examples of men of humble origins who made gigantic fortunes by fair means or foul.[2] And confirmation of the accuracy of Maupassant's portrait is underlined by the irony of life ultimately imitating art: not long after the appearance of his novel, one of the Third Republic's most prodigiously successful representatives—whose anonymity scholars once felt bound to respect—quickly found himself nicknamed 'Bel-Ami', so closely did the mechanisms of his acquired wealth and of his rise to power resemble those of Maupassant's central character.

Maupassant's realism

As a direct result of publishing 'Boule de Suif' in *Les Soirées de Médan* (1880), the volume put together by a group of writers consisting of Émile Zola and his circle, Maupassant has often been pigeon-holed as a Naturalist. Yet, within *Bel-Ami*, there is a belittling reference to 'the quarrels of the Romantics and the Naturalists' (p. 106) which better reflects Maupassant's aesthetic positioning. For there is, on his part, a consistent distancing from all literary schools, let alone from the furious doctrinal debates of the early 1880s. In the latter, faced with accusations of the gross exaggerations of *L'Assommoir*, Zola mounted a defence based on the argument that the veracity of his descriptions was supported by published sources and his own empirical observation of the social worlds represented in his novels. Polemical pressures so vitiated Zola's accounts of his own achievement (with the strategic analogy of the novelist and natural scientist hardening into a militant Naturalism) that, by 1880, in his best-known theoretical work, *Le Roman expérimental*, he was going so far as to claim that the documents assembled by Naturalist writers like himself were entirely responsible for the structure and content

[2] See vol. i (*Ambition, Love and Politics*) of Theodore Zeldin, *France 1848–1945*, 2 vols. (Oxford, Clarendon Press, 1973–7), especially chs. 5 and 6.

of their work: they both preceded the elaboration of character and plot, and were transposed so directly that the creative imagination was virtually redundant. However misleading such dogmatic statements are, they were in any case anathema to Maupassant. Indeed, as long ago as 1877, at the very moment he was about to become publicly associated with the most prestigious authors of his day (through his presence at the historic 'Dîner chez Trapp' held in honour of Flaubert, Zola, and Edmond de Goncourt), his private feelings on aesthetic labels are uncompromising: 'I don't believe in Naturalism any more than I do in Realism or Romanticism,' he wrote to a correspondent. 'In my view, all such terms are meaningless'. That the ambitious young writer should have contributed to *Les Soirées de Médan*, which in effect served as a Naturalist manifesto, is perfectly understandable; but there is no doubt that he continued to respect Gustave Flaubert's profound distaste for the collective ethos of such an enterprise.

That is not to deny that Maupassant's work as a whole is informed by a pervasive materialism and by a conception of the determinants of human behaviour which Zola would recognize as his own (leaving aside the latter's insistence on heredity as one of them). Maupassant deserves a place among the Naturalists by virtue of, in his own words (in *Le Gaulois* of 17 April 1880), 'a similar philosophical tendency'. Coloured by Maupassant's own reading of Schopenhauer, this 'tendency' is essentially the grimly secular vision of Man elaborated by the world-weary poet, Norbert de Varenne, during his evening stroll with Duroy in Part One, Chapter 6 (pp. 104–7). And *Bel-Ami* also shares with Zola's literary project the deliberate investigation of a particular social world. *Les Rougon-Macquart*, itself inspired by Balzac's earlier fictional reconstruction of the history of the Restoration (1815–30) and the July Monarchy (1830–48), is organized as a vast panorama of the Second Empire (1852–70). Most of the novels in Zola's twenty-volume series are individually focused on distinct worlds and key historical moments: the rebuilding of Paris (*La Curée*, 1872); the working-class (*L'Assommoir*, 1877, and *Germinal*, 1885); politics (provincial in *La Fortune des Rougon*, 1871, and *La Conquête de Plassans*, 1874, Parisian in *Son Excellence Eugène Rougon*, 1876); high-class prostitution (*Nana*, 1880), etc. To start itemizing Zola's subjects in this way is to do scant justice to the imaginative power of his writing. But it is revealing that the contemporary press, while it obviously figures in the margins of a number of Zola's novels, is not treated as a subject in its own right. Here, in other words, was a social, financial, and political world which Maupassant could explore while staking out a claim to originality, acutely aware as he was of working in the shadow of Zola's ambitions and achievement (with *Les Rougon-Macquart*, by 1884–5, well on the way to completion). *Bel-Ami* is not only Maupassant's longest novel. It is arguably the one which, in its detailed texture and internal organization, comes closest to Zola in providing us with a historical record of its times.

On the other hand, Maupassant never equates novelistic truth with quasi-scientific evidence and he eschews Zola's pedagogic perspective. Instead, he emphasizes the primacy of a necessarily subjective vision, retaining a preference for an 'objective mode' (as he puts it in the September 1887 preface to *Pierre et Jean*) which excludes the fracturing presence of authorial omniscience, while substituting for an absolute the notion of sincerity. In other words, he stresses that 'reality' is not an invariable; it is the construction of the individual. And the artist's role is to give a faithful rendering of his own version of it, without interposing judgements which would remind us that the novel we are reading is less a 'slice of life' than a commentary on it. It has to *seem* as if it is unmediated (or 'transparent'), giving us immediate access to the reality we are shown. The logic that 'to be truthful consists in rendering the complete illusion of truth', in distinguishing the literally accurate from the imperatives of verisimilitude, leads Maupassant to the strikingly modern conclusion that 'gifted Realists should really call themselves Illusionists'.

His own terminology apart, what such remarks reveal is a permanent debt to Flaubert. For most of the preferences expressed in this 1887 essay, as well as in his other forays into literary criticism, can be traced back to his seven-year literary apprenticeship under Flaubert, whose seminal influence Maupassant always explicitly acknowledges and which by no means came to an end with the former's sudden death on 8 May 1880. In particular, the 1887 essay repeats many of the points made in his articles on Flaubert in the winter of 1884–5, precisely at the time he was writing *Bel-Ami*. In discreet but significant ways, Maupassant's own version of a 'sentimental education' pays homage to the author of *L'Éducation sentimentale* (1869), not least in Norbert de Varenne's obliquely

autobiographical discourse punctuated by the emotional reference to
the exceptions to the general mediocrity of human beings: 'I've
known a few such men; they're dead' (p. 104). Nor does it seem by
chance that Duroy's return to his paternal origins takes him to Flaubert's hamlet of Croisset (p. 167), near Rouen. The panoptic view of
the city (pp. 162–3) transcribes, virtually word for word, the view
from Flaubert's window which Maupassant evoked in the 1884 preface to an edition of the former's letters to George Sand (1804–76).
So too, Duroy's erotic cab-rides (pp. 66–7, 200, 211), his euphoria at
having seduced a married woman (p. 67), the quasi-conjugal bliss
enacted in a rented room with Mme de Marelle (p. 73), and his
clandestine meeting with Mme Walter in a church (p. 203) all gesture
towards the corresponding episodes between Emma and Léon in
Madame Bovary (1857). Even in Madeleine's idealized, if hastily
revised, vision of rural life on her visit to Rouen (p. 166), we can
detect an ironically inverted echo of Emma Bovary's frustrations and
day-dreams. The initial view of the city itself is directly comparable
to the one which prefaces Emma's own 'honeymoon' there in
Madame Bovary. Suzanne Walter imagines 'nocturnal abductions'
(p. 271) in precisely the same romanticized terms (p. 273) which
Emma had drawn from her reading. And in the opening paragraphs
of *Bel-Ami*, Maupassant seems to 'take his hat off' to the Flaubert
who had said to him: 'When you pass by a shopkeeper sitting on his
doorstep, or a concierge smoking his pipe, next to a rank of carriages,
show me everything about that shopkeeper or concierge (how they
look, how they're sitting, and in those outward physical details—
thanks to the acuteness of your images—their inner character), and
in such a way that I would never confuse them with any other
shopkeeper or concierge.' How strange, to say the least, that, as we
accompany Duroy into the novel: 'Under arched carriage entrances,
shirt-sleeved concierges sat astride straw-bottomed chairs, smoking
pipes, while exhausted passers-by plodded along, bare-headed,
carrying their hats' (p. 4).

For it is ultimately Flaubert's conception of realism that marks
Maupassant's own, with its emphasis on the *recognizably* realistic,
the typical which is not exactly identifiable, an apprehension of reality so unique to the artist that it remains the only guarantee of
originality, the necessity of the writer being 'present everywhere,
but visible nowhere', the rejection of a realism in any sense

photographic, the key function of tiny details within an overall design, an autonomous *artistic* structure which is based on reality but which transcends it in its general implications. From Flaubert, Maupassant took his insistence on verbal clarity and precision (*le mot juste*), as well as the more overarching advice: 'In everything, there's something waiting to be discovered, simply because we tend to look at the world only through the eyes of those who have preceded us.' Maupassant's achievement in *Bel-Ami* is a result of seldom losing sight of these criteria.

The *reworking* of reality, without forfeiting the novel's realistic *effect*, takes a number of different forms. *Bel-Ami*'s historical co-ordinates, its references to contemporary figures, its setting in a recognizable Paris, all refer us to a world which undoubtedly (for the present tense of our reading) *exists*. But it is clearly not a history book, a biography, or a sociological treatise. For what Maupassant does, in the same way as he exploits his historical context, is disguise his reworkings. And he clearly takes a delight in doing so, not unlike Mme de Marelle whose origins can be detected through the incomplete disguises which allow her to move transgressively across boundaries and taboos (pp. 76–7). There is, indeed, almost a wilful deflection of the reader's recuperative temptations. Thus, for example, the transposition to Tunisia of the Moroccan campaign does not preclude separate references to the colonization of Tunisia itself. To identify Jacques Lenoble's gallery as that of Georges Petit is then to be put off the scent by finding Petit himself on the next page (pp. 242–3). In the case of the press, Maupassant places the fictional *La Plume*, *Le Salut*, *La Planète*, and *La Vie française* itself alongside an inventory of real newspapers like *Le Figaro*, the *Gil Blas*, *Le Gaulois*, *L'Événement*, *Le Rappel*, *Le Siècle*, *La Lanterne*, *Le Petit Parisien* (pp. 45–6) and *Le Voltaire* (p. 133), not least as a way of proving that they should not be confused. The manuscript of the novel confirms this: for the invented *La Planète*, for whom Forestier occasionally writes literary columns (p. 7), was originally the *Gil Blas*. And the same is true of Maupassant's fictional reporters: before deciding on the names of Garin and Montel (p. 10), he had inserted here two of the most famous journalists of the period, Albert Wolff (1833–91) and Aurélien Scholl (1833–1902), and, what is more, subsequently introduced the latter again before settling on 'Fervacques' (p. 50). Nor should names themselves be taken too

seriously: Laroche-Mathieu vaguely points to the real-life politician
Laroche-Joubert (1820–83); Rival may be based on the Baron de
Vaux, equally known as an author of a work on fencing, but his
onomastic potential matches that of the Vicomtesse de Percemur (p.
102) Crèvecœur, and Carvin (p. 190), to cite only the most obvious.
Maupassant's love of word-play (starting with his own name: 'je suis
le mauvais passant') is legendary, and should probably inflect conclu-
sions about the pre-emptive wisdom of his avoiding the prosecution
which might have resulted in 'naming names'. In any case, the mixture of real and imagined frigates sitting at anchor off Cannes (p.
136) offers a less litigious example of Maupassant's realist technique.
For his is essentially an art of allusion: it both intercalates the real
and the imaginary in a seamless narrative texture and, as Christopher
Lloyd has written, it allows the novelist 'a certain distance from
reality, a degree of fictional autonomy'.[3]

It remains to be asked, of course, how much of his own lived
experience Maupassant has put into *Bel-Ami*, thereby reinforcing its
credibility. Given his notorious personal promiscuity, such enquiries
have taken many a prurient turn. They include: the copies of the
novel he sent to female admirers signed by 'Bel-Ami' (not to mention the fact that he gave his yachts the same name!); a seductive
moustache at least as effective as Duroy's; mistresses who have
apparently contributed traits and personal habits to the protagonist's
conquests; a psychological profile complete with sexual proclivities.
Less sensationally, an entire network of parallels has been adduced to
elaborate on the title of Armand Lanoux's famous biography, *Maupassant le Bel-Ami* (1967): the people he knew; the papers he worked
for; the money he earned; the cafés he frequented; the addresses he
lived at; the furnishings he preferred. Yet, as Maupassant himself
wrote, if authors always put themselves into their books, 'the skill
consists in not allowing ourselves to be recognized by the reader
under the various masks we adopt'. It is thus too simple, or at least
misleading, to equate Duroy and his creator. For not only is the
self-portrait disguised, but it is also variegated across different
characters. On the one hand, Duroy displays characteristics entirely
foreign to Maupassant's nature; on the other, a figure like Norbert de
Varenne (who has also been identified with the poet Théodore de

---

[3] *Maupassant. 'Bel-Ami'* (London, Grant & Cutler, 1988), 77.

Banville (1823–91), amongst others) has a vision of experience which is patently Maupassant's own. But, there again, *both* the Forestiers share something with him, and even M. Walter collects some of his favourite painters. If it remains more interesting to discern how these 'various masks' reflect a shifting relationship with his text, it is relatively easy to confirm that one of the reasons why *Bel-Ami* persuades us to suspend our disbelief is its reworking of some of the fabric of Maupassant's life. But it is also true that what authenticates his art of illusion, whether in historical or autobiographical perspectives, is the novel's exceptional purchase on the materiality of the real.

Money, sex, and power

As a formula for readability, the triangulation of money, sex, and power is virtually irresistible. Maupassant is neither the first, nor the last, creative artist to explore, in these intertwined human appetites and desires, the dynamics of a modern society shorn of traditional values, metaphysical certainties, and constraining boundaries. Seldom in the French nineteenth-century novel, however, has a text so brutally and so precisely integrated the driving forces of such a newly unstable world. In exemplary fashion, *Bel-Ami* starts with the small change from a five-franc piece; its last word, with Duroy about to leap to political power, is 'bed'.

As far as money is concerned, the text's plausibility is less reliant on the standard mechanisms used by Maupassant to explain Duroy's transformation into a millionaire (a double dowry, a legacy, and a speculative operation) than on the concentration, in utterly prosaic detail, on the cost of things, the means of purchasing them, and the psychological vicissitudes of poverty and wealth. For this is a book saturated with monetary denominations, mental calculations, and even the feel and the colour of coins, with money itself less a theoretical system of economic exchange than the very stuff of survival, personal relationships, social standing, and identity. We are told the price of everything: a sausage, a glass of beer, a meal, a dinner, a cab, a newspaper, a dress-shirt, a cup-and-ball set, a room, a mansion, a painting. We learn the salaries of riding-instructors, clerks, and journalists; the rates of pay for a 200-line article; the amounts charged by paper-suppliers, different categories of prostitute and restaurant; the tips for waiters and coachmen, and for the concierge's son to run a message. One consequence of such a proliferation of price-tags is that, even when they are absent, they remain implicit: 'Thirty francs a day came to nine hundred by the end of the month. And that sum didn't allow for all those expenses of clothing, shoes, linen, laundry, and the like' (p. 78). *Bel-Ami* is a text full of objects shopped for, procured, bought on credit, or stolen, from the most basic necessities to those obtained by virtue of a whim, vanity, or pure greed: a cutlet, a bar of soap, a curling iron, a sponge, a bottle of perfume, two vases, silverware, a chafing-dish, finery, the entrance ticket to a *café-concert*, the 'gold buttons and scarlet facings' of servants' uniforms (p. 91), 'pistols from Gastine Renette' (p. 123), a villa, a splendid horse and carriage. And it is a text the very narrative of which is structured by budgetary pauses, in Duroy's rebalancing of income and expenditure with the rigour of an accountant, the feverish rescheduling of his debts, the fine-tuning of marriage-contracts, and the disbursement of an inheritance.

On Maupassant's part, there is less judgement than a sense of wonderment at such a world. Financial transactions are arbitrary and absurd. His Paris is the antithesis of the primeval desert 'where every drop of water is worth its weight in gold' and 'where commercial honesty is more highly developed than in civilized societies' (p. 23). The price of the same loan-bond moves by the hour; the same prostitute offers the same services for 20 or 30 francs to a local and 100 to a foreigner (p. 13); you can fill your stomach for 'a couple of francs' borrowed from a doorman (p. 79) or 130 at the Café Riche (p. 66) leaving as a gratuity the five francs on which Duroy had depended to eat and drink for a day. He spends on a watch and bracelet (p. 239) more than twice his entire annual 1,500 franc salary at the beginning of the novel. He haggles for those in much the way as he beats down the price of Rachel's body to less than that of a newspaper article or a round of beers (p. 16) and eventually to 50 per cent of the discounted rate at the very moment he could at last afford to pay more (p. 54). But it is precisely M. Walter's analogous avarice (p. 50) which secures discounts from his creditors and allows him to maintain a double-fronted house by letting half of it (p. 91). Notwithstanding the fact that Duroy's salary doubles, and then trebles again, he tells Suzanne that 'we can't even keep our own carriage' on 'an income of forty thousand' (p. 246); and he is still left feeling that

70,000 francs from an effortless scam is a humiliating trifle compared to the 100,000 which pays off Vaudrec's legitimate heir; and the half-a-million thereby acquired is an insult compared to M. Walter's 'real luxury' (p. 247). Receiving France's highest decoration thanks to Laroche-Mathieu, Duroy says of the cross of the Legion of Honour: 'I would rather have had ten million. This doesn't cost him much' (p. 254).

In the great scheme of things, as Norbert de Varenne insists, money is worthless: 'To do what with it? To buy women? What kind of happiness is that? To overeat, grow obese, and suffer the torments of gout all night long?' (p. 105). But, in the here-and-now, it seems supremely important: it shapes the limbs of impoverished peasants (p. 164); it determines the suffering of the 'desperately poor' woman vainly seeking compensatory salvation in the church (p. 202); it provides M. Walter with the opportunity to cash in on the 'financial straits' of the Prince de Carlsbourg by buying his house and garden at a knock-down price (p. 241), or to exploit the talents of 'starving' painters (p. 101). These contrasting destinies generate neither sympathy nor stricture. They are as indifferently noted as the levelling deviousness of petty swindles and grand larceny. Adjectives like 'pitiful', 'wretched', and 'clever' are always located within the point of view of fictional characters rather than offered as authorial comment. Money is simply the oil of envy, revenge, even happiness. There is little sign of generosity or altruism: a gift of 200 francs from Duroy is merely to 'placate' his covetous parents (p. 169); the 'faint clink of money dropping into bags' (p. 192), the 3,000 franc proceeds of a charity occasion, is drowned by laughter and people gorging themselves, leaving 'after all the expenses were paid, two hundred and twenty francs for the orphans of the sixth *arrondissement*' (p. 195). To obtain money, human beings are seen lying, 'cheating at cards' (p. 108), gambling away the savings of 'ordinary people' (p. 222) and the investments of the state. And consumerism for its own sake becomes a genuine pleasure: in the sensual delectation of 'oysters like tiny ears encased in shells, that melted between palate and tongue like salty bonbons' (p. 63); a celebratory 'tasty lunch' is followed by Duroy going 'into several shops to buy small things, purely for the pleasure of having them delivered to his place' (p. 47).

The relation between money and sexual pleasure is most obviously underlined by the theme of prostitution which informs

Bel-Ami from beginning to end. Duroy's initial 'urge to meet a woman' (p. 4) can only be paid for from the same purse which must satisfy his other physical needs. The theme itself, however, is extended well beyond his repeated encounters with women selling themselves on the streets. The irony of his contemptuous rejection of accosting whores who fail to note his frock-coat ('Couldn't those tarts tell the difference between men?' (p. 98)) is underlined by commodity exchanges in more bourgeois settings. When Duroy is overcome by lust, a bunch of flowers for Madeleine (pp. 170–3) or a bag of sweets for Mme de Marelle (p. 226) have their desired effect. And the association between money and sex is established at every level. Adultery is 'complicated by blackmail' (p. 21). Duroy's father (who 'had an eye for the ladies, in the old days') finds his son's expensively dressed new wife 'very much to his taste' (p. 165). But the luxury of the Café Riche and high society's drive back down the Champs Élysées from the Bois de Boulogne also lead directly to bed. Fortunes are made *from* wives and mistresses (p. 108). Duroy's concupiscent appraisal of Suzanne's 'slender waist, shapely hips and breasts' (p. 184) prefaces a marriage transformed into a business deal with her father, trumping those in which the latter would have 'sold' her in exchange for some 'rusty title' in the gift of the Marquis de Cazolles (p. 246) as her sister is handed over to the Comte de Latour-Yvelin. And, in a blatant inversion of roles, Duroy's affair with Mme de Marelle (in a room rented for *him*) is reliant on her paying the bills and her dropping coins into the lining of *his* clothes, which is entirely consistent with both his acclaiming the 'showy luxury' 'a well-known courtesan . . . had earned in bed' (p. 109) (aware of what they have in common) and his affinities with the prostitutes by profession, 'rubbing shoulders with them . . . feeling them around him' (p. 4).

As Duroy fails to 'feel for them any of the family man's innate contempt' (p. 4), *Bel-Ami* is certainly not a book designed to reassure those who subscribe to 'traditional family values'. Its parks (p. 33) and churches (p. 201) are the waiting-rooms for sex, peopled exclusively by those engaged in clandestine affairs. Monogamy is the exception rather than the rule. Mme Walter is astonishing precisely because, as Duroy is told, 'she's remained faithful' to her husband (p. 184). Mme de Marelle has an 'arrangement' with hers, and has clearly taken advantage of it prior to Duroy ('Of course she'd had lovers before', p. 76). Forestier's deathbed confession that he had been 'sinfully acquiescent' (p. 138) intimates the extent to which he too has allowed his wife her sexual freedom in return for Vaudrec's money. Madeleine, it almost goes without saying, is the daughter of a 'schoolmistress who'd been seduced' (p. 167). For this is a social world registered as sexual traffic: watching from the Avenue du Bois de Boulogne, Duroy enumerates the 'secret stories' of galloping riders and horsewomen: 'the names, titles, and qualities of the lovers they had had or were said to have had' (p. 108). In the brothel-like décor of the Café Riche, such generalizations include the admission that *all* women would cheat on their husbands if they could get away with it. Nor is this licence exclusively heterosexual: there are those 'of the lesbian persuasion' (p. 108); and Mme de Marelle loves dressing up 'as a schoolboy', allowing her the carnivalesque liberty of 'going to all these places single men go to, and women don't' (p. 76).

It has to be said, nevertheless, that this is a notably male-orientated (not to say misogynist) novel. In spite of an oft-avowed insistence on hiding an authorial point of view, *Bel-Ami* is punctuated by knowing aphorisms on the ways of women: their smiles promising imminent 'surrender' (p. 68); a look that 'reveals all the pain in a woman's heart' (p. 155); the 'manner' of 'a slighted woman' (p. 185); 'one of those attacks of hysteria that fling women to the ground' (p. 205). And the turns of phrase, whether clichéd or heart-felt, sometimes resemble those of a conversation between men: 'obsessed with her image, as occasionally happens when you have spent a delightful interlude with someone' (p. 60); 'one of those bright feminine glances that go straight to the heart' (p. 25); the 'satisfied sensuality, that comes from being loved by women' (p. 187); 'one of those rapid, grateful glances that make us their slaves' (p. 90); the 'fury smouldering in the heart of every male when faced with the capriciousness of female desire' (p. 181). And Madeleine Forestier seems to be the only exception in a cast of female characters who are largely swooning and empty-headed creatures. With her intelligence, political insight, and the financial acumen of a 'businessman' (p. 158), Madeleine is interesting precisely because she sees through Duroy and resists his seductiveness. But it is clear that her strength is likened by Maupassant to a properly masculine one. Even Rachel, who has the temerity to refuse Duroy on one occasion (p. 88) and challenge his adopted airs and graces (p. 85) reveals herself (p. 55) to be no more than a 'tart with a golden heart'.

The whimsical Mme de Marelle prattles and, at least when her
husband is out of town, is always available (lovers' tiffs apart). Mme
Walter is reduced to putty by Duroy's sweet-nothings and to an
infantile wreck by his manipulative cruelty. The doll-like Suzanne
returns from the chaste honeymoon of her abduction with her
naïvety untouched: 'I was so enjoying being your wife' (p. 280). For
Duroy himself, accordingly, virtually nothing seems to stand in the
way of a rampant promiscuity.

   Compared to the uncensored renderings of our times, Maupassant's description of all this sexual activity is notably discreet. It
usually stops at bedroom thresholds, leaving to the reader's imagination the intimacies sparked by flirtation and inviting caresses:
Madeleine 'followed him into their room, tickling his neck between
his collar and his hair with her fingertip, to make him go faster' (p.
173). Nothing more needs to be said. After Duroy is seen 'passionately kissing' Mme de Marelle's hair, there is a gap: 'an hour and half
later, he took her to the cab-stand' (p. 71). But that does not preclude the suggestion of a brutal physicality, whether in Mme de
Marelle's surrender in the cab (p. 67), the 'violent, clumsy coupling'
with Madeleine in a train-compartment (p. 161) or Duroy's stripping Mme Walter of her underwear 'with the light touch of a lady's
maid' before carrying her, naked but for her boots, to his bed (p.
212). In preparation, Duroy's predatory hands rove and fondle (pp.
67, 158), grab and maul (p. 197). His eyes feast on women's bodies,
picturing 'plump and warm' flesh (p. 35), making out through soft
gowns, 'froths of lace' or negligés, a 'supple figure' (p. 19) and 'generously rounded breasts' (p. 187). His nose picks up 'a faint fragrance' and 'the scent of someone who has just washed' (p. 35). And,
in spite of the text's many silences, euphemisms, circumlocutions,
and displacements ('the cab . . . was rocking like a ship', p. 200; or
the delicacies at the Café Riche as erotically consumed as in Field-
ing's *Tom Jones*), there are textual moments rich in sexual overtones,
such as the 'sensual aroma' given off by 'intertwined couples', those
'two creatures in every carriage, lying back silently on cushions and
clasping one another tightly, lost in the delusion of their desire,
trembling in anticipation of the approaching embrace' (p. 178). Yet it
is exactly here that Maupassant, in refusing to be taken in by such
delusions, refers to an 'ever-present *animal* desire', thereby alerting
the reader to the unpalatable fact that, beneath every expression of

tenderness in the novel, there are sexual drives indistinguishable from carnal appetites.

This reduction of 'passion' to bestiality serves as an ugly reminder of Maupassant's scatalogical and scabrous definitions: sexual intercourse as God's bad joke; a kiss as 'an exchange of spittle'; physical love as a 'disgusting' and 'ridiculous' mating. In *Bel-Ami* itself, Madeleine underlines for Duroy the distinction between the male and female of the species: "I know perfectly well that for you love is simply a kind of appetite' (p. 89). It is, therefore, at first sight almost surprising to find in the text an analysis of male sexual psychology not restricted to the frustration of Duroy's enforced chastity, when a two-week gap in his affair with Mme de Marelle makes him feel 'as if several years had elapsed since he had held a woman in his arms' (p. 87). Seduction is enjoyed as a refined game rather than simply a means to an end: running across his skin, Duroy feels the excitement of an imperceptible touch or of a glance of illicit attraction; along with the tactics of the chase, there is the heightened pleasure of deferral; and when satisfaction is achieved, there is (in the case of both his wife and Mme Walter) a loss of interest. There are contradictions: between Duroy's taste for defiling innocence, his paradoxical impatience with Mme Walter's awkward inexperience, and his curiously wounded pride at Mme de Marelle's allegation that he has slept with Suzanne (when, in fact, 'he knew how to control himself', p. 280); between icy-cold tactical acumen and losing his head. Selfish insistence is followed by pathetically sincere gratitude. Mme Walter's possessiveness is as dreaded as Madeleine's initiating tickle at the back of his neck. His sexual confidence is perilously close to a fear of rejection. Duroy's idyllic morning with Madeleine is chillingly deflated by Vaudrec's sudden entrance, leaving him miserably uncertain, 'haunted' by an indefinable anxiety (p. 40). He is tortured by jealousy and yet aroused by speculating about his mistresses' past lovers, obsessed by wanting to know whether Madeleine had cheated on her late husband, and what he was like in bed. The object of his desire is continually displaced, as he juxtaposes alternatives and thinks of Mme Walter while making love to Mme de Marelle. His pleasures come in different forms: savouring the 'delicious pleasure' (p. 110) of becoming M. de Marelle's trusted friend while sleeping with his wife; seeing in the priest (to whom Mme Walter turns) a sexual rival to be trounced: 'Today it's the priest's turn, tomorrow it'll be mine' (pp. 207–8).

While a feminist or psychoanalytical interpretation of the above might detect in these scenarios less a narrative of conquest than a virility under threat and an ambiguous sexuality seeking a Don Juan-esque reassurance, it is clear that Duroy's underlying motivation is one of possession and control. For power and potency, in *Bel-Ami*, are inseparable. It is at the very moment that Forestier reminds Duroy of his subordinate position that he plans to have Madeleine. Mme Walter is a target because she is 'the Director's wife', a further sign of her husband's dominating status. In making his play for Suzanne, Duroy sets his sights on money, sex, and power in the same throw of the dice. He follows Forestier's advice to make it to the top through women, with only Mme de Marelle and Rachel being used for pleasure rather than advancement. It goes without saying that, in this particular society, power is synonymous with wealth. This obvi-ously applies to the appropriation of colonial as much as to personal resources, underlined here in Duroy's consecration in the church of the Madeleine by 'the newly appointed bishop of Tangiers' (p. 287). And power in *Bel-Ami* is not simply ascribed, but performative in the most concrete as well as in the most minute ways: access to a box in the Folies-Bergère, the arrogance of presence in a *salon*, the positioning of a lolling chair, a look over a pair of glasses, a dismissive aside, the total lack of concern about those waiting for hours to make their entreaties. In the public domain it manifests itself in gawping crowds, fear, hushed tones, and grudging respect. In this novel, and whether in the portraits of individuals or in their relationships with others, power can be *felt*.

What Maupassant has also done, however, is relate sex and money to *political* power in its own right, as well as binding together these themes in the intersections of his plotting. For a number of narrative threads come together in the final chapters of Part Two. On the one hand, Mme Walter's infatuation with Duroy allows her to break a financial trust too by revealing to him what his own wife's lover and M. Walter had concealed from him in respect of the Moroccan adventure. On the other, there is Duroy's calculated revenge on Laroche-Mathieu for cutting him out of that colonial conspiracy, which takes the form of a sordid sexual humiliation that is also a political one. The result of this is to give Duroy plenty of reasons for jubilation: the profits from Mme Walter's privileged information; liberation from Madeleine and the freedom to aim higher; the downfall of the Minister for Foreign Affairs. These aligned narrative threads rely, of course, on coincidences of chronology and the concatenation of events. But that novelistic, and even melodramatic, design is substantiated by our immersion in the intensely physical details of power lost and power won (pp. 262–8); the half-full glasses on the mantelpiece in the room in which Laroche-Mathieu is discovered in bed; the remains of an incongruous supper; a pair of trousers cast aside; two pairs of shoes 'on their sides at the foot of the bed' (p. 263); the stale stench of past lives; the risibly naked politician divested of his authority; the *tone* of voice of those now in charge. Madeleine's pose, calmly smoking a cigarette to regain her composure, takes us back to another room, the neatly arranged setting of her controlling sensuality on a summer's morning (pp. 35–9). Behind the broken door of this one, eventually lit by 'ugly candelabra', the reader finds enacted both a reversal of fortunes and a persistence, in the intrusion of public officials in a private space, of those desires at the very centre of *Bel-Ami*.

Paris

A major reason, of course, why we suspend our disbelief is the quality of Maupassant's evocation of contemporary Paris. And we should not forget, in this respect, his deserved reputation for describing his native Normandy and the fact that he only arrived in Paris in 1872, remaining to some extent a less Parisian novelist than many of his contemporaries. The stage on which the dramas of money, sex, and power are played out is a very particular part of the French capital, inseparable from the very subject of *Bel-Ami*. The 'curtain rises' therefore on the Boulevard des Italiens: dividing the second and ninth *arrondissements*, and running between the Place de l'Opéra and the Boulevard Montmartre, this boulevard epitomized Parisian social values in the second half of the nineteenth century; it was the heart of the capital's theatre-land; at its northeastern end is the financial district around the stock exchange and where the main newspaper offices were to be found; it was the meeting-point of journalists and the rich and famous, lined as it was by the great cafés of the age; to be anybody (in Duroy's terms), it was there that one had to be seen. The private mansions of the *nouveaux-riches*, on the other hand, were further west, along the Boulevard Malesherbes. As he enters it from an impoverished Montmartre at the beginning of the novel, this lateral space is Duroy's territory; and at the far limits of his ambitions lie the Champs-Élysées with its Arc de Triomphe and the seat of political power, the Palais Bourbon across the river from the Place de la Concorde. Urban geography is thus precisely aligned to a fictional destiny.

Leaving aside its Norman interlude, this is not to say that *Bel-Ami* is set exclusively in this Right Bank triangle formed by the Place de Clichy, the Rue Druot, and the Arc de Triomphe. With Mme de Marelle (who herself lives on the Left Bank), he visits the outer boulevards with their working-class taverns, 'bare-headed girls', soldiers, cabbies and filthy drunks, almost in a calculated authorial acknowledgement of Zola's *L'Assommoir*. In Part Two, Chapter 9, there is an outing to Saint-Germain-en-Laye, preceding the elopement with Suzanne to La Roche-Guyon which replays, in a different mode, the earlier excursion along the Seine, to Rouen, with Madeleine. His duel, of course, is fought in the Bois du Vésinet outside the western fortifications. And there are interpolated references to Duroy's love of well-known riverside haunts to the west of Paris. But, to all extents and purposes, Maupassant's Parisian novel is firmly located in the eighth and ninth *arrondissements* of the city, allowing a focus on a specific *milieu* in both social and physical terms. Gradations of wealth and power within it are ranked by address, from the Rue Fontaine in the east to the Rue du Faubourg-Saint-Honoré where M. Walter asserts his social triumph. Particular cafés and restaurants are synonymous with the importance of their clienteles. Even the names of streets are used by Maupassant to symbolic effect, while Duroy's movements along them are seldom as arbitrary as they might seem. Paris is exploited, in other words, within a fictional design rather than simply being a picturesque or monumental backcloth. Assembled for our viewing at dinner-tables and receptions, and in their carriages returning from their 'playground' of the Bois de Boulogne, the social world described by Maupassant revolves *around* the *haute bourgeoisie*, but it remains one in which class itself is not distinct. For the social world he describes is in symptomatic flux reflecting, as much as Duroy himself, the mobilities and contaminations generated by new-found affluence and sexual alliances in a society in which butlers seem more assured than those they serve: a world of press barons and aristocratic residues; society ladies and riff-raff; politicians and common prostitutes elevated to the status of courtesans.

That hybrid world is identifiable at the Folies-Bergère, located just beyond the margins of the respectable *quartiers* of the city centre and exemplifying the juxtaposed, interpenetrating and blurred values of a modernity at a far remove from the nostalgically recalled elegance akin to Musard's or the orderly paths of the Parc Monceau (p. 11). Édouard Manet's *Bar at the Folies-Bergère* (painted in 1881–2 and dominating the Manet retrospective in the very year *Bel-Ami* was written) is the emblematic record of that social world. And Maupassant's wonderful description of it is both a set piece (pp. 12–14) and the one literary representation of the Folies-Bergère habitually cited in many pictorial analyses of Manet's own masterpiece.[4] What it also exemplifies is the novelist's talent, more generally, for creating an atmosphere, whether in the plunging view down on to the Gare Saint-Lazare in the approaching dusk or in his evocation of the escape from the 'overheated city' to the Bois de Boulogne, with the cool 'damp of the tiny creeks you could hear running under the boughs' (p. 179). And nowhere is this more evident than in the opening pages of *Bel-Ami*: the stifling early summer heat with its stale smells 'belched into the street'; the endlessly jostling and anonymous crowds, claustrophic and directionless in the collective rituals of individual evening strolls; the harshly lit cafés with tables spilling out over the pavement and loaded with ice-cold drinks shimmering in their reflected glare; the perfume-laden whores whispering their enticements to lonely men. As surely as its mist of tobacco smoke rising into the air and its 'illuminated clocks in the middle of the road' (p. 6) intimate the transience of this febrile and artificial urban scene, Maupassant's glittering jungle substantiates the hopes and fears of his characters and pulls the reader into a Paris vibrating with the intensity of the real.

[4] See Bradford R. Collins (ed.), *12 Views of Manet's 'Bar'* (Princeton, Princeton University Press, 1996), 193.

The art of illusion

Readers of *Bel-Ami* have seldom been in any doubt about the novel's significance. For it is seen as Maupassant's most fully developed novel of manners (or *roman de mœurs*) in the Balzacian tradition which explores the life of the French capital through the eyes of a young man leaving behind his provincial origins to make his fame and fortune in Paris. That tradition could in fact be extended all the way back to Marivaux's *Le Paysan parvenu* (1734–5). But its apogee in French nineteenth-century literature is obviously related to sociological realities which coincide with the contemporary novel's own historical ambitions. One need only think of Stendhal's *Le Rouge et le noir* (1830), with its famous analogy (of the novel as a mirror reflecting the route it travels) prefacing the narrative of Julien Sorel's picaresque ascent to the Parisian stage. Zola's *Rougon-Macquart* series charts a whole family's destiny in its relation to the wealth and power to be found there. And Flaubert's *L'Éducation sentimentale* reworks in an ironic mode the tropes and structures which we associate, above all, with Balzac. The author of so many *romans de mœurs parisiennes* is indeed the standard point of reference in assessments of *Bel-Ami*. The figure of M. Walter is 'straight out of Balzac' (p. 49), to the extent that he follows a succession of Jewish brokers of power and money who dominate the financial corridors of *La Comédie humaine*. The fact that *Bel-Ami*'s central protagonist makes his career in journalism inevitably invites comparisons with *Illusions perdues*, the second part of which (*Un grand homme de province à Paris*, 1839) brings Lucien de Rubempré into contact with a press as unscrupulous as the one described by Maupassant, and which, for Balzac's hero too, is the entry-point for a corrupting experience in the world of high society. On the other hand, Lucien is ultimately defeated by, and expelled from, that world. And, for that reason alone, it is instead the Rastignac of *Le Père Goriot* (1834–5) who is cited as the most pertinent model for *Bel-Ami* simply because, in the words of the most authoritative Maupassant scholar of his generation, 'Duroy, like Rastignac, is successful'.[5]

It is not difficult to understand why *Bel-Ami* should be seen as 'a

[5] André Vial, *Guy de Maupassant et l'art du roman* (Paris, Nizet, 1954), 358 (my translation).

novel of ascent'.[6] This can be qualified, of course, by the recognition that the success of a mediocre individual is simultaneously an indictment of the society which has allowed him to flourish. 'Wishing to analyse a scoundrel', Maupassant wrote in self-defence, 'I placed him in a world which would bring out his qualities' (*Gil Blas*, 1 June 1885). Jean-Paul Sartre goes so far as to compare Duroy to a mechanized figure in an equilibrium-chamber 'whose rise merely testifies to the decline of a whole society'.[7] The illusion of upward movement nevertheless remains a powerful one. Many critical guides to *Bel-Ami* include vertical diagrams which confirm that Duroy's apparent rise is minutely charted. The distance between the opening and closing pages of the novel seems self-evident: the unknown provincial eking out a living on the margins of society has a personal and material triumph consecrated in the fashionable heart of the capital; a Georges Duroy too poor to buy a drink has become the Baron Du Roy de Cantel, his sights now set on the political arena which seems to beckon the conquering hero. 'Challenging . . . the entire city' (p. 3) at the beginning, he ends the novel looking out towards the Palais Bourbon with an all-encompassing gaze reminiscent of Rastignac overlooking Paris from Père Lachaise and laying down that most famous of gauntlets: '*A nous deux, maintenant!*' There is a properly euphoric tone to the final chapter of *Bel-Ami*, so that Duroy's confidence is complemented both by the admiration of the assembled onlookers at his feet and the complicity of Maupassant's readers undeniably inscribed within this double point of view.

That we should suspend our disbelief in this way is, of course, Maupassant's realist achievement. His own literary techniques as one of those 'Illusionists' which he defines 'gifted Realists' as being, as has already been underlined, serve to erode the dividing-line between *Bel-Ami*'s imaginary world and the reality outside the novel to which the fiction effectively refers. He also stresses in that same 1887 essay, however, that, behind the resulting 'appearances', such techniques themselves disguise 'the real meaning of the work'. And, in inviting the perceptive reader to discover 'all the minute, hidden, virtually invisible threads which modern artists have substituted for The Plot', Maupassant alerts us to the potentially deceptive qualities

---

[6] Edward D. Sullivan, *Maupassant the Novelist* (Princeton, Princeton University Press, 1954), 74.

[7] *Situations II* (Paris, Gallimard, 1948), 173 (my translation).

of the latter. To base one's interpretation on the shape of such a conventional plot merely reveals how completely we have forfeited our critical detachment. And it is all the more ironic that we should subcribe to the illusions of *Bel-Ami* at the same time as being afforded a privileged view of the construction of such linguistic fictions. For one of the book's explicit preoccupations is, precisely, the *language* of duplicity. Forestier's advice to Duroy is couched in instructive terms: 'all you need in order to pull the wool over other people's eyes is a dictionary' (p. 8). Much of the novel demonstrates the efficacy of such a strategy, as the manipulation of words becomes synonymous with the manipulation of others, whether for speculative or seductive ends. What is true of sexual dalliance, marked by 'artful suggestiveness, of words lifting veils like a hand lifting a skirt' (p. 65), is equally true of the journalist's profession, 'insinuating rather than explicit' (p. 95). Above all, in both the private and public domain, language is seen as a substitute for reality rather than a reflection of it. The practices of *La Vie française* speak of an utter contempt for readers unable to differentiate between fact and fiction. The paper's very existence is inseparable from the fascination exerted by its frontage's 'three dazzling words' (p. 9). And, in the same way, Duroy's own identity literally depends on the self-assurance provided by seeing his name in print, perceived by others in the article he signs ('in large letters', p. 45) or the visiting cards he needs in order to confirm his new persona (p. 47). Conversely, self-doubt is equated with a blank where his name should be (p. 55), and an attempt to write is the immediate reaction to compensate for a threatening loss of outline (p. 121).

The significance of this preoccupation is considerably enlarged, indeed, by the fact that Duroy's gradual assimilation of social eloquence is reflected in an apprenticeship which takes him from creative impotence to the acknowledgement of his status as a writer (p. 288). Here the obviously autobiographical dimension of *Bel-Ami*, referred to earlier, is extended to a demystificatory stance, that ability to strip bare the pretensions, motives, and vanities around him (pp. 108–9); but also to those secretive verbal procedures (p. 143) which Maupassant insists elsewhere are the most prominent features of his own art. And this by no means precludes the irony of lucid self-appraisal. Duroy's lessons in grammar and style (pp. 36–8) point to Flaubert's former pupil as surely as his 'writer's sensitive pride and vanity' (p. 175) wounded by allegations that his texts are barely distinguishable from those of his mentor; so too does the detail that he 'found it hard to begin, and had difficulty finding the right words' (p. 172), and the reference to Duroy's habit of reworking earlier material (p. 209), within yet another novel in which Maupassant himself, on as many as thirty occasions, does precisely that. Potentially more problematic, however, is the way in which, once again, imaginative elaboration is seen to be divorced from experience, Duroy 'being unable to translate words into action' (p. 203) and being incapable of writing what he feels (p. 121). The novelistic 'pathetic tale' (p. 81) is a form of deceit, his 'dramatic story' (p. 126) of the duel a blatant fabrication, and his 'Recollections of an African Cavalryman' a self-conscious exercise in metaphor and rhetoric.

Much of this, it need hardly be said, is thematically consistent with the duplicity which informs the entire novel. Its emphasis on appearances embraces the poses and facial expressions characters adopt, the clothes Duroy hires, and the decorations he uses to hide the prosaic ugliness of his room. What lies behind the mask is mercilessly exposed. For *Bel-Ami* is no exception to Maupassant's familiar exploration of the theatrical. How things are *staged* for the spectator is the overriding concern of both the offices of *La Vie française*, with its 'showy staircase' (p. 40), and M. Walter's residence; within the latter's sumptuous décor we are treated to 'an endlessly rehearsed, decorous comedy of manners' (p. 92); when he moves to an even grander address, Parisian society made up of those 'who frequent opening nights' (p. 245) is invited to a public viewing advertised in the papers and organized with immaculate technical attention to the backcloth, foreground, lighting, and vanishing-points (pp. 244–8). Duroy's shock at realizing the two Walter daughters are in fact grown women is likened to witnessing a 'scene-change' (p. 99) not hidden behind the stage-curtain. Those privy to scandal fall into the category of 'protagonist [*acteur*], confidant, or just an onlooker' (p. 63). Love-affairs are similarly defined: Mme Walter surrenders with a 'mini-comedy of childish modesty', avowing her bliss 'like an ingénue in a play' (p. 218); and Mme de Marelle, faced with her husband's importunate return, announces to her lover: 'we must schedule a week's intermission' (p. 74) (with Maupassant using the specific theatrical term *relâche* to signal the temporary break). Duroy himself contemplates his reflection 'like an actor learning his part'

(p. 18), and becomes a consummate performer: 'speaking, now, with an actor's intonations and comic grimaces' (p. 160), as he parodies, with overlaid erotic connotations, his earlier inadequacies as a writer.

As Duroy's 'transparencies' (p. 70), however, also reflect his state of mind, so too, it can be suggested, *Bel-Ami* offers us more than a transparent screen through which the world's hypocrisy is revealed. For in the same way as a preoccupation with writing is potentially self-reflexive, the text intermittently mirrors its own design. The paintings which decorate the novel's interiors, for example, have not been innocently invented. Mme de Marelle's 'four second-rate pictures, depicting a boat on a river, a ship at sea, a mill on a plain, and a wood-cutter in a wood' (p. 58) all refer us back to Duroy's impoverished isolation at the time; at his parents' home, by contrast, 'two coloured pictures representing Paul and Virginie under a blue palm tree, and Napoleon I on a yellow horse' (p. 165) reflect the context of a triumphant honeymoon, as well as being subsequently, and ironically, echoed in the Virginie (Walter) he seduces, whose husband conceives 'an idea worthy of a Bonaparte' (p. 241). The latter's own series of pictures are significant in a rather different way, elaborated to the point where a number of them constitute a veritable microcosm (and a *mise-en-abîme*) of the novel's thematic concerns: apprenticeship in *The Lesson*, the struggle in *The Obstacle*, and, above all, vertical perspective in *Upper and Lower* (pp. 100–1).

It is a critical commonplace to point out that, throughout his career, the most prevalent of Maupassant's motifs is that of the mirror—both literally and as metaphor—which dramatizes the tension between self as identity and self as other. In *Bel-Ami* this is repeatedly used as a means of presenting the protagonist's introspection within the contraints of aesthetic objectivity. But Duroy's alienating self-spectacle is also emblematic. For the text too bears witness to what Maupassant calls in *Sur l'eau* (1888) 'a sort of doubling' transforming the writer into both 'actor and spectator of himself and of others'. This sense of watching himself 'in the mirror of my mind' in the very act of observing reality may well account for the ambivalence of the self-portrait located in Duroy. Yet that ambivalence is thereby extended to the novel itself, lodged between the realities it records and the imaginative construction it must necessarily be if it is to articulate a distinctive vision. In a society in which art is a commercial proposition and occupies a decorative space,

Bel-Ami thus provides alternative images of itself: on the one hand, as has been suggested, there are Duroy's empty journalistic inventions; on the other there is the Marcowitch painting, explicitly self-referential ('he looks like you, Bel-Ami', p. 256) and described as 'powerful and unexpected, indisputably the achievement of a master · . . . one of those works that turn your ideas upside down, and linger in the mind for years' (p. 248); but, as we are reminded, 'you had to look closely, in order to understand' (p. 247).

Maupassant's novel ultimately makes the same demands on us. For we are constantly made aware of Duroy's illusions and yet subscribe to his point of view. As the *Échos* of *La Vie française* lose none of their impact by being echoed in others, the reflections in Duroy's mirror tend to be confirmed rather than exploded by our perception of the mirroring process. The name 'Bel-Ami' is a conflation of *Bel-Homme* and *Bon-Ami* (a cross between 'Handsome' and 'Lover-Boy'); but even this frivolous product of childish adoration is finally the one through which the eponymous hero's story is authoritatively told. At his 'coronation' in the Rue Royale, we may well overlook the word-play (only caught in the original French) of the invisible narrator: Duroy 'se croyait un roi' ('felt like a king', p. 289). To do so is to be equally blind to the fact that this 'novel of ascent' is organized in patterns of stasis, circularity, and regression.

In so far as they end with his 'campaign . . . of conquest . . . begun' (p. 28), the opening chapters of *Bel-Ami* are exemplary in this respect. They appear to set in motion the dynamics of differentiation and future triumph, while simultaneously establishing a paradigm of subversive ironies. The scene at the Folies-Bergère thus functions as yet another mirror in which Duroy, with his own hair parted 'in the centre' (p. 4), fails to recognize himself in the figure of the trapeze artist:

You could see the muscles of his arms and legs outlined by his close-fitting costume; he puffed out his chest to disguise his all too-visible paunch, and he looked like a barber's assistant, for his hair was divided into two identical sections by a carefully drawn parting exactly in the centre of his skull. With a graceful leap he caught the trapeze, and, hanging from his hands, turned over like a whirling wheel; or else, his body straight and arms rigid, he remained motionless, lying horizontally in the void, connected to the stationary bar purely by the strength of his wrists. (p. 13)

Duroy has the same ease of movement (p. 5) and is also repeatedly admired for his strength; that immobility located within the trapeze artist's performance, however, punctutates his perambulations (pp. 3, 4, 6, 28) and his fearful contemplation of the duel (p. 120); and it anticipates the novel's close when he is transfixed on the steps of the Madeleine (p. 290). That, of course, was his original destination (p. 4), so that via another Madeleine (Forestier), he has come full circle. Asked where he is going, Duroy replies: 'Nowhere in particular, I'm taking a turn [*tour*] before going home' (p. 7), as a later walk does, taking him to a symbolic Arc de Triomphe (p. 51) and back again.

In a sense, the novel as a whole simply repeats Duroy's earlier experience, as we are told of his 'successes with women during his time in the army, mostly of the easy kind available to soldiers, but there had been a few in better circles. He had seduced a tax-collector's daughter who had wanted to give up everything and follow him, and a solicitor's wife who, when he abandoned her, had in her despair tried to drown herself' (p. 32), thereby prefiguring a sexual destiny which takes him from Rachel to Mme Walter and her daughter. In due course, Mme Walter is described as attaching herself to him 'with desperation, throwing herself into this love-affair the way people throw themselves into a river, with a stone tied round their necks' (p. 217). The underlying structure of *Bel-Ami* is itself reduplicative, with its repeated scenes of self-contemplation, its staircases and dinner-parties, and its complementary views of Paris and Rouen. Such symmetries serve to erode the illusion both of movement and difference. As the reporters at *La Vie française* are differentiated only by their flat-brimmed top hats, 'as if that shape set them apart from the rest of mankind' (p. 9), so the presence of prostitutes at all levels in the rising tiers of seats at the Folies-Bergère undermines the semblance of social hierarchy (pp. 12–15); and, in the same way, Duroy's dealings with categories as apparently distinct as cabinet-ministers and cab-drivers leave him 'not discriminating between them' (p. 56). Between the dinners at the Forestiers, the Café Riche, and the family tavern, equally characterized by smut, there is only the superficial difference of décor. Parallels between the text's female figures have an analogous function, in the pairing, for example, of Laurine and Suzanne and their respective mothers. The two prostitutes at the Folies-Bergère are recalled in Mme Forestier and Mme de Marelle (p. 19), and the sequence of early morning visits to the latter pair and to Mme Walter align them as surely as the process of substitution is confirmed by Duroy's subsequent return to Rachel when his society mistresses are not available. A 'portrait of a tall woman with large eyes reminded him of Mme Walter' (p. 187). 'A small woman' in the street 'who resembled Mme de Marelle' (p. 97) makes his heart pound as much as if he had not been mistaken. The hesitant seduction of the experienced Madeleine finds its inverted image in Mme Walter's virginal timidity, divested of its emotional particularity in Duroy's 'As if I care!' (p. 212) and his imbibing the same 'language of passion' (p. 226) irrespective of the object of desire.

As far as Duroy himself is concerned, a text which ends with the declaration that he is 'above others' (p. 288) in fact reveals that differentiation to be illusory. Others are judged by him as hypocritical and corrupt; he is only vaguely aware, however, that 'they had something in common, a natural bond, that they were of the same breed' (p. 109). He and Mme de Marelle are fellow-members of the same 'breed' too, of 'high-society vagabonds' (p. 220). His colleague Thomas also has an adopted name: 'they nicknamed me Saint-Potin at the paper' (p. 50). Duroy's status as 'one of the masters of the earth' (p. 288) simply echoes the description of M. Walter as 'one of the masters of the world' (p. 241). Another Duroy, in a sense (bearing in mind the reference to his residual 'interest in the affairs of the village', p. 98), is the contemptible Laroche-Mathieu, 'considered . . . very able' 'thanks to his village machiavellianism' (p. 174); as the former does in the Marelle household, he takes over in (to restore the French pun) the *maison Du Roy* the role of 'second master' (p. 243) vacated by the Vaudrec who had preceded Georges in Madeleine's extramarital affections. And we are told of her, in epilogue-like fashion, that Duroy's successor is a Jean Le Dol, 'a young man, good-looking, intelligent, who's of the same breed as our friend Georges' (p. 285). The most explicit surrogacy remains, of course, the pairing of Duroy and Forestier, with their double-act reflected in that of the two trapeze artists. From the moment he dogs his footsteps on the pavement when they renew their association, Duroy's illusions of individuality are subverted by the husband he eventually replaces. As his literary apprenticeship repeats Forestier's own, he appropriates his domestic chair and professional responsibilities, his newspaper column and his pen, his salary and decoration, his cup-and-ball set and his home, to the point where 'they never

called him anything but Forestier' (p. 175). Waiting for Mme Walter
in the church, he spots a stranger engaged on an identical mission,
only to imagine in this provincial reflection of himself 'that he
resembled Forestier' (p. 207). And, in his deteriorating relationship
with Madeleine, his retrospective jealousy foregrounds an obsession
with difference which Forestier's posthumous presence consistently
denies.

   What this network of parallels underlines is that though he may
seem self-assertive, thrusting 'his way roughly down the crowded
street' and 'jostling people, rather than deviate from his course' (p.
3), Duroy is ultimately, as this first glimpse of him already suggests, subordinate to the collective 'stream of promenaders' (p. 14).
Later, he is swept along in the procession of carriages likened to a
'vast river of lovers' (p. 178). Apparent conquest, in other words, is
merely surrender to those material and social determinants characteristic of the Naturalist aesthetic to which, as was indicated above,
Bel-Ami subscribes. In a fictional world elaborated in structures of
causality which make of individuals impotent victims of such fatal-
ities, Duroy's power is relativized by his passivity. If his motivation
is explained in terms of economic circumstances, he is equally subject to his chemistry and appetites. As he is unable to resist quench-
ing his thirst (p. 5), so his perception of triumph is figuratively
intoxicating ('draining his glass at one gulp', p. 25). Moving towards
the Champs-Élysées, he goes down the significantly entitled Rue
Notre-Dame-de-Lorette (see Explanatory Note to p. 3), his progress
checked by sexual desire (p. 4) and his aspirations for elegant love-
affairs interpolated by the temptations of the base; and his 'real
success with the ladies' (p. 15) is ironized by the bestiality which
attracts him to the 'fat brunette'. An unrefined violence lies only just
below the surface of the control he sometimes barely maintains,
'driven by a kind of malicious rage' (p. 182), 'overcome with rage at
that old bitch Mme Walter' (p. 228), exploding in the ugliness of
beating Mme de Marelle to the floor (p. 282). And Maupassant's
metaphorical assimilation of Duroy's superficially different conquests is particularly revealing. Each of them, ubiquitously in the
original French, is marked out as a prey: as Laurine is ensnared
(*apprivoisée*, p. 28) by his charm, he jumps on his new wife 'like a
sparrow-hawk on its prey' (p. 158) with the same savagery he displays in his treatment of Mme Walter; that she too is 'pounced on'

'like a bird of prey' (p. 212) further reminds us of his fantasy of wringing the necks of the rich as he had the chickens of the Arabs (on whom 'he used to prey', p. 5), themselves *la proie naturelle du soldat* ('more or less fair game for soldiers', p. 5). In the very first lines of the novel, what is underlined is Duroy's 'predatory glance' (p. 3). As Jean Béraud's *Upper and Lower* points to carnality, the novel's animal imagery is reflected in another invented painting, *A Rescue*, with its feline contemplation of a drowning fly (p. 100). Duroy himself later thinks of 'flies, that live a few hours, of animals that live a few days, of men who live a few years' (p. 141). Because it dramatizes such a struggle for life, *Bel-Ami* exemplified, for contemporary reviewers, 'literary Darwinism'. But the survival even of the fittest is framed by the biological destiny voiced by Norbert de Varenne: 'everything we do is part of dying. Indeed, to live is to die!' (p. 105).

The implications of the Duroy–Forestier substitution are inescapable. The advice that, given the necessary bearing, you can get away with anything (p. 8) is offered by a character whose substantial appearance only masks his inner disintegration. The warship the two ex-soldiers see off Cannes is appropriately called the *La Dévastation* (p. 136), and when Duroy climbs up to the Villa Jolie to begin his wooing of Madeleine, the spectacle of Forestier's death brings him face to face with a vision of his own. He is haunted throughout the novel by this *alter ego*; Forestier's imminent physical disappearance accordingly gives Duroy the illusion of freedom and a new-found independence, 'a feeling of deliverance, of space opening up before him' (p. 130). Yet that space is ultimately the same as 'the infinite . . . nothingness' he will perceive (p. 141), the 'deep chasm' (p. 29) below his own Rastignac-like view of Paris, the 'depths of the dark pit' of the station and the tunnels in which surrogate trains are buried, the sense of a 'tomb' experienced in the cellar in which he practises before the duel (p. 118), the 'cavern' of Rival's fencing chamber (p. 189), and the 'hollow' left by his body on the bed (on which his discarded clothes are likened to 'garments left unclaimed at the Morgue', p. 30), as Laroche Mathieu's shape in his wife's is that of a corpse (p. 264). For the sub-text of this 'novel of ascent' is the emptiness at its centre, the nothingness of human toil represented in another group of paintings whose titles are solemnly intoned (p. 100), and most fully articulated by Norbert de Varenne. Here,

Maupassant's ferocious pessimism receives expression in an almost embarrassingly explicit commentary. Norbert's discourse, however awkwardly inserted in the fiction, nevertheless illuminates the true significance of *Bel-Ami*'s vertical structures: 'Life is a hill. While you're climbing up, you look towards the summit, and you're happy; but when you reach the summit, suddenly you can see the slope down, and the bottom, which is death' (p. 104). This encroaching mortality, he tells us, has 'disfigured me so completely that I don't recognize myself'. In the same way, Duroy can barely recognize the dying Forestier (p. 131), and nowhere is that characteristic alienation in the mirror more uncompromisingly explored than on the night before the duel when 'he hardly recognized himself' (p. 120) in the contemplation of his own death. Norbert's speech opens up a 'pit full of bones, a hole into which he was inevitably destined one day to fall' (p. 107), prefigured in Duroy's sensation of 'falling down a hole' (p. 62) at the Café Riche and recalled as he finds himself 'staring straight into that tiny, deep, black hole in the barrel, from which a bullet would emerge' (p. 121). As his social persona is no more than the reverberation of his name in 'an empty room' (p. 91), so he and Madeleine's self-admiring 'triumphant laugh' is undercut by their spectral reflections in the glass, 'about to vanish into the night' (p. 240).

The force of these thematic patterns and remorseless symmetries is to equate all human activity with an illusion of the ego which seeks to assert its own reality in the face of nothingness. The repeated church scenes thus erode the apparent differences between an illicit liaison, a wedding, and a funeral. Like that of the trapeze artists, such behaviour is essentially a performance in 'the void' (p. 13). For the trivial games that people play, whether cup-and-ball or cards, are indisguishable from their overtly serious concerns. Colonial rapacity is an 'escapade' (p. 5) embracing the hunting metaphors of Duroy's later exploits. 'I play all day long', he tells Laurine (p. 60), and then engages in a game with her which exactly anticipates his chasing Mme Walter round her chairs (p. 197). Sophisticated conversations about elections to the Académie Française are reduced to a 'game of death and the forty old men' (p. 93). Related to its theatrical conception of experience, major episodes in *Bel-Ami* constitute a miming of action and a substitute for it. Complementing the visit to the Folies-Bergère, the 'frenzied display of gymnastics' (p. 191) of

the 'theatre' (p. 189) into which the fencing exhibition is transformed (Part Two, Chapter 3) also has more than an anecdotal function. For the combat enacted by 'two flesh-and-blood marionettes'
(p. 190) refers us back to the duel Duroy had imagined as real—in
spite of its absurd pretext and the overwhelming backcloth of an
indifferent nature (as in the landscape paintings, p. 100) which
invalidates its significance. Conversely, Norbert's existential musings
are set against the outline of the Palais-Bourbon (p. 107), the summit
of worthless political ambitions towards which Duroy looks at the
novel's close. His stabbing his rival's visiting card with a pair of
scissors (p. 119), his practice shooting at a dummy 'as if the duel
were actually taking place' (p. 117) and shadow-boxing against the
wall (p. 155) are all seen in a similarly ironic perspective. Where this
is again more problematic, in respect of *Bel-Ami*'s own mimetic
status, is Maupassant's extension of an oblique self-portrait to
include Duroy's 'game' of observing his society at play (p. 108) or
Madeleine's 'vague kind of game which never broke her concentration' (p. 38) while filling in the unwritten page.

Abstracted from it in this way, Maupassant's novel may well seem
to us as contrived as the geometry of its paintings or the
conservatory-arrangement of the Forestiers' drawing-room with its
plants which 'seemed improbable, artificial, too beautiful to be real'
(p. 26). The fact that we take the 'Illusionist''s artifice at face
value—at the level of appearances in spite of its thematic
subversion—is nevertheless revealing. Duroy's progress does indeed
seem uninterrupted in so far as we can discount his *return* to his
origins or to his first article, and are barely conscious, at its climax,
that the final image is of him going *down* yet another set of stairs,
subject once again to the animal sensuality of Mme de Marelle. Even
the text's internal rhythm sustains a forward momentum hardly
checked by its narrative interludes or the prosaic 'Georges Duroy
had resumed all his old habits' (p. 149) at the opening of Part Two,
which takes us back to the beginning. And Norbert's gloomy truths
introduce a merely temporary anxiety, not only on account of their
incongruous design, but above all because they are rapidly displaced
by the confidence of Duroy's alternative focus. Authorial self-
effacement leaves his as the privileged point of view within which
the reader shares the illusion of mastering the world of people and
events. For that reason, too, Duroy is not an unattractive figure. Or

at least Maupassant's refusal to direct our judgement (which is not inconsistent with an ambiguous moral neutrality) creates what Christopher Lloyd calls 'the central area of ambivalence in the book', in the contradictions located in the fascination exerted by 'a protagonist who, if considered dispassionately, seems somewhat repellent'.[8]

To acknowledge that a sneaking sympathy is not Maupassant's alone is to admit our enjoyment of both Duroy's demystificatory stance and the vicarious, albeit gendered, experience of domination and control. The text provocatively establishes the challenges to be overcome. Madeleine's declaration that she will never be his mistress (p. 89) is an invitation to read on as surely as Mme Walter's reputation as being 'beyond reproach' (p. 184) whets Duroy's appetite: 'it was precisely the difficulty of seducing the Director's wife which sexually excited him, as well as the novelty which men always want' (p. 198). Referred to here in the French as *La Patronne*, in that respect she is not unlike Mme Tourvel, the *présidente* of Laclos's *Les Liaisons dangereuses* (1782), whose virtue becomes a legitimate target in the same insidious way. Henry James, it must be said, was outraged by the Mme Walter episode. One is left wondering how many other readers of *Bel-Ami* can retain the same admirable moral rectitude faced with the choice between cynical intelligence and the blindness of piety. And in the comic scene in which Laroche-Mathieu is discovered *in flagrante delicto* (pp. 263–8), the reader long held in suspense about the basis of the rumours surrounding the awesome Madeleine is likely to identify with Duroy's machinations and the disappointed satisfaction of knowing the truth. The conventions of dramatic irony ensure that we do not take the side of the gullible; when we witness Duroy's financial trickery or his plans for the abduction of Suzanne, his stature is enhanced. He emerges in the reader's mind as somehow superior to those he dupes, so that when an individual as obviously successful as M. Walter marvels at Duroy's cunning, his 'All the same, he's strong' (p. 277) secures our assent and reinforces the character's subjective view of his own abilities. As we follow the underdog up the stairs of social values or the recurrent hills which afford an overview of the novel's topography, that subjectivity is itself validated. The self-deception we may not

---

[8] *Maupassant. 'Bel-Ami'*, 24.

notice is, in any case, relativized by the delusion of others. As Norbert puts it, 'in the kingdom of the blind the one-eyed man is king' (again with the punning on *roi* and Du*roy*, p. 104), as he in due course becomes 'a king . . . acclaimed by his people' (p. 289). In all these ways, it can be suggested, the rascal's illusion of ascent and superiority becomes a reality as difficult to resist as his charm.

The supreme irony of this modulation of our sympathies is that we therefore become as gullible as Mme Walter, as effectively stripped of her moral scruples as of her respectable clothes. She is seen prostrate and suspending her disbelief before the Marcowitch painting, unable to distinguish between reality and artistic representation, confusing the Son of God invoked in church (p. 289) and the Son of God located in the frame (p. 247) (the original French here, *L'Homme-Dieu*, better catches the convertibility of the human and the divine). As she is taken in by Duroy's 'banal music of love' (p. 199), so, by analogy, we may justifiably ask to what extent this corresponds to the reader's confrontation with *Bel-Ami* itself, so often considered an exemplary Naturalist text in its detailed and utterly prosaic recording of 'la vie française' epitomized by its fictional newspaper.

Whether such a definition is adequate is open to debate. For by involving us in the overlaid paradox that this construction of the 'Illusionist' both demystifies and confirms the illusions of experience, Maupassant certainly seems to enlarge the critical questions posed by his novel. And its moments of self-questioning tell us much about the nature of his achievement. Of Duroy we are told, for example, that 'as he found it extremely difficult to come up with ideas, he made it his speciality to rail against moral decline, a new weakness of character, the demise of patriotism, and the anaemia affecting the French sense of honour' (p. 129). As well as caricaturing a certain kind of journalism, here Maupassant alerts us to the fact that his own writing is not just that sort of facile polemic, and yet runs the risk of being no more than that in its similar castigations. Duroy's satirical pleasure is his own: 'He found this a highly amusing game, revelling in the excitement of, and somehow consoled by, the sense of putting on record the eternal and deep-seated infamy of man underlying outwardly respectable appearances' (p. 108). Alongside the recognition of hypocritical self-indulgence, however, there is Norbert de Varenne's 'behind everything you look at, what you see is death' (p. 104). In the 'mirror of my mind', mentioned earlier, Maupassant is uneasily situated behind the authority of the eccentric poet and the partial self-portrait offered by Duroy. That unease will receive its fullest examination in *L'Inutile Beauté* (1890), in which art is conceived as both the free-play of the imagination momentarily transcending deterministic forces, and yet ultimately as insubstantial as other human activities. Such an ambivalence towards his own writing, alternately asserted as a *raison d'être* and cynically dismissed as a way of earning a living, is undoubtedly registered in *Bel-Ami*. Norbert's lines are more instructive than they might seem:

> In the sombre void, to this dark mystery
> Where floats a pallid star, I seek the verbal key.
>
> (p. 107)

As the last words translate his *je cherche le mot*, they suggest the extent to which Maupassant is himself looking for a form in which to express the poet's intuitions: 'Oh! "Death". I know you don't even understand the word!' (*le mot*, p. 105). And Norbert's presence in the text, inserted as authorial spokesman, may testify to the uncertainty of Maupassant's achievement, to a fundamental lack of confidence, on his own part, that 'the real meaning of the work' will be understood by readers whose illusions will simply be confirmed in the mirror of Duroy's triumphant progress.

The distinctive quality of Maupassant's vision lies in the way *Bel-Ami*'s mirrors simultaneously effect a process of estrangement. For, as his self-appraisal is not synonymous with an undifferentiated self-reflection, that vision is the measure of the originality of the novelist's recognizably realist text which is not simply an identical copy of the particular reality it seems to transcribe. Duroy is himself disorientated by optical illusions: he mistakes his image for 'a gentleman in full evening dress' coming towards him (p. 17); entering another social world, 'at first he set off in the wrong direction, for the mirror had deceived him' (p. 91); and he misjudges heights: 'a seat onto which . . . he dropped heavily, imagining it to be much higher than it was' (pp. 91–2); but there is no mistaking the 'slight moral disquiet' occasioned by an optical re-adjustment (p. 99) and the significance of Mme Walter instinctively looking in the mirror 'as if to see whether she herself looked any different', given her impossibly altered situation (p. 275). In the same way, it can be argued, the reader finds in *Bel-Ami* an alienated version of himself, inviting him, as Norbert puts it, to 'see life differently' (p. 106).

The Marcowitch painting, too, is deceptive. Beneath the 'apparent simplicity' of its traditional subject, however, its composition brings together many of the significant details which underlie the novel's own. Thus, for example, the metaphorical infrastructure of *Bel-Ami*'s final chapter, with its 'sound of the distant sea' (p. 286) of the crowd and the waves of sound filling the church, is anticipated in the pictorial representation of *Jesus Walking on the Water*; what distinguishes it is the darkness surrounding the central figure and the vastness of the firmament, both integral to Norbert's poetic formulations of the insignificance of human activities (in a godless world) and Maupassant's pervasive relativization of fame and fortune. The fictional painting itself 'looked like a black hole surrounded by a fantastic, stunning background' (p. 247) thematically consistent with the recurrent focus, throughout the novel, on such emptiness; and the Folies-Bergère scene, with its performer 'motionless . . . in the void' (p. 13) is recalled in the 'man standing, motionless, on the sea' (p. 247). Above all, the impact of the painting derives from its theatrical lighting and the admiring gaze of the apostles, their faces 'overcome with astonishment' (p. 248). For Mme Walter, 'by the flickering light of the single candle illuminating him dimly from below, he looked so very like Bel-Ami that it was no longer God, but her lover who was gazing at her' (p. 278). And her illusions, as has been suggested, are potentially our own.

Her unthinking involvement can be contrasted with Maupassant's nostalgic evocation, in an essay exactly contemporary to the preparation of *Bel-Ami*, of an eighteenth-century reading-public appreciative of a writer's secretive procedures: 'It sought the underlying and inner meaning of words, delved into what the author was trying to say, read slowly so as not to miss a detail, and then, having understood a sentence, went back to discover whether there was more to it than might appear.' The cautionary 'you had to look closely, in order to understand' (p. 247), as far as the Marcowitch painting is concerned, has to be read in this wider context. For as Maupassant repeatedly stresses, the novelist's aim 'is not to tell us a story, to entertain us, or to appeal to our emotions, but rather to force us to think, and to understand the hidden and profound meaning of events'. And this necessitates both involvement in, and abstraction from, a recognizable fictional reality, neither exclusively symbolic, nor simply as anecdotal as Duroy's journalistic constructions which cater for the gullible. Mme Walter's suspension of disbelief leaves her, literally, unconscious. But there are more perceptive responses to the great work of art she confuses with life. 'How frightened these men are, and how they love him! Just look at his head, at his eyes, how he seems both simple and supernatural at the same time!' (p. 256). As adoring identification and fearful estrangement may be elicited in the complicitous mirrors held up to its hero, so, applied to the novel as a whole, that 'simple and supernatural at the same time' encourages the reader to see illustrated in *Bel-Ami* what is considered the most succinct statement of Maupassant's aesthetic: 'a work of art is only distinguished if it is at the same time both symbolic and exactly representative of reality' (*La Vie errante*, 1890).

It is far from certain that this ideal is fulfilled, or that the novel ranks as 'one of those works that turn your ideas upside down, and linger in the mind for years' (p. 248). Maupassant will not be alone in the doubts about his own achievement. Alongside the self-deprecating irony directed at Duroy's verbal facility and Norbert's intrusive discourse aimed at those readers unable to discern its 'hidden meaning' as well as believe in its 'events', unequivocal assessment of that achievement is not entirely pre-empted by the caricaturally philistine reaction of those who fail to understand the painting at its centre, 'and then had nothing to say except to comment on the value of the painting' in monetary terms (p. 248). It could be argued, indeed, that Maupassant's worst fears have been realized in the critical assimilation of *Bel-Ami* and the Balzacian tradition it is deemed to continue. André Vial writes that the novel 'is directly linked to Balzac',[9] and another important critic, Gérard Delaisement, cites the author of *Illusions perdues* as 'the uncontestable model'.[10] Such remarks implicitly minimize the distinctive qualities of the work and overlook the fact that the model *is* contested, specifically in the denial of the Balzacian point of reference in the curious mention of Duroy that he 'had never read any Balzac' (p. 50) but also, and more generally, in the text's demystification of the heroic ethos it seems to propose. Not the least intriguing aspect of *Bel-Ami*, and this is perhaps where its originality lies, is that in a

---

[9] *Guy de Maupassant et l'art du roman*, 358 (my translation).
[10] *Maupassant. 'Bel-Ami'* (Paris, Hatier, 1972), 46.

composition as stylized as that of its invented paintings, Maupassant's art of illusion generates a fiction not about the loss of illusions—that clichéd nineteenth-century theme—but about their construction and their reality.

NOTE ON THE TRANSLATION

This translation of *Bel-Ami*[1] is based on the 1988 Classiques Garnier text edited by Daniel Leuwers, with a few minor inaccuracies corrected against the 1987 Pléiade edition.

Translating Maupassant's wonderfully readable novel has been, for me, a fascinating but frustrating experience; I have found it extremely difficult to achieve the right tone in English. I have come to the conclusion, somewhat reluctantly, that I might have found this easier had I been a man. Robert Lethbridge, in his Introduction, speaks of the male-oriented, not to say misogynist, character of the narrative, which in places resembles 'a conversation between men'. Fortunately for me Professor Lethbridge supplied the necessary male point of view. His familiarity with the cultural and historical context of the novel, together with his experience as a translator, have been an invaluable resource. I am happy to have this opportunity to thank him for his substantial contributions to this English version of *Bel-Ami*.

I am also deeply indebted to friends and family members who have helped me with criticism and advice and suggestions, and have encouraged me to persevere at this solitary occupation of translating. In particular my loving thanks go to my daughter Jane Mauldon and my friends Rondi Gilbert and Sabra Macleod, and most especially to my husband Jim, who makes it fun to go on working.

MARGARET MAULDON

[1] This intriguing name is first mentioned in the novel on p. 70. For a discussion of its meaning see the Introduction, p. xxxv.

SELECT BIBLIOGRAPHY

Editions

Bel-Ami, in Louis Forestier's edition of Maupassant, *Romans* (Paris, Bibliothèque de la Pléiade, 1987); includes a synopsis of the novel's background and composition, notes on the text, and successive amendments from the manuscript to the final version of *Bel-Ami* in volume form. These 100 pages of material appended to the text constitute the most scholarly introduction to the novel. Readers wishing to go back to the original French text should note that, by contrast with occasional transcription errors which have crept into paperback reprintings of *Bel-Ami*, this Pléiade edition of the novel remains the most accurate and authoritative. Complementary to this edition of Maupassant's novels is his *Contes et nouvelles*, 2 vols., ed. Louis Forestier (Paris, Bibliothèque de la Pléiade, 1974–79).

Bel-Ami, ed. Marie-Claire Bancquart (Paris, Imprimerie Nationale, 1979); this luxury illustrated edition is also impressively scholarly.

Bel-Ami, ed. Daniel Leuwers (Paris, Garnier, 1988; repr. Garnier-Flammarion, 1993); as well as having very useful information about the novel, it is also generally reliable; it is the base text (with its occasional errors corrected against the Pléiade edition) for this Oxford World's Classics translation.

Bel-Ami, ed. Adeline Wrona (Paris, Garnier-Flammarion, 1999); this paperback edition contains some useful background information for readers of the novel.

Bel-Ami, ed. Jean-Louis Bory (Paris, Collection Folio, 1973); this is another generally reliable version of the text, but the appended notes are often inaccurate.

Bel-Ami, ed. Philippe Bonnefis (Paris, Livre de Poche, 1999); this is essentially the 1983 edition in Livre de Poche, with only the bibliography updated, but its introduction remains a highly stimulating one.

Biography

Ignotus, Paul, *The Paradox of Maupassant* (London, University of London Press, 1966).

Lanoux, Armand, *Maupassant le Bel-Ami* (Paris, Fayard, 1967; repr. Livre de Poche, 1983).

Lerner, Michael, *Maupassant* (London, Allen & Unwin, 1975).

Steegmuller, Francis, *Maupassant. A Lion in the Path* (New York, Collins, 1949; repr. London, Macmillan, 1972).

Troyat, Henri, *Maupassant* (Paris, Flammarion, 1989).

Readers should note that, while all the above are variably colourful and intelligent versions of Maupassant's life, none is wholly accurate and they tend to borrow inaccuracies from each other. His biographers lack a comprehensive edition of the writer's correspondence; and they face major problems in distinguishing fact from Maupassant's own autobiographical accounts (often somewhere between semi-fiction and fantasy). One exception to this is Roger Williams' exploitation of scientific evidence to reconstruct Maupassant's medical history, in his *The Horror of Life* (London, Weidenfeld & Nicolson 1980), 217–72.

Excellent collections of photos and images related to Maupassant's life are to be found in:

Album Maupassant, ed. Jacques Réda (Paris, Bibliothèque de la Pléiade, 1987).

Maupassant (1850–1893); catalogue of the centenary exhibition (Fécamp, 1993).

Maupassant inédit. Iconographie et documents, ed. Jacques Bienvenu (Aix-en-Provence, Édisud, 1993).

The most useful biographical background to *Bel-Ami* is to be found in:

Bancquart, Marie-Claire, 'Maupassant journaliste', in Joseph-Marc Bailbé and Jean Pierrot (eds.), *Flaubert et Maupassant. Écrivains normands* (Paris, Presses Universitaires de France, 1981), 155–66.

Critical Studies

General

Bury, Marianne, *La Poétique de Maupassant* (Paris, SEDES, 1994).

Donaldson-Evans, Mary, *A Woman's Revenge: The Chronology of Dispossession in Maupassant's Fiction* (Lexington, Ky., French Forum, 1986).

Sullivan, Edward D., *Maupassant the Novelist* (Princeton, Princeton University Press, 1954).

Vial, André, *Guy de Maupassant et l'art du roman* (Paris, Nizet, 1954); notwithstanding its date of publication, this remains the starting-point for any serious study of Maupassant the novelist.

On Bel-Ami

Bernardin, François, 'Le Scandale de *Bel-Ami*', *La Nouvelle Critique*, 7 (1955), 126–38.

Bismut, Roger, 'Quelques problèmes de la création littéraire dans

Bel-Ami', *Revue d'histoire littéraire de la France*, 67 (1967), 577–89; this essay traces textual moments in the novel back to the work of Maupassant's literary predecessors.

Chaikin, Milton, 'Maupassant's *Bel-Ami* and Balzac', *Romance Notes*, 1 (1960), 109–12.

Champagne, Roland, 'Revealing the Ideological Mask of Culture: The French New Philosophers, Maupassant and Literary Criticism', *Language and Style*, 18 (1985), 232–41; sees Duroy as the victim of ideological forces rather than heroic incarnation of masculine and capitalist values.

Delaisement, Gérard, 'L'Univers de *Bel-Ami*', *Revue des sciences humaines*, 87 (1953), 77–87; outlines the corruption of the social, financial and political reality which the novel represents.

—— '*Bel-Ami* et les écrits antérieurs de Maupassant', *Revue des sciences humaines*, 82 (1956), 195–228; traces Maupassant's reworking in the novel of earlier journalistic texts.

Giachetti, Claudine, 'Les Hauts et les bas: la conquête de l'espace dans *Bel-Ami* de Maupassant', *Revue romane*, 26 (1991), 219–29.

Grant, Richard B., 'The Function of the First Chapter of *Bel-Ami*', *Modern Language Notes*, 76 (1961), 748–52.

Haig, Stirling, 'The Mirror of Artifice: Maupassant's *Bel-Ami*', in his *The Madame Bovary Blues: The Pursuit of Illusion in Nineteenth-Century French Fiction* (Baton Rouge, La., Louisiana State University Press, 1987), pp. 152–62.

Hamilton, James F., 'The Impossible Return to Nature in Maupassant's *Bel-Ami*, or the Intellectual Heroine as Deviant', *Nineteenth-Century French Studies*, 10 (1982), 326–39; studies the complex inner life of Madeleine Forestier.

Hydak, M. G., 'Mars, Venus and Maupassant's *Bel-Ami*', *Romance Notes*, 18 (1977), 178–82; shows how classical allusion within M. Walter's tapestry is a subtle parallel to several episodes in the novel.

—— 'Door-imagery in Maupassant's *Bel-Ami*', *French Review*, 49 (1979), 337–41.

Lloyd, Christopher, *Maupassant. 'Bel-Ami'* (London, Grant & Cutler, 1988); the best critical introduction, in any language, to the novel.

Prince, Gerald, '*Bel-Ami* and Narrative as Antagonist', *French Forum*, 11 (1986), 217–26; challenging essay, arguing that the text is haunted self-reflexively by Maupassant's opposition to the conventional ordering of narrative.

White, Nicholas, '*Bel-Ami*: Fantasies of Seduction and Colonization', in his *The Family in Crisis in Late Nineteenth-Century French Fiction* (Cambridge, Cambridge University Press, 1999), 73–97.

Historical Background

Bancquart, Marie-Claire, *Images littéraires de Paris fin-de-siècle* (Paris, Éditions de la différence, 1979); particularly acute social geography elaborated from fictional lives, notably those in *Bel-Ami* (pp. 127–55).

Maupassant, Guy de, *A Selection of Political Journalism*, ed. Adrian Ritchie (Berne, P. Lang, 1999).

Vie et histoire du IXe arrondissement, ed. J. Van Deputte (Paris, Hervas, 1986); the volume of this Hervas series devoted to the Parisian setting of *Bel-Ami*, and an invaluable source of reference for its streets, cafés, churches, etc.

Zeldin, Theodore, *Ambition, Love and Politics*, vol. i of his *France 1848–1945*, 2 vols. (Oxford, Clarendon Press, 1973–77).

Further Reading in Oxford World's Classics

Maupassant, Guy de, *A Day in the Country and Other Stories*, trans. and ed. David Coward (1990).

—— *Mademoiselle Fifi and Other Stories*, trans. and ed. David Coward (1993).

—— *A Life*, trans. and ed. Roger Pearson (1999).

A CHRONOLOGY OF GUY DE MAUPASSANT

1850   5 August: Birth of Henry René Albert Guy de Maupassant, probably at Fécamp on the coast of Normandy, the first child of Gustave de Maupassant and Laure Le Poittevin.

1851–4   Comfortably off, the Maupassants live in a number of places in the Normandy area (Rouen, Fécamp, Étretat) before moving into the Château de Grainville-Ymauville near Goderville in the vicinity of Le Havre.

1856   Birth of Guy's brother, Hervé.

1859   Financial problems lead Gustave de Maupassant to enter employment with the Banque Stolz in Paris. Family move to Passy. October: Guy enters the Lycée Napoléon (now the Lycée Henri IV), where he remains for the academic year.

1860   Failure of the marriage between Gustave and Laure. Gustave remains in Paris, where he works for the Banque Évrard for the next twenty-five years. Laure and her two sons move to Étretat, where Laure has bought a house, Les Verguies.

1863   Legal separation of Gustave and Laure (divorce not being legalized until 1884). October: Guy becomes boarder at a Catholic school in Yvetot. Begins writing verse.

1863–8   Schooling at Yvetot, holidays swimming and boating at Étretat. On one occasion swims to the assistance of the poet Swinburne, who has got into difficulties. Following expulsion from school for some lewd verse, Maupassant is sent as a boarder to the Lycée Corneille in Rouen. His *correspondant* (a friend of the family chosen by parents of boarders to act as guardian) is Louis Bouilhet (b. 1821), the writer, city librarian, and close friend of Flaubert. Bouilhet and Flaubert encourage and advise him in his writing.

1869   18 July: death of Louis Bouilhet. 27 July: passes his *baccalauréat* ('mention passable'). August: meets the painter Gustave Courbet (1819–77). October: enrols as a law-student in Paris, and lives in the same apartment block as his father.

1870   15 July: France declares war on Germany. Maupassant is called

This Chronology is based on that provided by Louis Forestier in his edition of Maupassant's *Contes et nouvelles* in the Bibliothèque de la Pléiade.

up and, after training, posted as a clerk to Rouen. 1 September: French defeat at Sedan.

1871   28 January: Armistice signed. September: leaves the army.

1872   Applies to join the Ministry for the Navy and the Colonies as a civil servant. Application refused, then Maupassant offered an unpaid position pending a vacancy. Begins to be a frequent summer visitor to Argenteuil on the Seine, where boating and female company occupy his time.

1873   1 February: appointed to a position on a monthly salary of 125 francs, plus an annual bonus of 150 francs. Continues to spend time at Argenteuil when he can.

1874   25 March: confirmed in his post at the Ministry and salary increased. Continues to enjoy life at Argenteuil, and to write verse, stories, and plays.

1875   February: his first short story to be published, 'La Main d'écorché', appears under the pseudonym Joseph Prunier.

1876   Now fully involved in Parisian literary life (Flaubert, Mallarmé, Zola, Huysmans, Mendès, Turgenev). Consults doctor about chest pains.

1877   2 March: aware of having contracted syphilis. August: obtains two months' sick leave. Suffering from hair-loss, headaches, eye problems, stomach pains. December: tells Flaubert of his plans for a novel (*A Life*).

1878   Transfers to the Ministry of Education. Working on *A Life*. Leaves it to one side to concentrate on a long poem (*La Vénus rustique*) and some short stories. 10–13 October: invites Flaubert to his mother's house at Étretat and shows him his unfinished novel. Maupassant is now earning 2,000 francs a year, and receiving an annual allowance from his father of 600 francs.

1879   19 February: first night of his play *L'Histoire du vieux temps*, which is well received.

1880   January–February: accused of publishing an obscene poem ('Une fille'). A letter in his defence from Flaubert contributes to the case being dropped. Further health problems, including an eye lesion and renewed hair-loss. 16 April: Zola publishes the anthology of Naturalist writing *Les Soirées de Médan*, stories about the Franco-Prussian War including Maupassant's 'Boule de Suif', which Flaubert hails as a masterpiece. 8 May: sudden death of Flaubert. 1 June: obtains first of several periods of sick leave until he ceases work in 1882. September–October: visits Corsica with his mother.

1881　May: publication of *La Maison Tellier*, the first of his many collections of short stories. Resumes work on *A Life*. July–August: visits Algeria and writes commissioned newspaper articles. On his return continues work on *A Life*.

1882　1 October: a fragment from the beginning of *A Life* published in the review *Panurge*.

1883　27 February: birth of Lucien Litzelmann, son of Josephine Litzelmann and thought to be Maupassant's child. On the same day *A Life* begins to appear in serialized form in the magazine *Gil Blas*. The last instalment appears on 6 April. Maupassant's first novel is then published by Havard. Health problems continue, which his eye specialist relates to syphilis.

1884　Summer: starts work on *Bel-Ami*, his second novel.

1885　6 April–30 May: *Bel-Ami* appears in *Gil Blas* and is published by Havard on 22 May.

1886　19 January: marriage of Hervé. 1–15 August: visit to England. Stays with Baron Ferdinand de Rothschild at Waddesdon Manor, near Oxford. Visits Oxford, then London. 23 December: first instalment of *Mont-Oriol*, his third novel, appears in *Gil Blas*.

1887　January: *Mont-Oriol* published in book form.

1888　9 January: publication of *Pierre et Jean*, his fourth novel, together with an essay, 'Le Roman', by way of a preface. June: publication of *Sur l'eau*, his second travel book.

1889　May: publication by Ollendorff of *Fort comme la mort*, his fifth novel. August: takes brother to an asylum in Lyons. 13 November: death of Hervé.

1890　6–24 January: publication of *La Vie errante*, his third travel book, in series of articles in *L'Écho de Paris*, before its publication in book form in March. 15 May: his final completed novel, *Notre cœur*, begins to appear in the *Revue des deux mondes*: published in book form in June. His health is now giving serious cause for concern.

1891　January–March: begins another novel, *L'Angélus*. 4 March: first performance of his play *Musotte*.

1892　After visiting his mother on New Year's Day, he returns home (at Cannes); tries to kill himself that night by slitting his throat with a paper-knife. 8 January: taken to the clinic of Dr

Blanche in Passy (now part of Paris) and diagnosed as suffering from paresis (or general paralysis), the tertiary stage of syphilis.

1893   6 July: death of Maupassant. 8 July: burial in the cemetery of Montparnasse. Zola gives the funeral oration.

1903   8 December: death of Laure de Maupassant in Nice at the age of 82.

BEL-AMI

PART ONE

CHAPTER 1

When the cashier had handed him the change from his five-franc piece,* Georges Duroy left the restaurant.

Nature had given him a fine presence, enhanced by his bearing as a former NCO,* and he thrust out his chest, mechanically twirling his moustache in soldierly fashion, as he cast a rapid, sweeping glance over the remaining diners, the all-encompassing, predatory glance of a young and handsome man.

The women had raised their heads to look at him: three little seamstresses, an untidy, dowdy, middle-aged music teacher, wearing the inevitable frowzy hat and badly fitting dress, and a couple of middle-class housewives with their husbands, regular customers of this cheap little restaurant with its set meal.

Outside on the pavement, he stood still for a moment, wondering what to do. It was the 28th of June,* and he had left in his pocket exactly three francs forty to last the rest of the month. That meant two dinners but no lunches, or two lunches but no dinners, whichever he preferred. Since a midday meal cost twenty-two sous,* rather than the thirty which was the price for dinner, he would, by making do with just lunch, have one franc twenty centimes left over, sufficient to buy him two lots of bread and sausage and two beers, on the boulevard.* These were his main expense and the greatest pleasure of his evenings. And so he set off down the Rue Notre-Dame-de-Lorette.*

He walked exactly as he had walked when wearing the uniform of the hussars,* his chest out, his legs slightly straddled as if he had just got off his horse; and he thrust his way roughly down the crowded street, bumping into shoulders and jostling people, rather than deviate from his course. His rather shabby top hat was tilted slightly over one ear, and he clicked his heels sharply on the pavement as he strode along. With his cocky air* of a handsome soldier turned civilian, he seemed to be constantly challenging someone, the passers-by, the houses, the entire city.

Despite his sixty-franc outfit,* he still retained a certain flashy elegance, a trifle common, but genuine nevertheless. Tall and well built, he parted his naturally curly hair—dark blond faintly tinged with auburn—in the centre. With his curled-up moustache, which seemed to froth over his lip, and his clear blue eyes pierced by tiny pupils, he closely resembled the 'ne'er-do-well' of popular novels.*

It was one of those summer evenings when Paris is completely airless. The city, hot as an oven, seemed to swelter in the stifling night atmosphere. The stench of sewage rose up from the granite mouths of the drains, and through the low windows of basement kitchens the foul vapours of dishwater and stale sauces belched into the street.

Under arched carriage entrances, shirt-sleeved concierges sat astride straw-bottomed chairs, smoking pipes, while exhausted passers-by plodded along, bare-headed, carrying their hats.

When Georges Duroy reached the boulevard, he stopped once again, undecided what to do next. He felt tempted to make for the Champs-Élysées and the Avenue du Bois de Boulogne, where he might find a little fresh air under the trees, but he was tormented also by another desire, the urge to meet a woman.

How would this happen? He had no idea, but for three months now he had been waiting for it day and night. Sometimes, however, thanks to his handsome face and dashing air, he had managed to get a bit of love here and there for free, but he was always hoping for something more, for something better.

His pockets empty, his blood seething, he was excited by the whispers of the whores on the street-corners: 'Coming back with me, handsome?' Unable to pay, he dared not follow them; and also he was waiting for something different, for other, less common embraces.

Nevertheless he liked the places where prostitutes congregate, their dance-halls, their cafés, their streets; he liked rubbing shoulders with them, talking and chatting familiarly with them, sniffing their pungent scents, feeling them around him. They were women, after all, women meant for love. He did not feel for them any of the family man's innate contempt.

He turned towards the Madeleine* and followed the stream of people moving along, exhausted by the heat. The big cafés were crammed, overflowing onto the pavements, their customers drinking in the brilliant, harsh glare from the brightly lit façades. Before them, on little round or square tables, stood glasses of liquids in every shade of red, yellow, green, and brown; and in the carafes you could see the big transparent cylinders of ice shining, as they cooled the lovely clear water.

Duroy slowed down, his throat parched with longing for a drink. A burning thirst, the thirst you feel on a summer night, gripped him, and his thoughts lingered on the delicious sensation of chilled liquids slipping down his throat. But if he were to drink even two beers during the evening, it would mean kissing goodbye to tomorrow's meagre supper. And he knew only too well what it was like to go hungry at the end of the month.

He told himself: 'I must wait 'til ten, then I'll have my beer at L'Américain.* But, Hell! I'm so damn thirsty!' And he gazed at all those men sitting drinking at their tables, all those men able to satisfy their thirst to their heart's content. He walked boldly and jauntily past the cafés, assessing, with a single glance at a face or a coat, how much money each customer had on him.

And he was filled with rage at these men, sitting there so calmly. If you felt in their pockets you'd find gold and silver* and small change. Every one of them must have, on average, at least forty francs; there must be about a hundred customers per café; a hundred times forty was four thousand francs! He muttered: 'The swine!' as he swung stylishly past. Had he been able to grab hold of one of them in a nice dark corner of a street, he would have wrung his neck without a second thought, by God he would, just the way he used to wring the necks of the peasants' chickens, when he was out on army manœuvres.

And he remembered his two years in Africa, how he used to prey on the Arabs in the little outposts in the South.* And his mouth curled in a cruel, gleeful smile at the recollection of an escapade which had cost three Ouled-Alane tribesmen their lives,* and had netted, for him and his friends, twenty hens, two sheep, and some gold, not to mention something to laugh about for six months.

They had never found those responsible, indeed they had made very little effort to do so, Arabs being considered more or less fair game for soldiers.

In Paris, it was another matter entirely. You couldn't set off on a nice little looting expedition, with your sabre at your side and your revolver in your hand, safe from the arm of the law. In his heart he still had all the instincts of an NCO let loose in a conquered land. No question but that he missed them, those two years of his in the desert. Too bad he hadn't stayed over there! But there it was, he had expected something better when he came back. And now!... Oh yes, now he was in a fine mess! As he rolled his tongue round his mouth, it gave little clicks, as if to confirm how parched his palate was.

The crowd, exhausted and slow, flowed round him, as he thought to himself, 'What a bunch! All these half-wits have cash in their pockets!' He bumped into people, shouldering his way through as he whistled snatches of catchy tunes. Men he had jostled turned round, grumbling; women muttered: 'What an animal!'

He went past the front of the Vaudeville* and stopped opposite the Café Américain, wondering whether he shouldn't have his beer, his thirst was so agonizing. Before deciding, he looked to see what time it was by the illuminated clocks in the middle of the road. It was a quarter past nine. He knew himself: the moment the glass of beer was in front of him, he would gulp it down. Then what would he do until eleven?

He walked on; 'I'll go as far as the Madeleine,' he said to himself, 'and then I'll walk back very slowly.' As he reached the corner of the Place de l'Opéra, he passed a heavy young man, whose face he vaguely recalled having seen somewhere. He set off in pursuit, searching his memory and repeating under his breath: 'Where the devil have I met that chap before?'

He was digging about in his mind without managing to recall who he was; then, all of a sudden, by an extraordinary freak of memory, the same man appeared in his mind's eye, younger, not so heavy, wearing the uniform of a hussar. He exclaimed aloud: 'Goodness, it's Forestier!' and, lengthening his stride, he went and tapped the walker on the shoulder. The man turned round, looked at him, then said: 'What is it, Monsieur?'

Duroy began to laugh: 'Don't you recognize me?'

'No.'

'Georges Duroy, 6th Hussars.'

Forestier held out both hands: 'Georges! How are you, old man?'

'Fine, and how about you?'

'Oh, not so good; can you imagine, my chest's as delicate as a girl's; I've a cough six months out of twelve, ever since I got bronchitis at Bougival,* the year I came back to Paris, which is four years ago now.'

'Really! But you look in great form.'

And Forestier, taking his old comrade by the arm, talked about his illness, telling him of the consultations with the doctors, their diagnoses, their advice, and the difficulty of following their recommendations because of his job. They had ordered him to spend the winter in the South of France, but how could he do that? He was married, a journalist in a good position.

'I'm in charge of the political section at *La Vie française*. I cover the Senate for *Le Salut*, and occasionally I write literary columns for *La Planète*.* So you see, I've come a long way.'

Surprised, Duroy looked at him. He had certainly changed, matured. He now had the demeanour, bearing, and clothes of an established, self-confident man, and the paunch of a man who dines well. In the old days he had been a lean, slender, lithe fellow, scatterbrained, rowdy, and boisterous, always on the go. Three years in Paris had turned him into someone quite different, someone stout and sober, with a few white hairs at his temples, although he was only twenty-seven.

Forestier enquired: 'Where are you headed?'

'Nowhere in particular, I'm taking a turn before going home,' replied Duroy.

'Well, how about coming with me to *La Vie française*, where I've some proofs to correct; then we can go and have a beer together?'

'Lead on.'

And they set off walking arm in arm, with that easy familiarity of school friends or brothers-in-arms.

'What are you doing in Paris?' enquired Forestier.

Duroy shrugged: 'Starving, to put it bluntly. When I'd served my time, I wanted to come here to... to make my pile, or rather to live in Paris; and for six months now I've been working as a clerk for the Northern Railway, for a paltry fifteen hundred francs a year.'*

Forestier muttered: 'My God, that's not much!'

'You don't have to tell me. But what can I do about it? I'm on my own, I don't know a soul, I've got no contacts. It's not the will that's lacking, it's the means.'

His companion looked him over from head to foot, in the style of a practical man sizing someone up, then declared in a positive tone:

'You see, old chap, here everything depends on how much nerve you have. For someone with a little know-how it's easier to become a minister than a head clerk in an office. Never beg; you have to assert yourself. But why the devil couldn't you find something better than working for the Northern line?'

Duroy replied: 'I've searched everywhere, without finding anything. But I'm considering something at the moment, I've been asked to join the Pellerin riding-school* as an instructor. There I'll make three thousand at the very least.'

Forestier stopped dead: 'Don't do that, it's stupid, when you should be earning ten thousand. It would wreck your future on the spot. At your office, at least you're hidden away, nobody knows you, and if you've got what it takes you can leave and get ahead. But once you're a riding instructor, you're done for. It's as if you were to become head waiter in a restaurant where all Paris society dines. When you've given riding lessons to men of fashion, or to their sons, they couldn't ever get used to seeing you as their equal.'

He fell silent, thought for a few seconds, then enquired: 'Did you get your *baccalauréat*?'*

'No: I failed it, twice.'

'That doesn't matter, since you stayed on at school long enough to sit it. If someone mentions Cicero or Tiberius, you know more or less what they're talking about?'

'Yes, more or less.'

'Fine, that's all anybody knows, except for a handful of idiots who don't know how to use their knowledge. Believe me, it's not hard to appear clever; the whole trick is not to let yourself be shown up as ignorant. You wriggle out of it, you avoid the difficulty, you turn the question round, all you need in order to pull the wool over other people's eyes is a dictionary. All men are hopelessly stupid and don't know a thing.'

He spoke with the cheerful, easy confidence of a man who knows what's what, as he smilingly watched the crowds walking by. But, suddenly, he began to cough, stood still until the attack had passed, then said, in a disheartened tone:

'Isn't it exasperating, not being able to get rid of this bronchitis? And we're in the middle of summer. Oh, this winter, I'll go and recuperate at Menton.* There's nothing else for it, your health comes first, by God.'

Reaching the Boulevard Poissonnière,* they came to a big glass door, which had an open newspaper spread out on each of its panels. Three people had stopped to read it.

The words *La Vie française* were blazoned over the door like a challenge, spelt out in huge fiery letters by gas flares. The passers-by, moving abruptly into the brightness cast by these three dazzling words, would suddenly be bathed in light, as visible, clear, and distinct as if it were the middle of the day, before quickly passing back into the shadows.

Forestier pushed open the door: 'Come in,' he said. Duroy went inside, climbed a magnificent yet dirty staircase visible to the entire street, reached an anteroom where two messenger boys nodded to his companion, then came to a halt in a kind of waiting-room, a dusty, dilapidated place, hung with a dingy green imitation velvet that was covered with stains and worn through in places, as if mice had nibbled it.

'Sit down,' said Forestier; 'I'll be back in a minute or two.' He vanished through one of the three doors that led out of the room.

A strange, unique, indescribable smell, the smell of a newsroom, hung in the air. Duroy sat motionless, a little intimidated, but above all surprised. From time to time men raced past him, coming in by one door and leaving by another before he had time to get a good look at them.

Sometimes it would be a young man, very young, with a busy, preoccupied air, holding in his hand a sheet of paper which fluttered as he hurried by; sometimes it would be a typesetter wearing an ink-stained calico overall under which you could see a very white shirt-collar and cloth trousers like those gentlemen wear; they were carefully carrying strips of printed paper, fresh proofs which were still damp. Occasionally a little man would enter the room, dressed with overly conspicuous elegance, his waist too tightly moulded by his frock coat, his calf too shapely beneath the cloth of his trouser, his foot squeezed into too sharply pointed a shoe—some society reporter bringing that evening's latest items of gossip.

And then there were others who came in: solemn, self-important men, sporting flat-brimmed top hats, as if that shape set them apart from the rest of mankind.

Forestier reappeared, escorting a tall thin individual of between thirty and forty. Very dark-haired, dressed in tails and white tie, this man wore the ends of his moustache tightly curled and pointed. He had an insolent, self-satisfied air.

Forestier took his leave of him deferentially: 'Goodbye, my dear colleague.' The other shook his hand: 'Bye, my dear fellow.' And he went down the stairs whistling to himself, his walking-stick under his arm.

'Who's that?' enquired Duroy.

'It's Jacques Rival, you know, the well-known columnist, the duellist. He's just been correcting his proofs. Garin, Montel, and he are the three best, wittiest columnists on current affairs in Paris. He earns thirty thousand francs a year from us, for two articles a week.'*

As they were leaving, they met a short, fat, long-haired man of slovenly appearance, who puffed as he climbed the stairs.

Bowing very low, Forestier said: 'Norbert de Varenne, the poet, the author of *Dead Suns*, another one whose fees are enormous. Every story he gives us costs three hundred francs, and the longest are barely two hundred lines. But let's go to the Napolitain,* I'm beginning to die of thirst.'

The moment they were seated at the café table, Forestier shouted: 'two beers' and swallowed his in a single gulp, while Duroy drank his beer in slow mouthfuls, relishing and savouring it, as if it were something precious and rare. His companion was silent, apparently thinking, then suddenly said: 'Why don't you try your hand at journalism?'

Taken aback, the other stared at him, then replied: 'But... you know... I've never written anything.'

'Bah! You try it, you make a start. I could use you myself, to collect information, make contact with people, pay visits. You'd begin at two hundred and fifty a month, and your cabs paid. Would you like me to mention it to the boss?'

'Yes, of course I'd like that.'

'In that case, there's something you must do: come to my house for dinner tomorrow. There's only five or six coming, the boss, M. Walter, and his wife, Jacques Rival and Norbert de Varenne, whom you've just seen, plus a woman friend of my wife's. All right?'

Flushing, Duroy hesitated, disconcerted. Finally he muttered: 'The thing is... I haven't the right clothes.'

Forestier was dumbfounded. 'You've no evening clothes?

Goodness! But they're absolutely essential. In Paris, you know, it would be better not to have a bed than not to have evening clothes.'

Then, fishing in his waistcoat pocket, he quickly pulled out a handful of gold coins, selected two louis,* put them in front of his former comrade and said, in a friendly, familiar tone:

'Pay me back when you can. Hire the clothes you need or buy them with a down payment, but get them somehow, and come for dinner at my place tomorrow at seven-thirty, it's 17 rue Fontaine.'*

Duroy, flustered, stammered as he picked up the coins: 'You're too kind, thank you so much, you can be sure I won't forget...'

'Oh, that's all right,' the other interrupted. 'Let's have another beer, shall we?' And he shouted: 'Waiter, two beers.'

When they had drunk them, the journalist asked: 'How about a bit of a stroll, for an hour or so?'

'By all means.'

They set off again, in the direction of the Madeleine.

'What do you think we should do?' enquired Forestier. 'People say there's lots to occupy you just strolling round Paris; that's not so. Whenever I feel like taking a stroll for an hour or two in the evening, I never know where to go. A walk in the Bois* is no fun unless you're with a woman, and there isn't always one to hand; the *café-concert** may amuse my pharmacist and his wife, but not me. So, what is there to do? Nothing. There ought to be a summer pleasure garden here, like the Parc Monceau,* that's open at night, where you could listen to really good music while enjoying a cool drink under the trees. Not an amusement park, but a place for strolling, and they'd charge plenty for entrance, so as to attract pretty ladies. You could walk along nicely gravelled paths, lit by electric light, and sit down when you felt like it to listen to the music, either close by or from a distance. We used to have something of the sort, at Musard's,* but the band was too low class and played too much dance music; it wasn't spacious or shady enough, the lighting was too bright. You'd need a very beautiful garden, really enormous. It would be delightful. So where do you want to go?'

At a loss, Duroy hesitated, then made up his mind: 'I've never been to the Folies-Bergère.* I'd love to take a look at it.'

His companion exclaimed: 'My goodness, the Folies-Bergère! It'll be like an oven there, we'll roast. But all right, it's always fun.'

And they turned around and set off for the Rue du Faubourg-Montmartre.

The illuminated façade of the establishment cast a bright light down the four streets which met in front of it. A line of cabs stood waiting for people to leave.

As Forestier was walking in, Duroy stopped him: 'We haven't gone to the box-office.'

The other replied in a self-important tone: 'With me, you don't pay.'

As they reached the entrance, the three attendants nodded to him. The one in the centre shook his hand. The journalist enquired: 'Do you have a good box?'

'Certainly, M. Forestier.'

He took the proffered ticket, pushed open the padded, leather-furbished double doors, and they were in the theatre.

Like a very fine mist, a haze of tobacco smoke partially obscured the distant stage and the other side of the auditorium. Climbing endlessly into the air in thin whitish columns from all the cigars and all the cigarettes that all those people were smoking, this light mist went on rising, collecting at the ceiling where, under the wide dome, round the chandelier, and above the first-floor balcony thronged with spectators, it formed a sky heavy with smoke-laden clouds.

In the vast lobby that leads into the circular promenade, where the gaudily dressed pack of whores prowls about, mingling with the dark-suited crowd of men, a group of women waited for new arrivals in front of one of the three counters, over which three raddled and rouged vendors of drink and of love were presiding. Behind them, tall mirrors reflected their backs and the faces of the passers-by.

Threading his way rapidly through the crowds, like a man entitled to respect, Forestier went up to an attendant: 'Box 17?' he asked.

'This way, Monsieur.'

And they were shut into a little open box decorated in red, containing four chairs of the same colour, jammed so closely together that there was barely room to slide between them. The two friends sat down. To right and left of them, following a long curved line ending at either side of the stage, a series of similar compartments contained people who were seated like them, with only their heads and chests visible.

On the stage, three young men dressed in singlets and tights—one tall, one of medium height, and one short—were performing, each in turn, on a trapeze.

First, the tall one walked forward with short, rapid steps, smiling and greeting the audience with a movement of his hand, as though blowing them a kiss. You could see the muscles of his arms and legs outlined by his close-fitting costume; he puffed out his chest to disguise his all-too-visible paunch, and he looked like a barber's assistant, for his hair was divided into two identical sections by a carefully drawn parting exactly in the centre of his skull. With a graceful leap he caught the trapeze, and, hanging from his hands, turned over and over like a whirling wheel; or else, his body straight and his arms rigid, he remained motionless, lying horizontally in the void, connected to the stationary bar purely by the strength of his wrists.

Then, jumping down onto the floor, he bowed again, smiling, acknowledging the applause from the stalls, and went and stood beside the back-drop, taking care, at every step, to show off the musculature of his leg.

The second, less tall and of stockier build, came forward in his turn and went through the same routine, which the third man repeated again, to a more enthusiastic reception. But Duroy was paying no attention to the show and, turning his head, was constantly gazing over his shoulder at the spacious promenade area crowded with men and prostitutes.

Forestier said to him: 'Take a look at the orchestra stalls: nothing but solid citizens with their wives and children, well-meaning nitwits who've come to watch the show. In the boxes, some men-about-town, a handful of artists, a few fairly high-class tarts, and, behind us, the oddest mixture of men you'll see anywhere in Paris. Who are they? Look at them. There's every kind, from every profession and every class, but most are scum. There's bank clerks and government workers, shop assistants, reporters, pimps, officers out of uniform, nobs in evening clothes who've dined in town, then come out of the Opéra and will go on to the Italians;* then there's a whole mass of shady types who're impossible to pin down. As for the women, there's only one brand: the kind that haunts l'Américain, the girl who charges twenty or thirty francs, is on the lookout for a foreigner with a hundred, and gives her regulars the nod when she's free again. They've been around for a decade: you see them every evening, all year long, in the same spots, except when they're having a little rest at Saint-Lazare or Lourcine.'*

Duroy was no longer listening. One of those women was leaning on their box, looking at him. She was a large brunette, her skin plastered with white powder, her black eyes elongated and underlined with eye-liner and framed by huge, pencilled brows. Her massive breasts strained the dark silk of her dress, and her painted lips, red as a gaping wound, gave her a kind of feral, burning, excessive look that nevertheless excited desire.

With a jerk of her head she summoned one of her friends who was passing, a red-haired blonde, also plump, and said to her in a voice loud enough to be heard:

'Hey! Here's a good-looking chap; if he wants me for a couple of hundred francs, I wouldn't say no!'

Forestier turned round and, smiling, tapped his companion on the thigh: 'That's meant for you; you've made a hit, Duroy. Congratulations.'

The former NCO had gone red and was mechanically fingering the two gold pieces in his waistcoat pocket.

The curtain had been lowered, and the orchestra was now playing a waltz.

Duroy said: 'Shall we take a turn round the gallery?'

'If you like.'

They left the box and were immediately caught up in the stream of promenaders. Pushed, shoved, squashed, and jostled, they walked along, a multitude of hats before their eyes. And, two by two, the prostitutes moved about in this crowd of men, passing through it easily, sliding between elbows, chests, and backs, as if they were totally at home and at ease, like fish in the sea, in the midst of this tide of males.

Entranced, Duroy gave himself up to the moment, rapturously drinking in the air polluted by tobacco, by the smell of humanity, and by the scent of the whores. But Forestier was sweating, panting, coughing.

'Let's go into the garden,' he said.

Turning left, they entered a kind of covered garden cooled by a pair of big, garish fountains. Men and women were sitting drinking at zinc-topped tables, under yews and arborvitae growing in tubs.

'Another beer?' asked Forestier.

'Yes, I'd love one.'

They sat down and watched the passers-by. Now and again a whore making her rounds would stop and ask with a mechanical smile: 'Buy me a drink, Monsieur?' And at Forestier's reply: 'A glass of water from the fountain,' she would move away, muttering: 'Rotten bastard!'

But the fat brunette who had just been leaning on the back of their box appeared again, marching brazenly along arm in arm with the plump blonde. They certainly made a fine pair, well matched.

She smiled on catching sight of Duroy, as if their eyes had already exchanged intimate, secret messages; and she calmly drew up a chair opposite him, made her friend sit down too, then, in a carrying voice, ordered: 'Waiter, two grenadines!'

Forestier, taken aback, remarked: 'You've got a cheek, haven't you!'

She replied: 'It's your friend I fancy. He's such a pretty fellow. I believe I could lose my head over him!'

Duroy, intimidated, could think of nothing to say. He twisted his curly moustache, smiling foolishly. The waiter brought the cordials, which the women drank down in one gulp; then they stood up, and the brunette, with a friendly nod of the head and a light tap of her fan on Duroy's arm, said to him:

'Thanks, my pet. Not much of a talker, are you?'

And off they went, swaying their backsides.

Forestier began to laugh: 'My goodness, old chap, you're a real success with the ladies, aren't you? You should cultivate that. It could take you far.' After a moment's silence he said, in the abstracted tone of someone thinking out loud: 'They're still the quickest way to the top.'

And, as Duroy went on smiling without replying, he enquired: 'Are you going to stay? I'm going home, I've had enough.'

The other muttered: 'Yes, I'll stay for a bit. It isn't late.'

Forestier stood up: 'Well! I'll say goodnight then. See you tomorrow. You won't forget, will you? 17 rue Fontaine, seven-thirty.'

'Fine: see you tomorrow. Thank you.'

They shook hands, and the journalist left. The instant Forestier disappeared, Duroy felt a sense of freedom, and again gleefully fingered the two gold coins in his pocket; then, getting up, he began to thread his way through the crowd, scanning it with his eyes.

He soon caught sight of them both, the blonde and the brunette; they were still sweeping through the throng of men like a pair of disdainful beggars. He headed straight for them, but, on reaching them, lost his nerve.

The brunette said to him: 'Found your tongue again, have you?'

He stammered: 'Dammit, yes...' without managing to utter another word.

The three of them remained standing there, blocking the progress of the strollers, creating a little eddy around themselves.

Then she asked, all of a sudden: 'Are you coming back with me?'

And, trembling with lust, he answered crudely: 'Yes, but I've only twenty francs on me.'

She smiled, unconcerned: 'It doesn't matter.'

And she took his arm as a sign of possession.

As they walked out, he reflected that, with the other twenty francs, he could easily find himself an evening suit to hire for the next day.

CHAPTER 2

'M. Forestier, please?'

'Third floor,* on the left.'

The concierge had replied in a pleasant tone which showed his respect for his tenant. Georges Duroy climbed up the stairs.

He felt somewhat awkward, somewhat self-conscious and apprehensive. He was wearing evening dress for the first time in his life, and was uneasy about his whole appearance. He felt deficient in every respect—in his buttoned boots which, although not of patent leather, were nevertheless quite elegant, for he was vain about his feet; in the shirt bought at the Louvre* that very morning for four francs fifty, and whose very thin starched front was already cracking. Since his other, everyday, shirts were all more or less in a state of disrepair, he had been unable to use even the least shabby among them.

His trousers, a trifle too wide, did not show off his leg to advantage, and seemed to sag and wrinkle round his calves with that bedraggled air that second-hand clothes acquire on limbs they were not designed to cover. Only the coat fitted quite well, being almost exactly his size.

He was climbing slowly and nervously up the stairs, his heart pounding, tormented above all by the fear of seeming ridiculous, when he suddenly saw, opposite him, a gentleman in full evening dress gazing back at him. They were so close to one another that Duroy stepped backwards, then stopped, dumbfounded: it was his own reflection, in a tall, full-length mirror that made the first-floor landing look like a long gallery. He was suddenly overjoyed, he looked so much better than he could ever have believed.

Having nothing but a little shaving mirror in his lodgings, he had been unable to see himself full-length, and as he could get only a very imperfect view of the various parts of his improvised outfit, he had exaggerated its shortcomings, and was panic stricken at the idea of looking absurd.

But on catching sight of himself in the mirror he had not even recognized himself; he had taken himself for someone else, for a man of the world, whom he had, at first glance, thought very personable, very stylish. And now, examining himself carefully, he realized that, in fact, his outfit was perfectly acceptable.

Then he began to study himself like an actor learning his part. He smiled, offered himself his hand, gestured, registered various emotions: astonishment, pleasure, approval; and he tried out the different kinds of smile and meaningful looks that would convey his wish to please the ladies, and the fact that he admired and desired them. A door on the staircase opened. Afraid of being caught unawares, he began climbing very fast, alarmed that he might have been seen posturing like that by one of his friend's dinner-guests.

When he reached the second landing, he saw another mirror, and slowed his pace so he could watch himself walk past.

His bearing struck him as truly elegant. He walked well.

And he was filled with an inordinate feeling of self-confidence. Of course he would be successful, with that face of his, and that urge to get ahead, and the determination he knew he had, and his independence of spirit. He wanted to run, to leap, as he climbed the final flight of stairs. He halted in front of the third mirror, curled up his moustache in his habitual way, took off his hat to smooth his hair, and murmured softly, as he so often did: 'Such a wonderful invention.' Then, stretching out his hand, he rang the bell.

The door opened almost immediately, and he found himself in the presence of a black-suited, clean-shaven, unsmiling servant whose appearance was so perfect that Duroy felt renewed apprehension without understanding the cause of his vague unease: an unconscious comparison, perhaps, of the cut of their garments. This footman, whose shoes were of patent leather, asked, as he took the overcoat Duroy carried over his arm to hide its stains:

'Whom should I announce?'

And he fired off the name round a drawn-back door curtain, into a room which Duroy now had to enter.

But Duroy suddenly lost his nerve, and stood there paralysed with fright, breathing hard. He was about to take his first steps in the world for which he had longed, of which he had dreamed. He did go in, however. A young, fair-haired woman was standing alone waiting for him, in a large and well-lit room full of plants, like a conservatory.

He stopped dead, utterly disconcerted. Who was this smiling woman? Then he recalled that Forestier was married; and the thought that this pretty elegant blonde must be his friend's wife, put the finishing touch to his discomfiture.

He stammered: 'Madame, I am...'

She held out her hand: 'I know, Monsieur. Charles told me about your meeting yesterday evening, and I'm so pleased that he had the excellent idea of inviting you to dine with us tonight.'

He blushed to the roots of his hair, not knowing what to say, and feeling he was being examined, inspected from top to toe, sized up, assessed.

He wanted to apologize, to dream up something to explain the deficiencies of his appearance; but he could think of nothing, and shrank from broaching this difficult subject.

He sat down in an armchair she indicated, and when he felt the soft, resilient velvet of the seat yield beneath him, when he found himself enveloped by, supported by, enfolded in this soothing piece of furniture whose padded back and arms held him delicately, it seemed to him that he was embarking on a new, delightful life, that he was taking possession of something delicious, that he was becoming somebody, that he had found salvation; and he gazed at Mme Forestier, whose eyes had never left him.

She was wearing a gown of pale blue cashmere which showed off her supple figure and full breasts to advantage. The flesh of her arms and neck emerged from a froth of white lace with which the bodice and short sleeves were trimmed; and her hair, piled on the top of her head, curled a little at the nape of her neck, forming a faint cloud of blond fluff above her neck.

Duroy grew more relaxed beneath her gaze, which reminded him, for some unknown reason, of the prostitute he had met the night before at the Folies-Bergère. She had grey eyes, of a bluish grey which gave them a strange expression, a thin nose, full lips, a rather plump chin; her irregular, captivating countenance was full of sweetness and mischief. It was one of those feminine faces whose every line has its own particular charm, and seems to possess a meaning, whose every movement seems to reveal or to conceal something.

After a short silence, she asked: 'Have you been in Paris long?'

Gradually regaining his self-control, he replied: 'For only a few months, Madame. I'm working for the railway, but Forestier led me to hope that I may, through his good offices, be able to get into journalism.'

She smiled in a more open, more kindly manner, and murmured, lowering her voice: 'I know.'

The bell had rung again. The footman announced: 'Mme de Marelle.'

She was small and dark-haired, what people call a brunette.

As she walked rapidly in, he saw that she was wearing an extremely simple dark dress that fitted her like a skin from head to foot. A single red rose, tucked into her black hair, drew the eye irresistibly to her face, calling attention to its particular quality, adding the vivid, startling touch needed to set it off.

She was followed by a little girl in short skirts. Mme Forestier hurried forward:

'How are you, Clotilde.'

'Hallo, Madeleine.'

They kissed. Then, with the composure of an adult, the child proffered her forehead, saying:

'Good evening, cousin Madeleine.'

Mme Forestier kissed her, then made the introductions:

'M. Georges Duroy, a good friend of Charles's. My friend Mme de Marelle. We're distantly related.'

She added: 'You know, we don't stand on ceremony here, we're quite informal. I do hope that's understood!

The young man bowed.

But the door opened once more, admitting a fat little man, short and round, escorting on his arm a statuesque, beautiful woman, taller and much younger than himself, with patrician manners and a grave demeanour. It was M. Walter, member of the Chamber of Deputies, financier, money and business mogul, a Jew from the Midi,* Director of *La Vie française*, with his wife, née Basile-Ravalau, daughter of the banker of that name.

Then, right behind them, came Jacques Rival, looking very elegant, and Norbert de Varenne, the latter's coat collar shiny from contact with his long hair which brushed his shoulders, where it deposited a sprinkling of little white specks. His tie, badly knotted, looked well past its first youth. He advanced with the air of an ageing Don Juan, took Mme Forestier's hand, and planted a kiss on her wrist. As he bowed his head, his long hair spread like a sheet of water over the young woman's bare arm.

Finally Forestier himself arrived, apologizing for being late. He had been held up at the newspaper by the Morel affair. M. Morel, a radical deputy, had just asked the Minister a question about a request for funds relating to the colonization of Algeria.*

The servant announced: 'Dinner is served!' They went in to the dining-room.

Duroy found himself seated between Mme de Marelle and her daughter. Once again he was feeling awkward, terrified of using the wrong fork, spoon, or glass. He had four, one with a bluish tinge to it. What could that be for?

Nothing was said during the soup, then Norbert de Varenne enquired: 'Have you been reading about the Gauthier case? What an extraordinary business!'

And they discussed this case of adultery complicated by blackmail. They did not talk about it the way you might comment, around a family dinner-table, on events reported in the press, but rather the way doctors talk about diseases, or greengrocers about vegetables. They showed neither indignation nor astonishment over the facts; they searched for their deep-seated, hidden causes, with a professional curiosity and a complete lack of interest in the crime itself. They tried to find clear explanations in terms of underlying motive, trying to identify all the mental phenomena behind the tragedy, seeing it as the scientific consequence of a particular state of mind. The women, too, found this investigation, this task, deeply engrossing. And other recent events were analysed, commented upon, explored from every point of view, weighed up precisely, with that practised eye and that specialized approach of the dealer in news, the vendor of the human comedy by the line, just as a tradesman examines, scrutinizes, and weighs up the products he is going to sell to the public.

Then the conversation turned to duelling, and Jacques Rival took the floor. This subject was his: no one else was qualified to talk about it.

Duroy did not dare put in a word. He would glance occasionally at his neighbour, whose rounded breasts he found alluring. A diamond hung down below her ear on a golden wire, like a drop of water sliding over her skin. From time to time she would pass a remark that would make everyone smile. She had a funny, pleasing, unexpected turn of mind, the mind of a worldly-wise young creature who takes things as they come and views them with a light-hearted, easy-going scepticism.

Duroy searched in vain for some compliment to pay her and, unable to find one, devoted himself to her daughter, pouring out her drinks, holding the dishes for her and serving her. The child, more serious than her mother, kept thanking him in a solemn voice, giving little appreciative nods: 'You're most kind, Monsieur,' as she listened to the grown-ups with a thoughtful air.

Everyone praised the dinner, which was extremely good. M. Walter wolfed down his food, hardly saying a thing, and squinting under his glasses as he examined the dishes he was offered. Norbert de Varenne kept pace with him, occasionally letting drops of sauce fall on to his shirt front.

Forestier, smiling, serious and watchful, kept exchanging complicitous glances with his wife, like partners who together are carrying out a tricky task which is going perfectly.

Faces became flushed, voices were rising. From time to time the servant would whisper in the ear of each guest: 'Corton or Château Laroze?'*

Duroy had found the Corton to his taste, and allowed his glass to be refilled every time. He was beginning to experience a delicious sensation of happiness, a warm glow which, spreading from his stomach to his head and limbs, permeated his entire body. He felt himself possessed by a sense of total well-being, a well-being both physical and mental, of body and of mind.

And he was feeling, now, an urge to talk, to draw attention to himself, to be listened to and appreciated like those others whose slightest remarks were savoured to the full.

But the conversation flowed on without interruption, linking one idea with another, leaping from one subject to another at the prompting of a word or a trifling remark, until it had reviewed all the events of the day, and touching on countless topics, before returning at last to M. Morel's important parliamentary question on the colonization of Algeria.

M. Walter cracked a joke or two between courses; his mind had a coarse, sceptical bent. Forestier described his article which was to appear the next day, and Jacques Rival made the case for a military government, with grants of land for every officer with more than thirty years' service in the colonies.

'In that way,' he said, 'you'd build a dynamic community which had long since come to understand and love the country, would know its language and be familiar with all the serious local problems that newcomers inevitably run into.'

Norbert de Varenne interrupted him:

'Yes... they'll know about everything, except farming. They'll speak Arabic, but won't know how to thin out beetroot or how to sow wheat. They'll even be good at fencing, but very poor when it comes to fertilizers. On the contrary, this new country should be made freely available to everyone. Men with brains will find their feet, the others'll go under. That's the way the world works.'

A brief silence ensued. People were smiling.

Georges Duroy opened his mouth and spoke, surprised by the sound of his voice, as if he had never before heard himself talk: 'The main shortage over there is good land. Really fertile land is as expensive as it is in France, and it's bought up by very wealthy Parisians as an investment. The real settlers, the poor ones, who emigrate there because they can't make a living here, are forced into the desert, where nothing can grow, for lack of water.'

They were all looking at him. He felt himself blush. M. Walter enquired:

'Are you familiar with Algeria, Monsieur?'

He replied: 'Yes, Monsieur, I spent twenty-eight months there, and I've lived in all three provinces.'*

And suddenly, abandoning the Morel business, Norbert de Varenne asked him about a particular feature of Algerian life which he had heard about from an officer. It concerned the Mzab,* that strange little Arab republic which had sprung up in the heart of the Sahara, in the driest part of that scorchingly hot region.

Duroy had twice visited the Mzab, and he spoke about the customs of that extraordinary country, where every drop of water is worth its weight in gold, where every inhabitant is expected to help maintain the public services, where commercial honesty is more highly developed than in civilized societies.

He talked with a kind of exuberant verve, spurred on by the wine and by the wish to please, telling little stories about the regiment, describing features of the Arab way of life or adventures on the battlefield. He even found some evocative words to depict those barren yellow lands, everlastingly desolate beneath the all-consuming blaze of the sun.

The women were all gazing at him. Madame Walter said quietly in her unhurried way: 'With your experiences, you could write a delightful series of articles.'

Hearing this, Walter peered at the young man over the top of his glasses, as was his habit when he wanted to get a good look at a face. To inspect his food he looked under them.

Forestier seized his chance: 'I spoke to you earlier, Monsieur, about M. Georges Duroy, and asked you to take him on as my assistant for the political column. Ever since Marambot left, I've had no one to run around and collect information about urgent, confidential matters. The paper's suffering as a result.'

Turning serious, old Walter removed his glasses completely in order to look Duroy full in the face. He said: 'M. Duroy certainly has an original turn of mind. If he will be so good as to come to my office tomorrow at three, we'll see what we can arrange.' Then, after a pause, swivelling right round to face the young man: 'Let me have some entertaining little pieces on Algeria right away. Talk about your experiences, and relate them to the colonial question, as you did just now. It's topical, highly topical, and I'm sure it'll be just what our readers want. But hurry! I'll need the first article tomorrow or the day after, while the debate's going on in the Chamber, to get the public hooked.'

Mme Walter added, with that grave and gracious air which never left her and which made whatever she said seem like a special favour: 'And you have an excellent title: "Recollections of an African Cavalryman"; don't you agree, M. Norbert?'

The old poet, who had come to fame late in life, detested and feared the younger generation. He replied curtly: 'Yes, excellent, provided that the rest of the stories hit the right note, for that's what's so difficult: to hit the right note, what in music they call the right key.'

Mme Forestier was favouring Duroy with a protective, smiling gaze, an experienced gaze which seemed to say: 'You're going to succeed.' Mme de Marelle had several times turned towards him, and the diamond hanging from her ear kept quivering, as if the delicate drop of water was about to slide and fall off.

The little girl sat motionless and solemn, her head bent over her plate.

But the servant was going round the table, pouring a Johannisberg* into the blue glasses; and Forestier raised his glass to M. Walter in a toast, saying: 'Long life and prosperity to *La Vie française*!'

They all turned and bowed to the Director, who was smiling; Duroy, intoxicated with success, drained his glass at one gulp. He felt as if he could have drained a whole wine-cask in the same way; he could have devoured an ox or strangled a lion. His limbs were filled with superhuman strength, his spirit imbued with invincible determination and infinite hope. He felt at home, now, amongst these people; he had just secured his position, won his place. His eyes rested on their faces with new-found confidence, and for the first time he dared to address his neighbour.

'Your earrings, Madame, are the prettiest I have ever seen.'

She turned towards him with a smile: 'It was my own idea to wear diamonds in this way, just on a wire. You'd think they were drops of dew, wouldn't you?'

He whispered, amazed at his own audacity, and terrified of making a blunder:

'Yes, they're charming... but then the ears show them off so perfectly.'

She thanked him with a glance, one of those bright feminine glances that go straight to the heart.

And as he turned his head, his eyes again met Mme Forestier's still kindly gaze, but now he thought he saw in it a brighter sparkle, a flash of mischief, of encouragement.

The men were all talking together now, gesticulating and raising their voices; they were discussing the great project of the Paris Métro.* The subject was not exhausted until the end of dessert, for everyone had a great deal to say about the slowness of communications within Paris, the disadvantages of the trams, the problems with the omnibuses,* and the churlishness of the cab drivers.

Then they left the dining-room to have their coffee. Duroy jokingly offered the little girl his arm; she solemnly thanked him, standing on tip-toe to reach up to his elbow with her hand.

When they went into the drawing-room, he again had the impression of entering a conservatory. In each corner of the room a tall palm tree unfurled its elegant leaves, reaching high up to the ceiling, then fanning out like a fountain.

Rubber trees stood on either side of the fireplace, their trunks, like cylindrical columns, bearing layer upon layer of long, dark green leaves, while on the piano two round, unfamiliar plants, covered with

blossom, one all pink, the other all white, seemed improbable, artificial, too beautiful to be real.

The air was fresh and full of a vague, soft, indefinable perfume,
impossible to name.

And the young man, now feeling surer of himself, studied the
room attentively. It was not large; nothing, apart from the greenery,
drew the eye; there were no bright colours; but you felt at ease there,
calm and relaxed; it enveloped you gently, pleasingly, enfolding you
in something like a caress.

The walls were hung with an old-fashioned fabric of faded purple,
sprinkled with tiny yellow silk flowers no bigger than a fly. The
curtains over the doors, made of blue-grey military cloth, were decorated with a few carnations embroidered in red silk; chairs of every
shape and size, scattered haphazardly round the room, chaises
longues, enormous armchairs, tiny armchairs, pouffes, and foot-
stools were all covered in Louis XVI silk or a beautiful Utrecht
velvet, figured in garnet-red on a cream background.

'Will you take coffee, M. Duroy?' And Mme Forestier, as she
handed him a filled cup, gave him that invariably friendly smile of
hers.

'Yes, thank you, Madame.'

He accepted the cup, and as he leant anxiously forward to take,
with the silver sugar-tongs, a lump of sugar from the bowl the little
girl was carrying, the young woman said to him in a low voice:
'Now's your chance to make a good impression on Mme Walter.'

She moved away before he could say anything in reply.

Fearful of spilling his coffee on the carpet, he drank it immediately; then, feeling more relaxed, he cast about for an excuse to
approach the wife of his new employer, and begin a conversation.

All of a sudden he noticed that she was holding her empty cup in
her hand; and as she was not near a table, she had nowhere to put it
down. He leapt forward.

'Allow me, Madame.'

'Thank you, Monsieur.'

He took the cup away, then returned. 'You can have no idea,
Madame, how much I enjoyed reading *La Vie française* when I was
out there in the desert. It's really and truly the only paper to read
outside France, because it's more literary, it's wittier and less boring
than all the others. You can find a bit of everything in it.'

She gave him a politely amiable smile and replied gravely:

'M. Walter found it very difficult to start a newspaper of that kind, which filled a new need.'

And they began to chat. His small talk was fluent and trite, his voice attractive, his glance captivating and his moustache irresistibly seductive. Crinkly, curly, and delightful, it sprang thickly out over his lip, blond with auburn tints, slightly paler where it bristled at each end.

They spoke of Paris and its surroundings, the banks of the Seine, watering-places, the delights of summer, all those commonplace topics which you can discuss indefinitely without wearying the mind. Then, seeing M. Norbert de Varenne approaching with a glass of liqueur in his hand, Duroy moved discreetly away.

Mme de Marelle, who had been chatting to Mme Forestier, called him over: 'Well, Monsieur,' she said to him without preamble, 'so you want to have a go at journalism?'

He talked in vague terms of his plans, then began the same conversation with her that he had just had with Mme Walter; but, as he was now more in command of his subject, he acquitted himself better, repeating things he had heard as if they were his own. And all the time he gazed into his companion's eyes, as though seeking to confer some profound significance on what he was saying.

She, in her turn, told him a number of stories, in the easy, lively manner of a woman who knows she is witty and always wants to be amusing; then, laying her hand familiarly on his arm, she lowered her voice as she babbled on, thus bestowing a tone of intimacy on her inconsequential talk. Deep down, he felt excited by the proximity of this young woman who was taking such an interest in him. He would have liked to do her some signal service there on the spot, to spring to her defence, to show what he was made of; and the slowness of his replies revealed the preoccupation of his mind.

But suddenly, for no apparent reason, Mme de Marelle called 'Laurine!' and the little girl came over.

'Sit here, child; you'll be cold by the window.'

Duroy felt a fierce urge to kiss the little girl, as if some part of that kiss might transfer itself to the mother. He asked, in a flirtatious, fatherly tone: 'Would you allow me to kiss you, Mademoiselle?'

The child looked up at him in surprise. Mme de Marelle said with a laugh: 'Answer: "You may today, Monsieur, but don't imagine you can always do so."'

Duroy promptly sat down, taking Laurine on his knee, then brushed his lips over the soft curls of her forehead.

The mother was amazed: 'My goodness, that's extraordinary, she didn't run away. Usually she only lets herself be kissed by women. You're irresistible, M. Duroy.'

He blushed without replying, as he rocked the little girl gently on his knee.

Mme Forestier came up and exclaimed in astonishment: 'Heavens, you've made a conquest of Laurine, how very remarkable!'

Jacques Rival, a cigar in his mouth, was also approaching the group, and Duroy stood up to take his leave, afraid of ruining, by some inappropriate remark, the work he had accomplished, the campaign of conquest he had begun.

He bowed, softly pressing the small hands the women held out, then vigorously shaking those of the men. He noticed that Jacques Rival's hand was warm and dry, and responded cordially to his grasp; Norbert de Varenne's was damp and cold and slid away from between his fingers; old man Walter had a cold, flabby hand, quite without energy or character, while Forestier's was plump and warm. His friend whispered to him: 'Tomorrow at three, don't forget.'

'Oh, don't worry, I won't forget.'

When he was back on the stairs, his joy was so intense that he felt like running down them, and he began to take the steps two at a time; but, suddenly noticing, in the large mirror on the second floor landing, a gentleman who was coming bounding along to meet him, he stopped dead, as mortified as if he had been caught doing something wrong.

Then he stared at himself for a long time, astounded at being such a very handsome young man; then he smiled complacently at himself; then he took leave of his reflection with a low bow, a ceremonious bow, the kind of bow reserved for people of high rank.

CHAPTER 3

Once he was back in the street, Georges Duroy hesitated over what he should do next. He longed to keep moving, to dream, to walk on and on thinking about the future and breathing in the soft night air; but his mind kept returning to the series of articles old Walter had asked for, and he decided to go home immediately and set to work.

He strode rapidly along towards the outer boulevard, which he then followed as far as the Rue Boursault,* where he lived. His building, which had six floors, was inhabited by a score of small working-class or lower-middle-class households, and as he climbed upstairs, using taper matches to light the dirty steps littered with scraps of paper, cigarette ends, and kitchen refuse, he felt a nauseating wave of disgust and an urge to move out of there as soon as possible, to live as the rich do, in well-kept homes, with carpets. A heavy smell of food, privies, and humanity, a stagnant odour of filth and crumbling plaster walls that no draught of fresh air could have swept away, filled the building from top to bottom.

The young man's room was on the fifth floor, and looked out, as though over a deep chasm, onto the immense cutting of the Western Railway,* exactly above the point where it emerges from the tunnel by the Batignolles station.* Duroy opened his window and leant on the rusty iron railing.

Below him, in the depths of the dark pit, three motionless red signal lights glowed like the eyes of animals; further away, other lights were visible, and then, even further off, still others. Every moment, short or long blasts of train whistles were carried on the night air, some close by, others, from over by Asnières,* barely audible. They modulated, like voices calling out. One of them was coming nearer, still emitting its plaintive cry which grew louder by the instant, and soon a big yellow light appeared, hurtling along very noisily; Duroy watched as the long string of carriages was swallowed up by the tunnel.

Then he told himself: 'To work!' He put his lamp on the table; but just as he was about to start writing, he realized that all he had in his room was a folded sheet of notepaper.

Well, he would just have to open it out and manage with that. He dipped his pen into the ink and wrote at the top of the page, in his best handwriting, 'Recollections of an African Cavalryman'. Then he tried to think of how to begin his first sentence.

He sat there, leaning his head on his hand, his eyes fixed on the blank sheet spread out before him.

What was he going to say? He could no longer remember, now, anything he'd just been talking about, not a single incident, not a single fact, nothing. Suddenly he thought: 'I must begin with my departure.' So he wrote: 'It was in 1874, about the 15th of May, when an exhausted France was resting after the disasters of the terrible year...'* And there he stopped, not knowing how to lead into what followed, his boarding the ship, the voyage, his first reactions.

After thinking about it for ten minutes he decided to postpone the introductory page until the next day, and launch straight into a description of Algiers.

On his sheet of paper he wrote: 'The town of Algiers is completely white...' but was unable to say anything more.

In his mind's eye, he could see the lovely bright city, its low, flat-roofed houses cascading down the mountain into the sea; but he could no longer find a single word to express what he had seen, what he had felt. After a great struggle, he added: 'It is partly inhabited by Arabs...' Then he flung his pen down on the table, and stood up.

His little iron bed, where the weight of his body had made a hollow, was covered with his discarded everyday clothes, empty, tired, and limp, ugly as garments left unclaimed at the Morgue. And, on a straw-bottomed chair, his silk hat, his only hat, lay upturned as if ready to receive charitable coins.

His walls, papered in grey with a pattern of blue flowers, displayed quite as many stains as flowers, ancient, unidentifiable stains of dubious origin, which could have been squashed insects or splashes of oil, marks of fingers greasy with pomade, or soap scum splashed from the wash-basin. Everything reeked of shameful poverty, the poverty of Parisian furnished rooms. He was filled with rage at the wretchedness of his life. He told himself that he must escape from there without delay, that he must, the very next day, leave this impecunious existence behind him.

Suddenly feeling a renewed zeal for work, he sat down again at his table, and once more began searching for words to do justice to the strange charm of Algiers, that gateway to Africa with its impenetrable mysteries, the Africa of nomadic Arabs and strange black men, the undiscovered and seductive Africa whose incredible fauna we sometimes see displayed in zoos, fauna that might have been created for fairy-tales—the fantastic fowl the ostrich, the gazelle like a divine goat, the astounding, grotesque giraffe, the ponderous camel, the monstrous hippopotamus, the misshapen rhinoceros, and our alarming relative, the gorilla. A few ideas dimly began to take shape; he might perhaps have been able to talk about them, but he was quite unable to formulate them in writing. Feverish with frustration, he stood up once more, his hands damp with sweat and his temples throbbing.

His glance fell on his laundry bill, which the concierge had brought up that very evening, and he was suddenly overcome by a feeling of frantic despair. All his high spirits vanished in an instant, along with his self-confidence and his faith in the future. It was over, it was all over, he would achieve nothing, he would be nothing; he felt empty, ineffectual, useless, doomed to failure.

Duroy went back to the window and leant out, just at the very moment when a train emerged from the tunnel with a sudden, harsh blast of sound. It was heading over there, across the fields and the plains, to the sea.* And he found himself thinking of his parents.

That train would pass close by them, just a few miles from their house. He saw, in his mind's eye, the little building high up on the hill, overlooking Rouen and the immense valley of the Seine, on the outskirts of the village of Canteleu.*

His father and mother kept a small inn, *A la Belle Vue*, a country tavern where middle-class couples came from the city suburbs for their Sunday lunch. His parents had planned to make a gentleman of Duroy, and had sent him to secondary school. He had completed his schooling but failed the *baccalauréat*, so had gone off to do his military service, intending to become an officer, a colonel or a general. But, growing disenchanted with military life long before his five years were up, he began to dream of making his fortune in Paris.

When his time was up he had moved there, despite the entreaties of his parents, who, seeing their dreams evaporate, now wanted to keep him with them. He had his own hopes for his future; he foresaw a triumphal success, attained by means of circumstances which he could only vaguely imagine, but which he would surely be able to bring into being and use to his advantage.

He had had some successes with women during his time in the army, mostly of the easy kind available to soldiers, but there had been a few in better circles. He had seduced a tax-collector's daughter who had wanted to give up everything and follow him, and a solicitor's wife who, when he abandoned her, had in her despair tried to drown herself.

His fellow-soldiers said of him: 'He's a crafty, wily devil, he's got his wits about him and knows how to keep his nose clean.' And indeed he had promised himself to be crafty and wily and quick-witted.

His native Norman wit, whetted by daily contact with garrison life and broadened by the instances he saw in Africa of looting, illegal perks, and questionable deals, had been given a new edge by the notions of honour current in the army, by military bravado and patriotic sentiments, by tales of selfless heroism told in the sergeants' mess and by all the cheap glory of the profession; so that it had become like a box with multiple false bottoms, in which you could find a bit of everything.

But the passion to succeed was what predominated.

Without realizing it, he had begun day-dreaming again, as he did every night. He imagined a magnificent love-affair which would bring him, in one single move, to the fulfilment of his hopes. He would marry some banker or nobleman's daughter; they would meet in the street, and she would fall in love with him at first sight.

He was aroused from his dream by the strident whistle of an engine that, emerging on its own from the tunnel, like a big rabbit coming out of its burrow, was racing along the tracks at full steam, making for the depot, where it would be able to take its rest.

Then, once more under the spell of the vague, cheerful optimism that as a rule never left him, he blew a kiss, for luck, into the night, a kiss of love for the woman he was awaiting, a kiss of desire for the riches he coveted. Then, closing the window, he began to undress, muttering: 'Oh well, I'll find it easier in the morning. My mind's not clear tonight. And then, I may have had a bit too much to drink. You can't work properly in that state.'

He got into bed, blew out the light, and went to sleep almost immediately.

He awoke early, as you do when you are full of hope or anxiety, and, jumping out of bed, went to open his window, to drink in what he called a good cup of fresh air.

The houses of the Rue de Rome opposite, beyond the deep ditch made by the railway cutting, were shining in the rays of the rising sun, as if painted with a dazzling bright light. Over to the right, in the distance, you could make out the slopes of Argenteuil, the Sannois hills, and the mills of Orgemont,* through a bluish, thin mist that floated like a little transparent veil that someone had flung over the horizon.

Gazing for a few minutes at the distant countryside, Duroy murmured: 'It would be damn nice, out there, on a day like this.' Then he thought that he must get to work, and straight away, and also tip the concierge's son ten sous to go and tell them at the office that he was ill.

He sat down at his table, dipped his pen in the inkwell, leant his forehead on his hand and tried to think of some ideas. It was no use. Nothing came.

However, he did not feel discouraged. He thought: 'Oh well, I'm not used to this. It's a job you have to learn, like any other. I must have some help at the beginning. I'll go and find Forestier, who'll get my article into shape for me in no time.'

He dressed. Once in the street, he felt it was still too early to turn up at his friend's, who probably slept late. So he strolled about slowly under the trees of the outer boulevard. It was not yet nine o'clock when he reached the Parc Monceau,* which was still cool and damp from being watered. He sat down on a bench, and again began to day-dream. A young man was walking back and forth in front of him, a very elegant young man, no doubt waiting for a woman.

She appeared, her face veiled, her step rapid, took his arm after quickly shaking his hand, and they walked off.

Duroy's heart was filled with a fierce longing for love, for affairs that were elegant, perfumed, delicate. He stood up and started walking again, thinking about Forestier. What a lucky fellow he was!

He arrived at his door at the very moment his friend was coming out.

'You here! At this time of day! What do you want?'

Duroy, embarrassed at meeting him like this, just as he was leaving, stammered:

'It's um... it's... I can't manage to write my article, you know, the article that M. Walter asked me to do on Algeria. It's not very surprising, considering that I've never ever done any writing. It needs practice, like everything else. I'll pick it up fast, I'm sure, but, just at the beginning, I don't know how to set about it. I've lots of ideas, lots, but I can't put them into words.'

He stopped, hesitating a little. Forestier was smiling mischievously: 'I know just what you mean.'

Duroy continued: 'Yes, it must happen to everyone at the start. So, well, I've come... I've come to ask you to give me a hand... You'd get my article into shape for me in a couple of minutes, you'd show me the right approach. You could give me some pointers about style; without your help I'll never be able to pull it off.'

The other man was still smiling cheerfully. Tapping his former comrade on the arm, he said to him: 'Go and find my wife, she'll solve your problem for you as well as I could. I've trained her to do this work. I myself haven't the time this morning, otherwise I'd have been very glad to do it.'

Suddenly daunted, Duroy hesitated, not daring: 'But, surely I can't call and see her as early as this?...'

'Yes, you certainly may. She's up. You'll find her in my study, putting some notes in order for me.'

Duroy refused to go in. 'No, I can't possibly...'

Forestier took him by the shoulders, turned him around, and pushed him towards the stairs: 'Oh go on up, you great idiot, since I'm telling you to. Surely you're not going to force me to climb those three flights again, to take you in to her and explain what it is you want!'

So then Duroy agreed. 'Thanks, I'll go. I'll tell her that you forced me, literally forced me, to come and find her.'

'Yes. Calm down, she won't eat you. But don't you forget, this afternoon, at three.'

'Oh! Don't worry!'

And Forestier hurried away, while Duroy began climbing slowly up the stairs, step by step, wondering what he was going to say and uneasy about the welcome he might receive.

The servant came to open the door. He was wearing a blue apron and had a broom in his hands.

'Monsieur is out,' he said, without waiting for the question.

Duroy held his ground: 'Ask Mme Forestier if she can see me, and tell her that I come at the suggestion of her husband, whom I met in the street.'

Then he waited. The man returned, opened a door on the right, and announced: 'Madame will see you, Monsieur.'

She was sitting on an office chair, in a small room whose walls were entirely covered by books neatly arranged on black wooden shelves. The bindings of different shades, red, yellow, green, purple, and blue, added colour and brightness to this monotonous alignment of volumes.

She turned round, still smiling; she was enveloped in a white negligé edged with lace; and she held out her hand, revealing her bare arm through the wide opening of the sleeve.

'So soon?' she said. Then she went on: 'That's not a reproach, it's a simple question.'

He stammered: 'Oh, Madame, I didn't want to come up, but your husband, whom I met downstairs, made me. I feel so embarrassed that I daren't say what brings me here.'

She indicated a chair: 'Sit down and tell me.'

She was nimbly twirling a goose-feather quill between two fingers, and in front of her lay a large sheet of paper, half covered in writing which the young man's arrival had interrupted.

She seemed to feel at home seated at this writing-desk, as much at ease as if she were in her own drawing-room, busy with her normal duties. A faint fragrance arose from the negligé, the fresh scent of someone who has just washed. And Duroy tried to discern, fancied he could picture, the young, pale body, plump and warm, that was gently enveloped in the soft fabric.

As he sat silent, she repeated: 'Well, tell me, what's this all about?'

He murmured hesitantly: 'You see... No, really, I don't dare... It's just that I was working very late last night... and very early this morning... to do that article on Algeria that M. Walter asked me for... and I couldn't write anything good... I tore up all my efforts... I'm not used to this kind of work, so I came to ask Forestier to help me... just this once...'

Gratified and flattered, she interrupted him with a burst of happy laughter: 'And he told you to come and find me...? How very nice...'

'Yes, Madame. He told me that you'd help me out of my difficulties

better than he could... but I didn't dare, I didn't want to. Do you
know what I mean?'

She stood up. 'It'll be wonderful to work together like that. I love
your idea. Here, sit down in my chair, because they know my writing
at the paper. And we're going to do your article for you, one that's a
real hit, you'll see.'

He sat down, picked up a pen, spread a sheet of paper in front of
him, and waited.

Mme Forestier, still standing, watched him make these prepar-
ations; then she took a cigarette from the mantelpiece and lit it: 'I
can't work without smoking,' she said.

'Well, let's see; what do you want to say?'

He looked up at her in astonishment. 'But I don't know myself;
that's why I came to see you.'

She continued: 'Yes, I'll fix it up for you. I'll make the sauce, but
first I need the dish.'

He was nonplussed; finally he said, hesitating: 'I'd like to describe
my travels, right from the beginning...'

At that she took a seat opposite him, on the other side of the large
table, and, looking him in the face:

'All right, talk to me about it first, just to me, you understand, nice
and slowly, not leaving anything out, and I'll decide what to use.'

But as he did not know where to start, she began questioning him
like a priest in the confessional, asking precise questions which
reminded him of details he had forgotten, important people he had
encountered, faces he had merely glimpsed in passing.

When she had made him talk like that for a little while, she
suddenly interrupted him: 'Now we're going to begin. First, we'll
pretend you're sending your impressions to a friend, which will
allow you to put in a whole lot of nonsense, and make all kinds of
remarks, and be natural and funny, if we can manage it. Now begin:

'My dear Henri, you want to know what Algeria's like, well you're
about to find out. Having nothing to do, here in the little hut of dried
mud that serves as my home, I'm going to send you a kind of journal
of my life, day by day, hour by hour. It will be a bit coarse at times.
Well too bad, no one's forcing you to show it to your lady friends...'

She interrupted herself to relight her cigarette, which had gone
out; and, immediately, the high-pitched scratch of the goose quill on
the paper stopped.

'Let's go on,' she said.

'Algeria is a large French possession on the frontier of those vast unknown regions we call the desert, the Sahara, central Africa, and so on. Algiers is the gateway, the charming white gateway to this strange continent.

'But first you have to get there, which is not a piece of cake for every one. As you know, I'm a fine horseman—I train the colonel's horses—but you can be a good rider and a bad sailor. That's the case with me.

'Do you remember Major Simbretas, whom we used to call Doctor Ipecac?* When we felt we were ready for twenty-four hours in the blessed land of the infirmary, we would go to see him.

'He'd be sitting on his chair, his fat thighs in their red trousers thrust well apart, his hands on his knees, his arms akimbo and his elbows sticking out, rolling his big goggle-eyes and chewing on his white moustache.

'You'll remember his prescription: "This soldier is suffering from an upset stomach. Give him one of my number threes as an emetic, then twelve hours of rest; he will recover."

'This was a sovereign remedy, sovereign and infallible. So you swallowed it, since it was unavoidable. Then, when you had endured Doctor Ipecac's formula, you enjoyed twelve hours of well-deserved rest.

'Well, old chap, to reach Africa, you must endure, for forty hours, another kind of infallible emetic, the Transatlantic Shipping Company's formula...' She was rubbing her hands in delight at her idea.

She stood up, lit another cigarette, and began to walk about, still dictating, and blowing out thin trickles of smoke which at first rose straight up from a tiny round hole made by her pursed lips, then grew larger, evaporating, and leaving grey threads here and there in the air, a kind of transparent mist, a gossamer vapour. Sometimes, with a movement of her open hand, she would erase the more persistent of these faint traces; and sometimes she would cut across them with a slicing movement of her forefinger and then watch, with grave attention, as the two sections of barely perceptible vapour slowly disappeared.

And Duroy, raising his eyes, followed every gesture of hers, every attitude, every movement made by her body and her face, as she played this vague kind of game which never broke her concentration.

Now she was imagining incidents on the journey, portraying travel companions she herself had invented, and sketching in a love-affair with the wife of an infantry captain who was on her way to rejoin her husband.

Then, sitting down, she questioned Duroy on the topography of Algeria, of which she knew nothing. In ten minutes she knew as much about it as he did, and she wrote a brief section on political and colonial geography to bring the reader up to date, and prepare him to understand fully the serious questions that would be raised in future articles.

Next she continued with an expedition into the province of Oran, an entirely imaginary expedition which was mainly concerned with women, Moorish women, Jewish women, Spanish women.

'That's the only thing people are interested in,' she said.

She concluded with a visit to Saïda,* at the foot of the high table-land, and with a charming little affair between the NCO Georges Duroy and a Spanish girl employed at the esparto factory at Aïn-el-Hadjar.* She described nocturnal trysts on the bare stony mountain, with jackals, hyenas, and Arab dogs whining, barking, and howling among the rocks.

Then she announced cheerfully: 'To be continued tomorrow!' Next, rising to her feet: 'That, my dear M. Duroy, is how to write an article. Sign, please.'

He hesitated.

'Come on, sign!'

He began to laugh, and wrote at the foot of the page: 'Georges Duroy.'

She was still smoking as she walked about, and he was still gazing at her, finding nothing to say to thank her, happy to be near her, filled with gratitude and with the sensual pleasure of this budding intimacy. It seemed to him that everything that surrounded her was part of her, everything, even the walls covered with books. The chairs, the furniture, the air in which the smell of tobacco floated, had some special attribute, something good, sweet, and charming, that came from her.

She asked abruptly: 'What do you think of my friend Mme de Marelle?'

He was taken aback: 'Well... I find her... I find her extremely attractive.'

'Isn't she?'

'Yes, yes indeed.'

He wanted to add: 'But not as much as you.' He did not dare.

She went on: 'And if you knew how funny she is, how original, how intelligent! She's a bohemian, in fact, a real bohemian. That's why her husband isn't all that fond of her. He only sees her faults and doesn't appreciate her qualities.'

Duroy was dumbfounded to learn that Mme de Marelle was married. Yet it was perfectly natural.

He asked: 'Goodness... so she's married? And what does her husband do?'

Mme Forestier gave a little shrug and raised her eyebrows very slightly, in a single movement that was full of unfathomable meaning.

'Oh, he's an inspector in the Northern Railway. He spends a week per month in Paris. What his wife calls "compulsory service", or "the week of forced labour", or even "Holy Week". When you know her better, you'll realize how clever, how nice she is. So go and see her one of these days.'

Duroy was no longer thinking about leaving; he felt as if he would be staying for ever, as if he were in his own home.

But the door opened noiselessly, and a tall gentleman walked in, unannounced. On seeing another man, he halted. For an instant Mme Forestier looked embarrassed, then she said in her normal voice, although a trace of pink had spread from her shoulders to her face:

'Do come in, my dear man. Let me introduce a good friend of Charles, M. Georges Duroy, a future journalist.' Then, in a different tone, she announced: 'The Comte de Vaudrec, the best and closest of our friends.'

Eyeing one another, the two men bowed, and Duroy immediately made his farewells.

He was not urged to stay. He stammered his thanks, shook the hand the young woman held out him, bowed again to the new arrival, whose face still expressed the cold formality of those who move in the best circles, and departed, feeling thoroughly flustered, as though he had just committed a blunder.

Back in the street again, he felt depressed, ill-at-ease, gripped by an obscure awareness of some hidden sorrow. He walked along, wondering why this sudden melancholy had come over him; he could think of no reason, but the severe countenance of the Comte de Vaudrec, already rather elderly, with grey hair, and the calm, insolent air of a very wealthy, self-confident man, kept haunting him.

He realized that the arrival of this stranger, interrupting a delightful tête-à-tête to which his heart was already growing accustomed, had prompted in him this feeling of cold and despair that an overheard word, a glimpse of someone's wretchedness, the most trivial things are sometimes sufficient to inspire in us.

And he felt also that this man, for some unknown reason, had been displeased to find him there.

He had nothing further to do until three o'clock, and it was not yet noon. He had six francs fifty left in his pocket: so he went for lunch to a Duval restaurant.* Then, after wandering about on the boulevard, he climbed up that showy staircase at *La Vie française* just as three o'clock was striking.

The messengers sat waiting on a bench with arms crossed, while behind a kind of small professorial rostrum a clerk was sorting the mail that had just arrived. The setting was perfect for impressing visitors. Everyone looked decorous and personable, dignified and smart, as befitted the foyer of an important paper.

Duroy asked: 'M. Walter, please?'

The clerk replied: 'The editor is in conference. Kindly take a seat, Monsieur.' And he indicated the waiting-room, which was already full of people.

There were serious, important-looking men, wearing decorations, and slovenly men with well-hidden shirts and coats buttoned to the neck, the fronts of which were stained in patterns like the indentations of continents and oceans on geographical maps. Among these people were three women. One of them was pretty, smiling, overdressed, and had the look of a tart; her neighbour, with a tragic, wrinkled, mask-like face, was also dressed elaborately, though austerely, and had something shabby and false about her, typical of former actresses, a kind of bogus, musty youthfulness, like an erotic perfume that has turned sour. The third woman, wearing mourning, was sitting in a corner, and looked like a widow in distress. Duroy supposed that she had come to ask for charity.

But no one was being shown in, and more than twenty minutes had passed.

Then Duroy had an idea, and went back to find the clerk: 'M. Walter told me to come at three,' he said. 'In any case, go and see if my friend M. Forestier is here.'

This time he was shown into a long corridor leading into a big room where four men sat round a broad green table, writing.

Forestier was standing in front of the fireplace, smoking a cigarette and playing cup-and-ball.* He was very skilful at this game, catching the huge yellow boxwood ball on the little wooden spike every time. He was counting: 'Twenty-two, twenty-three, twenty-four, twenty-five...' Duroy said: 'Twenty-six.' And, without interrupting the regular movement of his arm, his friend looked up. 'Ah, here you are! Yesterday I caught it fifty-seven times in a row. The only person here who's better than me is Saint-Potin. Have you seen the boss? There's nothing so funny as watching that old half-wit Norbert playing cup-and-ball. He opens his mouth as if he's going to swallow the thing.'

One of the sub-editors turned his head in his direction: 'I say, Forestier, I know of one for sale, a splendid one in West Indian hardwood; it's said to have belonged to the Queen of Spain. They're asking sixty francs for it. That's not a lot.'

Forestier enquired: 'Where is it?' And, as he had missed his thirty-seventh shot, he opened a cupboard in which Duroy caught sight of about twenty superb cups-and-balls, arranged and numbered like a collection of curios. Then, having put his instrument in its usual place, he said again: 'Where is this gem?'

The journalist replied: 'A ticket-seller for the Vaudeville has it. I'll bring it to you tomorrow, if you like.'

'Yes, all right. If it's really beautiful, I'll take it; you can never have too many cups-and-balls.' Then, turning to Duroy: 'Come with me, I'm going to take you in to see the boss, otherwise you could still be cooling your heels here at seven tonight.'

Again they passed through the waiting-room, where the same people still sat in the same order. The moment Forestier appeared, the young woman and the old actress sprang to their feet and came up to him. One after the other, he led them over to the window recess, and although they were careful to speak quietly, Duroy noticed that he addressed both of them familiarly. Then, after pushing open a couple of padded doors, they went into the Director's office.

The conference, which had been going on for an hour, consisted of a game of écarté* with some of those gentlemen in flat hats whom Duroy had noticed the previous evening.

M. Walter was holding his cards and playing with concentrated attention and cautious gestures, while his opponent was putting down, picking up, and handling the light painted cards with the ease, skill, and grace of an experienced player. Norbert de Varenne was writing an article, sitting in the Director's chair, and Jacques Rival lay stretched out full length on a divan, smoking a cigar with his eyes closed.

The room was stuffy, smelling of leather furniture and stale tobacco and printer's ink; it had that special smell of newspaper offices familiar to every journalist.

On the table of dark wood inlaid with brass lay an incredible pile of papers: letters, cards, newspapers, magazines, tradesmen's invoices, printed matter of every sort.

Forestier shook the hands of the punters who were standing behind the players, and watched the game in complete silence; then, as soon as M. Walter had won, he made the introduction. 'Here's my friend Duroy.'

The Director gave the young man a rapid glance over the top of his glasses, then enquired: 'Have you brought my article? That would fit in very well today, along with the Morel debate.'

Duroy pulled the sheets of paper, folded in four, from his pocket: 'Here you are, Monsieur.'

The Director, delighted, smiled: 'Very good, very good. You're a man of your word. You'll have to take a look at this for me, Forestier?'

But Forestier hurriedly replied: 'No need, M. Walter, I wrote the story with him to show him the ropes. It's very good.'

And Walter, who now was picking up a hand dealt by a tall, thin man, a left-of-centre deputy, said casually: 'That's fine, then.'

Forestier did not let him begin his new game, but murmured, bending down close to his ear: 'You know that you promised me to take on Duroy, in Marambot's place. Would you like me to engage him on the same terms?'

'Yes, certainly.'

And, taking his friend by the arm, the journalist led him away as M. Walter resumed his game.

Norbert de Varenne had not looked up, he appeared not to have seen or recognized Duroy. Jacques Rival, on the other hand, had shaken his hand with the open, deliberate warmth of a good friend whom you can count on in a tight corner.

They re-crossed the waiting-room and, as everyone looked up, Forestier said to the youngest of the women, loud enough to be heard by the other people waiting: 'The Director will see you very shortly. He's in conference at the moment, with two members of the Budget Commission.'*

Then he walked rapidly on, his manner hurried and self-important, as if he were just about to draft a dispatch of the gravest significance.

Once they were back in the newsroom, Forestier promptly picked up his cup-and-ball once more, and, beginning to play again, said to Duroy, interrupting his sentences to keep score: 'So. You'll come here at three every day, and I'll tell you what errands there are and what people you must see, either during the day or in the evening or in the morning—one—I'll begin by giving you a letter of introduction to the Police Chief at Division One of Police Headquarters—two—who'll put you in touch with one of his staff And you'll make arrangements with him to get all the important news—three—from headquarters, I mean of course official or semi-official news. For the details, you must ask Saint-Potin, who knows what's what—four—you'll be seeing him shortly, or else tomorrow. What you'll have to get used to, above all, is pumping the people I'll send you to see—five—and pushing your way in everywhere, regardless of closed doors—six. For that you'll be paid two hundred francs a month basic, plus two sous per line for any interesting news items you come up with—seven—plus two sous per line, also, for the articles that you'll be commissioned to write on various topics—eight.'

After that, he concentrated solely on his game, still counting slowly: 'nine—ten—eleven—twelve—thirteen.' He missed the four-teenth, and swore: 'Damn and blast that thirteen; the bastard always brings me bad luck. I'll die on the thirteenth, for sure.'

One of the sub-editors, having finished what he was doing, also took a cup-and-ball from the cupboard; he was a very small man who looked like a child, although he was thirty-five; then several other journalists who had come in, went in turn to collect their own toy. Soon there were six of them, standing side by side with their backs to the wall, tossing into the air, with identical, regular movements, the balls which, depending on the wood from which they were made, were red, yellow, or black. A competition was set up, so the two sub-editors who were still working came over to judge it.

Forestier won by eleven points. Then the tiny child-like man, who had lost, rang for a messenger and ordered: 'Nine beers.' And, while they waited for the drinks, they started playing again.

Duroy drank a glass of beer with his new colleagues, then asked his friend: 'What is there for me to do?' The other replied: 'I've nothing for you today. You can go if you like.'

'And... our... our article... will it go in tonight?'

'Yes, but don't worry about it, I'll correct the proofs. Do the next instalment for tomorrow, and be here at three, same as today.'

And Duroy, after shaking all the hands without even knowing the names of their owners, walked blithely down the handsome staircase, his heart full of jubilation.

CHAPTER 4

Georges Duroy slept badly, he was so excited at the prospect of seeing his article in print. He got up with the dawn, and was loitering in the street long before the time when newsboys race from kiosk to kiosk delivering the papers.

Knowing that *La Vie française* would appear at the Gare Saint-Lazare before it reached his own district, he went to the station. As it was still too early, he wandered about on the pavement. He watched the vendor arrive and open her glass-sided kiosk, then he caught sight of a man carrying on his head a huge pile of folded newspapers. Dashing over, he saw *Le Figaro*, the *Gil Blas*, *Le Gaulois*, *L'Événement*, and two or three other morning papers, but not *La Vie française*.

Suddenly he was filled with alarm: suppose the 'Recollections of an African Cavalryman' had been held over till the next day, or perhaps, at the last moment, old Walter hadn't liked it?

Returning again to the kiosk, he realized that the paper was already on sale, although he had not seen it delivered. Flinging down his three sous, he hurriedly unfolded it, and skimmed the titles on the front page. Nothing. His heart began to pound as he opened out the paper and, filled with intense excitement, read at the bottom of a column, in large letters, 'Georges Duroy.' It was in! What a thrill!

He walked off unthinkingly, the paper in his hand, his hat at an angle, longing to stop the passers-by and tell them: 'This is the paper to buy—this one here. There's an article of mine in it.' He would have liked to shout at the top of his voice, the way those paper-sellers on the boulevards do, in the evening: 'Read *La Vie française*, read Georges Duroy's article "Recollections of an African Cavalryman!"' And he suddenly felt an urge to read the article himself, to read it in a public place, in a café where people would see him. So he looked for somewhere that was already busy. He had to walk for a long time. Eventually he sat down in front of a sort of wine-merchant's where several customers were already seated, and ordered a rum, just as he might have ordered an absinthe, without giving a thought to the time of day. Then he called: 'Waiter, give me *La Vie française*.'

A man in a white apron hurried over: 'We haven't got it, Monsieur, we only take *Le Rappel*, *Le Siècle*, *La Lanterne* and *Le Petit Parisien.*'

His voice angry and indignant, Duroy retorted: 'What sort of a place is this! Well, go and buy me a copy.' The waiter hurried off and came back with it. Duroy began to read his article, saying loudly several times: 'Very good! Very good!' to attract his neighbours' attention and make them long to know what was in the paper. Then, as he went out, he left it behind on the table. Noticing this, the proprietor called him back: 'Monsieur, Monsieur, you've forgotten your paper!'

And Duroy replied: 'You can have it, I've read it. By the way, there's something very interesting in it today.'

He did not specify what, but as he walked off he saw someone sitting nearby pick up *La Vie française* from the table where he had left it.

'What shall I do now?' he wondered. Deciding to go to his office to collect his wages and hand in his resignation, he tingled with pleasurable anticipation at the thought of the expression on the faces of his boss and his fellow workers. The idea of his boss's bewilderment, in particular, filled him with delight.

He walked slowly, so as not to arrive before nine-thirty, since the cashier's desk did not open until ten. His office was a large, gloomy room where the gas had to be kept lit almost all day long in winter. It overlooked a narrow courtyard, and faced onto other offices. Eight clerks worked in it, as well as a deputy chief clerk, hidden behind a screen.

First, Duroy went to collect his one hundred and eighteen francs, twenty-five centimes, which were in a yellow envelope in the pay clerk's drawer; next, he walked triumphantly into the vast office where he had, in the past, spent so many days.

As soon as he came in, the deputy chief clerk, M. Potel, called to him: 'Ah, it's you, M. Duroy. The boss has asked for you several times. You know that he doesn't permit anyone to be off sick two days running without a doctor's certificate.'

Duroy, standing in the middle of the room for maximum effect, replied in carrying tones: 'Really! I don't give a damn!'

Amid the general stupefaction, the head of a bewildered M. Potel appeared over the screen which shut him in like a box. He was subject to rheumatism, and barricaded himself behind it for fear of draughts. He had simply pierced two holes in the paper in order to keep an eye on his staff.

You could have heard a pin drop. Finally, the deputy chief clerk asked hesitantly: 'What did you say?'

'I said that I didn't give a damn. I've only come today to hand in my resignation. I've joined the editorial staff of *La Vie française* at five hundred francs a month, plus so much per line. In fact, my first article is in this morning's paper.'

He had promised himself to spin out the pleasure of his announcement, but could not resist the temptation to blurt everything out at once. In any case, the effect was perfect. Not a soul stirred.

Then Duroy announced: 'I'll go and tell M. Perthuis, then I'll come back and say goodbye.'

He went in search of the boss, who exclaimed on seeing him: 'Ah! There you are. You know I won't have...'

His employee interrupted him: 'There's no point in bellowing like that...'

M. Perthuis, a big man with a beet-red face, was speechless with astonishment.

Duroy went on: 'I've had enough of this dump of yours. I've started in journalism this morning, with a very nice salary. Good day to you.'

He then left the room. He had had his revenge.

He did go and shake hands with his former colleagues, who scarcely dared address a word to him, for fear of compromising themselves, because, as the door had been left open, they had overheard his exchange with the boss.

He found himself out in the street again, with his pay in his pocket. He treated himself to a tasty lunch at a good, moderately priced restaurant he knew; then, having bought *La Vie française* and again left it on his table at the restaurant, he went into several shops to buy small things, purely for the pleasure of having them delivered to his place and saying his name: Georges Duroy, adding: 'I'm a sub-editor at *La Vie française*.' Then he gave the street and the number, being careful to stipulate: 'Leave it with the concierge.'

As he still had plenty of time, he stopped at an engraver's who made visiting cards on the spot, under the gaze of passers-by, and had a hundred printed there and then, showing his name and, below his name, his new position.

Then he went along to the paper.

Forestier greeted him condescendingly, as one greets an inferior: 'Ah, here you are, good. I've a number of things for you to do. Wait, I'll be about ten minutes. I've got this to finish first.'

And he went on with a letter he had started. At the other end of the large table, a very pale little man, very fat and bloated, his hairless skull white and shiny, sat writing, his nose right down on the paper because of his extreme myopia.

Forestier asked him: 'Tell me, Saint-Potin, what time are you going to interview those fellows?'

'At four.'

'Take young Duroy here with you, and show him the tricks of the trade.'

'Right.'

Then, turning to his friend, Forestier added: 'Did you bring the next piece on Algeria? This morning's opener was a great success.'

Disconcerted, Duroy stammered: 'No... I thought I'd have time during the afternoon... I had so much to do, and I couldn't...'

Forestier gave an exasperated shrug: 'If you can't be more dependable than that, you'll wreck your chances here. Old Walter was relying on getting your copy. I'll tell him he'll have it tomorrow. If you think you're going to be paid for doing nothing, you're wrong.'

Then, after a silence, he added: 'Damn it, you have to strike while the iron is hot!'

Saint-Potin stood up: 'I'm ready,' he said.

Forestier leant back in his chair and, assuming an almost pontifical pose to give his instructions, turned towards Duroy: 'Well now. For the past couple of days we've had the Chinese General Li-Theng-Fao staying at the Continental, and the Rajah Taposahib Ramaderao Pali at the Hotel Bristol.* You're going to interview them.'

Then, turning to Saint-Potin: 'Don't forget the main points I mentioned. Ask the General and the Rajah what they think about England's dealings in the Far East, what they think of her system of colonization and colonial domination, and what their hopes are of European, and particularly French, intervention in their affairs.'

He fell silent, then added, speaking to no one in particular: 'Our readers will find it extremely interesting to learn, at the same time, about the views held in China and in India on these topics, which are of such vital concern to the public at present.'

He added, for Duroy's benefit: 'Watch the way Saint-Potin goes about it, he's an excellent reporter, try to learn how to get everything out of someone in five minutes.'

Then he solemnly started writing again, with the obvious intention of establishing a clear distance, of putting his former friend and new colleague well and truly in his place.

The moment they were through the door, Saint-Potin began to laugh, and said to Duroy: 'What a fraud! He's trying to put one over on us. Anyone would think he takes us for his readers.'

They walked down towards the boulevard, and the reporter asked: 'How about a drink?'

'Yes, good idea. It's very hot.'

They went into a café and ordered cold drinks. Saint-Potin began to talk. He talked about everybody and about the paper with an abundance of surprising detail.

'The boss? A real Jew! And you know, the Jews, you'll never change 'em. What a race!' And he quoted some astonishing examples of avarice, of that avarice peculiar to the sons of Israel, savings of ten centimes, haggling worthy of a cook, shamefully small discounts asked for and obtained, all their money-lending, pawn-broking approach.

'And yet, at the same time, he's a good chap who doesn't believe in anything and swindles everybody. His paper, which is semi-official, Catholic, liberal, republican, Orléanist,* one-size-fits-all, and has something for everyone, was only founded to further his dealings on the stock market and all his various other enterprises. He's really good at that, and makes millions through companies that haven't a sou of capital...'

He talked on and on, calling Duroy 'my dear fellow'.

'The old skinflint says things straight out of Balzac. Just imagine, the other day I was in his office with that halfwitted antique, Norbert, and our Don Quixote, Rival, when our business manager Montelin walks in with his morocco leather briefcase under his arm—the whole of Paris knows that briefcase. Walter squints up at him and says: "What's the latest?" Montelin artlessly replies: "I've just paid the sixteen thousand francs we owe the paper supplier."

'The boss nearly jumped out of his skin. "What did you say?"

' "That I've just paid M. Privas."

' "But you're out of your mind!"

' "Why?"

' "Why... why... why." He took off his glasses and wiped them. Then he smiled, an odd little smile that flutters round his fat cheeks whenever he's going to say something cunning or outrageous, and in a mocking, emphatic tone he said: "Why? Because we could have got it reduced by four or five thousand francs."

'Montelin, astonished, retorted: "But Monsieur, all the bills were in order; they'd been checked by me and approved by you..."

'Then the boss, growing serious again, declared: "I didn't know anyone could be that naïve. Please remember, M. Montelin, always incur debts; they enable you to negotiate." '

And, giving an appreciative nod, Saint-Potin added: 'Well? Straight out of Balzac isn't he?'

Duroy had never read any Balzac, but he replied with conviction: 'My God, yes.'

Then the reporter talked about Mme Walter, a dull, stupid woman, about Norbert de Varenne, an old has-been, about Rival, a rehash of Fervacques.* Finally he came to Forestier.

'As for him, he's had the good luck to marry his wife, that's all.'

Duroy asked: 'What's his wife like, really?'

Saint-Potin rubbed his hands together: 'Oh, she's a cunning woman, she's quite a one. She's the mistress of an old lecher named Vaudrec, the Comte de Vaudrec, who gave her a dowry and married her off...'

Duroy suddenly felt a chill, a kind of nervous constriction, an urge to insult and slap the face of this gossip-monger. Instead he just interrupted him to ask:

'Is Saint-Potin your real name?'

The other answered quite simply:

'No, my name's Thomas. They nicknamed me Saint-Potin at the paper.'

Duroy, as he paid for the drinks, went on:

'It seems to me that it's getting late, and we've two most distinguished gentlemen to see.'

Saint-Potin began to laugh: 'You're still very naïve, aren't you! Do you really believe that I'm going to ask that Chinaman and that Indian what they think of England? As if I didn't know better than they do what they're supposed to think for the readers of *La Vie française*! I've already interviewed hundreds of those Chinese, Persians, Hindus, Chileans, Japanese, and suchlike. As far as I can see, they all tell me the same thing. I simply have to take the article I wrote most recently and copy it word for word. What does change, naturally, is their appearance, their names, their titles, their age, their staff. Oh! I mustn't make a single mistake there, because *Le Figaro* or *Le Gaulois* would come down on me like a ton of bricks. But I'll get what I need on that subject in five minutes from the concierges of the Continental and the Bristol. We can walk there while we have a cigar. Total: a five franc cab fare I can charge to the paper. That's the way to go about it, old man, when you know your way around.'

'It must be quite profitable, being a reporter on that basis?' enquired Duroy.

The journalist replied cryptically: 'Yes, but nothing's as profitable as writing the gossip column,* because of the self-publicity* you can sneak in.'

They had got up from their table and were walking along the boulevard towards the Madeleine. Saint-Potin suddenly said to his companion: 'You know, if you've got things to do, I really don't need you.' So Duroy shook his hand and left him.

The thought of the article he had to write that evening was worrying him, and he began turning it over in his mind. As he walked along, he was storing up ideas, impressions, opinions, and anecdotes, and he went right to the end of the Champs-Élysées, where only the occasional stroller was to be seen. Paris was deserted during the hot weather.

After dining in a cheap restaurant near the Arc de Triomphe, he walked home slowly along the outer boulevards, then sat down at his table to work. But the instant his gaze fell upon the big sheet of white paper spread out before him, all the material he had amassed vanished from his head, as if his brain had melted into thin air. He tried to grab hold again of the odds and ends he had recalled, and fix them in his memory; just as fast as he remembered them they disappeared again, or else they came rushing into his head in a jumble, and he could not work out how to introduce them, how to present them, or with which to begin.

After struggling for an hour, and covering five pages with opening sentences which led nowhere, he thought: 'I still haven't got the hang of this. I need another lesson.' And, immediately, the prospect of another morning spent working with Mme Forestier, the expectation of that long, warm, intimate tête-à-tête that was so sweet, made him tremble with desire. He quickly went to bed, almost afraid, now, of trying again, lest he should suddenly succeed.

The next morning he stayed in bed quite late, postponing, and relishing in advance, the pleasure of the visit.

It was past ten when he rang his friend's doorbell.

The servant replied: 'I'm afraid M. Forestier is busy.'

It had not occurred to Duroy that the husband might be there. Nevertheless he persevered: 'Tell him it's me; I've come on urgent business.'

After waiting for five minutes, he was shown into the study where he had spent such a delightful morning.

Forestier, now, was sitting writing in the place he had occupied; he wore a dressing-gown and slippers, and on his head a little cap, while his wife, dressed in the same white wrap as before, was leaning on the mantelpiece with a cigarette in her mouth, dictating.

Duroy stopped on the threshold and murmured: 'I'm very sorry; am I interrupting you?'

His friend had turned his head and, scowling angrily, snarled: 'Whatever do you want now? Get a move on, we've a lot to do.'

Nonplussed, Duroy stammered: 'No, I beg your pardon, it's nothing.'

But Forestier, annoyed, went on: 'Damn it all, man! Hurry up; surely you didn't barge your way in here just for the pleasure of saying "Good morning" to us.'

At that Duroy, feeling very uncomfortable, took the plunge:

'No... well... it's just that I still can't seem to manage to write my article... and you were so... you were both so kind last time... that I was hoping... that is I took the liberty of coming...'

Forestier interrupted him: 'Well, you've got some cheek, haven't you! So you think I'm going to do your job, and all you have to do is go and pick up your pay at the end of the month! No! What a nerve!'

The young woman went on smoking without saying a word, a vague, set smile, like a friendly mask, on her face, hiding the irony of her thoughts.

Duroy, blushing, stammered: 'I'm sorry... I had thought... I had supposed...' Then, abruptly, in a clear voice: 'I most humbly beg your pardon, Madame, and I thank you again, most sincerely, for the charming article you wrote for me yesterday.'

Then he said to Charles: 'I'll be at the paper at three,' and left.

He strode rapidly home, muttering: 'Well, I'm going to do this one, and I'll do it all by myself, and then they'll see...'

The moment he was home, spurred on by anger, he began to write.

He went on with the romantic story Mme Forestier had begun, piling up extravagantly unrealistic details, astonishing reversals of fortune, and flowery descriptions, his style as clumsy as a schoolboy's and as trite as a sergeant's. In an hour he had completed a story that was a hotchpotch of absurdities, which he then took confidently round to *La Vie française*.

The first person he encountered was Saint-Potin, who shook his hand with conspiratorial fervour and asked:

'Have you read my interview with the Chinaman and the Hindu? Don't you think it's funny? I've made the whole of Paris laugh. And I didn't see so much as the tips of their noses.'

Duroy, who had not read any of it, promptly took the paper and skimmed through a long article entitled 'India and China', while the reporter pointed out and emphasized the most interesting passages.

A breathless Forestier came bustling hurriedly up to them.

'Oh, good, I need you two.'

And he gave them a list of political questions he wanted answered that very evening.

Duroy handed him his article. 'Here's the next instalment on Algeria.'

'Fine, give it to me. I'll see the boss gets it.'

That was all.

Saint-Potin led his new colleague away and, when they were in the corridor, said to him:

'Have you been to see the cashier?'

'No. Why?'

'Why? To collect your pay. You see, you should always draw a month's pay in advance. You never know what might happen.'

'Well... I've no quarrel with that.'

'I'll introduce you to the cashier. He won't have any objection. The pay's good here.'

And Duroy went and drew his two hundred francs, plus the

twenty-eight for his previous day's article, which, together with what was left of his railway company pay, meant that he had a total of three hundred and forty francs in his pocket.

Never had he owned such a sum, and he felt it was enough to keep him flush indefinitely.

Then Saint-Potin took him off for a chat in the newsrooms of four or five rival papers, hoping that the information he had been told to track down would already have been unearthed by others, and that his fluent and crafty tongue would easily enable him to filch it from them.

In the evening Duroy, who had nothing more to do, decided to return to the Folies-Bergère, where he brazenly presented himself at the box office: 'My name's Georges Duroy, I'm a sub-editor at *La Vie française*. I came the other evening with M. Forestier, and he promised he would see that I got complimentary tickets. I don't know if he's remembered to do that?'

They consulted a list. His name was not on it. However, the extremely friendly box-office clerk said: 'Go in anyway, Monsieur, and ask the manager yourself. I'm sure he'll be pleased to oblige.'

He went in, and almost immediately met Rachel, the woman he had been with that first night.

She came up to him: 'Hallo, darling. You well?'

'Fine, and you?'

'Oh, not too bad. Just imagine, I've dreamt of you twice, since the other day.'

Duroy smiled, feeling flattered: 'Aha! And what does that prove?'

'That proves that I like you, you silly fool, and that we can do it again whenever you like.'

'How about today?'

'Suits me.'

'Good, but listen...' He hesitated, somewhat embarrassed at what he was about to do. 'The thing is, this time, I haven't a sou, I've just come from a club,* where I blew it all.'

She gave him a sharp look, suspecting, with her prostitute's instincts, and her experience of how men swindle and haggle, that he was lying. 'You're having me on! That's not a very nice thing to do, you know!'

He gave an embarrassed smile. 'If you want ten francs, that's what I've got left.'

She murmured, with the disinterest of a whore indulging her fancy: 'Whatever suits you, darling, it's just you I want.'

And, her longing gaze fixed on the young man's moustache, she took his arm and, clinging to it lovingly:

'Let's go and have a grenadine first. I'd like to walk down to the Opéra with you, to show you off. And then we'll go home early, what d'you say?'

He slept late at her place. It was daylight when he left, and he immediately had the idea of buying *La Vie française*. He opened the paper with a feverish hand; his article was not in it; he stood there on the pavement, anxiously scanning the columns of print in the hope that he would, in the end, find what he was looking for.

He was suddenly conscious of a feeling of intense depression. After an exhausting night of love-making, this setback, added to his fatigue, seemed like a major disaster.

He returned home and fell asleep, fully dressed, on his bed.

Upon his arrival, some hours later, at the newspaper office, he presented himself at M. Walter's door. 'I was very surprised this morning, Monsieur, not to find my second article on Algeria.'

The editor looked up and said in a dry voice: 'I gave it to your friend Forestier and asked him to read it; he did not consider it satisfactory; you'll have to rewrite it.'

Duroy walked out in a fury without replying, and burst into his colleague's office: 'Why did you stop my article from appearing, this morning?'

The journalist was smoking a cigarette, sitting well back in his armchair with his feet on the table, his heels smudging an article he had begun. He declared calmly, the tone of his voice bored and distant, as though coming from the bottom of a hole: 'The boss thought it poor, and told me to return it to you to be rewritten. Here it is.' He pointed with his finger to some sheets that lay under a paperweight.

Disconcerted, Duroy could find nothing to say; as he was putting his composition in his pocket, Forestier went on: 'Today I want you to go first of all to police headquarters.' And he listed a series of errands to be run and news items to be collected. Duroy departed, without having been able to come up with the scathing comment he was looking for.

He took his article back the next day. It was returned to him once again. Having rewritten it for the third time and had it returned, he realized that he was moving too fast, and that Forestier was the only person who could help him make his way. He therefore said no more about 'The Recollections of an African Cavalryman', resolving to be flexible and crafty, since that was what was required. He would do his job as a reporter zealously, while waiting for better things.

He learnt his way around behind the scenes in the theatre and the world of politics; he grew familiar with the corridors and the waiting-rooms of statesmen and deputies, with the pompous countenances of cabinet secretaries and the sullen faces of drowsy ushers.

He dealt constantly with ministers and concierges, generals and policemen, princes, pimps, prostitutes and ambassadors, bishops and procurers, foreign con men, men-about-town, card-sharps, cabbies, waiters and countless others. He was the friend—at once self-serving and neutral—of all of them, not discriminating between them in his regard, measuring them by the same standard, judging them with the same impartial eye, as a consequence of meeting them every day, every hour, without ever changing his approach, and talking to them all about the same topics connected with his job. He likened himself to someone who tastes, one after another, samples of every wine, and is soon unable to tell a Château-Margaux from an Argenteuil.*

In a very short time he became a remarkable reporter, sure of his facts, cunning, fast, subtle, a real asset to the paper, as old man Walter, who knew a thing or two about reporters, used to say.

However, as he drew only ten centimes a line, plus his basic two hundred francs, and as the life of a man-about-town, an habitué of cafés and restaurants, is expensive, he never had a sou to his name, and was depressed about his abject poverty.

It's a trick I'll have to learn, he thought, seeing how certain of his colleagues had money to burn, although he was never able to grasp by what hidden means they had acquired their wealth. And, full of envy, he suspected them of all sorts of subterfuges, of services rendered, of a whole system of underhand dealings that was accepted and condoned. So he would have to penetrate the mystery, become part of the secret circle, force his colleagues to let him have his share.

And often as he sat at his window in the evening, watching the trains pass by, he would ponder over different ways of doing just that.

CHAPTER 5

Two months had passed; September was approaching, and it seemed to Duroy that the rapid rise in fortune he had been hoping for was very slow indeed in coming. He was particularly disquieted by his humble position, and could not see how to make his way to the top where you find respect, power, and wealth.

He felt confined by his mediocre job as a reporter, isolated in it, with no possibility of escape. He was appreciated, but the respect accorded him was proportionate to his rank. Even Forestier, for whom he performed countless little services, no longer invited him to dinner, and treated him in every way as an inferior, although he still addressed him familiarly, like a friend.

It was true that from time to time Duroy saw his chance and had a little piece published. As reporting news snippets had given him a facility with words and a sense of what was appropriate that he lacked when he wrote his second article on Algeria, he no longer risked having his work on current affairs rejected. But there was as much difference between that kind of writing, and reporting on whatever he fancied or authoritatively reviewing political issues, as there was between driving along the avenues of the Bois as a cabbie, and driving yourself in a carriage of your own. What humiliated him most was to feel the doors of society closed to him, to have no connections whom he could treat as equals, to have no close relationships with women, although occasionally various well-known actresses had, for reasons of their own, made themselves accessible.

Moreover, he knew from personal experience that all these women, whether society ladies or third-rate actresses, felt a peculiar attraction towards him, an instantaneous liking, and because he did not know any who might ensure his future success, he felt as impatient as a hobbled horse.

He had often considered visiting Mme Forestier, but he was stopped by the thought of their last, humiliating encounter; and moreover he was waiting for her husband to invite him. Then he remembered Mme de Marelle and that she had invited him to come and see her, so he called on her one afternoon when he had nothing to do.

'I'm always at home until three o'clock,' she had said.

He rang her doorbell at two-thirty.

She lived in the Rue de Verneuil,* on the fourth floor. At the sound of the bell the door was opened by a maid, an unkempt little servant-girl who was tying on her cap as she replied: 'Yes, Madame's at home, but I don't know if she's up.'

And she pushed open the drawing-room door, which was standing ajar.

Duroy went in. The rather large room was inadequately furnished, and had a neglected air. The armchairs, shabby and old, stood in rows along the walls in an order determined by the maid, for nowhere could you detect the elegant touch of a woman who loves her home. Four second-rate pictures, depicting a boat on a river, a ship at sea, a mill on a plain, and a wood-cutter in a wood, hung in the centre of the four wall panels from cords of different lengths; all four were askew. You could tell that they had been hanging like that for some considerable time, beneath the casual gaze of a woman quite indifferent to such things.

Duroy sat down and waited. He waited a long time. Then a door opened and Mme de Marelle hurried in, dressed in a pink silk Japanese kimono embroidered with golden landscapes, blue flowers, and white birds; she exclaimed:

'Just imagine, I was still in bed. How nice of you to come and see me. I was sure you'd forgotten me.'

With a gesture of delight she offered him both her hands, and Duroy, put at ease by the scruffy appearance of the apartment, took them and kissed one, as he had seen Norbert de Varenne do.

She asked him to sit down and then, looking him over from head to foot: 'How you've changed! You've got more of an air. Paris is doing you good. Come, tell me all the news.'

At once they began to chat as if they were old friends, feeling an immediate mutual sympathy develop, conscious of the birth of one of those currents of trust, intimacy, and affection that in five minutes can make friends out of two creatures of similar character and type.

The young woman suddenly broke off what she was saying, and remarked in astonishment: 'It's odd how I feel about you. It's as though I've known you for ten years. I'm sure we're going to be good friends. Would you like that?' He replied: 'Of course'—with a smile that said more.

He found her utterly enticing in her dazzling, soft kimono, less subtle than the other one in her white negligé, less tender, less delicate, but more exciting, spicier.

When he had been close to Mme Forestier, with her steady, gracious smile which simultaneously attracted and restrained you, which seemed to say: 'I like you' but also: 'Be careful', and the true meaning of which you never fathomed, he felt above all the longing to prostrate himself at her feet, or to kiss the exquisite lace of her bodice and slowly breathe in the warm, fragrant scent that surely came from there, sliding between her breasts. When he was close to Mme de Marelle, he was conscious of a coarser, more specific desire in himself, a desire that made his hands tremble as he watched the moulded contours of the thin silk.

She was still talking, sprinkling each sentence with that facile wit at which she was so adept, just as a craftsman acquires the knack of carrying out a task widely held to be difficult, and which other people find astonishing. He listened to her, thinking: 'I must remember all this. One could write a delightful "Paris Diary" by listening to her gossip about what's going on.'

But someone was knocking softly—very softly—on the door through which she had entered, and she called: 'You can come in, darling.' The little girl came in, went straight to Duroy, and offered him her hand.

The astonished mother murmured: 'You've really made a conquest. I can hardly recognize her.' The young man kissed the child, sat her down beside him, and, his manner serious, enquired kindly about what she had been doing since they had last met. She answered him with her little piping voice, in her solemn, adult way.

The clock struck three. The journalist stood up.

'Come often,' said Mme de Marelle, 'and we'll chat just as we've done today, I'll always be glad to see you. But why do you no longer go to the Forestiers'?'

He replied: 'Oh, no reason. I've been very busy. I certainly hope that we'll meet there again one of these days.'

He left, feeling full of hope, although he could not say why.

He told Forestier nothing about this visit.

But the memory of it lingered throughout the days that followed, more than the memory, a kind of awareness of the intangible yet persistent presence of this woman. He felt as if he had brought something of her away with him, the image of her body still present in his vision, and the flavour of her personality still present in his heart. He remained obsessed by her image, as occasionally happens when you have spent a delightful interlude with someone. You feel as if you are bewitched by a very private spell that is strange, ambiguous, and disturbing, exquisite in its mystery.

A few days later he paid her a second visit.

The servant showed him into the drawing-room, and Laurine immediately appeared. This time she offered him not her hand, but her forehead, and said: 'Mama told me to ask you to wait. She'll be a few minutes, because she's not dressed. I'll keep you company.'

Duroy, amused by the little girl's ceremonious manners, replied: 'Certainly, mademoiselle, I'll be delighted to spend time with you, but let me warn you that I'm am not in the least serious. I play all day long; so what about playing a game of tag?'

The child seemed very surprised, then she smiled, as a woman would have done, at this idea that she found somewhat shocking, and also astonishing, and she murmured:

'Flats aren't for playing in.'

He said: 'I don't mind. I play everywhere. Come on, try to catch me.' And he began going round and round the table, urging her on to chase him, while she followed behind, still smiling with a kind of polite condescension, and occasionally reaching out her hand to touch him but never going so far as to run.

He would stop and crouch down, and when her tiny hesitant steps brought her close, he would spring into the air like a jack-in-the-box, then give a great leap to the other end of the drawing-room. This struck her as funny and after a while she started to laugh; growing excited, she began trotting along behind him, giving happy, fearful little cries whenever she thought she was on the point of catching him. He moved the chairs about, turning them into obstacles, making her dodge back and forth round the same chair for a moment, and then, abandoning that one, would seize another. Laurine was running now, surrendering herself completely to the pleasure of this new game and, her face rosy red, springing forward with all the eagerness of a delighted child at each retreat, each ruse, each feint made by her companion.

Suddenly, just as she thought she was going to catch him, he seized her in his arms, lifted her up to the ceiling and exclaimed:

'Got you!' The delighted little girl was thrashing her legs about, struggling to escape, and laughing with all her might.

Coming into the room, Mme de Marelle cried in astonishment: 'Ah! Laurine... Laurine's playing... You're a sorcerer, M. Duroy.'

He put the child down, kissed the mother's hand, and they sat down with the child between them. They tried to chat; but Laurine, normally so silent, was over-excited, and talked all the time; they had to send her to her room.

She obeyed without a word, but there were tears in her eyes.

As soon as they were alone, Mme de Marelle lowered her voice: 'Let me tell you something, I've a special plan, and you're involved. It's this: as I have dinner every week at the Forestiers', from time to time I return their hospitality at a restaurant. I don't like entertaining here at home. I'm not organized for it, and in any case I'm no good in the house, no good in the kitchen, no good at anything. I like living in a topsy-turvy way. So now and again I take them to a restaurant, but it's not very lively when there's just the three of us, and my own friends aren't their type at all. I'm telling you this to explain a somewhat unconventional invitation. What I mean is, I'm inviting you to join us on Saturday, at the Café Riche,* seven-thirty. Do you know the place?'

He accepted with pleasure. She went on: 'We'll be just a foursome, two men and two women. That sort of little party is such fun for us women who don't often get the chance.'

The chestnut brown dress she was wearing clung to her waist, her hips, her breasts, and her arms in a tantalizing, alluring way, and Duroy was aware of a feeling of perplexed astonishment, almost of embarrassment, the cause of which eluded him, at the contrast between this fastidious, refined elegance and her obvious indifference towards the home she inhabited.

Everything that clothed her body, everything that touched her flesh directly and intimately, was delicate and fine, but her surroundings were no longer of any importance to her.

He left her, retaining, like the other time, the impression of her continuing presence, in a sort of hallucination of the senses. And he awaited the day of the dinner-party with ever-increasing impatience.

Having again rented a black suit—for his means did not yet enable him to buy evening dress—he arrived first at the restaurant, a few minutes before the time they'd agreed.

He was shown up to the second floor, and ushered into a small private dining-room* draped in red; its solitary window gave onto the boulevard.

A white tablecloth, so glossy that it might have been varnished, was spread over a square table on which four places were set; the glasses, the silverware, the chafing dish glittered brightly in the light of a dozen candles in two tall candelabra.

Outside, you could see a great splash of pale green, made by the leaves of a tree illuminated by the brilliant light from the private dining-rooms.

Duroy sat down on a very low sofa, red like the walls; its worn-out springs gave way beneath him, so that he felt as if he was falling down a hole. He could hear, throughout the huge building, an indefinable noise, that soft hum of a big restaurant, that clatter of china and silverware, the sound of the waiters' rapid footsteps muffled by the carpets in the corridors, and of doors being opened momentarily, letting out the murmur of voices of the diners enclosed in all those small rooms. Forestier came in, shaking his hand with a cordial familiarity that he never showed him in the offices of *La Vie française*.

'The two ladies are coming together,' he said. 'Aren't these dinners fun!'

Then he studied the table, asked for a gas light that had been left burning dimly to be extinguished completely, closed one of the shutters because of a draught, and selected a sheltered seat for himself, remarking: 'I have to be very careful; I felt better for a month, but now I've been sick again these last few days. I must have caught cold on Tuesday when I was leaving the theatre.'

The door opened and the two young women appeared, followed by the head waiter. Discreetly veiled and cloaked, they had that alluring air of mystery that women assume in the kind of place where they are likely to have around them, or meet, disreputable individuals.

When Duroy greeted Mme Forestier, she scolded him severely for not having been back to see her, then she added, turning to her friend with a smile: 'I know what it is, you prefer Mme de Marelle to me, you've plenty of time for her.'

Then they all sat down, and as the head waiter presented the wine-list to Forestier, Mme de Marelle exclaimed: 'Give these gentlemen whatever they want; as for us, we'll have some chilled

champagne, the best you have, a sweet one of course, nothing else.'
When the man had gone, she declared with an excited laugh: 'I feel
like getting tipsy tonight, let's have a fling, a real fling.'

Forestier, who seemed not to have heard, enquired: 'Would you
mind if the window was closed? My chest's not been too good the
last few days.'

'No, not at all.'

So he went and closed the window that had been left ajar, and
returned to his seat, his expression more composed and relaxed.

His wife sat silently, apparently lost in thought; her eyes fixed on
the table, she was smiling at the glasses with that vague smile which
seemed always to tender a promise that was never fulfilled.

Ostend oysters were served, dainty plump oysters like tiny ears
encased in shells, that melted between palate and tongue like salty
bonbons.

Then, after the soup, came a trout with flesh as pink as a young
girl's; and they all began to chat.

They talked first about a bit of scandal that was going round, the
story of a woman of high social standing who had been caught, by a
friend of her husband's, having supper in a private dining-room with
a foreign prince.

Forestier laughed heartily at the story; the two women were of the
opinion that the tactless gossip-monger was nothing but a craven
cad. Duroy agreed with them, declaring loudly that it's a man's duty
to bring to these sorts of affairs—be he protagonist, confidant, or
just an onlooker—the silence of the grave. He added: 'How full of
delights life would be if we could rely on one another's absolute
discretion. What often, very often, almost always stops women, is the
fear of having their secret revealed.'

Then, smiling, he went on: 'Come, isn't that so? How many
women are there who would not indulge a passing fancy, a sudden,
fierce, momentary passion, an amorous fantasy, if they weren't afraid
that this brief, unimportant happiness would cost them irremediable
scandal and bitter tears!' He spoke with infectious conviction, as if
he were pleading a cause, his cause, as if he were saying: 'With me
you'd have no reason to fear such dangers. Try it and see.'

They were both gazing at him, approving with their eyes, thinking that he spoke well and that he was right, admitting by their
friendly silence that the flexible morality of Parisian wives would

have accommodated anything, given an absolute assurance of silence.

And Forestier, who was almost lying on the sofa, with one leg doubled under him and his napkin tucked into his waistcoat to protect his coat from stains, suddenly declared, with the laugh of a confirmed sceptic: 'Oh! yes, they'd have a good time if they were sure of secrecy. My God, yes! The poor old husbands!'

And the conversation turned to love. Without admitting that it might be eternal, Duroy believed that it could last, creating a bond, a kind of tender friendship, a mutual trust. The union of the senses was just a seal set upon the union of two hearts. But he waxed indignant about the storms of jealousy, the dramas, scenes, and anguish that almost always accompany the end of an affair.

When he fell silent, Mme de Marelle sighed: 'Yes, it's the only good thing in life, and we often spoil it by asking the impossible.'

Mme Forestier, who was playing with a knife, added: 'Yes... yes... it's good to be loved...' And she seemed to be pursuing her dream further—to be thinking of things she did not dare put into words.

And because the first entrée was slow in coming, they kept sipping champagne and nibbling bits of crust torn from the little rolls. And, slowly and insinuatingly, the thought of love took hold of them, intoxicating them in the same way that the pale wine excited their blood and confused their minds, as it slipped down their throats drop by drop.

Lamb cutlets were brought in, tender and delicate, lying on a deep bed of tiny asparagus heads.

'My God! This looks good!' exclaimed Forestier. They ate slowly, relishing the choice meat and the soft, buttery vegetable.

Duroy continued: 'When I'm in love with a woman, everything in the world vanishes but her.'

He spoke with conviction, carried away by the thought of the pleasures of love in his enjoyment of the pleasures of the table.

Mme Forestier murmured, in that detached way of hers, 'Nothing is as wonderful as the first time one hand presses another, when one person asks "Do you love me?" and the other replies "yes, I love you".'

Mme de Marelle, who had just drunk a fresh glass of champagne in a single gulp, said brightly as she put down her glass: 'I'm not quite so platonic.'

And, their eyes gleaming, the others all began to snigger, concurring with this remark.

Forestier stretched out on the sofa, leant back with his arms on the cushions and said in a serious tone: 'Your frankness does you credit, and proves that you are a practical woman. But may one enquire what M. de Marelle thinks of this?'

Slowly, with immeasurable, lingering contempt, she shrugged her shoulders, then said in an emphatic tone: 'M. de Marelle has no opinion on this subject. He simply... abstains.'

And, coming down from lofty theories of love, the conversation then descended into a profusion of elegant smut.

They had now reached the stage of artful suggestiveness, of words lifting veils like a hand lifting a skirt, the stage of plays on meaning, cleverly disguised improprieties and every kind of unblushing hypocrisy, a covert language revealing naked images, generating in the mind's eye a fleeting vision of all that cannot be said, and enabling sophisticated society to indulge in a subtle, mysterious sort of love, a kind of impure contact of the mind, by the simultaneous evocation—as disturbing and sensual as a sexual embrace—of a secretly and shamefully desired intertwining of bodies. The roast had been served, partridges flanked by quail, followed by peas, then a terrine of *foie gras* accompanied by a salad of frilly leaves that filled a great basin-shaped salad bowl with a froth of green. They had eaten these things without tasting them, totally unaware, totally preoccupied by what they were saying, immersed in a bath of love.

The two women, now, were making quite bawdy remarks; Mme de Marelle with a natural audacity that was almost a provocation, Mme Forestier with a charming reserve, a modesty of tone, of voice, of smile, of her whole self, that seemed to mitigate, while actually emphasizing, the daring utterances of her mouth.

Forestier was lying sprawled on the cushions, laughing, drinking and eating without respite, and from time to time coming out with some remark that was so bold or so coarse that the women, a trifle shocked both for form's sake and by the words' form, would assume a little pretence of embarrassment lasting two or three seconds. Whenever he made a joke that was particularly dirty, he would add: 'You're doing very well, my dears. If you go on like this you'll end up doing something you'll regret.'

Dessert was served, followed by coffee; and then the liqueurs trickled into their veins a more intense excitement.

Just as she had promised on sitting down to dinner, Mme de Marelle was tipsy. She cheerfully admitted as much, with the loquacious grace of a woman who, to entertain her guests, overplays her slight, but real, degree of intoxication. Mme Forestier was quiet now, perhaps out of prudence; and Duroy, aware that his drunkenness might make him indiscreet, shrewdly kept silent.

They lit cigarettes, and suddenly Forestier began to cough.

The spasm of coughing—a dreadful spasm—tore at his chest; with scarlet face and brow pouring sweat, he coughed and choked into his napkin. When the attack had passed, he growled angrily: 'They don't do me any good at all, these parties; they're idiotic.' All his good humour had vanished, in the terror of the disease that haunted his thoughts.

'Let's go home,' he said.

Mme de Marelle rang for the waiter and asked for the bill. It was brought to her almost immediately. She tried to read it, but the figures danced before her eyes, and she passed the paper to Duroy, telling him: 'Here, pay it for me, I can't see a thing, I've had too much.' And as she said this, she tossed her purse into his hands.

The bill totalled a hundred and thirty francs. Duroy studied and checked the bill, then put down two notes, asking quietly as he picked up the change: 'How much should I leave for the waiters?'

'Whatever you like; I don't know.'

He put five francs on the plate, then enquired, as he handed back the purse to the young woman, 'Would you like me to see you home?'

'Yes, of course; I'm not capable of finding my own front door.'

They shook hands with the Forestiers, and Duroy found himself alone with Mme de Marelle in a moving cab.

He could feel her beside him, so close beside him, shut up with him in this dark box which the gas lights on the pavements would suddenly, for an instant, illuminate. He could feel the warmth of her shoulder through his sleeve, and he could think of nothing to say to her, absolutely nothing, for his wits were paralysed by the overriding desire to clasp her in his arms. 'What would she do if I dared?' he wondered. The memory of all those indelicacies whispered during dinner encouraged him, but, at the same time, the fear of a scene held him back.

She too was silent, and sat motionless, huddled into her corner. He might have thought she was asleep had he not seen her eyes glitter each time a ray of light shone into the cab.

What was she thinking? He was certain that he ought to remain silent, that a word, a single word, by breaking the silence, would destroy all his hopes; but he lacked daring, the daring to act swiftly and decisively.

Suddenly, he felt her foot move. She had made a movement, a sharp, sudden twitch of impatience or perhaps of entreaty. This almost imperceptible movement electrified him from head to foot, and, turning rapidly, he threw himself on her, seeking her mouth with his lips and her bare flesh with his hands.

She gave a cry, a little cry, tried to draw away, to resist, to push him off, then she surrendered, as if she did not have the strength to resist any longer.

The carriage soon drew up in front of the house where she lived, and Duroy, taken by surprise, did not need to search for passionate words of thanks, devotion, and love. But, dazed by what had just occurred, she did not get up, she did not stir. So, afraid that the driver might suspect something, he got out first in order to help the young woman down.

Eventually she stumbled out of the cab without uttering a word. He rang the bell and, as the door opened, he asked her in a trembling voice: 'When shall I see you again?'

So quietly that she could hardly be heard, she whispered: 'Come and have lunch with me tomorrow.' And she disappeared into the shadowy hallway, pushing the heavy door to; it shut with a sound like a cannon shot.

He gave the driver a hundred sous and walked on, his step rapid and triumphant, filled with joy.

At last he had one, a married woman, a society woman, from real society! Paris society! How easy it had been, how unexpected!

Until then, he had imagined that to approach and conquer one of those intensely desirable creatures would require interminable attentiveness, endless patience, and a skilful campaign involving compliments, words of love, tender sighs, and gifts. And yet here, quite suddenly, with minimal effort on his part, the first one he'd met had given herself to him, with an alacrity that left him stunned.

'She was tipsy,' he thought. 'Tomorrow it'll be a different story.

There'll be tears.' This idea worried him, then he told himself: 'Well, too bad. Now that I've got her, I'm certainly going to keep her.'

And, in the jumbled mirage of his roving hopes—hopes of greatness, of success, of fame, wealth, and love—he suddenly glimpsed, like those garlands of dancing figures that decorate the sky in triumphal scenes, a procession of elegant, rich, powerful women who moved past him smiling, before disappearing, one behind the other, into the golden mist of his dreams.

And his sleep was peopled with visions.

He felt a trifle nervous, the following day, as he climbed Mme de Marelle's staircase. How would she receive him? And what if she did not receive him? What if she had given orders for him not to be admitted? What if she were to tell...? But no, she couldn't say anything without running the risk of revealing everything. So he was in control of the situation.

The little maid opened the door. Her expression was quite normal. He felt reassured, as if he had been expecting the servant to look upset.

He asked: 'Is Madame well?'

She replied: 'Yes, Monsieur, the same as ever.' And she showed him into the drawing-room.

He walked straight over to the mantelpiece to check the appearance of his hair and his clothes, and he was adjusting his cravat in the mirror when he saw, reflected in it, the young woman standing on the threshold of the room, looking at him. He pretended he had not seen her. For a few seconds they appraised one another in the mirror, each observing and studying the other, before they came face to face.

He turned round. She had not moved, and seemed to be waiting. He leapt forward, stammering: 'I love you so much! I love you so much!' She opened her arms and fell into his; then, when she had lifted up her head, they kissed for a long time.

He thought: 'It's easier than I had imagined. This is going beautifully.' And, when their lips parted, he smiled, not saying anything, but trying to express infinite love by the look in his eyes. She was smiling too, smiling the way women smile in offering their desire, their consent, their readiness to surrender. She whispered: 'We're alone. I've sent Laurine off to lunch with a friend.'

He sighed, as he kissed her wrists: 'Thank you. I adore you.'

Then she took his arm, as if he were her husband, to walk over to the sofa where they sat down side by side.

He would have liked to open the conversation with some clever, fascinating remark, but, unable to think of anything suitable, he stammered: 'So, you're not too angry with me?'

She put a hand over his mouth: 'Be quiet!'

They sat in silence, gazing at one another, their fingers intertwined, burning hot.

'I wanted you so much!'

She said again: 'Hush!'

They could hear the maid moving plates about in the dining-room, on the other side of the wall.

He stood up: 'I'd better not sit so close to you. I might lose my head.'

The door opened: 'Lunch is served, Madame.'

He solemnly offered her his arm.

They had lunch sitting face to face, constantly looking at one another and smiling, wholly absorbed in one another, enthralled by the sweet charm of the beginning of a love-affair. They had no idea what they were eating. He felt a foot, a small foot, roaming about under the table. He caught it between his and kept it there, pressing it with all his might.

The maid came and went, nonchalantly bringing in and removing dishes without appearing to notice anything.

When they had finished eating, they returned to the drawing-room and sat down again on the sofa, side by side.

Little by little he pressed closer up against her, and tried to embrace her. But she pushed him away calmly: 'Be careful. Someone might come in.'

He murmured: 'When can I see you really alone, to tell you how much I love you?'

She leant towards his ear and said very softly: 'One of these days I'll pay you a little visit at home.'

He felt himself blush: 'But... it's just that... my room... my room's nothing much.'

She smiled: 'That doesn't matter. It's you I'll be visiting and not your room.'

So then he begged her to tell him when she would come. She named a day at the end of the following week, and he begged her to advance the date, stammering out the words, his eyes glittering as he kneaded and squeezed her hands, his face red, feverish, contorted with desire, with that impetuous desire that follows an intimate meal.

She enjoyed seeing him plead, and, a day at a time, she slowly advanced the date. But he kept repeating: 'Tomorrow... please... tomorrow.'

Finally she consented: 'Yes, Tomorrow. Five o'clock.'

He gave a long sigh of happiness; and they chatted away almost peacefully, in an intimate way, as if they had known each other for twenty years.

A ring on the bell made them jump, and they moved apart.

She whispered: 'That will be Laurine.'

The child came in, and, disconcerted, stopped dead; then she ran towards Duroy, clapping her hands, overjoyed at seeing him, and cried: 'Ah! Bel-Ami!'*

Mme de Marelle began to laugh: 'Goodness! Bel-Ami! Laurine's christened you! That's a nice friendly little nickname for you; I'll call you Bel-Ami too!'

He had taken the child on his knee, and had to play all those little games with her that he had taught her.

At twenty to three he took his leave, to go to the newspaper; on the landing, through the half-open door, he whispered again, barely moving his lips: 'Tomorrow. Five o'clock.'

The young woman answered 'Yes' with a smile, and disappeared.

His jobs for the day completed, he thought about how to arrange his room to receive his mistress, and how best to disguise the poverty of his surroundings. He had the idea of pinning some trifling Japanese bric-à-brac on the walls, and for five francs bought a lot of crêpe paper hangings, tiny fans, and decorations, with which he hid the more obvious stains on the wallpaper. On the window panes he stuck transparencies depicting boats on rivers, birds flying across red skies, multicoloured ladies on balconies, and processions of little black men moving across snow-covered plains.

Soon his room, which was barely large enough to sleep and sit in, looked like the inside of a painted paper lantern. He was pleased with the general effect, and spent the evening sticking on the ceiling some birds cut out of the remaining coloured sheets.

Then he went to bed, lulled by the whistle of the trains. The following day he came home early, with a bag of little cakes and a bottle of Madeira from the grocer's. He had to go out again to buy two plates and two glasses; and he set all this out on his dressing-table, whose dirty wooden top he covered with a napkin, after stowing away the wash-basin and ewer underneath.

Then he waited.

She arrived about a quarter past five, and, captivated by the multi-coloured brilliance of the decorations, exclaimed: 'My, your room is nice. But what a lot of people live on the staircase.'

He had taken her in his arms, and was passionately kissing her hair between her brow and her hat, through the veil.

An hour and a half later, he took her to the cab-stand in the Rue de Rome. When she had got in, he whispered: 'Tuesday, same time.' She said: 'Same time, Tuesday.' And as night had fallen, she pulled his head into the window and kissed him on the lips. Then, as the driver was whipping up the horse, she cried: 'Goodbye, Bel-Ami!' and the old cab set off, to the weary trotting of a white horse.

For the next three weeks, this was how Duroy received Mme de Marelle every two or three days, sometimes in the morning, sometimes in the evening.

As he was waiting for her one afternoon, a tremendous noise on the staircase drew him to his door. A child was screaming. A furious voice—a man's voice—shouted: 'What the devil is that little bugger bellowing about now?' A woman replied in strident, exasperated tones: 'That dirty tart that visits the journalist upstairs pushed Nicholas over, on the landing. Sluts like that what don't watch out for kids shouldn't be let into the building!'

Disconcerted, Duroy stepped back inside, for he could hear a rapid rustling of skirts and a swift step climbing up the flight of stairs beneath him.

Soon there was a knock on his door, which he had closed behind him. He opened it, and Mme de Marelle, breathless and dreadfully upset, flung herself into the room, stammering: 'Did you hear?'

He pretended to know nothing. 'No, what?'

'The way they insulted me?'

'Who?'

'Those dreadful people downstairs.'

'No, what's the matter, tell me.'

Unable to utter a word, she began to sob.

He had to remove her hat, undo her laces, lay her on the bed, dab her temples with a damp cloth; she was choking; then, when she was a little calmer, all her indignant rage exploded.

She wanted him to go down straight away, fight them, kill them.

He kept repeating: 'But they're working people, peasants. Remember, the law would be called in, you might be recognized, arrested, ruined. You don't get involved with people like that.'

She turned to something else: 'How are we going to manage now? I can't come back here.' He replied: 'It's perfectly simple, I'll move.'

She murmured: 'Yes, but that would take a long time.' Then, suddenly struck by an idea, she quickly regained her composure: 'No, listen, I know what to do, leave it to me, don't you worry about a thing; I'll send you an "express"* tomorrow morning.' 'Express' was her name for the personal telegrams that could be sent within Paris.

Now she was smiling, thrilled with her brainwave, that she refused to divulge; and, wild with passion, she made love to him without restraint.

Nevertheless she felt extremely nervous as she went down the stairs, and her legs were so shaky she had to lean heavily on her lover's arm. They did not meet a soul.

As he got up late, he was still in bed when, about eleven the next morning, the telegraph boy delivered the promised 'express'.

Duroy opened it and read: 'Meet me this afternoon, five o'clock, 127 rue de Constantinople.* Ask for Mme Duroy's apartment. Your loving Clo.'

At exactly five o'clock, he arrived at a large building of furnished flats and enquired of the concierge: 'It's here that Mme Duroy has taken an apartment?'

'Yes, Monsieur.'

'Would you show me in, please.'

The man, no doubt accustomed to delicate situations where discretion is required, looked him straight in the eye and asked, as he selected one of the long row of keys: 'I take it you are M. Duroy?'

'Yes, of course,'

And he opened a small two-room apartment located on the ground floor, opposite the concierge's lodge.

The drawing-room, decorated with a reasonably clean floral wallpaper, contained a mahogany couch upholstered in a greenish rep patterned in yellow, and a skimpy flowered carpet, so thin that you could feel the wooden floor through it.

The bedroom was so tiny that three-quarters of the space was taken up by the bed, which filled the far end from one wall to the other; it was the sort of big bed you find in furnished rooms, draped in heavy blue curtains also made of rep, and engulfed by a red silk eiderdown spotted with suspicious stains.

Duroy, uneasy and annoyed, was thinking: 'This flat's going to cost me a fortune. I'll have to borrow more money. It's absurd, what she's done.'

The door opened and Clotilde burst into the room with a great rustling of skirts, her arms wide open. She was delighted. 'Isn't this nice, don't you think this is nice? And no stairs to climb, it's on the ground floor, looking onto the street! You can come and go through the window without the concierge seeing you. Oh, how we're going to love each other in here!'

He kissed her coldly, not daring to voice the question on his lips.

She had put down a large parcel on the pedestal table in the middle of the room. Opening it, she took out a bar of soap, a bottle of Lubin water,* a sponge, a box of hair pins, a bottle opener, and a tiny curling iron for arranging the curls on her forehead, which came undone every single time.

She made a game of settling in, deciding where to put everything, enjoying herself enormously.

She chatted while opening drawers: 'I'll have to bring some underwear, so I can change if necessary. It will be so handy. If I happen to get soaked, for example, when I'm out shopping, I'll come here to dry off. We'll each have our own key, apart from the one we leave with the concierge in case we forget ours. I've rented it for three months, in your name of course, since I couldn't give mine.'

So then he asked: 'You'll tell me when I must pay, won't you?'

She replied simply: 'But it's already paid, my dearest!'

He went on: 'So I owe it to you?'

'No, my pet, it's nothing to do with you, this little escapade is entirely my idea.'

He gave the appearance of being annoyed: 'Oh! No, absolutely not. I won't allow that.'

She came and pleaded with him, putting her hands on his

shoulders: 'I beg you, Georges, it would make me so happy, so very happy if it's mine, if our nest is really mine! That doesn't offend you, does it? Why should it? I wanted to do this for our love. Say you would like it, please, darling Georges, say yes?' She was begging him with her eyes, with her lips, with her whole being.

He let her go on imploring, frowning angrily in refusal, then he gave in, feeling that, after all, it was only fair.

When she had left, he murmured, rubbing his hands, and without searching the depths of his heart to discover why he should have thought this on this particular day: 'When all's said and done, she really is nice.'

A few days later he received another 'express' that said: 'My husband returns this evening after a six weeks' tour of inspection. So we must schedule a week's intermission. What a chore, my darling! Your Clo.'

Duroy was dumbfounded. He no longer ever thought of her as married. Now there was a man whose face he'd like to see, just once, so as to know what he looked like!

He did, however, patiently await the departure of the husband, although he spent two evenings at the Folies-Bergère, evenings which ended at Rachel's.

Then, one morning, another telegram came, containing five words: 'Five o'clock this afternoon.—Clo.'

They both arrived early at the rendezvous. She flung herself into his arms with a great outburst of love, kissing him passionately all over his face, then she said: 'If you like, when we've made love, you can take me somewhere for dinner. I've arranged it so I'm free.'

It was the beginning of the month, and although his salary was pledged far in advance and he was living from hand to mouth on cash he picked up here and there, Duroy happened to be in funds; and he was pleased to have the opportunity to spend something on her.

He replied: 'Yes, my love, wherever you want.'

So they set off around seven o'clock and made for the outer boulevard. Clinging tightly to his arm, she said in his ear: 'If you knew how happy it makes me to take your arm when we're walking, how I love to feel you close to me.'

He asked: 'Would you like to go to Père Lathuile's?'*

'Oh no, that's too fashionable,' she replied. 'I'd like something fun, something common, like a restaurant where clerks and working girls go; I adore going to little places on the outskirts! Oh, if only we could have gone into the country!'

As he knew of nowhere like that in the area, they wandered right along the boulevard, and eventually went into a wine merchant's where food was served in a separate room. Through the window, she had seen two bare-headed girls* sitting at a table opposite a pair of soldiers.

Three cab drivers were having their dinner in the rear of the long, narrow room, and another man, whose profession it was impossible to determine, was smoking his pipe with his legs stretched out and his hands tucked into the band of his trousers, lounging in his chair with his head lolling over the back. His coat was a repository of stains, and in its pockets—which bulged like swollen bellies—the neck of a bottle could be seen, along with a piece of bread, a parcel wrapped in a newspaper and a trailing length of string. His hair was thick, frizzy, tousled, grey with dirt; his cap lay on the ground, under his chair.

The entry of Clotilde in her elegant outfit caused a sensation. The two couples stopped whispering, the three cabbies stopped arguing, and the fellow who was smoking, having removed his pipe from his mouth and spat in front of him, turned his head a little to look.

Mme de Marelle murmured: 'This is really lovely! We'll be fine here; another time, I'll dress up as a working girl.'

And, without any embarrassment or distaste, she sat down at the table, the wood of which had been varnished by grease from the food, rinsed by spilt drinks, and wiped down with a waiter's cursory rag. Duroy, somewhat ill-at-ease and ashamed, was searching for a peg on which to hang his top hat. Not finding one, he put it on a chair.

They ate mutton stew, and a slice of leg of mutton with a salad. Clotilde kept repeating: 'I just adore this. I like slumming. I find this more fun than the Café Anglais.'* Then she said: 'If you want to give me a special treat, you'll take me to a dance hall. I know one near here that's great fun—it's called La Reine Blanche.'*

Surprised, Duroy enquired: 'Who was it took you there?'

He was watching her, and saw her blush and look a trifle discomfited, as if this sudden question had sparked a sensitive memory. After one of those feminine hesitations so transient as to be barely noticeable, she answered: 'Someone I knew...' Then, after a silence, she added: 'who died.'

And she lowered her eyes with a sadness that was perfectly natural. And, for the first time, Duroy thought of all the things in this woman's past about which he knew nothing; and he wondered. Of course she'd had lovers before, but what kind? From what social class? A vague kind of jealousy, a sort of hostility towards her was stirring in him, a hostility towards everything he did not know about her, towards everything in her feelings and in her life that had never belonged to him. He gazed at her, exasperated by the mystery locked inside this pretty, silent head that was thinking—perhaps at this very moment—of the other man, of other men, with regret. How he would have loved to see into her memory, to search through it, and find out everything, know everything!...

She repeated: 'Will you take me to La Reine Blanche? That would really top off the evening.'

He thought: 'Bah! What does the past matter? I'm being very stupid to let it bother me.' And he answered with a smile: 'Yes, of course, sweetheart.'

When they were out in the street, she continued, very softly, in that mysterious tone people use for confiding secrets: 'Until now I haven't dared ask you this; but you can't imagine how I love these adventures—going to all these places single men go to, and women don't. At carnival time I'll dress up as a schoolboy. I look priceless as a schoolboy.'

When they went into the dance-hall, she pressed up against him, frightened and happy, gazing delightedly at the prostitutes and pimps and, from time to time, as if to reassure herself against potential danger, remarking, upon noticing a solemn, motionless military policeman: 'There's a constable who looks a reliable type.' After a quarter of an hour she had had enough, and he took her home.

Then began a series of expeditions to all the seedy haunts where working people go for a good time; and Duroy discovered in his mistress a remarkable appetite for roaming round the town like a student on a spree.

She would arrive at their usual meeting place wearing a coarse cotton dress, her head covered by a bonnet like that worn by the lady's maid in a farce, and, despite the elegant and studied simplicity of her outfit, she would still be wearing her diamond rings, bracelets

and earrings, explaining, when he begged her to remove them: 'Nonsense! They'll think they're rhinestones.'*

She believed herself to be wonderfully disguised, and, although in
fact she was merely concealed ostrich-fashion, she would go into the
most disreputable taverns.

She had wanted Duroy to dress as a workman, but he refused,
keeping his conventional man-about-town clothes, not even agreeing
to replace his top hat with a soft felt one. She had consoled herself at
this obstinacy by reasoning that 'they'll think I'm a servant girl
who's got off with a young man of good family'. She thought this a
delicious joke.

In this way they would go into working-class cafés, sitting down at
the back of the smoky hovel, on rickety chairs, at an old wooden
table. A cloud of acrid smoke permeated by the smell of the fried fish
served at dinner filled the room; men in overalls shouted as they
downed their tots of spirit, and the waiter would stare in astonishment at this strange couple, as he placed before them two glasses of
brandied cherries.

Trembling, frightened, and enthralled, she would begin sipping
the fruity red juice, gazing round her with uneasy, excited eyes. Every
cherry she swallowed gave her the feeling of committing a sin, every
drop of the burning, spicy liquid going down her throat gave her a
fierce pleasure, the pleasure of a wicked, forbidden gratification.

Then she would say in a low voice: 'Let's go.' And they would
leave. She walked out quickly with her head bent, the way an actress
walks off the stage, passing between the drinkers who, leaning their
elbows on the tables, watched her with a suspicious, annoyed air; and
when she was through the door she would give a great sigh, as if she
had just escaped from some terrible danger.

Sometimes, with a shiver, she would ask Duroy: 'What would you
do if I was insulted in one of those places?' and he would reply in a
blustering tone: 'I'd defend you, by God!'

And she would give his arm a delighted squeeze, feeling, perhaps,
a vague longing to be insulted and defended, to see men fighting over
her, even that kind of men, fighting with her beloved.

But these expeditions, which were repeated two or three times a
week, began to bore Duroy, who moreover found it very hard to lay
his hands on the ten francs needed to pay for the carriage and the
drinks.

His circumstances were now severely straitened, worse than in the days when he was employed by the railway, for, having spent money freely, heedlessly, during his first months as a journalist, in the continual expectation of earning large sums in the very near future, he had used up all his resources and every possible way of raising money.

A very simple technique—that of borrowing from the cashier— had rapidly been exhausted, and he already owed the paper four months' salary, plus six hundred francs against what he earned for his writing. In addition, he owed a hundred francs to Forestier, three hundred to Jacques Rival, who was very open-handed, and he was bothered by a pile of embarrassing little debts, ranging from twenty francs to five.

Saint-Potin, whom he had consulted about ways to find another hundred francs, had been unable, despite his resourcefulness, to come up with any suggestion; and Duroy was increasingly frustrated by this poverty of which he was more conscious than in the past, because his needs were greater. A feeling of repressed rage against the whole world festered in him, and a constant irritation, which manifested itself at every moment, for the most trifling reasons.

He sometimes wondered how, without indulging in any extravagance or whim, he had managed to spend an average of a thousand francs a month, but then he would work out that if you added together eight francs for lunch and twelve for dinner in any big café on the boulevard, that alone came to twenty, which, along with ten francs' pocket money—those coins that just trickle away on nothing in particular—you reached a total of thirty francs. Thirty francs a day came to nine hundred by the end of the month. And that sum didn't allow for all those expenses of clothing, shoes, linen, laundry, and the like.

So, on the 14th of December, there he was without a sou in his pocket, and without the faintest notion of how to get his hands on any money.

As he had so often done in the past, he went without lunch; then, irritable and uneasy, he spent the afternoon at the office. About four o'clock, he received an 'express' from his mistress, which said: 'How about dinner tonight? We can go on one of our jaunts afterwards.' He replied immediately: 'Dinner impossible.' Then he reflected that it would be very stupid indeed to deprive himself of the pleasant interlude she could afford him, and added: 'But I'll expect you at nine at our place.' And having dispatched one of the office boys with the note, to save the cost of the telegram, he began thinking how to set about paying for his dinner that evening. By seven he still had not come up with a solution, and his stomach was being racked by dreadful hunger pangs. So he resorted to a desperate stratagem. He waited until, one by one, all his colleagues had left, and, when he was alone, rang the bell sharply. The Director's doorman, who looked after the offices, appeared.

Duroy was on his feet, nervously searching through his pockets, and said in a brusque tone, 'Look here, Foucart, I've left my purse at home, and I've got to go to the Luxembourg* for dinner. Lend me a couple of francs for a cab.'

The man took three francs from his waistcoat pocket, enquiring: 'Would you like more than that, Monsieur?'

'No, no, that's enough. Thanks very much.'

And, snatching up the coins, Duroy ran down the stairs, then went for dinner to a cheap eatery he used to frequent when he was penniless.

At nine, he was waiting for his mistress, warming his feet by the fire in the little sitting-room.

In she came, very lively and cheerful, invigorated by the cold air of the street, saying: 'We could go out for a bit first, if you like, then come back here at eleven. It's wonderful weather for walking.'

He replied in a peevish tone: 'Why go out? We're very comfortable here.'

She continued, without removing her hat: 'You know, the moonlight's heavenly. It's a real pleasure to be out, tonight.'

'That may be, but I don't want to go out.'

He had said this in a very angry manner. Startled and offended, she asked: 'What's the matter with you? Why are you speaking to me like that? I'd like to go for a bit of a walk, I don't see why that should make you cross.'

He stood up in exasperation: 'It doesn't make me cross. It bores me, that's all.'

She was one of those women who are irritated by opposition and exasperated by rudeness. She said, with scornful, icy anger: 'I'm not accustomed to being spoken to like that. I'll go out by myself, then: goodbye!'

He realized that he had made a serious mistake, and rushing towards her he took her hands, kissed them, and stammered: 'Forgive me, darling, forgive me. I'm feeling very on edge tonight, very touchy. I've problems, you see, worries—things connected with the paper.'

Somewhat mollified, but not entirely soothed, she replied: 'That's nothing to do with me; and I'm not going to put up with the effects of your bad temper.'

He took her in his arms, drawing her towards the sofa: 'Listen, my pet, I didn't mean to hurt you; I wasn't thinking what I was saying.'

He had made her sit down, and, kneeling in front of her, asked: 'Have you forgiven me? Tell me you've forgiven me.'

She murmured, in a cold voice: 'All right; but don't do that again.' And, standing up, she added: 'Now let's go out for a walk.'

He was still on his knees, encircling her hips with his arms; he mumbled: 'Please, let's stay here. Please. Do this for me. I would so love to keep you all to myself this evening, here, by the fire. Say yes, please, please say yes.'

She answered in a sharp, cold voice: 'No. I really want to go out, and I'm not going to give in to your whims.'

He insisted: 'Please, I have a reason, a very good reason...'

Again she said: 'No. And if you don't want to go out with me, I'm leaving. Goodbye!'

She had shaken herself free, and was making for the door. He ran towards her, enveloping her in his arms: 'Listen, Clo, my little Clo, do this for me...' She was shaking her head in refusal, without replying, avoiding his kisses and trying to escape from his grasp so that she could leave.

He was stammering: 'Clo, my little Clo, I have a reason.'

She stopped, looking him full in the face: 'You're lying... What is it?'

He blushed, not knowing what to say. And she went on indignantly: 'You see... it's obvious you're lying... You filthy beast.'

Her eyes brimming with tears, she freed herself from him with an angry gesture. He grabbed hold of her again by the shoulders, and, utterly miserable, ready to confess everything to avoid losing her, declared in desperate tones: 'The thing is... I'm flat broke. There.'

She stopped dead, gazing deep into his eyes, trying to read the truth in them: 'What did you say?'

He had blushed to the roots of his hair: 'I said I'm flat broke. Do you understand? I haven't twenty sous, I haven't ten, I haven't got enough to buy us a cassis when we go into a café. You're forcing me to confess things I'm ashamed of. But it just wasn't possible for me to go out with you, and then when we were sitting down with two drinks in front of us, calmly tell you that I couldn't pay for them...'

She was still looking directly at him: 'So... it really is true... what you said?'

Instantly he turned out all his pockets, those in his trousers, those in his waistcoat, those in his jacket, muttering: 'There... now are you satisfied?'

Suddenly, spreading wide her arms in a burst of passion, she flung them round his neck, stammering: 'Oh, my poor darling, my poor darling, if only I'd known! How did this happen?'

She made him sit down, and sat herself on his knees, then, with her arms round his neck, kissed him repeatedly, kissing his moustache, his mouth, his eyes, as she forced him to tell her how this misfortune had come about.

He invented a pathetic tale. He had had to come to the assistance of his father, who had found himself in difficulties. Not only had he given him all his savings, but he himself was now heavily in debt. He added: 'It will mean starving for six months, because I've used up all my reserves. It's too bad, but these things happen in life. After all, money's not worth worrying about.'

She whispered in his ear: 'Would you like me to lend you some?'

He answered with dignity: 'You're very sweet, my pet, but please, don't let's talk about this any more. You'll offend me.'

She was silent; then, clasping him in her arms, she whispered: 'You'll never know how much I love you.'

That was one of their best evenings of love-making.

When she was leaving, she said with a smile: 'Georges! When you're in a spot like yours, isn't it fun to find a coin you've forgotten about in a pocket, something that's slipped down into the lining!'

His reply was emphatic: 'You're damn right!'

She wanted to return home on foot, claiming that the moon was superb, and she went into ecstasies gazing at it. It was a cold, calm night in early winter. Passers-by and horses moved swiftly, spurred on by the clear frosty air. The sound of heels echoed on the sidewalks.

As they parted, she asked: 'Would you like to meet the day after tomorrow?'

'Yes, of course.'

'Same time?'

'Same time.'

'Goodbye, my darling.' And they kissed, tenderly.

Then he walked home, striding along, wondering what he would be able to think up the next day, to solve his problem. But when, on opening his door, he fumbled in his waistcoat pocket for some matches, he was dumbfounded to discover that his fingers were touching a coin. The moment he had some light, he seized the coin and examined it. It was a louis, a twenty-franc piece!

He thought he must have gone mad. He turned it over and over, trying to work out by what miracle this coin could be in his pocket. After all, it could hardly have fallen there out of the sky. Then, suddenly, he guessed, and was filled with angry indignation. His mistress had indeed spoken of coins that slip into linings, that you come upon in moments of need. She must have been the one who had given him this handout! How mortifying!

He swore: 'Fine! I'll see her, all right, day after tomorrow! She'll have something to remember me by!' And he went to bed, his feelings in a turmoil of fury and humiliation.

He woke late. He felt hungry. He tried to go back to sleep so as not to get up before two o'clock; then he said to himself: 'This isn't going to help me, in the end I'll still have to find some money.' He went out, hoping that an idea would come to him in the street.

It didn't, but as he passed each restaurant a fierce longing for food made his mouth water. At midday, as he had not thought of anything, he suddenly made up his mind: 'Bah! I'll have lunch with Clotilde's twenty francs. That won't stop me giving them back to her tomorrow.'

So he lunched in a brasserie, for two francs fifty. On arriving at the paper, he handed over three more francs to the doorman. 'Here, Foucart, here's what you lent me yesterday evening for my cab.'

He worked until seven o'clock. Then he went out for dinner, taking another three francs out of the same money. His two evening beers brought his day's expenses to a total of nine francs thirty centimes. But, since he could not obtain any more credit nor discover a fresh source of funds in twenty-four hours, he borrowed another six francs fifty the following day from the twenty he planned to repay that same evening, so that he arrived at the agreed rendezvous with four francs twenty in his pocket.

He was in a foul temper, and had promised himself he would instantly make the situation very clear indeed. He would tell his mistress: 'You know, I found the twenty francs you put in my pocket the other day. I'm not returning them to you today because my position hasn't changed, and I haven't had any time to devote to money matters. But I'll repay it the next time we see each other.'

She came in, loving, attentive, and very nervous. How would he receive her? She kissed him repeatedly so to avoid an immediate explanation. For his part, he kept telling himself: 'It will be soon enough if I raise the matter later on. I'll wait for the right moment.'

He never found the right moment and said nothing, shying away from uttering the first words on this delicate subject. She never said a word about going out, and was charming in every way.

They separated towards midnight, arranging their next meeting only for the Wednesday of the following week, because Mme de Marelle had dinner engagements on several consecutive evenings.

Duroy, as he was paying for his lunch the next day and feeling for the four coins he should have left, discovered that they were five; one of them was gold. At first he supposed that he had accidentally been given a twenty-franc piece in change, the previous evening; but then he understood, and felt his heart pound at the humiliation of this persistent charity.

How sorry he was that he had said nothing! If he had spoken forcefully, this would not have happened.

For four days he attempted to raise five louis, trying various means and embarking on endeavours as numerous as they were futile, and so he ran through Clotilde's second louis.

On their next meeting, she found a way—despite his saying, in furious tones: 'Don' t try that trick again that you played those other evenings, because I'll get angry'—to slip another twenty francs into his trouser pocket. When he discovered the money, he swore 'for Christ's sake!'—and put the coin in his waistcoat so that it would be ready to hand; he was absolutely broke. He appeased his conscience by reasoning that: 'I'll repay it all at once. After all, it's really only a loan.'

Eventually, the cashier at the newspaper, in response to his desperate pleas, agreed to let him have five francs a day. It was just enough for his meals, but not enough to repay the sixty francs.

So, as Clotilde was again seized by her wild urge to spend evenings going round all the unsavoury night-spots of Paris, in the end he did not become too irritated when, after these expeditions, he would find a coin in one of his pockets, even, on one occasion, in his boot, or, another time, inside his watch-case.

Since she had fancies that he could not, at present, satisfy, wasn't it only natural that she should pay for them, rather than go without? Besides, he kept count of everything that he received in this way, so that one day he could repay it.

She said to him one evening: 'Would you believe that I've never been to the Folies-Bergère? Will you take me there?' He hesitated, afraid that he might meet Rachel. Then he thought: 'Bah! After all, I'm not married. If she sees me, she'll understand the situation and won't speak to me. Besides, we'll take a box.'

Something else decided the matter. He was very pleased to have this opportunity to treat Mme de Marelle to a box at the theatre without parting with any money. It was a kind of repayment.

He left Clotilde in the cab at first while he collected the tickets, so that she would not see that they were complimentary; then he fetched her. They were greeted by the doormen as they walked in. An enormous crowd filled the lobby, and they made their way with difficulty through the throng of men and prostitutes. Eventually they reached their box and settled down in it, sandwiched between the staid orchestra stalls and the bustling gallery.

But Mme de Marelle scarcely looked at the stage, for she was utterly engrossed by the prostitutes parading round behind her back; and she turned to watch them, wanting to touch them, to feel their breasts, their cheeks, their hair, to discover what those creatures were made of.

Suddenly she said: 'There's a great big brunette who's watching us all the time. I thought she was going to speak to us just now. Did you see her?'

'No, you must be mistaken,' he replied. But he had already caught sight of her. It was Rachel, with rage in her eyes and angry words on her lips, loitering about close by. Duroy had brushed past her in the crowd, just a few minutes earlier, and she had said 'Hallo' very softly, giving him a wink that meant 'I understand.' But, afraid of being seen by his mistress, he had not acknowledged this thoughtfulness, and had passed by in icy silence, his head held high and his expression disdainful. Rachel, goaded now by unconscious jealousy, came back, brushed against him again, and said in a louder voice: 'Hallo, Georges.'

He had still made no reply. At that she grew stubbornly determined to be recognized and greeted, and she returned constantly to the back of the box, waiting for an opportunity.

As soon as she noticed Mme de Marelle looking at her, she prodded Duroy in the shoulder with her finger: 'Hallo. How are you?'

But he did not turn round.

She went on: 'Well? Have you gone deaf since last Thursday?'

He made no reply, affecting a contemptuous air that prevented his lowering himself by saying one single word to this slut. She gave a laugh—a furious laugh—and asked: 'Lost your tongue, have you? Perhaps Madame bit it off for you?'

With an angry gesture he said in an exasperated voice: 'Who gave you permission to speak to me? Be off, or I'll have you arrested.'

Then, her eyes blazing and her breasts heaving, she bellowed: 'Ah! So that's how it is! You rotten bastard! When you go to bed with a woman, at least you say 'hallo' to her. Just because you're with someone else is no reason to cut me dead. If you'd simply nodded to me just now, when I passed right by you, I'd have left you in peace. But you wanted to play the high and mighty, well you just wait! I'm gonna show you what's what! So, you won't even say "hallo" when we meet...'

She would have gone on and on screaming, but Mme de Marelle had opened the door of the box, and was disappearing through the crowd, desperately seeking the exit. Duroy rushed after her, trying to catch her up.

Then Rachel, seeing them take flight, yelled triumphantly: 'Stop her! Stop her! She's pinched my lover.'

The crowd began to laugh. Two men, as a joke, seized the fugitive by the shoulders, trying to kiss her and take her off with them. But Duroy, catching up with her, freed her violently and pulled her into the street. She threw herself into an empty cab that was waiting in front of the building. He jumped in after her, and when the coachman enquired: 'Where to, mister?' he answered: 'Wherever you like.'

Slowly the cab began to move, jolting over the cobblestones. Clotilde, in a state bordering on hysteria, sat gasping and choking with sobs, her hands over her face; Duroy did not know what to do, or what to say.

Finally, as he could hear her crying, he faltered: 'Listen, Clo, my little Clo, let me explain! It's not my fault... I knew that woman before... in the early days...'

She suddenly took her hands away from her face and, filled with the rage of a betrayed lover, a passionate rage which restored her voice to her, she stammered out some rapid, staccato, breathless phrases: 'Ah! you wretch... you wretch... How vile you are... Is this possible?... How shameful! Oh, God! How shameful!'

Then, growing angrier and angrier as her ideas became clearer and arguments occurred to her: 'It was my money you paid her with, wasn't it? I was giving him money for that prostitute... Oh, the wretch!'

For a few seconds she seemed to be searching for a stronger word that would not come to her, then, suddenly, she spat out—going through the motions of actually spitting: 'Oh... you pig... pig... pig. You were paying her with my money... you pig... you pig!' She could think of no other word and went on repeating: 'You pig... you pig...'

All of a sudden, leaning out, she grabbed the driver by the sleeve: 'Stop!' Then, opening the door, she jumped into the street. Georges tried to follow, but she cried: 'I forbid you to get out,' in such a loud voice that passers-by gathered round her; and Duroy, afraid of a public scene, did not move.

Then she took her purse from her pocket and looked for some coins by the light of the street-lamp; having found two francs fifty she put them into the driver's hand, telling him in carrying tones: 'Here... this is for your time... I'm the one that pays... and drive this skunk back to the Rue Boursault, in the Batignolles.'*

A ripple of laughter ran through the group that surrounded her. A man said: 'Bravo, my love!' and a young lout standing between the cab wheels stuck his head through the open door and shouted in a high, shrill voice: 'Goodnight, my little pet!'

The cab set off again, pursued by roars of laughter.

CHAPTER 6

Duroy woke up the next morning feeling miserable. He dressed slowly, then sat down by his window and began to think. His whole body ached, as if he had been beaten up the night before.

Eventually, the necessity of finding some money spurred him into action, and he went first to visit Forestier.

His friend received him in his study, where he was sitting in front of the fire.

'What's got you up so early?'

'Something very serious, I've a debt of honour.'

'A gambling debt?'

He hesitated, then confessed: 'Yes, a gambling debt.'

'A lot?'

'Five hundred francs.'

He owed only two hundred and eighty.

Forestier asked distrustfully: 'Whom do you owe it to?'

Duroy could not give an immediate answer: 'Well... um... to a M. de Carleville.'

'Oh yes. And where does he live?'

'Rue... Rue...'

Forestier began to laugh. 'Come on, I've heard that one before. I know that man, my dear fellow. If you'd like twenty francs, I'm still prepared to lend you that, but not more.' Duroy accepted the gold coin.

Then he went from door to door, calling on all his acquaintances, and finally, by five o'clock, had gathered together eighty francs. As he still needed to lay his hands on two hundred francs, he decided to hold on to what he had collected, muttering: 'Hell, I'm not going to get all upset over that bitch. I'll pay her when I can.'

For two weeks he lived a frugal, regular, chaste life, full of energetic determination. Then he was seized by a fierce wave of desire. He felt as if several years had elapsed since he had held a woman in his arms, and, like the sailor who goes beserk on sighting land again, he trembled at every skirt he passed.

So one evening he returned to the Folies-Bergère, hoping to find Rachel there. He did indeed see her as soon as he went in, for she rarely left the place. He went up to her with a smile, holding out his hand. But, looking him up and down, she asked:

'What do you want with me?'

He tried to laugh it off: 'Come on, don't give yourself airs.'

She turned her back on him, announcing: 'I don't go with pimps.'

She had deliberately come up with the worst possible insult. He felt his face go scarlet, and returned home alone.

Forestier, weak and ill and constantly coughing, made his life a burden at the paper, apparently racking his brains to find him irksome assignments. One day, in a moment of nervous exasperation following a long spasm of coughing, as Duroy had not brought him some information he had requested, he even snarled: 'Damn it all, you're stupider than I'd have thought possible.'

Duroy almost hit him, but, controlling himself, moved away, muttering: 'You wait, I'll get you.' A sudden thought flashed across his mind and mentally he added: 'I'm going to have your wife, old man.' And he walked off rubbing his hands, delighted with this plan.

The very next day, intending to start carrying it out, he paid Mme Forestier an exploratory visit.

He found her lying full length on her sofa, reading a book. She offered him her hand without moving, simply turning her head, and said: 'Hallo, Bel-Ami!'

He felt as if he had been slapped: 'Why did you call me that?'

She replied with a smile: 'I saw Mme de Marelle the other week, and heard how they'd christened you, over at her place.'

The young woman's friendly manner reassured him. Besides, what had he to fear? She went on: 'You spoil her! As for me, people come and see me when they think of it, once in a blue moon, just about!'

He had sat down beside her and was looking at her with a new kind of curiosity, the curiosity of a collector of pretty objects. She was charming, warmly and delicately fair, made to be caressed; and he thought: 'She's certainly better than the other one.' He never doubted he would succeed, it seemed to him that he had only to stretch out his hand and pluck her like a ripe fruit. He said resolutely: 'I didn't come to see you because it was better not to.'

She asked, not understanding: 'What? Why?'

'Why? Can't you guess?'

'No, not at all.'

'Because I'm in love with you... Oh, a bit, only a bit... And I don't want to fall really in love with you...'

She seemed neither surprised, nor shocked, nor flattered; she went on smiling the same dispassionate smile, as she calmly replied: 'Oh, you can come just the same. No one's ever in love with me for long.'

Surprised by the tone even more than by the words, he asked: 'Why?'

'Because it's pointless, and I make that clear straight away. If you had told me earlier about your fear, I would have reassured you, and on the contrary pressed you to come as often as possible.'

He exclaimed, in a pathetic tone: 'As if one's feelings could be controlled at will!'

She turned towards him: 'My dear friend, for me, a man who's in love is erased from the roll of the living. He becomes a half-wit, and not just a half-wit, but a dangerous one. With men who are really in love with me, or who claim they are, I break off any close relationship, first because they bore me, but also because I don't trust them, just as I don't trust a rabid dog who might go on the rampage. So I put them into moral quarantine until their sickness is over. Don't ever forget this. I know perfectly well that for you love is simply a kind of appetite, whereas for me it would be, on the contrary, a kind of... of spiritual communion that has no place in the religion of men! For you it's the letter that counts, but for us it's the spirit. But... look at me please...'

She was no longer smiling. Her face was calm and impassive, and she said, emphasizing each word: 'You must understand that I shall never, ever be your mistress. Therefore it's absolutely pointless, it would even be bad for you to persist in this desire... And now that that's over and done with... do you want us to be friends, good friends, I mean true friends, without any ulterior motives?'

He had realized that any attempt on his part would be fruitless, in the face of this irrevocable decision. He promptly and openly resigned himself, and, delighted at being able to secure himself this ally in life, he reached both hands out to her: 'I am yours, Mme Forestier, in whatever way you wish.'

She heard the sincerity of the thought in the voice, and gave him her hands. He kissed them one after the other, then, raising his head, said simply: 'Lord, if I'd found a woman like you, how happy I'd have been to marry her!'

She was touched, this time, gratified by his remark, as women are by compliments that speak directly to their heart, and she gave him one of those rapid, grateful glances that make us their slaves. Then, as he could find no suitable topic with which to continue the conversation, she said in a gentle voice, placing a finger on his arm: 'And I shall start immediately in my role as your friend. You've made some blunders, my dear man...' She hesitated, and asked: 'May I speak frankly?'

'Yes.'

'Quite frankly?'

'Quite frankly.'

'Well! Then go and see Mme Walter, who thinks highly of you, and make yourself agreeable to her. You'll get the chance, with her, to pay your compliments, although she's a virtuous woman, make no mistake, absolutely virtuous. Oh! There's not a chance of... poaching there either. But you might do yourself some good by making a favourable impression there. I know that you're still in a modest position at the paper. But don't worry, they welcome all their editorial staff in the same friendly way. Take my advice, go.'

He smiled and said: 'Thank you, you're an angel... a guardian angel.' Then they talked of this and that. He stayed a long time, wanting to prove that he enjoyed being with her, and, on leaving, he asked again: 'We're friends, agreed?'

'Agreed.'

As, earlier, he had noticed the effect of his compliment, he underscored it, by adding: 'In case you should ever become a widow, I'm putting my name down.' Then he left, quickly, so that she would not have the time to be annoyed.

Duroy was a little uneasy at visiting Mme Walter, for he had not received permission to call on her, and was afraid of committing a *faux pas*. But the Director treated him benevolently, appreciated his work, and made a point of choosing him for difficult assignments, so why should he not take advantage of this favour to get inside the house?

So one day, having got up early, he went off to Les Halles as the markets opened, and for about ten francs obtained some twenty splendid pears. He packed them up carefully in a hamper to make them look as if they had been sent from a distance, and took them to the concierge at the Walters', together with his card on which he had written:

'Georges Duroy humbly begs Mme Walter to accept these pears, which he received from Normandy this morning.'

The next day, in his mail box at the paper, he found in exchange an envelope containing a card from Mme Walter, 'who thanked M. Georges Duroy most warmly, and was always at home on Saturdays.'

The following Saturday he presented himself.

M. Walter lived on the Boulevard Malesherbes,* in a double-fronted house owned by him, part of which he rented out—an economical practice favoured by the thrifty. A single concierge, housed between the two entry-ways, served as porter for both owner and tenant, giving each entrance the imposing air of a wealthy, respectable establishment, thanks to his handsome porter's uniform, with his solid calves encased in white hose, and his ceremonial coat complete with gold buttons and scarlet facings.

The reception rooms were on the first floor, leading out of a vestibule hung with tapestries and closed off by heavy curtains over the doors. Two valets sat dozing on benches. One of them took Duroy's overcoat, the other seized his walking-stick, opened a door, preceded the visitor by a few paces, and then stood aside to let him pass, while shouting his name into an empty room.

The embarrassed young man looked all round, then noticed, reflected in a mirror, a number of seated people who seemed a long way away. At first he set off in the wrong direction, for the mirror had deceived him, then he crossed two more empty rooms to reach a sort of small parlour hung with blue silk patterned with buttercups, where four ladies were chatting in low voices at a round table on which stood cups of tea.

Despite the confidence he had gained in the course of his life in Paris, and especially through his work as a reporter, which put him in frequent contact with prominent people, Duroy felt somewhat intimidated by the circumstances of his entrance, and by having had to walk through empty drawing-rooms. He stammered: 'Madame, I've taken the liberty...' as his eyes sought the mistress of the house.

She offered him her hand which he bowed over, then, saying: 'It's very kind of you, Monsieur, to come and see me,' she indicated a seat onto which, in sitting down, he dropped heavily, imagining it to be much higher than it was. Silence had fallen. One of the women began talking again. The topic was the cold weather, which was growing severe, although not sufficiently so to put a stop to the epidemic of typhoid fever, nor to make skating possible. And each of them gave her opinion about this first appearance of frost in Paris; then each explained which season she preferred, giving all the hack-neyed reasons that hang about in people's minds in the way dust hangs about in rooms.

A faint sound of an opening door made Duroy turn his head and he saw, through two panes of plate glass, a large lady approaching. As soon as she appeared in the parlour one of the visitors rose, shook hands, then departed; and the young man's gaze followed her black back, glistening with beads of jet, through the other drawing-rooms.

When the excitement generated by this interchange of persons had subsided, the conversation turned spontaneously, without tran-sition, to the Moroccan question and the war in the East, as well as to the problems England was encountering in the southernmost tip of Africa.*

The ladies discussed these matters by rote, as if they were repeat-ing lines from an endlessly rehearsed, decorous comedy of manners.

A fresh entrance now occurred, of a little curly-headed blonde, and this triggered the departure of a tall dried-up person of middle age.

They talked of M. Linet's chances of entering the Academy.* The most recent arrival was convinced that he would be beaten by M. Cabanon-Lebas, author of the fine French verse adaptation for the theatre of *Don Quixote*.*

'You know that it's going to be put on at the Odéon* next winter?'

'Really? I'll certainly go and see such a very literary experiment.'

Mme Walter replied graciously, her manner calm and indifferent, never hesitating over what she should say, for her opinions were always ready in advance. Noticing that darkness was approaching, she rang for the lamps, while she listened to the chatter which flowed on in a stream of syrupy platitudes, and reflected that she had forgot-ten to call at the engraver's for the invitations to her next dinner-party.

A trifle too plump but still beautiful, she had reached the danger-ous age at which rapid decay is imminent. She kept her looks by dint of care, precautions, hygiene, and creams for the skin. She seemed sensible in every way, moderate and reasonable, one of those women whose mind runs on orderly lines like a French garden. There are no surprises when you walk around one, but it does possess a certain charm. She had judgement, subtle, discreet, reliable judgement, that in her took the place of imagination; she was good, loyal, calmly benevolent, generous to everyone and in everything.

She noticed that Duroy had said nothing, that no one had addressed him, and that he seemed somewhat ill at ease; and as the ladies had not abandoned the Academy—a favourite subject upon which they invariably dwelt—she asked: 'You must be better informed than any of us, M. Duroy, whom do you favour?'

He replied without hesitation: 'In this matter, Madame, I would never consider the merits—which are always debatable—of the candidates, but their age and their health. I would not ask about their qualifications, but about their illnesses. I would not enquire whether they have made a verse translation of Lope de Vega,* but I would take pains to find out about the state of their liver, their heart, their kidneys, and their spinal cord. For me, a nice hypertrophy, a nice albuminuria, and especially a nice incipient ataxia would be a hundred times more valuable than forty volumes' worth of disquisitions on the concept of patriotism in Berber poetry.'

An astonished silence greeted this statement.

Smiling, Mme Walter went on: 'Yes, but why?' He replied: 'Because my sole concern is to give pleasure to the ladies. Now, Madame, the Academy really only interests you when an Academician dies. The more Academicians die, the happier you must be. But in order for them to die quickly, they must be appointed when they're old and sick.'

As the ladies still seemed a bit taken aback, he added: 'Moreover I feel just as you do; I love reading of the death of an Academician in the Paris gossip columns. I immediately wonder: "Who's going to take his place?" And I make up my list. It's a game, a very agreeable little game people play in every Parisian drawing-room each time one of the Immortals dies: "The game of death and the forty old men."'

The ladies, still a trifle disconcerted, nevertheless began to smile, his remark was so true. He concluded, rising from his seat: 'It is you who appoint them, Mesdames, and you appoint them in order to see them die. Therefore choose those who are old, very old, as old as possible, and don't ever concern yourselves about anything else.' Then, with considerable grace, he took his leave.

As soon as he had gone, one of the women declared: 'That young man is amusing. Who is he?' Mme Walter replied: 'One of our sub-editors; so far his job at the paper is a modest one, but I've no doubt he'll soon make a name for himself.'

A cheerful Duroy strode rhythmically down the Boulevard Males-herbes, well satisfied with his outing and murmuring to himself: 'Good beginning.'

That same evening he made it up with Rachel.

The following week two things happened to him. He was appointed head of the gossip column,* and he was invited to dinner by Mme Walter. He immediately saw a connection between the two events.

La Vie française was above all a financial paper, since the owner was a financier who had used the press and the deputies as a means of influence. Making a weapon of his affability, he had always done his scheming from behind a smiling, good-natured mask, but in the tasks he delegated—whatever they might be—he employed only those whom he had probed, tested, sniffed out, who he sensed were wily, audacious, and flexible. He thought Duroy, the new head of the gossip column, a real asset.

Up to that time, the position had been filled by the chief sub-editor, M. Boisrenard, an elderly journalist who was as correct, as conscientious, and as meticulous as a clerk. Over the last thirty years he had served as chief sub-editor for eleven different papers, without making the slightest modification in the way he operated or how he looked at things. He moved from one newspaper office to another in the way one changes restaurants, barely aware that the food did not taste exactly the same. Political or religious opinions were a closed book to him. He was devoted to whatever paper he worked for, very capable at his job, and highly valued because of his experience. In his work he was like a blind man who sees nothing, a deaf man who hears nothing, and a mute who never says a word about anything. He was intensely loyal, however, and would never have been party to anything that he did not consider professionally honourable, honest, and correct.

M. Walter, who appreciated him nevertheless, had often wished there was someone else to whom he could entrust the gossip column, which was, he used to say, the nerve centre of the paper. That is where news is first reported, where rumours are born, where influence can be exerted on the public and on the stock exchange. You need to know how to slip the important piece of news in between two fashionable evening parties, as though it is of no significance, insinuating rather than explicit. You have to hint at what you want to say, letting readers guess what you have in mind, issuing denials in terms which confirm a rumour, or confirming in such a way that no one believes it. It is essential that every reader, every day, should find at least one item of gossip that is of interest to him, so that everyone will read the column. You must think of everything and everybody, of every class, of every profession, of Paris and the provinces, of the military, the arts, the clergy, the university, the magistrature, and the world of high-class prostitution.

The man in control of the column and in command of the legion of reporters must be always on the alert, always on his guard, distrustful, far-sighted, cunning, vigilant, and flexible, capable of every kind of guile and endowed with an infallible gift for uncovering a bogus news item at a glance, for judging what should be communicated and what should be kept quiet, for guessing what will make an impression on the public; and he must know how to present it in such a manner that its effect will be intensified.

M. Boisrenard, who was thoroughly competent in his way, lacked adroitness and style; above all, he lacked the innate, amoral wiliness needed to sense what the boss was secretly thinking every day. Duroy was to fill the bill perfectly, and he made an excellent addition to the editorial staff of this paper which, in the words of Norbert de Varenne, 'navigated the deep waters of state finance and the shallows of politics.'

The inspiration behind *La Vie française*, and its *de facto* editors, were a half-dozen deputies who were involved in all the speculations that the Director either launched or supported. In the Chamber they were known as 'the Walter gang', and they were envied because of the money they must be making with him and through him. Forestier, the political editor, was merely a front for these businessmen; he carried out projects they suggested. They gave him the ideas for his leaders, which he always went home to write, so he could work in peace, as he put it.

However, in order to give the paper a more literary, Parisian character, two writers, well known in their different fields, had been taken on: Jacques Rival, who specialized in current events, and Norbert de Varenne, a poet and chronicler of the imaginary or, to use the modern literary term, a short-story writer. Then the paper had acquired, at low cost, critics of art, of painting, of music, and of theatre, and editors for crime and for racing, from among the vast tribe of mercenaries made up of writers willing to turn their hand to anything. Two society women, 'Domino Rose' and 'Patte Blanche',* contributed items of social news and wrote about fashion, fashionable society, elegant entertaining, etiquette, and good breeding, and passed on indiscreet bits of gossip about socially prominent ladies.

And *La Vie française* 'navigated the deep waters and the shallows,' manœuvred by all these different hands.

Duroy was revelling in the pleasure of his appointment as editor-in-chief of the gossip column when he received a small engraved card on which he read: 'M. and Mme Walter request the pleasure of the company of M. Georges Duroy at dinner on Thursday, the 20th of January.'

This new favour, coming on the heels of the other, filled him with such joy that he kissed the invitation as if it were a love letter. Then he went to find the cashier, to deal with the important matter of funds.

A head of the gossip column section generally has a budget from which he pays his reporters, and also pays for news items—whether important or run-of-the-mill—that different people may bring him, just as market-gardeners bring their produce to a vegetable stall.

Initially, twelve hundred francs a month were allocated to Duroy, who had every intention of keeping a large proportion for himself. In response to his urgent requests, the cashier had finally advanced him four hundred francs. At first he had been absolutely determined to return to Mme de Marelle the two hundred and eighty francs he owed her, but, realizing almost immediately that he would then have left only a hundred and twenty francs, a sum that was quite inadequate for starting up his new department in a suitable manner, he postponed repaying her to some future time.

He spent two days settling in, for he had inherited a particular table and a set of pigeon-holes in the enormous room shared by all the reporters. He occupied one end of this room, while Boisrenard, whose head—still ebony-black despite his age—was invariably bent over a sheet of paper, occupied the other end. The long table in the centre was the domain of the itinerant reporters. As a rule it served as a bench to sit on, either with one's legs swinging over the edge, or cross-legged on the top. There were sometimes five or six of them squatting on this table, like a lot of little Chinamen, doggedly playing at cup-and-ball.

After a time Duroy had come to enjoy this pastime, and, thanks to Saint-Potin's instructions and advice, he was beginning to be very skilled at it. Forestier, whose condition was worsening, had entrusted to him his fine cup-and-ball made out of wood from the Antilles,* the one he had bought most recently and found rather heavy. Duroy, with a vigorous arm, would manipulate the heavy black ball on the cord, quietly counting: 'one—two—three—four—five—six.'

It so happened that he managed, for the first time, to score twenty points in a row on the very day when he was dining at Mme Walter's. 'This is a lucky day,' he thought, 'I'm doing well at everything.' Skill at cup-and-ball did actually confer a kind of distinction at *La Vie française*.

He left the paper early so as to have time to dress, and he was walking up the Rue de Londres* when he saw, trotting along in front of him, a small woman who resembled Mme de Marelle. He felt his face going hot and his heart begin to pound. He crossed the road in order to see her from the side. She too stopped to cross over. He was mistaken; he breathed again.

He had often wondered how he ought to behave if he met her face to face. Should he greet her, or should he pretend not to see her? 'I'll pretend not to see her,' he thought.

It was cold, the gutters were thick with ice. The pavements looked dry and grey in the light of the gas lamps.

When the young man got home, he reflected: 'I'll have to move. This won't do for me now.' He felt nervous and elated, capable of leaping from roof to roof, and he kept saying out loud, as he moved between his bed and the window: 'I'm going to be rich! Rich! I must write to Papa.'

He wrote to his father from time to time, and the letter always brought great joy to the little Normandy inn standing by the highway, at the summit of the big hill overlooking Rouen and the broad valley of the Seine.

And from time to time, he himself received a blue envelope

addressed in a large tremulous hand, and invariably, at the beginning of his father's letter, he would read these lines: 'My dear son: This letter is to let you know that your mother and I are well. There's not much in the way of news here. However, I must tell you...' And in his heart he still felt an interest in the affairs of the village, in news about neighbours, in the state of the soil and of the harvests.

He kept saying to himself, as he tied his white tie in front of his tiny mirror: 'I must write to Papa tomorrow. If he could see me this evening, in the house where I'm going, wouldn't the old boy be flabbergasted! Lord! I'll soon be having a dinner the like of which he's never had!' And, suddenly, he saw again that dark kitchen, behind the empty café, the saucepans casting yellow glints onto the walls, the cat sitting in the hearth with his nose to the fire, in the pose of a crouching Chimera, the wooden table thick with years of accumulated grease and spilt liquids, a soup bowl steaming in the centre, and a lighted candle standing between two plates. And he saw them as well, the man and woman, the father and mother, the two peasants with their slow gestures, drinking their soup in little sips. He was familiar with the tiniest creases in their old faces, with the smallest movements of their arms and their heads. He even knew what they said to one another, every evening, as they ate their supper sitting opposite each other.

Again he thought: 'Still, I really must go and see them one day.' But he had finished dressing, so he blew out the light and went down.

Prostitutes accosted him as he walked along the outer boulevard.

Pulling his arm away, he snapped at them: 'For God's sake leave me alone!' in tones of fierce contempt, as if they had insulted him, mistaken him for someone else... Who did they think he was? Couldn't those tarts tell the difference between men? The feeling of his black coat, donned for a dinner in the home of very rich, very well-known, very important people, gave him the sense of having a new personality, the consciousness of being a different person, a man of the world, of real high society.

He walked confidently into the hallway, which was lit by the great bronze candelabra, and with an easy gesture handed his walking-stick and overcoat to the two valets who had approached him. All the drawing-rooms were illuminated.

Mme Walter was receiving in the second, which was the largest.

She welcomed him with a charming smile, and he shook hands with the two men who had arrived before him, M. Firmin and M. Laroche-Mathieu,* both deputies and unacknowledged editors of *La Vie française*. M. Laroche-Mathieu had a particular authority in the paper because of his great influence in the Chamber. No one doubted that he would become a minister some day.

Then the Forestiers arrived, Mme Forestier, in pink, looking enchanting. Duroy was amazed to see her on intimate terms with the two national representatives. She spent more than five minutes standing by the fireplace with M. Laroche-Mathieu, talking very quietly. Charles seemed exhausted. He had lost a great deal of weight over the past month, he coughed incessantly, and kept saying: 'I really ought to make up my mind to go south for the rest of the winter.'

Norbert de Varenne and Jacques Rival arrived together. Then, a door having opened at the far end of the room, M. Walter entered with two tall young girls of sixteen and eighteen, one ugly, the other pretty. Although Duroy was aware that the Director had a family, he was filled with astonishment. He had never thought of the daughters of the Director except in the way you think about distant lands you will never see. And then, also, he had imagined them still to be tiny children, and here before him were two women. He experienced the slight moral disquiet occasioned by a scene-change not hidden from view.

When they had been introduced, they shook his hand in turn, and then went and sat at a little table which was obviously for them, where they began sorting through a pile of reels of silk thread in a small basket.

Another person had yet to arrive, and the company fell silent, feeling the kind of constraint that precedes dinners where the guests are all in different moods, after spending the day doing different things.

Duroy had raised his eyes idly to the wall, and M. Walter, prompted by an obvious wish to show off his possessions, addressed him from a distance: 'You' re looking at *my* pictures?' The 'my' rang out. 'I'll show them to you.' And he picked up a lamp so that they could make out all the details.

'These are the landscapes,'* he said.

In the middle of the panel hung a large canvas by Guillemet,

showing a Normandy beach under a stormy sky. Beneath it a wood
by Harpignies was displayed, then a plain in Algeria by Guillaumet,
with a camel on the horizon, a big camel with long legs, resembling
some strange monument.

M. Walter moved on to the neighbouring wall and declared in a
solemn tone, like a master of ceremonies: 'Major paintings.'* There
were four canvases: *A Visit to the Poorhouse*, by Gervex; *A Woman
Reaping*, by Bastien-Lepage; *A Widow*, by Bouguereau, and *An
Execution* by Jean-Paul Laurens. This last work depicted a priest of
the Vendée* being executed against the wall of his church by a
detachment of the French Republican Army.

A smile flitted across the owner's grave face as he indicated the
next panel: 'Here we have the lighter works.'* First there was a small
canvas by Jean Béraud, entitled *Upper and Lower*. It showed a pretty
Parisian woman climbing up the stairs of a moving tram. As her head
appeared at the level of the upper deck, the men seated on the
benches were gazing, with avid delight, at the young face approaching them, while the men standing on the lower platform were studying the young woman's legs with a different expression—one of
disappointment and lust.

Holding the lamp out as far as he could, M. Walter kept saying,
with a lecherous laugh, 'Well? Isn't that great? Quite something, isn't
it?'

Next he announced: *A Rescue*, by Lambert. There, in the middle
of a dining-table that had been cleared away, a young cat sat on its
haunches, examining with perplexed astonishment a fly drowning in
a glass of water. He had one paw raised, ready to snatch the insect
with a quick swipe. But he hadn't made up his mind. He was hesitating. What was he going to do? Then M. Walter, pointing to a
Detaille: *The Lesson*, which portrayed a soldier in a barracks teaching
a poodle to play the drum, declared: 'Now that's witty!' Duroy was
laughing approvingly and enthusing: 'It's charming, absolutely
charming, charm...' when he stopped dead, hearing behind him the
voice of Mme de Marelle, who had just entered the room.

M. Walter continued to hold the lamp up to the canvases, as he
explained them. Now he was showing a watercolour of Maurice
Leloir's *The Obstacle*. It depicted a sedan chair which had been
obliged to halt, because the street was blocked by a brawl between
two working men, a hefty pair who were battling like Titans. You

could see, emerging from the sedan chair's window, the exquisite face of a woman who was intently watching, with neither impatience nor fear, but with a certain admiration, this struggle between two brutes.

M. Walter was still talking: 'I've others in the next rooms, but they're by people who aren't so well known, and aren't prizewinners yet. This is my Salon Carré.* At present I'm buying up young artists, very young, and putting them in reserve in our family rooms, against the day when they become famous.' Then he added, in a whisper: 'Now's the time to buy pictures. Painters are starving. They haven't a penny, not a penny...' But Duroy was seeing nothing, was listening without understanding. Mme de Marelle was there, behind him. What should he do? If he greeted her might she not turn her back on him or lash out at him with some insolent remark? If he ignored her, what would people think?

He told himself: 'I'll play for time.' He was so agitated that for an instant he thought of pretending that he had suddenly been taken ill, so that he could leave.

The tour of the walls was over. M. Walter replaced the lamp and went to greet the latest arrival, while Duroy began to study the canvases again, on his own, as if he had not yet wearied of admiring them. His mind was in a whirl. What should he do? He could hear people's voices, he could make out what was being said. Mme Forestier called to him: 'By the way, M. Duroy...' He hurried over to her. It was to tell him about a friend of hers who was giving a reception and would really love a reference to it in the gossip column of *La Vie française*. He stammered: 'But of course, Madame, of course...'

Mme de Marelle was now very close to him. He did not dare turn round and move away. All of a sudden he thought he must have lost his mind; she had said, in a loud voice: 'Hallo, Bel-Ami, don't you recognize me any more?' He quickly spun round on his heels. She was standing in front of him, smiling, her eyes full of laughter and affection. She offered him her hand. He shook it nervously, still fearing some trick, some treachery. She calmly went on: 'What have you been doing with yourself? You're quite a stranger.'

He was stammering, unable to regain his composure. 'I've been very busy, Madame, very busy. M. Walter has put me in charge of a different section, which keeps me very fully occupied.'

She replied, still looking him in the face, without his being able to detect anything other than benevolence in her eyes: 'So I heard. But that's not a reason for forgetting your friends.'

They were separated by the entrance of a portly lady, a portly lady in a low-cut gown, with red arms and red cheeks, who was pretentiously dressed and coiffured and walked with so heavy a tread that, watching her move, you could feel the weight and solidity of her thighs.

As everyone seemed to be treating her with great respect, Duroy asked Mme Forestier: 'Who's that?'

'The Vicomtesse de Percemur,* the one who signs herself "Patte Blanche".'

He was dumbfounded, and wanted to laugh. 'Patte Blanche! Patte Blanche! And there was I, imagining a young woman like yourself! She's Patte Blanche? Oh, that's rich, really rich!'

A servant appeared at the door and announced: 'Dinner is served.'

The dinner was banal and lively, one of those dinners where people talk about everything without saying anything. Duroy found himself between the editor's elder daughter, Rose, the ugly one, and Mme de Marelle. Being quite so close to the latter unsettled him somewhat, although she seemed very much at ease and chatted in her usual witty manner. At first he floundered about, unrelaxed and hesitant, like a musician who has lost the key. Little by little, however, his confidence returned, and their eyes, meeting continually, questioned one another, their gazes mingling intimately, almost sensually, as they used to do.

Suddenly he thought he felt, under the table, something brush his foot. He gently advanced his leg and encountered that of his neighbour, who did not shrink away from this contact. They were not conversing at this particular juncture, both having turned away to speak to their other neighbour. His heart pounding, Duroy thrust his knee a little closer. A slight pressure answered him. Then he realized that their love-affair was beginning once again.

What did they say after this? Nothing very much; but their lips trembled each time they looked at one another.

The young man, however, anxious to be nice to his boss's daughter, addressed a remark to her from time to time. She replied just as her mother would have done, never hesitating over what she ought to say.

On M. Walter's right, the Vicomtesse de Percemur had adopted a regal pose; and Duroy, enjoying watching her, asked Mme de Marelle softly:

'Do you know the other one, the one who signs herself "Domino Rose"?'

'Yes, certainly, the Baronne de Livar?'

'Is she the same type?'

'No, but just as funny. A tall dried-up creature of sixty, with false curls, horsy teeth, ideas dating from the Restoration and dressed to match.'

'Where did they dig up these literary freaks?'

'Bourgeois social climbers have always tended to collect the left-overs of the nobility.'

'No other reason?'

'No, no other reason.'

Then a political discussion began between the host, the two deputies, Norbert de Varenne and Jacques Rival; it lasted until the dessert.

When they returned to the drawing-room, Duroy went up to Mme de Marelle again, and, looking deep into her eyes: 'Would you like me to see you home this evening?'

'No.'

'Why not?'

'Because whenever I dine here, M. Laroche-Mathieu, who's my neighbour, drops me at my door.'

'When shall I see you?'

'Come and lunch with me tomorrow.' They separated without saying another word.

Duroy found the evening dull, and did not stay late. Going down the stairs, he caught up with Norbert de Varenne, who had also just left. The old poet took his arm. No longer fearing competition in the paper—for their contributions were fundamentally different—he now treated the young man with a grandfatherly benevolence.

'Well, will you keep me company part of the way?'

'With the greatest pleasure, my dear sir.'

And they set off walking slowly down the Boulevard Malesherbes. The night was cold, and Paris almost deserted. It was one of those nights that seem vaster than others, when the stars seem higher up in the sky and the air seems to carry on its icy breath something that comes from further away than the heavenly bodies.

At first the two men did not speak at all. Then Duroy, to break the silence, remarked: 'That M. Laroche-Mathieu strikes me as very intelligent and well-informed.'

The old poet murmured: 'You think so, do you?'

Surprised, Duroy hesitated: 'Yes, I do; besides, he is said to be one of the most capable men in the Chamber.'

'Possibly. In the kingdom of the blind the one-eyed man is king. All those men, you see, are second-rate, because their minds are confined within two boundaries: money and politics. They're boors, my dear boy, with whom it's impossible to talk about anything, anything we care about. Their intelligence has a foundation of sludge, or more precisely of sewage, like the Seine at Asnières.*

'Ah! It's hard to find a man whose thoughts have depth and breadth, who gives you the feeling of being on the coast breathing in those great sea-breezes. I've known a few such men; they're dead.'

Norbert de Varenne spoke in a voice that was clear but restrained, that would have rung out into the silence of the night had he let it do so. He seemed keyed-up and melancholy, with that kind of melancholy which sometimes falls upon the soul and makes it as resonant as ground that is frozen hard.

He went on: 'What does it matter, anyway, if there's a little more or a little less genius, since everything must come to an end!' He fell silent. Duroy, who on that particular evening was feeling light-hearted, said with a smile: 'You're in a black mood, tonight, my dear sir.'

The poet replied: 'I always am, my boy, and you will be too, just like me, in a few years' time. Life is a hill. While you're climbing up, you look towards the summit, and you're happy; but when you reach the summit, suddenly you can see the slope down, and the bottom, which is death. It's slow going up, but coming down is quick. At your age, you're happy. You hope for so many things, which more-over never happen. At my age, you don't hope for anything any more... except death.'

Duroy began to laugh: 'My God, you're giving me the shivers.'

Norbert de Varenne continued: 'No, you don't understand me now, but later you'll remember what I'm telling you at this moment. The day will come, you'll see, and for many it comes before you know it, when the laughter's over, as they say, because behind every-thing you look at, what you see is death. Oh! "Death." I know you don't even understand the word! At your age it has no meaning. At mine, it's terrifying.

'Yes, suddenly you understand it, you don't know why nor in response to what, and then everything in life looks different. In my case, for the past fifteen years I've felt it wearing me down like some creature gnawing away at my being. Little by little, month by month, hour by hour, I've felt it undermine me like a house that's falling in. It's disfigured me so completely that I don't recognize myself. There's nothing left of me, of the me that was a joyful, vigorous young man of thirty. I've seen it dye my black hair white, and with such cruel, cunning slowness! It's taken from me my firm skin, my muscles, my teeth, the whole of my former body, leaving me only my despairing soul which will soon be taken from me too.

'Yes, the wretch has worn me down, has quietly and horribly, second by second, completed the long destruction of my being. Now I feel myself dying in everything that I do. Every step brings me nearer to it, every movement, every breath hastens its odious task. Breathing, sleeping, eating, drinking, working, dreaming, everything we do is part of dying. Indeed, to live is to die!

'Ah! You'll find out! If you thought about it for just a few moments, you'd understand. What are you hoping for? Love? A few more kisses, and you'll be impotent. And then, what else? Money? To do what with? To buy women? What kind of happiness is that? To overeat, grow obese, and suffer the torments of gout all night long? And what else is there? Fame? What's the point of that when you can no longer reap its rewards in the shape of love? And after that? Death is always there, at the end.

'I myself, now, see it so close to me that I often feel like stretching out my arms to push it away. It covers the earth and fills the void. I find it everywhere. Tiny creatures run over on the road, falling leaves, a white hair noticed in a friend's beard; these things fill my heart with despair and cry out to me: "It's here!" For me it spoils everything I do, everything I see, what I eat and what I drink, everything I love, moonlight, sunrise, the open sea, the lovely rivers, and the summer night air, which is so sweet to breathe!'

He was walking slowly along, a little out of breath, dreaming aloud, forgetting, almost, that someone was listening.

He went on: 'And no one ever comes back again, ever... Casts of statues can be kept, and moulds that go on producing identical objects; but my body, my face, my thoughts, my desires will never return. And yet there'll be millions, billions of individuals born who will all have, within the space of a few centimetres, a nose, eyes, a forehead, cheeks, and a mouth as I have, and also a soul as I have, without my self ever returning, without anything recognizable as part of me reappearing in those innumerable, different beings— different in indefinable ways, yet all approximately similar.

'What can we depend on? To whom should we cry out in our anguish? What can we believe in? All the religions are stupid, with their puerile morality and selfish, monstrously imbecilic promises.

'Only death is certain.'

He stopped, grasped Duroy by his overcoat lapels, and, in a slow voice, said: 'Think about all this, young man, think about it for days, for months, and for years, and you'll see life differently. So try to free yourself of everything that confines you, make that supreme effort, while you are still living, to dissociate yourself from your body, your concerns, your thoughts, and all of mankind, and look elsewhere; then you'll understand how unimportant are the quarrels of the Romantics and the Naturalists, and the debate on the budget.'

He began to walk again, faster.

'But you'll also feel the terrible anguish of despair. You'll flounder about, bewildered, drowning in uncertainty. You'll call for help in every direction, and no one will answer you. You'll stretch up your arms, you'll cry out to be helped, loved, consoled, saved! And no one will come.

'Why do we suffer like this? Probably because we were born to live more in our material bodies and less in our minds; but by dint of thinking, a disproportion has arisen between the state of our over-developed intelligence and the immutable conditions of this life. Look at the average man: unless dreadful disasters befall him, he's content, he doesn't suffer from this general unhappiness. Nor are animals conscious of it.'

He stopped again, thought for a few seconds, then went on, his manner weary and resigned: 'As for me, I'm a lost soul. I've neither father, nor mother, nor brother, nor sister, nor wife, nor children, nor God.' He added, after a silence: 'I've nothing but poetry.'

Then, looking up at the sky, where the pallid face of the full moon was shining, he declaimed:

'In the sombre void, to this dark mystery
Where floats a pallid star, I seek the verbal key.'

They were coming up to the Pont de la Concorde, which they crossed in silence, then they walked along beside the Palais-Bourbon.* Norbert de Varenne began speaking again: 'Get married, my friend, you don't know what it means to live alone, at my age. Nowadays being alone fills me with appalling anguish; being alone at home, by the fire, in the evening. It seems to me then that I'm alone on the earth, dreadfully alone, but surrounded by indeterminate dangers, by unknown, terrible things; and the wall which divides me from my neighbour, whom I do not know, separates me from him by as great a distance as that which separates me from the stars I see through my window. A kind of fever comes over me, a fever of pain and fear, and the silence of the walls terrifies me. It is so profound, so sad, the silence of the room in which you live alone. It isn't just a silence of the body, but a silence of the soul, and, when a piece of furniture creaks, a shiver runs through your whole body, for in that dismal place you expect to hear no sound.'

He fell silent once more, then added: 'Really, though, when you're old, it would be good to have children!'

They had reached a point about half way along the Rue de Bourgogne.* The poet stopped in front of a tall house, rang the bell, shook Duroy's hand and said to him: 'Forget all this senile rambling, young man, and live the way the young should live; goodbye!'

And he vanished into the darkness of the passage.

Duroy set off again, his heart heavy. He felt as if he had just been shown some pit full of bones, a hole into which he was inevitably destined one day to fall. He murmured: 'My God, it can't be much fun, being him. I'm damned if I'd care to have a ring-side seat, to watch what goes on in his head!'

But, having stopped to give way to a perfumed woman who emerged from a cab and went into her house, he breathed deeply and greedily, inhaling the scent of verbena and iris wafted on the air. Suddenly, hope and joy set his lungs and heart pounding; and the memory of Mme de Marelle, whom he was to see again the following day, flooded his being from head to foot.

Everything was smiling at him, life was welcoming him warmly. How good it was, to see your hopes fulfilled!

He fell asleep with his head spinning, and rose early to take a walk in the Avenue du Bois de Boulogne, before going to his rendezvous. The wind had changed, and the weather had moderated during the night; it was warm and sunny, like a day in April. All the regulars of the Bois were out that morning, enticed by the clear, soft sky. Duroy walked slowly, drinking in the gentle air, as delicious as a spring delicacy. He passed the Arc de Triomphe of the Étoile and turned into the enormous avenue, on the opposite side from the riders. He watched them as they trotted or galloped past, both men and women, the wealthy of the world, but now he felt scarcely any envy. He knew nearly all of them by name, knew the amounts of their fortunes and the secret stories of their lives, for his job had turned him into a kind of register of Parisian celebrities and scandals.

Women riders went by, their slender waists tightly encased in dark cloth, with that indefinable air of arrogance and unapproachability typical of so many horsewomen; and Duroy entertained himself reciting in a low voice, the way litanies are recited in church, the names, titles, and qualities of the lovers they had had or were said to have had; and sometimes, even, instead of saying: 'Baron de Tanquelet, Prince de la Tour-Enguerrand,' he would murmur: 'Of the lesbian persuasion, Louise Michot, of the Vaudeville, Rose Marquetin, of the Opéra.'

He found this a highly amusing game, revelling in the excitement of, and somehow consoled by, the sense of putting on record the eternal and deep-seated infamy of man underlying outwardly respectable appearances.

Then he said, out loud: 'Bunch of hypocrites!' and looked around to spot the riders about whom the worst stories were circulating. He saw many who were suspected of cheating at cards, for whom at all events gambling clubs were a major source of income, the only source, and obviously a questionable one. Others, very prominent men, were widely known to live solely on their wife's income; yet others on the income of their mistress, so people said. Many had settled their debts (an honourable act) without anyone ever being able to guess where they had found the necessary money (a highly suspicious mystery). He saw financiers whose immense fortunes had originated in theft, and who were received everywhere, in the most noble houses, and other men so respected that tradespeople doffed their hats to them as they went by, yet whose shameless speculation in the principal state-controlled companies was an open book to anyone familiar with the shady side of what went on.

They were all haughty in demeanour, with arrogant mouths and insolent eyes, whether they favoured side-whiskers or moustaches. Still laughing, Duroy said again: 'What a filthy lot, they're all scoundrels, all crooks!'

But a carriage passed him, an open, low, charming vehicle pulled at a fast trot by two svelte greys with flying manes and tails, and driven by a young, petite blonde, a well-known courtesan with two grooms seated behind her. Duroy halted, feeling an urge to raise his hat to and applaud this upstart paramour who was obviously flaunting, in a place and at a time that were the preserve of hypocritical aristocrats, the showy luxury she had earned in bed. Perhaps he felt, vaguely, that they had something in common, a natural bond, that they were of the same breed, that they were basically the same, and that his success would be achieved by methods equally bold.

He returned more slowly, his heart glowing with satisfaction, and arrived a little ahead of time at his former mistress's door.

She offered him her lips on greeting him, as if they had never been estranged, even forgetting, for a few seconds, the sensible caution with which, in her own home, she avoided his arms. Then she said to him, as she kissed the curly ends of his moustache: 'You can't imagine what an annoying thing has happened, my darling. I was looking forward to a real honeymoon, and now here's my husband turned up, I'm stuck with him for six weeks, he's taken some leave. But I don't want to spend six weeks without seeing you, especially after our little quarrel, so here's what I've fixed up. You must come to dinner on Monday, I've already told him about you. I'll introduce you.'

Duroy hesitated, somewhat at a loss; until then he had never found himself in the presence of a man whose wife was his mistress. He feared that something might betray him, a little awkwardness, a look, anything. He stammered: 'No, I'd rather not meet your husband.' Greatly surprised, she insisted, standing before him with wide-open, artless eyes. 'But why? What a funny thing! This goes on all the time, it does really! I'd never have thought you such a fool, never.'

He was hurt. 'All right, fine, I'll come for dinner on Monday.'

She added: 'So that it will seem quite natural, I'll ask the

Forestiers. Although I don't find it any fun, having people to dinner here.'

Until Monday arrived, Duroy hardly thought about this meeting; but as he climbed up Mme de Marelle's stairs, he felt strangely uneasy, not that he was averse to shaking the husband's hand, to drinking his wine and eating his bread, but he was afraid of something, without knowing what.

He was shown into the drawing-room, and, as usual, he waited. Then the door of the room opened, and he saw a tall, white-bearded man, serious and gentlemanly in appearance and wearing a decoration, approach him with punctilious politeness: 'My wife has often spoken to me of you, Monsieur, and I am delighted to make your acquaintance.'

Duroy walked forward, trying to give to his features an expression of real cordiality, and shook his host's outstretched hand with exaggerated energy. Then, having taken a seat, he could think of nothing to say to him.

M. de Marelle replaced a piece of wood on the fire, and enquired: 'Have you been in journalism long?'

Duroy replied: 'Just a few months.'

'Ah! You've got ahead fast.'

'Yes, quite fast;' and he began talking at random, without paying too much attention to what he was saying, trotting out all the banalities employed by people who do not know one another. He was feeling more relaxed now, and beginning to think the situation extremely entertaining. He gazed at M. de Marelle's serious, respectable face, his lips twitching with an urge to laugh, and thinking: 'I'm sleeping with your wife, old chap, I'm having her.' And he was filled with a very private, vicious satisfaction, the joy of a successful thief who is not suspected, a duplicitous, delicious pleasure. Quite suddenly he wanted to become this man's friend, to gain his trust, to persuade him to confide his secrets to him.

Hurrying into the room, Mme de Marelle gave them a smiling, inscrutable glance, then went up to Duroy who, in the presence of the husband, did not dare kiss her hand in his usual way.

She was composed and cheerful, like someone who could deal with any situation, whose instinctive, artless duplicity made her see this meeting as natural and straightforward. Laurine appeared, and came over to Georges more sedately than usual to offer her brow for a kiss, for she was intimidated by the presence of her father. Her mother said to her: 'So, today you're no longer calling him Bel-Ami.' The child blushed, as if someone had committed a serious indiscretion, revealed something that should not be mentioned, a private, slightly guilty secret of her heart.

When the Forestiers arrived, they were all alarmed by the state of Charles's health. He had grown dreadfully thin and pale in the course of one week, and he coughed incessantly. Moreover he told them that, on strict orders from the doctor, they were leaving for Cannes the following Thursday.

They went home early, and Duroy remarked, shaking his head: 'I think he's in a really bad way. He'll never make old bones.' Mme de Marelle serenely agreed: 'Oh! He's done for. And he was so lucky, to find a wife like his.'

Duroy enquired: 'She helps him a lot?'

'Actually, she does everything. She knows everything that's going on, she knows everybody without seeming to see anybody; she gets what she wants, in the way she wants, when she wants. Oh! She hasn't her equal for subtlety, shrewdness, and cunning. She'd be a treasure for a man who wants to succeed.'

Georges went on: 'She'll marry again very soon, I imagine?'

Mme de Marelle replied: 'Oh, I wouldn't even be surprised if she had someone in mind... a deputy... unless... he didn't care for the idea... because there might perhaps be... serious moral... obstacles. Well, there you are. I really don't know.'

M. de Marelle muttered, with contained impatience: 'You're always hinting at all sorts of things I don't like. We shouldn't involve ourselves in other people's business. We should follow our own conscience. That ought to be a rule for everybody.'

Duroy left, feeling uneasy, his mind full of vague plans.

The following day he paid a visit to the Forestiers, and found them finishing their packing. Charles, lying stretched out on a sofa, was breathing with exaggerated difficulty and kept repeating: 'I should have left a month ago'; then he gave Duroy a lot of advice about the paper, although everything had been discussed and agreed with M. Walter.

When Georges left, he shook his friend's hands vigorously: 'Well, old chap, see you soon!' But as Mme Forestier was seeing him to the door, he said to her earnestly: 'You haven't forgotten our agreement?

We're friends and allies, aren't we? So, if you need me, no matter what for, don't hesitate. A wire or a letter, and I'll come.'

She murmured: 'Thank you, I won't forget.' Her eyes thanked him too, in a more meaningful and tender way.

As Duroy was going down the stairs, he met M. de Vaudrec climbing slowly up; he had seen him at Mme Forestier's once before. The count looked sad—might it be because of this departure?

Anxious to appear socially adept, the journalist greeted him with alacrity. The other man returned his bow politely, but with a certain haughtiness.

The Forestiers left on Thursday evening.

CHAPTER 7

The disappearance of Charles increased Duroy's importance on the editorial staff of *La Vie française*. He put his name to some leading articles, while still continuing to sign his gossip column, for the Director wanted each of them to be responsible for his own copy. He was involved in a few controversies from which he extricated himself cleverly; and his regular dealings with statesmen gradually prepared him to become, in his turn, a skilful and shrewd political sub-editor.

On the whole horizon he could see only one cloud. This was caused by an insignificant and irreverent publication that attacked him constantly, or rather attacked, through him, the editor responsible for the gossip column in *La Vie française*, or M. Walter's 'surprises,' as the anonymous editor of this paper, *La Plume*,* liked to call it. Every day brought nasty digs, acid comments, insinuations of every kind.

One day Jacques Rival remarked to Duroy: 'You're very patient.'

The other man stammered: 'What can I do, there's no direct attack.'

However, when he entered the reporters' room one afternoon, Boisrenard handed him the latest issue of *La Plume*.

'Here, there's another nasty crack at you.'

'Oh! What about?'

'Nothing really, the arrest of some Mme Aubert by an officer of the vice squad.'

Georges took the paper he was handed and read, under the title *'Duroy enjoys himself'*:*

'The distinguished reporter of *La Vie française* informs us today that Mme Aubert, whose arrest by an agent of the hateful vice squad we reported, exists only in our imagination. Now the person in question lives at 18 rue de l'Écureuil, in Montmartre. We understand only too well, however, the advantage or advantages that the agents of the Walter Bank may find in supporting the agents of the Police, who condone their transactions. As for the reporter concerned, he would do better to give us one of those sensational news flashes he alone can provide: reports of deaths denied the following day, news of battles that never took place, reports of momentous

statements by sovereigns who have said nothing, in a word all the
news that helps swell Walter's profits, or even one of those little
indiscretions about parties given by ladies in the public eye, or about
the excellence of certain products that are such a valuable "resource"
to some of our colleagues.'

The young man was nonplussed rather than infuriated, realizing
only that this article contained something extremely disagreeable for
him personally.

Boisrenard went on: 'Who gave you this news item?'

Duroy reflected, but could no longer recall. Suddenly, however, he
remembered: 'Oh, yes, it was Saint-Potin.'

Then, rereading the paragraph in *La Plume*, he abruptly turned
scarlet, outraged at the accusation of venality.

He exclaimed: 'What! They're saying I'm paid to...' Boisrenard
interrupted him: 'Yes, they are. It's most annoying for you. The boss
is extremely sensitive on that subject. With a gossip column it could
happen so easily...'

Saint-Potin happened to come in just then. Duroy rushed over to
him: 'You've read the bit in *La Plume*?'

'Yes, and I've just come from seeing the Aubert woman. She does
indeed exist, but she wasn't arrested. That rumour has no foundation.'

Duroy then hurried to the boss, who was rather chilly, and eyed
him suspiciously. After listening to Duroy's story, M. Walter replied:
'Go and see this woman yourself, and word your denial in such a way
that they won't write about you like that again. I'm talking about the
end part. It's extremely annoying for the paper, for me, and for you.
Like Caesar's wife, a journalist must be above suspicion.'

Duroy, with Saint-Potin as guide, got into a cab and shouted to the
driver: '18 rue de l'Écureuil, in Montmartre.'

It was an enormous house with six floors, which they had to climb
up. An old woman wearing a loose wool jacket opened the door to
them: 'What do you want now?' she asked, on seeing Saint-Potin.

He replied: 'I've brought this gentleman to see you, he's a police
inspector and would like to hear your story.'

So she invited them in, saying: 'Two more come after you, for
some paper—I don't know which.' Then, turning to Duroy: 'So, you
was wanting to know about it?'

'Yes. Were you arrested by an officer of the vice squad?'

She raised up her arms: 'Never in me born days, Monsieur, never in me born days. Here's what happened. I've a butcher that serves good stuff but weighs short. I've often noticed without saying nothing, but t'other day when I was asking for two pounds of cutlets, 'cos me daughter and son-in-law's coming, I see that he's weighing in scrap bones with them, they was cutlet bones it's true, but not from my cutlets. I could have made 'em into a stew, that's true as well, but when I ask for cutlets it's not to be given other people's scraps. So I refused to take 'em, an' he called me a stingy old thing, an' I call him an old rogue; in a word, one thing leads to another, we had such an argy-bargy that there was more'n a hundred people round the shop laughing fit to bust! In the end a policeman noticed and asked us to go round an' explain to the superintendent. We went, an' they sent us home without saying nothing 'bout who was right. Now I'm getting me meat from another butcher, an' I don't even pass his door, so as not to make a scene.'

She stopped talking. Duroy asked: 'That's all?' 'It's the whole truth, Monsieur'—and, having offered him a glass of cassis which he refused, the old woman insisted that he mention in his report that the butcher gave short weight.

Back at the newspaper, Duroy composed his reply:

'An anonymous scribbler for *La Plume*, who bears me a grudge, is picking a quarrel with me over an old woman who, he claims, was arrested by the vice squad, which I deny. I have myself seen Mme Aubert, who is at least sixty years of age, and she has described to me in great detail her quarrel with a butcher over the weighing of some cutlets, which necessitated sorting out the matter with the police-superintendent.

'That is the whole truth.

'As for the other insinuations of the writer for *La Plume*, I consider them beneath contempt. Besides, one does not answer such things when they are anonymous.

'Georges Duroy.'

M. Walter and Jacques Rival, who had just come in, thought this note sufficient, and it was decided that it would be printed that very day, at the foot of the gossip column.

Duroy went home early, rather worried and uneasy. How would the other man reply? Who was he? What was behind this brutal attack? In view of the blunt ways of journalists, this idiotic affair could go far, very far. He slept badly.

On rereading his note in the paper the next day, he found it looked more aggressive in print than in handwriting. He felt he could have toned down some of the expressions.

He passed the day in restless agitation, and that night slept badly again. He rose with the dawn, to buy the issue of *La Plume* which should respond to his reply.

The weather had grown cold again; there was a hard frost. The gutters, frozen while water still flowed in them, edged the pavements with two ribbons of ice.

The papers had not arrived at the news-stands and Duroy remembered the day of his first article: 'Recollections of an African Cavalryman'. His hands and his feet were growing numb and painful, especially his fingertips; and he began running round the glass kiosk, where, through the little window, all you could see of the newspaper-vendor huddled over her foot-warmer was a red nose and cheeks beneath a woollen hood.

Finally the boy with the newspapers handed the expected bundle through the opening in the window, and the woman passed *La Plume*, already spread open, to Duroy. He glanced over it rapidly, searching for his name, and at first saw nothing. He was already breathing again when he noticed it, set off by two dashes.

'Monsieur Duroy, of *La Vie française*, flatly contradicts us and, in so doing, is himself lying. He does, however, admit that a woman named Aubert exists, and that an officer took her to the police station. All that is missing is the addition of the four words: "of the vice squad" after the word "officer" and the matter is settled.

'But the conscience of certain journalists is of the same calibre as their talent.

'And I sign my name:

'Louis Langremont.'

Georges's heart began to beat violently, and he returned home to dress without really knowing what he was doing. So he had been insulted, and in such a fashion that there could be no doubt about it. Why? Over nothing. Over an old woman who had quarrelled with her butcher.

He dressed very fast and went to see M. Walter, although it was barely eight in the morning. M. Walter, already up, was reading *La Plume*. 'Well,' he said, on seeing Duroy, 'you can't back out now, can you?'

The young man made no reply. The Director went on: 'Go straight away and find Rival; he'll see to things for you.'

Duroy stammered a few vague words and left for the home of the journalist, who was still asleep. He jumped out of bed at the sound of the bell, and, after reading the item: 'Lord, you'll have to do it. Who might be the other second?'

'Really, I've no idea.'

'Boisrenard? What d'you think?'

'Yes, Boisrenard.'

'Are you good at fencing?'

'No, not at all.'

'Hell! And with a pistol?'

'I shoot a bit.'

'Good. You must go and practise while I take care of everything. Wait for me for a few minutes.'

He went into his dressing-room and soon reappeared, washed, shaved, and meticulously dressed.

'Come with me,' he said.

He lived on the ground floor of a small town house, and he took Duroy down into the cellar, an enormous cellar which, by walling up all the openings onto the street, had been converted into an area for fencing and shooting.

After lighting a row of gas lights that stretched to the far end of a second cellar, where there stood an iron figure of a man, painted in red and blue, he put on a table two pairs of pistols—of a modern, breech-loading style—and began barking out orders as if the duel were actually taking place.

'Ready?'

'Fire! One, two, three.'

Quite overwhelmed, Duroy obeyed, raising his arm, aiming, firing, and as he frequently hit the figure right in the belly—for in his early youth he had often used an old horse pistol of his father's to kill birds in their courtyard—Jacques Rival declared in a satisfied voice: 'Good, very good... very good... you'll do, you'll do.'

Then he left him. 'Go on shooting like this until noon. Here's some ammunition, don't worry about using it all. I'll come and fetch you for lunch, and tell you what's happening.' Then he went away.

Left alone, Duroy tried a few more shots, then sat down and began to think. Really, how stupid these things were! What did they prove? Was a rogue any less of a rogue after fighting a duel? What had an honest man who'd been insulted to gain by risking his life against a scoundrel? And, his thoughts wandering gloomily on, he remembered what Norbert de Varenne had said about the barrenness of men's minds, the banality of their ideas and their concerns, the inanity of their moral principles!

And he declared out loud: 'My God, how right he is!'

He was feeling thirsty, and, hearing the sound of water dripping behind him, he saw there was a shower. He went and drank directly from the shower-head. Then he continued to think. It was depressing in this cellar, as depressing as the tomb. The far-off, muted rumbling of carriages was like the rumbling of a distant storm. What might be the time?

In that place the hours were passing the way they must pass deep inside a prison, without anything to indicate or mark them, except for the arrival of the gaoler bringing plates of food. He waited, for a long, long time.

Then, suddenly, he heard steps, and voices, and Jacques Rival reappeared, accompanied by Boisrenard. As soon as he caught sight of Duroy he cried: 'It's all arranged!'

Duroy imagined the affair had been settled by some letter of apology; his heart gave a leap, and he stammered: 'Ah! Thank you.' The journalist replied: 'This Langremont is very straightforward, he accepted all our conditions. Twenty-five paces, one shot, bringing the pistol up at the command. That way, your arm is much steadier than if you're lowering it. Look, Boisrenard, this is what I've been telling you.'

Picking up a pistol, he began to shoot, demonstrating how you could keep your aim much straighter by bringing your arm up.

Then he said: 'Come on, let's have lunch, it's gone twelve.'

They went into a nearby restaurant. Duroy hardly spoke at all. He ate, so as not to seem afraid, then in the afternoon went to the newspaper with Boisrenard and did his work in an abstracted, mechanical way. People thought him brave.

Towards mid-afternoon Jacques Rival came in and shook his hand; it was agreed that his seconds would fetch him in a landau at seven the following morning, to go to the Bois du Vésinet,* where the duel was to take place. All this had happened so suddenly, without his playing any part in it, or saying a word, or giving his opinion, without his accepting or refusing, and so fast, that he was left dazed and bewildered, not really understanding what was going on.

He found himself back home about nine o'clock, after dining with Boisrenard, who, as a loyal friend, had stayed with him the entire day.

Once he was alone, he strode rapidly up and down his room for a few minutes. He was too upset to think about anything. A single idea filled his mind—tomorrow he would fight a duel—without this thought evoking in him anything other than a confused but powerful emotion. He had been a soldier, he had shot at Arabs, though without incurring much danger to himself, certainly, rather like shooting a wild boar on a hunt.

In a word, he had done what he ought to do. He had demonstrated that he was what he ought to be. People would talk about it, they would praise him, they would congratulate him. Then, speaking out loud, as people do when in the grip of an overpowering idea, he declared: 'What a swine that man is!'

Sitting down, he began to reflect. He had tossed onto his small table a card of his adversary's that Rival had given him, so he would have the address. He reread it, as he had done twenty times in the course of the day. *Louis Langremont, 176 rue Montmartre.* Nothing else.

He examined this collection of letters which to him seemed mysterious, full of menace. 'Louis Langremont'; who was this man? How old was he? How tall? With what sort of face? Was it not disgusting that a stranger, someone you didn't know, should disrupt your life like this, for no reason, on a pure impulse, because of an old woman who had quarrelled with her butcher?

Again he repeated, aloud, 'What a swine!'

He sat there without moving, thinking, his gaze still fixed on the card. Anger was stirring in him, an anger full of hatred into which was blended a strange feeling of unease. This business was so stupid! He picked up a pair of nail scissors that lay there and dug them into the middle of the printed name, as if he were stabbing someone.

So he was going to fight, and fight with pistols? Why hadn't he chosen swords? He would have got off with a jab in the arm or the hand, whereas with a pistol one never knew what might be the result.

He said: 'Come on, be a man.'

The sound of his voice made him jump, and he looked all around.

He was beginning to feel extremely nervous. He drank a glass of water, then went to bed.

As soon as he was in his bed, he blew out the light and closed his eyes.

He felt very warm under the bedding, although it was very cold in his room, but he could not fall asleep. He turned over and over, lay for five minutes on his back, then tried his left side, then rolled over onto the right.

He was thirsty again. He got out of bed for a drink, and was struck by a nasty thought: 'Might I be afraid?'

Why did his heart begin pounding madly at every familiar sound in his room? When his cuckoo clock was about to strike, the little creak of the spring made him start, and for a few seconds he had to open his mouth in order to breathe, he felt so overcome.

He began to consider, as a philosopher might, the question: 'Might I be afraid?'

No, certainly, he would not be afraid, since he was determined to carry the thing through to the end, since he was firmly resolved to fight, and not to vacillate. But he felt so profoundly agitated that he wondered: 'Can you be afraid in spite of yourself?' And he was overwhelmed by doubt, by dread, by terror. If he was overpowered by a force stronger than his will, a force which dominated him, was irresistible, what would happen? Yes, indeed, what might happen!

To be sure, he would appear for the duel since that was what he wanted to do. But what if he trembled with fear? What if he lost consciousness? And he thought about his position, his reputation, his future.

And suddenly he was seized by a strange compulsion to get up and look at himself in the mirror. He relit the candle. When he saw his face reflected in the polished glass, he hardly recognized himself; he felt as if he had never seen himself before. His eyes looked enormous; and he was pale, yes, certainly, he was pale, extremely pale.

An unexpected thought entered his head with the speed of a bullet: 'Tomorrow at this time I may be dead.' And once again his heart began pounding furiously.

He turned towards his bed, and clearly saw himself stretched out on his back, in these same sheets he had just left. He had the sunken face of a corpse, and those white hands that will never move again.

So then he felt afraid of his bed, and in order not to see it any longer he opened his window and looked out.

A blast of frigid air lacerated his flesh from head to foot, and he recoiled, gasping.

He thought of lighting a fire. Slowly, never turning round, he got it to burn. His hands shook with a slight nervous tremor whenever they touched anything. He felt he was losing his mind, and his whirling, disjointed, fleeting thoughts were making his head ache; a kind of intoxication was permeating his spirit, as if he had been drinking.

And all the time he kept wondering: 'What am I going to do? What will become of me?' He began again to walk about, repeating constantly and mechanically: 'I must be strong, very strong...' Then he said to himself: 'I'll write to my parents, in case something happens.'

He sat down again, took some writing-paper, and wrote: 'My dear Papa, my dear Mama...' Then he thought these terms too familiar to use in such tragic circumstances. He tore up the first sheet and began again: 'My dear Father, my dear Mother; I am going to fight a duel at dawn, and since it may happen that...' He could not bring himself to write the rest, and leapt to his feet.

The idea of fighting a duel was now like a dead weight pressing heavily upon him. He could no longer avoid going through with it. So what was happening to him? He wanted to fight; his intention, his determination were quite unshakeable; and it seemed to him, in spite of all the force of his will, that he would not even have the strength needed to get to the place where they were to meet.

From time to time, in his mouth, his teeth would begin chattering, making a tiny sharp clicking sound, and he wondered: 'Has my adversary ever fought a duel? Has he done much target shooting? Has he a reputation? Has he been ranked?' He had never heard the name mentioned. And yet, if this man were not an exceptional shot, he would surely never have agreed, without hesitation or discussion, to this dangerous weapon.

Then Duroy began visualizing their encounter, his own demeanour, and how his enemy might behave. He racked his brains imagining the smallest details of the duel, and quite suddenly he found himself staring straight into that tiny, deep, black hole in the barrel, from which a bullet would emerge.

And without warning, he was overwhelmed by a terrible wave of despair. His entire body shook, convulsive shudders running through it. He clenched his teeth so as not to cry out, feeling a fierce urge to roll on the ground, to tear something, to bite. But then, catching sight of a glass on his mantelpiece, he recalled that he had in his cupboard almost a full litre of brandy, for he had kept up the military habit of taking 'a hair of the dog' each morning.

He grabbed the bottle and drank from it directly, in long greedy gulps. He did not put it down until he ran out of breath. The bottle was a third empty.

A flame-like warmth was soon burning his stomach, spreading through his limbs, bolstering his spirits and making him dizzy. He told himself: 'That's the answer.' And since his skin, now, was burning hot, he reopened the window.

Day was breaking, calm and icy-cold. Up above, in the depths of the lightened sky, the stars seemed to be dying, and in the deep cutting of the railway the green, red, and white signals were growing paler. The first locomotives emerged from the sidings, whistling as they came in search of the first trains. Others, far away, gave shrill, repeated cries, their cries of awakening, like cockerels out in the countryside.

Duroy thought: 'Perhaps I won't ever see this again.' But, sensing that he was starting to feel sorry for himself once more, he reacted forcefully: 'Come on, you musn't think of anything before the moment of the duel, it's the only way to keep your courage up.'

And he began his toilet. While shaving he again experienced a moment of weakness, when he thought that it was perhaps the last time he would look at his face. But he swallowed another mouthful of brandy, and finished dressing.

The hour that followed was difficult to get through. He walked up and down, forcing his mind into a state of total quiescence. When he heard someone knock at his door, he very nearly collapsed, so violent was the shock. It was his seconds. Already!

They were enveloped in fur coats. Rival announced, after shaking his charge's hand: 'It's as cold as Siberia.' Then he enquired: 'Everything all right?'

'Yes, fine.'

'You're feeling calm?'

'Yes, very calm.'

'Good, you'll do. Have you had something to eat and drink?'

'Yes, I don't need anything.'

In honour of the occasion, Boisrenard was wearing a foreign decoration in green and yellow, that Duroy had never seen on him before.

They went down. A gentleman was waiting for them in the landau. Rival introduced him: 'Doctor Le Brument.' Duroy shook hands, stammering: 'Thank you,' then tried to take his place on the front bench, where he sat down on top of something hard that made him leap to his feet as if he were on a spring. It was the case containing the pistols.

Rival kept saying: 'No! The principal and the doctor sit in the back!' Eventually Duroy understood and sank down beside the doctor. Then the two seconds climbed in and the coachman set off. He knew where to go.

But the pistol-case was in everybody's way, and particularly bothered Duroy, who would have preferred not to be able to see it. They tried putting it behind their backs, which was terribly uncomfortable; then they stood it between Rival and Boisrenard, and it fell over constantly. Finally they slipped it under their feet.

Conversation flagged, although the doctor told some stories. Only Rival answered him. Duroy would have liked to demonstrate his self-possession, but he was afraid of losing the thread of his ideas and revealing the agitation of his mind; and he was haunted by the agonizing fear that he might start trembling.

Soon the carriage was in open country. It was about nine in the morning. It was one of those bitter winter mornings when the whole of nature is shiny, brittle, and hard, like crystal. The trees, decked out in frost, seem to have sweated ice; the earth resounds beneath one's feet; the tiniest sounds carry a long way in the dry air; the blue sky is bright as a mirror, and the sun moves through space in icy brilliance, casting on the frozen world rays which bestow no warmth upon anything.

Rival was telling Duroy: 'I got the pistols from Gastine Renette.* He himself loaded them, the case is sealed. In any case, we'll draw lots for which we use, these or your opponent's.'

Duroy replied automatically: 'Thank you.'

Then Rival gave him very detailed advice, for he was determined that his charge should commit no error. He repeated each point several times: 'When you're asked: "Are you ready, gentlemen?"' you'll answer in a loud voice: "Yes!"

'When you hear the order: "Fire!" you'll quickly raise your arm, and fire before they get to three.'

And Duroy repeated to himself: 'When I hear the order "fire!", I'll raise my arm. When I hear the order "fire!", I'll raise my arm.' He was learning this the way children learn their lessons, muttering it over and over again to get it firmly fixed in his memory. 'When I hear the order "fire!", I'll raise my arm.'

The landau entered a wood, turned right into an avenue, then right again. Rival suddenly opened the door to shout to the coachman: 'There, up that little track.' The carriage started along a rutted path between two thickets quivering with dead, ice-rimmed leaves.

Duroy was still mumbling: 'When I hear the order to fire, I'll raise my arm.' And it occurred to him that an accident with the carriage would solve everything. Oh, what luck if they could overturn! If he could break his leg!...

But he saw another carriage halted at the end of a clearing, and four gentlemen who were stamping their feet to keep them warm; and he was forced to keep his mouth open, it was so difficult to breathe.

The seconds got out first, then the doctor and the principal. Rival had picked up the case of pistols, and, with Boisrenard, approached two of the strangers who were coming towards them. Duroy saw them bow ceremoniously to one another, then walk together through the clearing, examining now the ground, now the trees, as if they were looking for something that might perhaps have fallen, or been blown away. Then they counted out the paces, and with great difficulty stuck two walking-sticks into the frozen ground. Then they collected in a group and went through the motions of tossing for heads or tails, like children at play.

Doctor Le Brument asked Duroy:

'Do you feel all right? Is there anything you need?'

'No, nothing, thank you.'

He felt as if he'd gone mad, or was sleeping, or dreaming, as if something supernatural had occurred, in which he was swept up. Was he afraid? Possibly. But he did not know. Everything around him was different.

Jacques Rival came back and in a gratified voice quietly informed him: 'Everything's ready. Luck was on our side over the pistols.'

That was a matter of indifference to Duroy. They removed his overcoat. He made no objection. They felt the pockets of his jacket to make sure that he was not carrying any papers or wallet that might protect him.

He kept repeating to himself, like a prayer: 'When I hear the order to fire, I'll raise my arm.'

Next they led him to one of the walking-sticks stuck into the ground, and gave him his pistol. Then he saw a man standing opposite him, very close, a bald, pot-bellied little man wearing glasses. It was his adversary.

He could see him very clearly, but he was thinking only of this: 'When I hear the order to fire, I'll raise my arm and shoot.' A voice rang out in the deep empty silence, a voice that seemed to come from a long way off; it asked:

'Are you ready, gentlemen?'

Georges cried: 'Yes!'

Then the same voice ordered: 'Fire!'

He listened to nothing more, he noticed nothing more, he was aware of nothing more, he felt only that he was raising his arm and pressing as hard as he could on the trigger.

And he heard nothing.

But, instantly, he saw a small amount of smoke at the end of the barrel of his pistol; and, seeing that the man opposite was still standing upright, also in the same posture, he noticed another little white cloud flying up over the head of his adversary.

Both of them had fired. It was over.

His seconds and the doctor were touching him, feeling him, unbuttoning his clothes as they anxiously enquired: 'You're not wounded?' He answered without thinking: 'No, I don't believe so.'

Moreover Langremont was as unscathed as his enemy, and Jacques Rival muttered in a dissatisfied tone: 'With a confounded pistol, that's what it's always like, you either miss each other or kill each other. What a damnable weapon!'

Duroy was standing motionless, paralysed with surprise and joy: 'It was over!' They had to take his pistol, which he was still clutching tightly, away from him. It seemed to him now that he would have fought the entire universe. It was over. How wonderful! Suddenly he felt brave enough to challenge absolutely anybody.

The seconds conferred for a few moments, arranging a time to meet later in the day to draw up an official report of the proceedings, then they got back into the landau; and the cabbie, who was laughing up there on his seat, set off again, cracking his whip.

The four of them had lunch on the boulevard, and talked over the event. Duroy described his impressions: 'It had no effect on me, none whatever. Anyway, you must have seen that?'

Rival replied: 'Yes, you acquitted yourself well.'

When the report had been drawn up it was given to Duroy to put into the gossip column. He was astonished to see that he had exchanged two shots with M. Louis Langremont, and, somewhat uneasy, he questioned Rival: 'But we only fired one shot.'

The other smiled: 'Yes, one shot... one each... that makes two shots.'

And Duroy, satisfied with this explanation, let the matter drop. Old Walter embraced him: 'Well done, well done! You've defended the flag of *La Vie française*, well done!'

That evening Georges put in an appearance at the principal large newspaper offices and at the principal large cafés on the boulevard. Twice he met his adversary, who was doing the rounds in similar fashion. They did not greet one another. If one of them had been wounded, they would have shaken hands. Moreover each solemnly swore that he had heard the other man's bullet whistle past.

About eleven the following day Duroy received a telegram: 'My God, I've been so frightened! Please come right away to the Rue de Constantinople, so I can kiss you, my love. How brave you are—I adore you. Clo.'

He went to the rendezvous and she flung herself into his arms, covering him with kisses: 'Oh, sweetheart, if you knew how agitated I was this morning when I read the papers. Oh, do describe it to me. Tell me everything. I want to know.'

He had to tell her every tiny detail. She asked: 'What an awful night you must have spent, before the duel!'

'No, I slept well.'

'If it had been me, I shouldn't have slept a wink. And at the actual duel, tell me how that went.'

He made a dramatic story of it: 'When we were face to face, at a distance of twenty paces—that's only four times the length of this room—Jacques, after asking whether we were ready, gave the order:

"Fire." I raised my arm immediately, nice and straight, but I made the mistake of trying to aim at the head. I had a weapon with an extremely stiff trigger, and I'm used to pistols with very light ones, so that the resistance of the trigger pulled up the shot. It doesn't matter, it can't have been far out. The other devil's a good shot too. His bullet skimmed past my temple. I felt the draught of air from it.'

She was sitting on his knee with her arms round him, as if to share in his danger. She said falteringly: 'Oh, my poor darling, my poor darling...'

Then, when he had finished his story, she told him: 'You know, I can't do without you any longer. I must see you; and with my husband in Paris, it's not easy to arrange. I'll often be free for an hour in the morning, before you're up, and I could come and give you a kiss, but I don't want to go into that dreadful house of yours again. What are we to do?'

He had a sudden inspiration and enquired: 'How much do you pay here?'

'A hundred francs a month.'

'Well, I'll take these rooms myself and I'll live here all the time. My place is no longer adequate for me, in my new position.'

She thought for a few moments, then replied: 'No. I don't want that.'

He was astonished: 'Why ever not?'

'Because...'

'That's not a reason. These rooms suit me very well. Here I am, and here I stay.' He began to laugh. 'Besides, they're in my name.'

But she still refused. 'No, no, I don't want you to...'

'But why not, for goodness' sake?'

Then, softly and tenderly, she whispered: 'Because you'd bring women here, and I don't want that.'

Indignantly he protested: 'Heavens, I wouldn't dream of doing that, never, I promise you.'

'No, you would bring them, just the same.'

'I swear I wouldn't.'

'Really and truly?'

'Really and truly. Word of honour. This is our place, just ours.'

Overcome with emotion, she gave him a hug. 'Then yes, I'd really like that, my love. But you know, if ever you cheat on me, even just once, everything will be finished between us, finished for good.'

He again gave her his solemn word, repeating his protestations, and it was agreed that he would move in that very day, so that she could visit him when she passed by the door. Then she said to him: 'In any case, come for dinner on Sunday. My husband thinks you're charming.'

He was flattered. 'Really?'

'Yes, you've made a conquest. And listen, you told me you'd been brought up in a chateau in the country, isn't that so?'

'Yes, why?'

'So you must know a bit about agriculture?'

'Yes.'

'Well, talk to him about gardening and crops, he loves that.'

'All right. I won't forget.'

She left him, after showering him with endless kisses, for the duel had intensified her love.

Duroy was thinking, as he made his way to the paper: 'What a strange creature she is! What a birdbrain! Who knows what she wants or what she likes? And what a strange couple! Whatever kind of prankster can it be that arranged to pair that old man with that giddy little thing! Whatever can have induced that surveyor to marry that schoolgirl? What a mystery! Who knows? Perhaps it was love.'

Then he concluded: 'Anyway, she's a most delightful mistress; I'd be a real idiot to let her go.'

CHAPTER 8

His duel had established Duroy as one of the principal staff writers on *La Vie française*; however, as he found it extremely difficult to come up with ideas, he made it his speciality to rail against moral decline, a new weakness of character, the demise of patriotism, and the anaemia affecting the French sense of honour. (He himself had discovered the word 'anaemia,' and was very proud of it.)

And when Mme de Marelle, in that teasing, sceptical, mocking style that is called Parisian wit, poked fun at his tirades that she would deflate with an epigram, he replied with a smile: 'Bah! It's giving me a good reputation for later on.'

He was living now in the Rue de Constantinople, where he had conveyed his trunk, his hairbrush, his razor, and his soap, which was all his removal had entailed. Two or three times a week, the young woman arrived before he was up, undressed in an instant and, shivering all over from the cold outside, slipped into his bed.

Duroy, by contrast, went for dinner every Thursday at the couple's home and made up to the husband by talking to him about agriculture; and as he himself loved things to do with the land, both of them sometimes became so absorbed in their conversation that they forgot all about their woman, sitting dozing on the sofa.

Laurine, too, would fall asleep, sometimes on her father's lap, sometimes on Bel-Ami's.

And when the journalist had left, M. de Marelle never failed to declare in that doctrinaire tone which he used for even the most trivial remarks: 'That young man is really most agreeable. He has a very good mind.'

It was almost the end of February. In the streets, now, in the morning, you could smell violets as you passed the flower-vendors' barrows.

For Duroy, there was not a cloud in the sky.

On returning home one night, however, he found a letter slipped under his door. He looked at the stamp, and saw 'Cannes'. Opening it, he read:

Cannes, Villa Jolie.

Dear friend,

You told me, didn't you, that I could rely on you for absolutely anything? Well I am asking a grim favour of your friendship: to come and help me, so that I am not alone during Charles's last hours, for he is dying. He may not live through the week, although he is still able to get up; but the doctor has warned me.

I no longer have the strength or the courage to watch this agony day and night. And I am terrified when I think of his last moments, which are very close. You are the only person of whom I can ask a thing like this, for my husband has no family left. You were his comrade; he gave you your start at the newspaper. Come, I beg you. I have no one to turn to.

Your most devoted friend,
Madeleine Forestier.

Like a breath of air, an extraordinary feeling filled Georges's heart, a feeling of deliverance, of space opening up before him, and he murmured: 'Of course I'll go. That poor Charles! But, really, isn't life strange!'

The Director, to whom he showed the young woman's letter, grumblingly gave his permission. He kept repeating: 'But come back quickly, we can't do without you.'

Georges Duroy left for Cannes the following day by the seven o'clock express, after letting the Marelles know by telegram. He arrived the next afternoon about four.

A porter showed him the way to the Villa Jolie, which was built half-way up the hill, in the pine-wood dotted with white villas which stretches from Le Cannet to Golfe Juan.*

Italian in style, the house was small and low, and stood on the edge of the road that zigzags up through the trees, affording superb views at every bend.

The servant opened the door, and exclaimed: 'Oh, Monsieur, Madame has been so anxious for you to get here.'

Duroy asked: 'How's your master?'

'Oh, not at all well, Monsieur. It won't be long now.'

The drawing-room the young man entered was hung with rose-pink chintz patterned in blue. The tall, wide window looked over the town and the sea.

Duroy muttered: 'My goodness, this is very elegant for a country villa. Where the devil do they get the money?' At the sound of a gown he turned round.

Mme Forestier was holding out her hands: 'How kind you are, how kind to have come!' And suddenly she gave him a kiss. Then they looked at one another.

She was a little paler, a little thinner, but still glowingly fresh, and perhaps, with her air of greater fragility, prettier than ever. She murmured: 'He's terrible, you see, he knows he's dying and he bullies me atrociously. I've told him you've come. But where's your trunk?'

Duroy replied: 'I left it at the station, not knowing which hotel you would suggest I should stay at, so as to be near you.'

She hesitated, then went on: 'You must stay here, in the villa. In any case, your room is prepared. He may die at any moment, and if that were to happen at night, I should be alone. I'll send for your luggage.'

He bowed. 'As you wish.'

'Now let's go up,' she said.

He followed her. She opened a door on the first floor, and Duroy saw, enveloped in blankets in an armchair beside a window, a kind of corpse that sat there gazing at him, ghastly pale in the red glow of the setting sun. He scarcely recognized him; he guessed, rather, that it was his friend.

The room smelled of fever, infusions, ether, and tar-water, that indefinable, oppressive odour of a room where a consumptive breathes the air.

Forestier raised his hand in a painful, slow gesture: 'Here you are,' he said. 'You've come to watch me die. Good of you.'

Duroy forced a laugh. 'Watch you die! That wouldn't be an amusing sight, and I'd never pick that as a reason for coming to Cannes. I've come to see you, and to have a bit of a rest.'

The other mumbled: 'Sit down.' And he bent his head, as if sunk in despairing thoughts. He was breathing in a rapid, shallow way, occasionally giving a kind of moan, as though to remind others of how ill he was.

Seeing he was not going to talk, his wife came up and leaned on the window, saying, as she nodded at the horizon: 'Look at that! Isn't it beautiful?'

In front of them, the hillside dotted with villas sloped down to the

town which lay curved in a semi-circle along the shore, stretching,
on the right, up to the jetty over which loomed the old city surmounted by its ancient belfry, and on the left as far as Pointe de la
Croisette, opposite the Îles de Lérins.* These islands looked like two
green stains on the pure blue water. From that height they seemed so
flat that they might have been two huge, floating leaves.

In the far distance, closing out the horizon on the other side of the
bay, above the jetty and the belfry, a long range of bluish mountains
traced across the brilliant sky an erratic, charming line of peaks,
domed, crooked, and jagged in shape, which ended in a great
pyramid-shaped mountain that plunged steeply down into the open
sea.

Mme Forestier pointed to it: 'That's the Esterel.'*

The sky behind the dark summits was red, a blood-red tinged
with gold that the eye could not bear to look at.

In spite of himself, Duroy was stirred by the majesty of this close
of day. Unable to think of any other phrase sufficiently vivid to
express his admiration, he murmured: 'Oh, yes, that's stunning!'

Forestier looked up at his wife and said: 'Give me a little air.'

She replied: 'Be careful, it's late, the sun's setting, you'll catch
cold again and you know that's not a good idea in your state of
health.'

With his right hand he sketched a febrile, ineffectual gesture that
might have been an attempt to hit her, and he muttered with an
angry grimace—a dying man's grimace that revealed the fleshless
lips, the sunken cheeks and the way every bone protruded: 'I'm
stifling, I tell you. What can it matter to you if I turn my toes up a
day sooner or a day later, since I'm done for.'

She flung the window wide open.

The air that came in took them all by surprise, like a caress. It was
a gentle, warm, quiet breeze, a springtime breeze already rich with
the scents of the shrubs and intoxicating flowers that grow along that
coast. In it you could distinguish the strong scent of resin and the
bitter aroma of eucalyptus.

Forestier drank it in in short, feverish gasps. Digging his nails into
the arms of his chair, he said in a low, wheezy, waspish voice: 'Close
the window. It's bad for me. I'd sooner die in a cellar.'

And his wife slowly closed the window, then, her forehead against
the glass, gazed out at the distance.

Ill at ease, Duroy would have liked to talk to the sick man, to cheer him up. But he could not think of anything likely to comfort him. He stammered: 'So you haven't been any better since getting here?'

The other shrugged his shoulders with weary impatience: 'As you can see.' He bent his head once more.

Duroy went on: 'My goodness, it's awfully nice here compared with Paris. It's still the middle of winter there. We've got snow, and hail, and rain, and it's dark enough for the lamps to be lit at three in the afternoon.'

Forestier enquired: 'Nothing new at the paper?'

'Nothing new. To replace you they've taken on that little Lacrin who used to be with *Le Voltaire*,* but he hasn't enough experience. It's time you came back!'

The sick man muttered: 'Me? Where I'll soon be writing articles is six feet under the ground.'

No matter what the subject, his fixation came back again like a bell tolling, constantly reappearing in every thought, in every sentence.

There was a long silence, a painful, profound silence. The fiery sunset was slowly fading away; the mountains were turning black against the deepening red sky. Glowing shadows, a beginning of darkness which still held gleams of dying embers was coming into the room, tinting furniture, walls, draperies, and corners in shades of inky purple. The mirror over the mantelpiece, where the horizon was reflected, looked like a disc of blood.

Mme Forestier remained motionless, standing with her back to the room and her face pressed against the window-pane.

And Forestier began speaking in a staccato, breathless voice, heart-rending to listen to. 'How many more of them shall I see — how many more sunsets? Eight... ten... fifteen or twenty... perhaps thirty... not more. You have time, you others do... but for me, it's over. And it'll go on after me, as if I were still here...'

He said nothing for a few moments, then began again: 'Everything I see reminds me that in a few days I shall no longer see it... It's horrible... I shall see nothing more... nothing of what exists... the smallest objects that we use... glasses... plates... beds where people sleep so comfortably... carriages. It's so lovely, going out in a carriage, in the evening... How much I enjoyed all that!'

He was moving the fingers of both hands in a rapid, restless fashion, as if playing the piano on the arms of his chair. And each of his silences was more painful than what he said, so conscious were his companions that he must be thinking appalling thoughts.

Suddenly, Duroy remembered what Norbert de Varenne had been saying to him just a few weeks earlier. 'For my part, now, I see it so close to me that I often feel like stretching out my arms to push it away... I find it everywhere. Tiny creatures run over on the road, leaves that fall, a white hair I notice in a friend's beard, these things fill my heart with despair, and cry out to me: "It's here!"'

He hadn't understood, then; but now, as he watched Forestier, he did understand. And he began to feel an unknown, dreadful anguish, as though he could sense right there beside him, within his reach, in the armchair where that man sat gasping for breath, the hideous presence of death. He wanted to jump to his feet, to leave, to run away, to return to Paris that very instant! Oh, had he known, he would never have come!

Night was spreading now throughout the room, like a mourning garment cast prematurely over this dying man. Only the window was still visible, with the motionless silhouette of the young woman outlined against its paler rectangle.

And Forestier asked in an exasperated voice: 'Well, aren't we going to have the lamp brought in today? So this is how you look after an invalid!'

The shadow of the body outlined against the window disappeared, and an electric bell echoed through the house.

Soon a servant entered and placed a lamp on the mantelpiece. Mme Forestier said to her husband: 'Do you want to go to bed, or will you come down for dinner?' He murmured: 'I'll come down.'

All three of them, as they waited for the meal, remained motionless for almost an hour, saying only an occasional word, an unnecessary, banal word spoken at random, as if there might have been danger, some mysterious danger, in letting that stillness last too long, in letting the silent atmosphere solidify in that room, that room where death was lurking.

And then, finally, dinner was announced. It seemed long to Duroy, interminable. They did not speak, they ate noiselessly, then crumbled bread with the tips of their fingers. The servant, waiting on them, walked about, came and went without his feet making any sound, for, because the noise of his soles irritated Charles, the man wore slippers. Only the sharp tic-toc of a wooden clock, with its mechanical, regular motion, disturbed the quiet of the walls.

As soon as they had finished eating, Duroy, on the pretext of fatigue, withdrew to his room; leaning on his window-sill, he watched as, high up in the sky, the full moon, like the huge globe of a lamp, cast its dry, dim light on the white walls of the villas, and spread a scaly coat of gently moving radiance over the sea. He tried to think up an excuse for leaving very soon, devising strategies, telegrams he would receive, a summons from M. Walter.

But when he woke up the next morning, his plans of escape seemed to him more difficult to put into effect. Mme Forestier would not be taken in by his schemes, and he would lose, through his cowardice, all the advantages gained by his devotion. He said to himself: 'Bah! It's a nuisance; still, nothing to be done about it, life has its unpleasant moments, and then, perhaps it won't be for long.'

The sky was blue, that southern blue that fills your heart with joy; and Duroy walked down to the sea, thinking it would be soon enough if he saw Forestier later in the day.

When he returned for lunch, the servant said to him: 'The master has already asked for you two or three times, Monsieur. If you would be so good as to go up and see him?'

He went upstairs. Forestier was sitting in an armchair, apparently asleep. His wife, stretched out on a sofa, was reading. The invalid raised his head. Duroy asked: 'Well, how are you? You look in great form this morning.'

The other replied: 'Yes, I'm feeling better, my strength has come back. Have lunch quickly with Madeleine, because we're going out for a drive in the carriage.'

As soon as she was alone with Duroy, Madeleine said to him: 'You see! Today he believes he's cured. He's been making plans all morning. Right after lunch we're going to Golfe Juan to buy pottery for our flat in Paris. He's absolutely determined to go out, but I'm horribly afraid something may happen. He won't be able to stand the jolting on the drive.'

When the landau arrived, Forestier went downstairs one step at a time, supported by his servant. But as soon as he saw the carriage, he asked for the hood to be opened.

His wife objected: 'You'll catch cold. It's madness.'

He was determined: 'No, I'm much better. I know I am.'

At first they drove along those shady lanes which all have gardens on either side, and make of Cannes a sort of English park, then they turned into the road to Antibes and drove along the sea-shore.

Forestier described the area. He had already pointed out the villa belonging to the Comte de Paris,* and he identified several others. He was cheerful, with the forced, artificial, feeble cheerfulness of a dying man. He would raise his finger, no longer having the strength to extend his arm. 'Look, there's the Île Sainte-Marguerite and the castle that Bazaine* escaped from. He certainly pulled a fast one there!'

Then he began reminiscing about the regiment; he mentioned a number of officers, and that reminded him and Duroy of various incidents. But suddenly, at a turning of the road, they saw the whole of Golfe Juan, with its white village in the distance and the Cap d'Antibes at the other end.

And Forestier, abruptly filled with childish delight, stammered: 'Oh, the squadron, you're going to see the squadron!'

In the middle of the vast bay there were indeed a half-dozen large ships; they resembled rocks covered with branches. They were bizarre, deformed, enormous, with excrescences, and towers, and rams that plunged into the water as if intending to take root under the sea. You could not imagine how they could shift about and move, they seemed so heavy, so fixed to the sea-bed. A floating battery, round and tall and shaped like an observatory, resembled one of those beacons that are built on rocks.

A tall, three-masted schooner passed near them with all its white, joyful sails spread, making for the open sea. It looked graceful and pretty beside those monsters of war, those monsters of iron, those hideous monsters crouching on the water. Forestier tried to identify them. He gave their names: *Le Colbert, Le Suffren, L'Amiral-Duperré, Le Redoutable, La Dévastation,** then he corrected himself: 'No, I'm wrong, that one's *La Dévastation.*'

They arrived before a large outbuilding with a sign announcing: 'Golfe Juan Pottery Artworks', and the carriage, having circled a lawn, stopped in front of the door.

Forestier wanted to buy two vases to stand on his bookcase. As he could not really leave the carriage, various types were brought out to him, one after another. He spent a long time choosing, consulting his wife and Duroy. 'You know, it's for that piece of furniture at the far end of my study. When I'm sitting in my chair, I can see it all the time. I've set my heart on a classical shape, a Greek shape.' He studied the samples, made them bring others, went back to the first ones. Finally, he made up his mind and, having paid, insisted that the vases should be dispatched immediately. 'I'm returning to Paris in a few days,' he said. They turned back; but, on the road along the bay, they were suddenly hit by a chill wind blowing down the fold of a small valley, and the sick man began to cough.

At first it was nothing, a slight attack; but it grew, became a relentless paroxysm, then a kind of hiccup, a death-rattle.

Forestier was choking, and each time he struggled to draw breath the cough, coming from deep down in his chest, tore at his throat. Nothing could calm him, nothing could relieve him. He had to be carried from the landau to his bedroom, and Duroy, who was holding his legs, felt his feet jerk at every spasm of his lungs.

The warmth of his bed did not stop the attack, which lasted until midnight; then, at last, narcotics pacified the mortal spasms of the cough. The sick man remained sitting up in bed, his eyes wide open, until dawn. The first words he spoke were to ask for the barber, because he insisted on being shaved every morning. He got up for this part of his toilet, but he had to be put back to bed immediately, and he began to breathe in such a shallow, harsh, laborious manner that Mme Forestier, terrified, had Duroy—who had just gone to bed—woken up, with a request that he should fetch the doctor.

Almost immediately, he brought back Dr Gavaut, who prescribed a draught and gave some advice; but when the journalist saw him to the door and asked for his opinion: 'His last moments have come, he'll be dead tomorrow,' he said. 'Warn that poor young woman and send for a priest. There's nothing more for me to do. But I'm entirely at your service should you need me.'

Duroy asked to see Mme Forestier. 'He's dying. The doctor advises sending for a priest. What do you want to do?'

She hesitated for a long time, thinking everything over; then she replied slowly: 'Yes, that would be best... for all sorts of reasons... I'll go and prepare him, tell him that the curé wants to see him... Well, I don't know, something or other. It would be so kind if you would go and find me a priest, and choose him carefully. Find one that won't make a lot of fuss. Try to get one who'll be satisfied with hearing confession and let us off the rest.'

Duroy brought back an obliging old priest who agreed to this arrangement. As soon as he had entered the dying man's bedroom, Mme Forestier came out and sat with Duroy in the adjoining room.

'He's horribly upset,' she said. 'When I mentioned a priest, a dreadful expression came over his face as if... as if he had felt... felt a breath... you know... He realized that it's over, at last, that it's a matter of hours...' She was extremely pale. She continued: 'I'll never forget the look on his face. There's no doubt that at that moment he saw death. He saw it...'

They could hear the priest who, being slightly deaf, was speaking rather loudly. He was saying: 'No, no, you're not as bad as that. You're ill, but in no danger. And the proof is that I've come as a friend, as a neighbour.'

They could not make out Forestier's reply. The old man went on: 'No, I'm not going to give you communion. We'll talk about that when you're well. But if you want to take advantage of my visit to make your confession, there's nothing I'd like better. I'm a pastor, and I seize every opportunity to bring my lambs into the fold.'

A long silence ensued. Forestier must have been speaking in his gasping, toneless voice.

Then, all of a sudden, the priest declared in a different tone, the tone of a priest officiating at the altar:

'God's mercy is infinite, recite the *Confiteor*, my son. You may perhaps have forgotten it, I'll help you. Repeat after me: "*Confiteor Deo omnipotenti... Beatae Mariae semper virgini...*"'

He would stop from time to time, to allow the dying man to catch up. Then he said:

'Now, make your confession. . .'

The young woman and Duroy were sitting absolutely still as they waited uneasily, gripped by a strange emotion.

The sick man had muttered something. The priest repeated: 'You have been sinfully acquiescent: in what way, my son?'

The young woman stood up and said simply: 'Let's go into the garden for a little while. We mustn't listen to his secrets.'

They went and sat on a bench, in front of the door, underneath a flowering rose and beside a circular bed of carnations which filled the air with its strong, sweet perfume.

Duroy, after a few moments of silence, enquired: 'Will it be long before you return to Paris?'

She replied: 'Oh, no. As soon as everything's seen to, I'll come back.'

'In about ten days?'

'Yes, at most.'

He went on: 'So there are no relatives?'

'Not one, apart from cousins. His father and mother died when he was quite young.'

They both watched a butterfly gathering its food from the carnations, going from one to another with a rapid fluttering of its wings, which continued beating slowly after it had settled on the flower. They were silent for a long time.

The servant came to tell them that the priest had finished. They went back upstairs together.

Forestier seemed to have grown even thinner since the previous day. The priest was holding his hand. 'Goodbye, my son, I'll return tomorrow morning.' And he departed.

The instant he had left, the dying man, panting, tried to raise his two hands to his wife and stammered: 'Save me, save me, darling... I don't want to die... I don't want to die... Oh, save me! Tell me what I must do, go and get the doctor... I'll take anything I'm told to... I don't want to... I don't want to...'

He was crying. Big tears ran down from his eyes over his sunken cheeks; and the emaciated corners of his mouth were puckered up, like the mouth of a miserable little child.

Then his hands, which had fallen back onto the bed, began an incessant, slow, regular movement, as if trying to pluck something off the sheets.

His wife, who had also begun to cry, was stammering: 'But no, this isn't serious. It's a bad attack, but you'll feel better tomorrow, you got tired yesterday, on that outing.'

Forestier's breathing was faster than that of a dog who's been running, so fast that it couldn't be counted, and so weak that it was barely audible.

He was still repeating: 'I don't want to die! Oh! My God... my God... my God... what's going to happen to me? I shall see nothing more... nothing more... ever again... Oh! My God!'

He was gazing in front of him at something invisible to the others, something hideous, the terror of which was reflected in his staring eyes. His two hands continued their dreadful and exhausting movement.

All at once he gave a sudden shudder which, as they watched, ran right down his body from head to foot, and he stammered: 'The cemetery... me... my God!'

And he did not speak again. He lay motionless, haggard and gasping for breath.

Time passed; the clock of a neighbouring convent struck noon. Duroy left the room to go and eat something. He returned an hour later. Mme Forestier refused to have anything. The sick man had not moved. He was still dragging his thin fingers over the sheet as if to pull it up towards his face.

The young woman was sitting in an armchair at the foot of the bed. Duroy took another beside her, and they waited in silence.

A nurse had come, sent by the doctor; she was dozing near the window.

Duroy himself was beginning to doze off when he had a feeling that something was happening. He opened his eyes just in time to see Forestier close his, like two lights that are going out. A little hiccup shook the dying man's throat, and two trickles of blood appeared at the corners of his mouth and ran down on to his nightshirt. His hands ceased their grotesque roaming. He had stopped breathing.

Realizing what had happened, his wife gave a kind of cry, and fell on her knees, sobbing into the sheet. Georges, surprised and frightened, automatically made the sign of the cross. The nurse had woken up and went over to the bed: 'That's it,' she said. And Duroy, his composure returning, murmured with a sigh of relief: 'It didn't take as long as I expected.'

Once the first shock was over and the first tears shed, they began to deal with all the tasks and various procedures that a death entails. Duroy was kept busy running errands until nightfall.

He was extremely hungry when he returned to the villa. Mme Forestier ate a little; then both of them settled down in the dead man's room to watch over the corpse.

Two candles were burning on the night table, beside a dish where a spray of mimosa lay in a little water, for they had been unable to find the requisite sprig of box.

The young woman and the young man were alone, beside this man who no longer existed. They sat without speaking, deep in thought, looking at him.

But Georges, who felt uneasy in the shadowy darkness surrounding this dead body, was staring at it doggedly. His eyes as well as his thoughts were drawn in fascination to this gaunt face which, in the uncertain light, appeared even more emaciated; and his gaze remained fixed there. That was his friend, there, Charles Forestier, who was talking to him only yesterday! What a strange and terrible thing it was, this complete cessation of a being! Oh! Now he remembered the words of Norbert de Varenne, who was haunted by the fear of death. 'No one ever comes back.' Millions, billions of beings would be born, more or less alike, with eyes, a nose, a mouth, a skull, and thoughts within it, without that particular one who was lying in that bed ever reappearing.

For a number of years he had lived, eaten, laughed, loved, hoped, like everyone else. And for him it was over, over for good. A life! A few days, and then nothing! You're born, you grow up, you're happy, you wait, then you die. Goodbye! Man or woman, you'll never return to this earth! And yet each of us bears within him the fierce, unrealizable longing for eternity, each of us is a kind of universe within the universe, and each of us soon vanishes completely into the dunghill of new organisms. Plants, animals, men, stars, worlds, everything quickens, then dies, in order to transform itself. And nothing ever returns, whether insect, man, or planet!

A confused, immense, crushing terror was weighing upon Duroy's soul, the terror of this infinite, inevitable nothingness, endlessly destroying each fleeting, miserable life. Already, he was bowing his head before its threat. He thought of flies, that live a few hours, of animals, that live a few days, of men who live a few years, of worlds that live a few centuries. So what difference was there between them? Only one or two more dawns, nothing else.

He turned away his eyes so as to look no longer at the corpse.

Mme Forestier, her head bent, also seemed to be absorbed in painful thoughts. Her fair hair looked so pretty round her sad face, that a sweet sensation like the presence of hope stirred in the young man's heart. Why grieve when he still had so many years ahead of him?

He began to gaze at her. Lost in meditation, she was unaware of him. He was thinking: 'Yes, this is the only good thing in life: love! To hold a woman you love in your arms! That is the ultimate in human happiness.'

What luck he'd had, the dead man, to find this intelligent,

charming companion. How had they met? How had she come to agree to marry this commonplace, impecunious young man? How had she eventually succeeded in making something of him?

Then he thought about all the hidden mysteries in people's lives. He recalled all the rumours about the Comte de Vaudrec, how it had been said that he had arranged her dowry and marriage. What would she do now? Whom would she marry? A deputy, as Mme de Marelle believed, or some fine young fellow with a future, a superior Forestier? Had she schemes, plans, definite ideas? How he would have loved to know! But why was he concerned about what she might do? He asked himself that question, and realized that his anxiety came from one of those elusive, confused, secret thoughts that we conceal from ourselves, and uncover only by probing deep into our hearts.

Yes, why should he himself not try to win her? How strong he would be, with her beside him, how formidable! How rapidly and far he would advance, and how surely!

And why should he not succeed? He was convinced that she was drawn to him, that what she felt for him was more than just liking, that it was one of those affections that arise between two people with similar natures, and that derive both from a mutual attraction and from a sort of wordless complicity. She knew him to be intelligent, determined, and tenacious; she could rely on him.

Had she not sent for him at this difficult time? And why had she done so? Ought he not to see in it some sort of choice, of admission, of signal? If she had thought of him, at the very moment when she was about to become a widow, might it not be, perhaps, that she had thought of the man who was to be her new companion and ally?

He was seized by an impatient urge to know the facts, to question her, to learn what her intentions were. He had to leave in two days' time, since he could not remain alone with that young woman in that house. So he must be quick; before going back to Paris, by employing tact and skill he must get her to reveal her plans, and not let her return home and perhaps, by yielding to another's pleas, commit herself irrevocably.

The silence in the room was profound; you could hear nothing but the metallic, regular beat of the clock's pendulum, ticking on the mantelpiece.

He whispered: 'You must be very tired?'

She replied: 'Yes, but most of all I feel terribly depressed.'

The sound of their voices astonished them, echoing strangely in that ill-omened room. And, rapidly, they glanced at the face of the dead man, as if expecting to see him move, to hear him speak to them, as he had been doing a few hours earlier.

Duroy went on: 'Oh, it's a dreadful blow for you, and such a complete change in your life, a real upheaval for your feelings and your whole existence.'

She gave a long sigh, without replying.

He continued: 'It's so sad for a young woman to find herself alone, as you are going to be.'

Then he fell silent. She said nothing. He stammered: 'In any case, you know the agreement we made. You can count on me in any way you wish. I am yours.'

She stretched out her hand to him, giving him one of those sad, sweet looks that stir us to the marrow of our bones: 'Thank you, you are so good, so very good. If I dared, and if there was something I could do for you, I too would say: You can count on me.'

He had grasped the proffered hand and kept it in his, squeezing it and longing desperately to kiss it. Finally deciding to do so, he raised it slowly to his mouth, for a long time holding the warm, delicate, febrile, perfumed skin against his lips.

Then, when he felt that this friendly caress was becoming too prolonged, he had the good sense to release the little hand. It returned gently to the lap of the young woman, who said gravely: 'Yes, I shall certainly be very lonely, but I'm going to try to be brave.'

He did not know how to make her understand that he would be happy, most happy, to become her husband in his turn. He certainly could not tell her that, now, at this moment, in this place, in the presence of this corpse; nevertheless he could, he believed, find one of those ambiguous, acceptable, complicated statements whose words have a hidden significance, and which can, by their calculated reservations, express everything you intend.

But the corpse inhibited him, the corpse that lay rigidly in front of them and that he could feel between them. Besides, for some time he had thought he could detect a suspicious odour in the stuffy air of the room, a fetid breath coming from those rotted lungs, the first carrion breath that the poor dead bodies lying on their beds exhale over the relatives keeping vigil beside them, a foul breath with which they soon fill the hollow box that is their coffin.

Duroy asked: 'Might we open the window a little? The air seems to me to be tainted.'

She said: 'Of course. I'd just noticed it too.'

He went to the window and opened it. All the scented freshness of the night came in, making the flames of the two bedside candles flicker. Just as it had done on the previous evening, the moon spread its calm, generous light over the white walls of the villas and the vast shining expanse of the sea. Duroy, breathing deeply, unexpectedly felt a great surge of hope, as if he were being buoyed up by the tremulous approach of happiness.

He turned round: 'Come and breathe some fresh air,' he said. 'It's a beautiful night.'

She came calmly over and leant on the sill beside him.

Then, in a low voice, he murmured: 'Listen to me, and please don't misunderstand what I say. Above all, don't be angry with me for speaking of such a matter at a moment like this; but I'll be leaving you the day after tomorrow, and when you return to Paris it might be too late. So... I'm just a poor devil with no money who still has his career to make, as you know. But I have the will, I believe I'm quite intelligent, and I've made a beginning, a good beginning. With a man who's made it you know what you're getting; with a man who's starting out you don't know where he'll go. So much the worse, or so much the better. To come to the point—I once told you, in your home, that my dearest wish would have been to marry a woman like you. Today, I am telling you again that that is my wish. Don't answer. Let me go on. I am not asking you to marry me. The place and the time would make such a proposal revolting. It's just that I do not want you to be unaware that a word from you can make me happy, that you can make of me either a devoted friend or a husband, as you prefer, that my heart and my whole self are yours. I do not want you to answer me now; nor do I want us to speak of this again, here. When we meet again, in Paris, you can let me know what you have decided. Not another word until then, do you agree?'

He had said this without looking at her, as if he were scattering his words into the night before him. And she seemed not to have heard, so motionless had she remained, she too gazing out, with eyes that were fixed and vague, at the broad pale landscape lit up by the moon.

For a long time they continued there side by side, elbow by elbow, silent and thoughtful.

Then, whispering: 'It's a little cold,' she turned and came back towards the bed. He followed her.

As he approached, he realized that Forestier actually was beginning to smell; he moved his chair away, for he could not have stood that odour of decay for long. He said: 'He must be put in his coffin in the morning.'

She replied: 'Yes, yes, of course; the carpenter's coming about eight.'

And, when Duroy sighed: 'Poor fellow!' she in her turn gave a long sigh of heart-broken resignation.

They were looking at him less often now, already used to the idea of this death, beginning to accept, in their minds, this disappearance, which only a short while before had shocked and angered them, they who were mortal also.

They said no more, but continued to keep vigil in the traditional way, without falling asleep. But, towards midnight, Duroy was the first to doze off. When he awoke, he saw that Mme Forestier was also dozing, and, settling himself more comfortably, he closed his eyes again, grumbling: 'It's a hell of a lot more comfortable in a bed!'

A sudden noise made him start. The nurse was entering the room. It was broad daylight. The young woman, in the armchair opposite him, seemed as surprised as he was. She was rather pale, but still pretty, fresh, pleasing, in spite of having spent the night sitting up.

Then, glancing at the corpse, Duroy gave a shudder, crying: 'Oh! His beard!' In a few hours the beard had grown, on that decaying flesh, as much as it would have grown in a few days on the face of a living man. And they were shocked and bewildered by this evidence of life still persisting on the corpse, as if they were witnessing some horrifying trick of nature, some supernatural intimation of resurrection, one of those abnormal, terrifying things that overwhelm and confound the mind.

They both went to rest until eleven. Then they put Charles in his coffin, and immediately felt relieved and soothed. They sat down opposite one another for lunch with an eager readiness to talk of comforting, more cheerful subjects, to get back into life, now that they had finished dealing with death.

Through the window, which stood wide open, came the sweet warmth of spring, bringing with it the perfumed breath of the carnations flowering in the bed in front of the door.

Mme Forestier suggested that they take a turn together in the garden, and they began to walk slowly around the little lawn, delightedly breathing in the mild air that was full of the fragrance of pine and eucalyptus. And, suddenly, she spoke to him, without turning her head towards him, just as he had done during the night, in the room up there. She spoke slowly, in a quiet, grave voice:

'Listen, my dear; I've already thought carefully... about what you proposed, and I don't want to let you leave without giving you some kind of reply. I shall not, however, say either yes or no. We'll wait, we'll see what happens, we'll get to know each other better. For your part, think about it carefully. Don't let yourself be carried away by a superficial attraction. But, if I speak to you about this even before my poor Charles is in his grave, it's because it's important, after what you said to me, that you should really understand what kind of person I am, so that you may not continue to cherish the hope you spoke of, if your... character... is such that you cannot understand me and give me your support.

'You must understand me. Marriage, for me, is not a bond, but a partnership. I expect to be free, completely free, in what I do, whom I see, where I go, always. I could not tolerate either supervision, or jealousy, or any discussion of my behaviour. I would of course under-take never to compromise the name of the man I had married, never to make him seem hateful or ridiculous. But that man would also have to see me as an equal, an ally, not as an inferior or an obedient, submissive wife. I know my ideas are not shared by everyone, but I shan't change them. So that's the way it is.

'I'll also add: Don't answer me, it would be pointless, and unseemly. We shall see each other again, and we may perhaps speak again about all this, later. Why don't you go out for a walk now. As for me, I'm going back to him. I'll see you this evening.'

He gave her hand a lingering kiss, and left without saying a word.

In the evening, they met only at dinner time. Afterwards they went up to their rooms, for they were both utterly exhausted.

The next morning Charles Forestier was buried without any pomp, in the cemetery at Cannes. Georges Duroy decided to catch the Paris express that stops at one-thirty.

Mme Forestier went with him to the station. They walked calmly up and down the platform, talking of indifferent matters, as they waited for the time of departure. The train, a very short one, drew up; it was a genuine express, with only five carriages.

The journalist chose his seat, then got out again to chat a little longer with her, feeling unexpectedly overcome with sadness and regret and an intense sense of loss at leaving her, as if he were about to lose her for ever.

A railway employee shouted: 'All aboard for Marseilles, Lyons, Paris!' Duroy climbed up, then leant on the window-sill to say a few more words to her. The engine whistled and the train gently began to move. The young man, leaning out of the carriage, gazed at the young woman standing motionless on the platform, following him with her eyes. And suddenly, when she was almost out of sight, he threw her a kiss with both hands. She returned it hesitantly, with a more discreet gesture, a mere suggestion of a kiss.

PART TWO

CHAPTER 1

Georges Duroy had resumed all his old habits.

Now installed in the little ground-floor apartment of the Rue de Constantinople, he was leading a quiet life, as befitted a man preparing for a new existence. His relations with Mme de Marelle had even assumed a conjugal air, as if he were practising, in advance, for the approaching event; and his mistress, often amazed at the tranquil regularity of their union, would say laughingly: 'You're even more of a home body than my husband, it wasn't worth the bother of changing.'

Mme Forestier had not returned, she was still in Cannes. He received a letter from her, telling him she would not be back before the middle of April, and making no reference to their farewells. He waited. He was now quite determined to go to any lengths to marry her, if she seemed hesitant. But he had confidence in his luck, confidence in that seductive power he knew he possessed, a vague but irresistible power to which every woman responded.

A brief note informed him that the decisive moment was at hand.

I'm in Paris. Come and see me.
   Madeleine Forestier.

Nothing more. It arrived by the nine a.m. post. By three o'clock the same day he was at her door. She stretched out both her hands to him, smiling her pretty, friendly smile; and for a few seconds they looked deep into one another's eyes.

She murmured: 'How good it was of you to come down there in those terrible circumstances!'

He replied: 'I would have done anything you told me to do.'

And they sat down. She asked for news of the Walters, of all the journalists, and of the newspaper. She thought about the paper often, she said.

'I miss it badly, really badly. I had become a journalist in spirit. Well, what can you expect, I love the profession.'

Then she fell silent. He thought he understood, he thought he could see a kind of invitation in her smile, in her tone of voice, in her very words; and although he had promised himself not to rush things, he stammered:

'Well then... why... why not get back into it again... into journalism... under... under the name of Duroy?'

Abruptly, she grew serious again, and, putting her hand on his arm, said softly: 'Don't let's talk about that yet.'

But he sensed that she was accepting, and, falling to his knees, he began to kiss her hands passionately, stammering over and over again: 'Thank you, thank you, oh, how I love you!'

She stood up. He did likewise, and saw that she was extremely pale. Then he realized that she found him attractive, had done so, perhaps, for a long time; and as they were face to face, he took her in his arms, and gravely gave her a long, tender kiss on the forehead.

When she had freed herself, slipping from his embrace, she went on in a serious tone: 'Listen, Georges, I haven't yet decided anything. However it's possible that was a "yes". But, you must promise me absolute secrecy until I give you leave.'

He made the promise and departed, his heart overflowing with happiness.

From then on he behaved with great circumspection during his visits to her, not seeking a more definite acceptance, for she had a way of talking about the future, of saying 'later on', of making plans in which their two existences were intermingled, that continually gave him an answer, in a better, more subtle manner than would a formal acceptance.

Duroy worked hard and spent little, trying to save up some money so as not to be penniless when the time came for his marriage; he became as miserly as he had formerly been extravagant.

The summer passed, and then the autumn, without anyone having the slightest suspicion, for they met rarely, and in the most natural way possible.

One evening Madeleine said to him, looking him straight in the eye: 'You haven't told Mme de Marelle of our plans?'

'No, my dear. Having promised you to keep it a secret, I haven't breathed a word to a soul.'

'Well, it's time to let her know. I myself will tell the Walters. You'll do it this week, won't you?'

He had blushed. 'Yes, tomorrow.'

She gently averted her eyes, as if to avoid seeing his embarrassment, and continued: 'If you like, we could get married at the beginning of May. That would be very suitable.'

'It gives me the greatest happiness to obey you.'

'May the 10th, which is a Saturday,* would please me very much, because it's my birthday.'

'May the 10th it is.'

'Your parents live near Rouen, don't they? At least that's what you told me.'

'Yes, near Rouen, in Canteleu.'

'What do they do?'

'They... they have a modest income.'

'Ah! I'd love to meet them.'

He hesitated, completely at a loss. 'But, the thing is... they're...' Then he went on, with manly decisiveness: 'My dear, they're peasants, tavern-keepers, who bled themselves white to get me educated. I'm not ashamed of them myself, but their... simplicity... their lack of refinement might perhaps embarrass you.'

She gave an enchanting smile, that lit up her face with a gentle goodness.

'No, I shall like them very much. We'll go and see them. I want to. I'll talk of this later. I too am the child of humble people... but I've lost mine, my parents are dead. I no longer have anybody in the whole world'—she gave him her hand and added—'except you.'

He felt himself moved, stirred, won over, to a degree he had never before experienced with any woman.

'I've thought of something else,' she said, 'but it's a bit difficult to explain.'

He asked: 'What is it?'

'Well, you see, Georges, I'm just like other women, I've my little weaknesses, my foibles, I love things that look and sound impressive. I'd have adored to have a title. Might you not be able—to mark the occasion of our marriage—to get yourself a bit of a title?'

She, in her turn, had blushed, as if she had suggested something faintly discreditable.

He replied simply: 'I've often thought of it, but I don't think it would be easy.'

'Why not?'

He began to laugh. 'Because I'm afraid of looking ridiculous.'

She shrugged. 'No, not at all, not at all. Everybody does it and nobody laughs at it. Divide your name in two: "Du Roy". That sounds very good.'

He replied immediately, like an expert on such matters: 'No, that won't do. It's too simple a way, too common, too well-known. I myself had thought of taking the name of the place I come from, at first as a pseudonym, then add it—very gradually—to my name, and then, later, even break my name in two as you suggested.'

She enquired: 'You come from Canteleu?'

'Yes.'

But she hesitated. 'No. I don't like the ending. Let's see, couldn't we change that word a bit... Canteleu?'

She had picked up a pen from the table and was scribbling names, studying how they looked. Suddenly she exclaimed: 'Wait, wait, what about this.'

And she handed him a sheet of paper on which he read: 'Madame Duroy de Cantel.'

He considered for a few seconds, then gravely announced: 'Yes, that's very good.'

And she, delighted, kept repeating: 'Duroy de Cantel, Duroy de Cantel, Mme Duroy de Cantel. It's very good, very!'

She added, with great conviction: 'You'll see how easy it is to get everybody to accept it. But you mustn't miss your chance. It would be too late afterwards. From tomorrow you'll sign your reports D. de Cantel, and your gossip items Duroy pure and simple. In journalism people do it all the time, and no one will be surprised to see you using a pseudonym. At the time of our marriage we can modify it a little more, and tell our friends that you had given up your "du" out of modesty, in view of your position, or even not say anything at all. What's your father's first name?'

'Alexandre.'

Two or three times she murmured 'Alexandre, Alexandre,' listening to the resonance of the syllables, then she wrote on a completely clean sheet of paper:

'Monsieur and Madame Alexandre du Roy de Cantel have the honour to inform you of the marriage of their son, Monsieur Georges du Roy de Cantel, to Madame Madeleine Forestier.'

Thrilled with the effect of what she had written, she studied it from a distance, and declared: 'If you just put your mind to it, you can do anything you want.'

When he was outside in the street, fully determined to call himself 'du Roy' or even 'du Roy de Cantel' from then on, it seemed to him that he had just acquired a new importance. He walked along more jauntily, his head higher, his moustache bolder, the way a gentleman should walk. He felt a kind of joyful urge to tell passers-by: 'My name is du Roy de Cantel.'

But hardly was he back home, than he was overcome with anxiety at the thought of Mme de Marelle, and he wrote to her immediately, asking for a meeting the following day.

'It's going to be very difficult,' he thought. 'I'm in for a first-class tongue-lashing.'

Then, with that innate heedlessness that made him ignore the disagreeable things in life, he pushed it aside and settled down to writing a playful article on the new taxes that should be introduced to balance the budget. The upper classes would be taxed a hundred francs per annum for a name with 'de' in it, while the tax on titles would range from five hundred francs for Baron to five thousand francs for Prince. He signed it: D. de Cantel.

The next morning he received an 'express' from his mistress stating that she would come at one o'clock.

He waited for her a little feverishly, resolved, however, to be blunt, to tell her everything straight away, then, when the first shock had passed, to present her with clever arguments proving that he could not remain a bachelor indefinitely, and that as M. de Marelle seemed determined to stay alive, he had had to think of someone else to be his lawful companion.

But all the same, he felt anxious. When he heard the bell ring, his heart began to pound.

She threw herself into his arms. 'Hallo, Bel-Ami.' Then, finding his embrace lacked warmth, she looked at him, and asked:

'What's the matter?'

'Sit down', he said. 'We must have a serious talk.'

She sat down without removing her hat, simply raising her veil from her forehead, and waited.

He had lowered his eyes; he was working out what to say first. In a slow voice, he began: 'My dear, as you can see, I feel very upset, very sad and very embarrassed by what I have to confess to you. I love you very much, I truly love you from the bottom of my heart, so that the fear of hurting you distresses me even more than what I'm actually going to tell you.'

Turning white, and feeling herself start to tremble, she stammered: 'What is it? Tell me quickly!'

He declared in a sad but resolute tone, with that feigned dejection people assume to announce bad news they rejoice over: 'I'm getting married.'

She gave a sigh as if she were about to faint, an anguished sigh that came from deep down in her breast, then she began to choke, gasping so for breath that she could not speak.

Seeing that she was saying nothing, he went on: 'You can have no idea how much I've suffered in making this decision. But I've neither position nor money. I'm entirely alone, lost in Paris. I needed someone at my side, someone who above all will give me advice, comfort and support. It's a partner, an ally, that I've been looking for, and that's what I've found!'

He stopped, waiting for her to reply, expecting raging anger, violence, abuse.

She had placed one hand on her heart as if to calm it, and her breath was still coming in painful, heaving gasps that lifted her breasts and made her head jerk spasmodically.

He took the hand resting on the arm of the chair, but she abruptly pulled it away. Then, as though in a stupor, she murmured: 'Oh!... My God...'

He knelt down in front of her, but without daring to touch her, and, more moved by this silence than he would have been by passionate outbursts, he stammered: 'Clo, my little Clo, think carefully about my situation, think carefully about what I am. Oh, if I'd been able to marry you, Clo, how happy I'd have been! But you're married. What could I do? Consider, please consider! I need to establish myself in society, and I can't do that as long as I haven't a home. If you only knew... There've been moments when I've wanted to kill your husband...'

His voice as he spoke was gentle, husky, seductive, a voice that fell like music upon the ear.

He watched as, in his mistress's staring eyes, two tears slowly grew larger, then ran down her cheeks, while two others were already forming on the edge of her lids.

He whispered: 'Oh! Don't cry, Clo, don't cry, I beg you. You're breaking my heart.'

So then she made an effort, a tremendous effort to behave with dignity and pride; and she asked, in that tremulous voice of a woman on the verge of tears: 'Who is it?'

He hesitated for a moment, then, realizing that he had no choice: 'Madeleine Forestier.'

A shudder ran through Mme de Marelle's whole body, then she sat absolutely silent, so lost in thought that she seemed to have forgotten he was kneeling at her feet.

And, in her eyes, two transparent drops continued to form, to fall, and to reform again.

She stood up. Duroy sensed that she was going to leave without saying a word, without reproach or forgiveness; and he felt hurt, humiliated, to the depths of his soul. In an attempt to stop her, he put his arms round the skirt of her dress, embracing, through the fabric, her shapely legs which stiffened in resistance.

He begged her: 'Please, please, don't leave like this.'

Then she looked down at him, she looked down with that tearful, despairing look—so charming and so sad—that reveals all the pain in a woman's heart, and stammered: "I've nothing... nothing to say... there's nothing... nothing I can do... You're right... you've... you've chosen exactly what you needed...'

And, stepping back to free herself, she went out of the room, without his trying to detain her any longer.

Left alone, he got to his feet, feeling as dazed as if he had been hit on the head; then, making the best of it, he muttered: 'Oh well, it could have been worse! It's over, and without any fuss. That suits me.' And, relieved of a great burden, feeling suddenly free, liberated, comfortable with his new life, he began pounding the wall with great blows of his fist, as if intoxicated with his success and strength, as if he had been fighting against Destiny.

When Mme Forestier asked him: 'Have you told Mme de Marelle?' he replied calmly: 'Of course...'

Her clear eyes gazed at him searchingly.

'And she wasn't upset?'

'No, not at all. On the contrary, she thought it a good idea.'

The news was soon common knowledge. Some expressed

astonishment, others claimed to have foreseen it, while yet others smiled, letting it be understood that it did not surprise them.

The young man, who now signed his reports D. de Cantel, his gossip column Duroy, and du Roy for the political articles that he was beginning occasionally to produce, spent half his time with his fiancée who treated him with a sisterly familiarity which nevertheless comprised a genuine, though concealed, affection, a kind of desire she hid as though it were a weakness. She had decided that the marriage would take place privately, with only the witnesses present, and that they would leave that very evening for Rouen. The following morning they would go to receive the congratulations of the journalist's elderly parents, with whom they were to spend a few days. Duroy had done his best to make her abandon this plan, but, meeting with no success, he had finally given way.

Therefore, on the 10th of May, the newly married couple, having deemed a religious ceremony pointless since they had not invited anyone, went home to finish their packing after a brief trip to the town hall, and then, from the Gare Saint Lazare, caught the six o'clock evening train, which carried them off towards Normandy.

They had barely exchanged twenty words up to the moment of finding themselves alone in the carriage. As soon as they felt the train begin to move, they looked at one another and began laughing, to disguise a certain unease that they did not want to show.

The train travelled slowly through the long station at Les Batignolles, then crossed the desolate plain which stretches from the fortifications* to the Seine. From time to time Duroy and his wife exchanged a few meaningless words, then turned back to the window.

When they crossed the bridge at Asnières, they were filled with elation by the sight of the river thronged with boats, anglers, and people rowing. The sun, a powerful May sun, cast its slanting rays over the boats and over the calm river which lay motionless, without currents or eddies, solidified by the heat and brightness of the dying day. In the middle of the river, a sailing boat had unfurled a huge triangle of white canvas over either side, to catch the smallest breath of a breeze. It looked like a giant bird about to fly away.

Duroy murmured: 'I adore the outskirts of Paris, I can remember meals of fried fish that were the best in my whole life.'

She replied: 'And the boats! It's so lovely to glide over the water as the sun is setting!'

Then, falling silent, as if they did not dare continue these revelations about the past, they sat without speaking, already, perhaps, savouring the poetry of regret.

Duroy, opposite his wife, took her hand and kissed it, slowly.

'After we come back,' he said, "we'll go to Chatou* for dinner sometimes.'

She murmured: 'We'll have so much to do!' in a tone which seemed to mean: 'We'll have to put duty before pleasure!'

He was still holding her hand, wondering anxiously how to make the transition to more intimate caresses. The inexperience of a young girl would not have troubled him in the same way, but the lively, subtle intelligence that he sensed in Madeleine disconcerted him. He was afraid of seeming inept in her eyes, too timid or too rough, too slow or too fast. He kept giving her hand little squeezes, but without eliciting any response. He said:

'It seems really funny that you're my wife.'

She seemed surprised. 'Why?'

'I don't know. It just seems funny. I want to kiss you, and I'm amazed that I should have that right.'

Calmly she offered him her cheek, which he kissed as he would have kissed the cheek of a sister.

He went on: 'The first time I saw you—you know, at that dinner Forestier invited me to—I thought: "God!, if only I could find a woman like that." Well! I've done it. I've got her.'

She said softly: 'That's nice.' And she gave him a straight, penetrating look, her eyes smiling as usual.

He thought: 'I'm being too distant. I'm being stupid. I ought to be moving faster than this.' And he asked: 'So how did you meet Forestier?'

She replied, mockingly provocative: 'Are we going to Rouen to talk about him?'

He blushed: 'I'm an idiot. You make me very nervous.'

She was delighted: 'Who, me? Surely not! Why should I?'

He had sat down beside her, very close. She exclaimed: 'Oh! A stag!'

The train was travelling through the forest of Saint-Germain,* and she had seen a frightened deer spring clear across a path. Duroy, who had bent forward while she was looking through the open window, gave the hair on her neck a prolonged kiss, a lover's kiss.

For a few moments she remained motionless, then, raising her head: 'Stop it, you're tickling me.' But he did not stop, gently moving his curly moustache over the white flesh in a tantalizing, protracted caress.

She roused herself: 'Do stop it.'

He had seized her head with his right hand which he had slipped round her, and was turning her towards him. Then he fell upon her mouth like a sparrow-hawk on its prey.

She was struggling and pushing him away, attempting to free herself. Finally succeeding, she repeated: 'Do please stop.'

He no longer listened to her, but clasped her in his arms, kissing her with avid, trembling lips, trying to push her down onto the carriage cushions.

With a great effort she freed herself and, standing up quickly: 'Oh, really, Georges, stop that. After all, we're not children any more, we can perfectly well wait till Rouen.'

Very red in the face, he remained in his seat, chilled by these reasonable words; then, having regained some self-possession: 'Right, I'll wait,' he said cheerfully, 'but I shan't be capable of stringing twenty words together until we get there. And remember, we're only now passing through Poissy.'*

'I'll do the talking,' she said. And she sat down quietly at his side.

She spoke, in great detail, of what they would do on their return. They were going to keep the apartment that she had occupied with her first husband, and Duroy would also inherit Forestier's responsibilities and salary at *La Vie française*.

Moreover, Madeleine herself, before their marriage, had settled all the financial details of their union as confidently as any businessman. The settlement stipulated that they each administer their separate properties, and every eventuality was foreseen: death, divorce, the birth of one or several children. Duroy claimed to be contributing four thousand francs, but of this amount fifteen hundred were borrowed. The remainder came from savings made during the year, in expectation of the marriage. The young woman brought forty thousand francs that Forestier, she said, had left her.

She returned to the subject of Forestier, citing him as an example:

'He was very thrifty, very steady and hardworking. He would soon have made a lot of money.'

Duroy was no longer listening; his mind was on other matters.

She would stop, from time to time, to pursue some private fancy, then begin again: 'Three or four years from now, you may easily be earning thirty to forty thousand a year. That's what Charles would have made, if he'd lived.'

Georges was beginning to tire of being lectured, and replied: 'I didn't think we were going to Rouen to talk about him.'

She gave him a little pat on the cheek: 'I'm in the wrong, I'll admit it.' She laughed.

He was making a show of keeping his hands on his knees, like a good little boy.

'You look so silly, like that,' she remarked.

He replied: 'It's my role, as, indeed, you've just reminded me, and I won't depart from it again.'

'Why?' she asked.

'Because you're the person responsible for managing the household, and even for managing me. Indeed, as a widow, that's your responsibility!'

Astonished, she enquired: 'What exactly do you mean?'

'That you, with your experience, must dispel my ignorance, and with your practical knowledge of marriage enlighten my bachelor's innocence—so there!'

'That's a bit much!' she exclaimed.

He answered: 'That's the way it is. I myself don't know women, whereas you, being a widow, do know men—so there! You're the one who's going to instruct me... tonight... and you can even start right away, if you want to... so there!'

Highly amused, she cried: 'Oh, well now, really, if you're counting on me for that!'

He replied, in the tone of a schoolboy reciting his lesson: 'Oh yes... I'm counting on you. I'm even counting on you to give me a solid course of instruction... in twenty lessons... ten for the elementary stuff... reading and grammar... ten for more advanced subjects and refinements of style... I myself don't know anything... So there!'

Finding this very entertaining, she exclaimed, using the familiar 'tu': 'What an idiot you are.'

He went on: 'Since you've started calling me "tu", I shall follow your example, and tell you, my love, that I adore you more every second, and I'm beginning to find Rouen a long way off!'

He was speaking, now, with an actor's intonations and comic grimaces; this amused Madeleine, who was accustomed to the manners and humour of the bohemian world of writers.

She gave him a sidelong glance, finding him altogether delightful, feeling the urge we have to eat a fruit straight from the tree, while common sense tells us to wait until dinner, and eat it at the proper time.

So then she said, blushing faintly at the thoughts running through her head: 'My little student, trust to my experience, my broad experience. Kisses in a railway carriage are no good. They turn sour.'

Then she blushed even more, murmuring: 'You should never harvest unripe corn.'

He sniggered, excited by the ambiguity of the remarks slipping out of that pretty mouth; and, making the sign of the cross, he moved his lips as if mumbling a prayer, and announced: 'I've just put myself under the protection of St Anthony, patron saint of temptation. I'm made of stone, now.'

Night was falling softly, enveloping the vast plain stretching over to the right in translucent shadows, like a gauzy mourning veil. The train was travelling along the Seine, and the young people began watching as, on the river that unwound beside the track like a broad ribbon of burnished metal, glints of red appeared, patches fallen from a sky that the departing sun had daubed with tones of purple and flame. These glimmers were gradually fading, turning a deeper shade, growing dark and sad. The plain was sinking into blackness with an ominous shudder, that shudder of death which every twilight visits upon the earth.

Through the open window, the melancholy of evening permeated the souls of the newly weds, who, for all their recent high spirits, were now silent. They had moved closer to one another to watch the dying moments of the day, this beautiful bright May day. At Mantes,* the tiny oil lamp had been lit; it cast its yellow, flickering light over the grey cloth of the head-rests. Duroy had his arm round his wife and was holding her close. The intense desire he had just felt was turning to tenderness, a languid tenderness, a soft yearning for small comforting caresses, the kind of caresses with which you soothe a child.

He murmured very softly: 'I'm going to love you very much, my little Made.'

The gentleness of this voice moved the young woman, sending a quick tremor though her flesh, and she gave him her mouth, bending over him, for he had rested his head on the warm cushion of her breasts.

A very long kiss, silent and deep, was followed by a start, a sudden, frenzied embrace, a short, breathless struggle and a violent, clumsy coupling. Then they remained in each other's arms, both a little disappointed, weary and still full of tenderness, until the train whistle announced the approach of the next station.

Smoothing the tousled hair on her temples with her finger tips, she declared: 'That was very silly. We're behaving like kids.'

But he was kissing her hands, moving from one to the other with feverish speed, and he replied: 'I adore you, my little Made.'

Until Rouen they sat almost motionless, cheek to cheek, their eyes on the dark window where the lights of passing houses were sometimes to be seen; they were sunk in dreams, happy to be so close to one another, in the ever-growing expectation of a more intimate, freer embrace.

They put up at an hotel whose windows overlooked the waterfront, and went to bed after a very quick bite of supper.

The chamber maid woke them the next morning, just after eight o'clock had struck.

When they had drunk the cups of tea left on the night table, Duroy looked at his wife, then suddenly, with the joyful impulse of a happy man who has just found a treasure, he grasped her in his arms, stammering: 'My little Made, I feel so much love for you, so much... so much...' With that trusting, contented smile of hers she murmured, as she returned his kiss: 'And I for you... I think...'

But he was still anxious about that visit to his parents. He had already warned his wife several times; he had prepared her, lectured her. He felt he should do so again.

'They're peasants, you know, real country peasants, not out of a comic opera.'

She was laughing: 'But I know that, you've told me often enough. Come on, get up and let me get up as well.'

He jumped out of bed, and, as he put on his socks: 'We'll be very uncomfortable in the house, very uncomfortable. There's only an old pallet bed in my room. They've never heard of bed-springs, in Canteleu.'

She seemed delighted. 'All the better. It will be lovely to sleep badly... with... with you... and be woken up by the cocks crowing.'

She had put on her negligé, a commodious garment made of white flannel, that Duroy instantly recognized. He found the sight of it disagreeable. Why? His wife possessed, as he knew very well, a full dozen of these early morning garments. She couldn't just destroy her trousseau and buy a new one, could she? No matter, he would have preferred that her intimate garments, those she wore at night, for love, were not the same as with the other one. He felt that the velvety, warm cloth must have preserved something of its contact with Forestier.

And he walked over to the window, lighting a cigarette.

The sight of the port, of the broad river filled with slender-masted vessels and squat steamers which derricks were very noisily unloading onto the quay, stirred him, although he had long been familiar with it. He exclaimed:

'My God! It's beautiful!'

Madeleine hurried over, put both hands on one of her husband's shoulders and, leaning towards him in a movement of loving abandon, was filled with delight and emotion. She kept repeating: 'Oh! How lovely! How lovely! I didn't know there would be as many ships as that!'

They left an hour later, for they were to lunch with the old people, who had been forewarned some days before. They made the journey in an open, rusty carriage with rattling metalwork. They followed a long, rather ugly boulevard, crossed fields through which a river ran, then began to climb the hill. Madeleine, who was tired, had dozed off under the penetrating caress of the sun, which was warming her deliciously where she sat at the very back of the ancient vehicle, as if she were resting in a tepid bath of light and country air.

Her husband woke her up: 'Look,' he said.

They had just halted two thirds of the way up, at a spot famous for the view, to which every tourist is taken.

They were looking down over the immense valley, wide and long, across which the limpid river flowed in sweeping, shallow curves. They could see it approaching from the distance, dotted with numerous islands and swinging round before it crossed through

Rouen. Then the city appeared on the right bank, lightly veiled by the morning mist, with flashes of sunlight glinting on its roofs, and its thousand airy belfries, pointed or squat, delicate and highly wrought like giant jewels, its square or round towers crowned with heraldic decorations, its belfries and its turrets, the throng of Gothic church-tops, dominated by the cathedral's narrow spire, an amazing needle of bronze, ugly, bizarre, and excessive, the tallest in the world.

But opposite, on the other side of the river, rose up the thin, round chimneys, bulging out at the top, of the factories of the vast suburb of Saint-Sever. They were more numerous than their siblings the belfries, and their tall brick columns appeared even in distant fields, puffing out into the blue sky their black, coal-laden breath.

And, tallest of them all, as tall as the Cheops pyramid,* second highest of the man-made peaks and almost the equal of her proud counterpart the cathedral spire, the great flaming chimney of La Foudre* seemed to be the queen of the labouring, smoky horde of factories, just as her neighbour was the queen of the pointed throng of sacred monuments.

Over beyond, behind the industrial part of the city, stretched a forest of pine trees; and the Seine, after passing between the two towns, continued on its way, skirting a large, undulating hillside wooded along the top, with occasional bare patches of chalky ground showing like white bones, then the river disappeared into the horizon after tracing another long, rounded curve. They could see ships moving up and down the river, drawn by steam boats the size of flies, belching forth a viscous smoke. There were islands spread out along the water, always either lined up one immediately behind the next, or else leaving a large gap in between, like the unevenly strung beads of a verdant rosary.

The cab driver waited until the travellers had finished enthusing. He knew, from experience, how long the admiration of every kind of tourist would last.

But when he set off again, Duroy suddenly noticed, at a distance of several hundred metres, two old people approaching, and he jumped out of the vehicle, crying: 'It's them. I recognize them.'

Two peasants, a man and a woman, were walking along with an irregular, lurching gait, their shoulders occasionally bumping. The man was short, stocky, red-faced, and slightly pot-bellied, still vigorous despite his age. The woman was tall, dried-up, bent and sad, the typical farm woman-of-all-work, who has laboured since childhood and never laughed, while her husband would be drinking and swapping jokes with his customers.

Madeleine, who also had got down from the carriage, watched with an aching heart, with a sadness that she had not foreseen, as these two pitiful creatures drew near. They did not recognize their son in this fine gentleman, and would never have guessed that this fine lady wearing a light-coloured dress was their daughter-in-law.

They were walking fast, not talking, to meet their son, never sparing a glance for these city folk who were being followed by a carriage.

They were going past. Georges called out laughingly: 'Morning to you, old Duroy.'

Both of them stopped dead, at first amazed, then struck dumb with astonishment. The old woman recovered first, and, without moving, stuttered: 'It ain't you, son?'

The young man replied: 'Yes, it's me, mother Duroy!' And striding up to her, he gave her a son's hearty kiss on both of her cheeks. Then he rubbed his face against his father's, the latter having removed his cap, which was made in the Rouen style, of black silk and very tall, like those worn by cattle merchants.

Then Georges announced: 'This is my wife.' And the rustic pair gazed at Madeleine. They gazed at her the way people gaze at a curiosity, with an uneasy fear, tinged, in the father's case, with a sort of satisfied approval, and, in the mother's, with jealous hostility.

The man, whose natural high spirits were enhanced by being steeped in sweet cider and alcohol, felt emboldened to ask, with a mischievous gleam in the corner of his eye: 'All right if I gives her a kiss?'

The son replied: 'Good Lord, yes!' And Madeleine, ill at ease, offered both cheeks to the noisy salutes of the old man, who wiped his lips with the back of his hand, afterwards. The old woman, in her turn, kissed her daughter-in-law with cold reserve. No, this was not the daughter-in-law of her dreams, the plump, fresh farm girl, red as an apple and round as a brood mare. She looked like a tart, this lady did, with her furbelows and her musk. For the old woman, every scent was musk.

And they set off again, following the cab carrying the newly weds' trunk. The old man took his son's arm, holding him back, and enquired with interest:

'So, how's business? Doin' nicely?'

'Yes, very nicely.'

'Well, fine, good. Tell me, your wife, she well fixed?'

Georges replied: 'Forty thousand francs.'

His father gave a little whistle of admiration and could only mutter: 'Christ!' he was so impressed by the sum. Then, with profound conviction, he added: 'By God, but she's a fine-looking woman.' For he found her very much to his taste. And he was said to have had an eye for the ladies, in the old days.

Madeleine and the mother were walking side by side, not saying a word. The two men joined them.

They were coming to the village, a little village that bordered the road, with ten houses on either side, some solid and brick-built, others dilapidated farm structures made of clay, the former with slate roofs, the latter thatched. Old Duroy's bar, *A la Belle Vue*, a small, poky building composed of a ground floor and a garret, stood at the approach to the village, on the left. A pine branch tacked over the door indicated, in the old style, that thirsty people would find a welcome there.

The meal had been laid in the bar, on two tables that had been pushed together and covered with two large napkins. A neighbour who had come to help serve gave a low curtsy on seeing so handsome a lady, then, recognizing Georges, she exclaimed: 'Lord, be it you, lad?'

He replied cheerfully: 'Yes, it's me, Mother Brulin!'

And he promptly kissed her, as he had kissed his father and mother.

Then he turned to his wife: 'Come into our room, you can take off your hat.'

He took her through the door on the right into an entirely white room with a tiled floor, whitewashed walls and a bed with cotton curtains. A crucifix above a stoup for holy water, and two coloured pictures representing Paul and Virginie* under a blue palm tree, and Napoleon I on a yellow horse,* were the only ornaments in that clean and desolate room.

As soon as they were alone, he kissed Madeleine. 'Hallo, Made. I'm pleased to see the old folks again. When you're in Paris, you don't think of them, and then when you're back with them it's actually very nice.'

But his father was shouting and banging on the wall with his fist: 'Come on, come on, soup's up.' And they had to take their seats at the table.

It was a long, countrified meal consisting of a series of ill-assorted dishes, sausages served after a leg of lamb, an omelette after the sausages. Old Duroy, filled with good cheer by cider and several glasses of wine, let loose a stream of his best jokes, those that he saved for special occasions, coarse, bawdy stories involving, he claimed, friends of his. Georges, who had heard them all, laughed nevertheless, intoxicated by his native air, gripped afresh by his innate love of the area, of the familiar places of his childhood, by all the sensations, returning memories, and rediscovered things of the past, tiny little things, the knife-mark on a door frame, a wobbly chair that recalled a trivial event, earthy smells, the strong scent of resin and trees from the nearby forest, the redolence of the house, of the brook, of the dunghill.

Georges's old mother, still stern-faced and sombre, said nothing, eyeing her daughter-in-law with a heart full of fierce hostility, the hostility of an old working woman, an old peasant with worn fingers and limbs deformed by harsh labour, towards this city woman, who aroused in her a feeling of revulsion for this cursed, damned, tainted being who was made for idleness and sin. She continually got up to fetch dishes and to pour into their glasses the yellow, sour contents of the carafe, or the sugary, reddish, frothy cider from bottles whose corks popped out like the corks of fizzy lemonade.

Madeleine, who was eating and saying almost nothing, went on sitting despondently with her lips set in her usual smile, but a smile that was cheerless and resigned. She felt disappointed, heart-broken. Why? She had wanted to come. She had known quite well that she was going to visit peasants, very simple peasants. So what had she dreamed they would be like, she who ordinarily did not indulge in daydreaming?

Did she herself know? As if women do not always hope for something other than what actually is! From a distance, had she imagined them as more poetic? No, but, perhaps, as more literary, more noble, more loving, more decorative. Yet she did not want them to be distinguished, like those shown in novels. So how did it come about that they shocked her in countless tiny, imperceptible ways, by countless indefinable vulgarities, by their very natures as peasants, by their words, their gestures, and their laughter?

She remembered her own mother, of whom she never spoke to anyone, a schoolmistress who'd been seduced, and had grown up in Saint-Denis,* dying in destitution and misery when Madeleine was twelve. A stranger had paid for the little girl's education. Her father, most probably? Who was he? She did not know precisely, although she had vague suspicions.

The meal dragged on and on. Now there were customers coming in, shaking old Duroy by the hand, exclaiming on seeing the son, then, as they gave the young woman a sidelong glance, winking maliciously, as if to say: 'Christ almighty! She's not half bad, Georges Duroy's wife ain't.'

Others, not such close friends, sat down at the wooden tables, shouting: 'A litre! A handle! Two brandies! A raspail!'* And they began playing dominoes, very noisily banging down the little squares of black and white bone.

Old Mme Duroy was constantly on the go, serving the customers with her mournful air, taking the money, wiping the tables with the corner of her blue apron. Smoke from clay pipes and cheap cigars was filling the room. Madeleine began to cough and asked: 'Shall we go outside? I can't stand this any more.'

They had not yet finished. Old Duroy was annoyed. So she got up and went to sit on a chair in front of the door, on the road, waiting for her father-in-law and her husband to finish their coffee and liqueurs.

Georges soon joined her. 'How about heading down to the Seine?' he said. She agreed joyfully: 'Oh, yes! Let's go.'

They walked down the hillside, hired a boat at Croisset, and spent the rest of the afternoon alongside an island, under the willows, both of them dozing in the gentle spring warmth, rocked by the river's little waves. Then, at nightfall, they climbed back up again.

The evening meal, lit by a single candle, was even more trying for Madeleine than the morning one had been. Old Duroy, who was half drunk, no longer spoke. The mother still had her sour expression. The dim light projected the shadows of heads with enormous noses and exaggerated gestures onto the grey walls. From time to time, you could see a giant hand lift something that resembled a pitchfork up to a mouth that opened like the jaws of a monster, when someone, turning slightly sideways, presented a profile to the yellow, flickering flame.

As soon as supper was over, Madeleine drew her husband outside, so as not to have to stay in that gloomy room where the pungent smell of old pipes and spilt drinks hung permanently in the air.

When they were outside: 'You're already bored,' he said.

She started to protest. He stopped her: 'No. I could see it clearly. If you like, we can leave again tomorrow.'

She murmured: 'Yes. I'd like that.'

They walked slowly on. It was a warm night, whose deep, caressing darkness seemed full of tiny sounds, of rustlings and murmurings. They had turned onto a narrow pathway that ran beneath some very tall trees, between two impenetrably dark thickets.

She enquired: 'Where are we?' 'In the forest,' he told her. 'Is it big?' 'Very big, one of the biggest in France.'*

A smell of earth, of trees, of moss, that fresh, ancient scent of thickly wooded forests, made up of the sap of shoots and the dead, mouldy greenery of the underbrush, seemed to lie slumbering in that avenue. When she looked up, Madeleine could see stars between the tree-tops, and although no breeze stirred the branches, she sensed all around her the vague pulsation of that ocean of leaves.

A strange shiver ran through her soul and over her body; an obscure feeling of anguish wrung her heart. Why? She had no idea. But it seemed to her that she was lost, overwhelmed, surrounded by dangers, abandoned by everyone, alone, alone in the world, beneath this living canopy which rustled high up above.

She whispered: 'I feel a bit scared. I'd like to go back.'

'All right, let's go back.'

'And... we'll leave again for Paris tomorrow?'

'Yes, tomorrow.'

'Tomorrow morning.'

'Tomorrow morning, if you like.'

They returned. The old people had gone to bed. She slept badly, constantly awakened by all the noises of the country that were new to her, the hooting of owls, the grunting of a pig shut up in a shed next to the wall, and the crowing of the rooster who began trumpeting at midnight. She was up and ready to leave at first light.

When Georges informed his parents that he was going back to

Paris, they were both startled, then they realized where this decision had originated.

The father asked simply: 'Ye'll come an' see us agin soon?'

'Of course. Some time in the summer.'

'Well, good.'

The old woman growled: 'I hope ye don't live to be sorry fer what ye've been an' done.'

He left them a present of two hundred francs to placate them, and when the cab, which a lad had gone to fetch, appeared about ten o'clock, the newly weds kissed the old peasants and set off again.

As they were going down the hill, Duroy began to laugh: 'There, you see,' he said, 'I warned you. I ought never to have introduced you to M. and Mme du Roy de Cantel senior.'

She too began to laugh, and replied: 'I'm delighted, now. They're fine people, of whom I'm beginning to be very fond. I'll send them some little presents from Paris.'

Then she murmured: ' "Du Roy de Cantel..." You'll see, no one will be surprised by our wedding announcements. We'll say that we spent a week on your parents' estate.'

And, moving closer to him, she brushed the tip of his moustache with a kiss: 'Good morning, Georges!'

He answered: 'Good morning, Made,' as he slipped a hand round her waist.

Far away, in the depths of the valley, they could see the great river stretched out like a ribbon of silver under the morning sun, and all the factory chimneys puffing their clouds of coal into the sky, and all the pointed belfries rising up above the old city.

CHAPTER 2

The Du Roys had been back in Paris for two days and the journalist was carrying on with his former duties, pending the day when he would leave the gossip section and permanently take over Forestier's responsibilities, devoting himself entirely to politics.

On that particular evening, as he was walking home in high spirits to have dinner in his predecessor's apartment, he felt an intense desire to kiss his wife there and then, for he was totally under the sway of her physical charms and subtle domination. Passing a florist's at the bottom of the Rue Notre-Dame-de-Lorette, he had the idea of buying flowers for Madeleine, and he chose a large bunch of barely opened roses, a cluster of perfumed buds.

On each landing of his new staircase, he observed himself complacently in the mirror which constantly reminded him of the first time he had entered that house.

He rang, as he had forgotten his key, and the same servant, whom, on his wife's advice, he had also kept, opened the door.

Georges enquired: 'Is Madame back?'

'Yes, Monsieur.'

But when he crossed the dining-room he was very surprised to see three places laid; and, as the curtain dividing off the drawing-room was drawn back, he saw Madeleine arranging, in a vase on the mantelpiece, a bunch of roses exactly like his own. He felt upset and irritated, as if his idea, his thoughtfulness, and all the pleasure he expected from it, had been stolen from him.

As he came in he asked: 'So you've invited someone?'

She replied without turning round, while continuing to arrange the flowers: 'Yes and no. It's my old friend the Comte de Vaudrec who has always dined here on Mondays, and who's coming as usual.'

Georges muttered: 'Oh! Fine.'

He was still standing behind her, with his bouquet in his hand, feeling an urge to hide it or throw it away. However he said: 'Here, I've brought you some roses.'

And she turned round quickly, all smiles, exclaiming: 'Oh, how sweet of you to think of that!' And she held out her arms and offered him her lips with so spontaneous and genuine a pleasure that he felt consoled.

She took the flowers, smelt them, and, with the vivacity of a delighted child, put them in the empty vase that stood opposite the first one. Then, gazing at the effect, she murmured:

'Oh, how wonderful! Now my mantelpiece is all nicely arranged.'

Almost immediately, she added, with an air of conviction: 'You know, Vaudrec is charming, you'll feel he's an old friend right away.'

A ring of the bell announced the Comte's arrival. He walked calmly in, very much at his ease, as if entirely at home. After gallantly kissing the young woman's fingers, he turned to her husband and cordially offered him his hand, enquiring: 'Everything going well, my dear Du Roy?'

His manner was no longer stiff and starchy, as it had been before, but affable, demonstrating clearly that the situation had now changed. Taken aback, the journalist made an effort to appear friendly, and respond to Vaudrec's overtures. Five minutes later one might have supposed that the two of them had been dear friends for at least a decade.

Then Madeleine, her face radiant, said to them: 'I'll leave you together. I must give an eye to my dinner.' And she went out, followed by the gaze of both men.

When she came back, she found them talking about the theatre, discussing a new play, and so completely of one mind that a kind of instant friendship was awakening in their eyes, as they discovered how perfectly their ideas concurred.

The dinner was delightful, very intimate and warm; and Vaudrec stayed late into the evening, so comfortable did he feel in this household, in the company of this charming newly wedded couple.

As soon as he had left, Madeleine said to her husband: 'He's perfect, isn't he? He improves immeasurably on better acquaintance. Now there's a good friend, dependable, devoted, loyal. Ah! Had it not been for him...'

She left her thought unfinished, and Georges answered:

'Yes, I find him very agreeable. I believe we shall get on together very well.'

But she went on immediately: 'You didn't know, but we've got work to do this evening, before we go to bed. I didn't have time to tell you about this before dinner, because Vaudrec arrived straight away.

I've just heard some important news, news about Morocco. I have it from Laroche-Mathieu, the deputy, the future minister. We must write a major article about this, a sensational scoop. I have facts and figures. We must get to work at once. Here, you take the lamp.'

He took it and they went into the study.

The same books stood in the bookcase, which now bore on its top shelf the three vases Forestier had bought in Golfe Juan, the day before his death. Under the table, the dead man's foot-warmer awaited the feet of Du Roy who, after taking a seat, picked up the ivory pen-holder, the end of which had been slightly chewed by the teeth of the other.

Madeleine, leaning on the mantelpiece, lit a cigarette and related the news, then expounded her ideas, and the outline of the article she had in mind.

He listened to her attentively, while he scribbled some notes; and when she had finished he raised some objections, re-examined the question, enlarged its scope, and in his turn expounded not the plan of an article, but the plan of a campaign against the current ministry. This attack would be the beginning. His wife had stopped smoking, so greatly had her interest been aroused, so wide and far could she see as she followed Georges's thinking.

She muttered from time to time: 'Yes... yes... Very good... Excellent... That's very powerful...'

And, when he in his turn had finished speaking: 'Now, let's begin to write,' she said.

But he still found it hard to begin, and had difficulty finding the right words. So she quietly came up and leant over his shoulder, softly whispering his sentences into his ear. From time to time she would hesitate, and ask: 'That is what you want to say, isn't it?' and he would reply: 'Yes, exactly.'

She came up with some stinging barbs, venomous, feminine barbs aimed at wounding the head of the Cabinet; and she mixed ridicule of his face with ridicule of his politics, in a comic way that made the reader laugh even as it hit home with the accuracy of its observation.

Du Roy, occasionally, would add a few lines to deepen and strengthen the implications of an attack. Furthermore he was adept at the art of perfidious insinuation, which he had learnt while perfecting his technique in the gossip column; and when something that Madeleine reported as a fact struck him as doubtful or compromising, he excelled at leaving it for the reader to deduce, in such a way that it carried far greater conviction than if he had stated it positively.

When their article was completed, Georges reread it, declaiming it like a speech. They were in complete agreement as to its excellence, and each smiled at the other in delight and surprise, as if they had just discovered one another. Gazing with admiration and tenderness deep into each other's eyes, they embraced fervently, with a passionate ardour that communicated itself from their minds to their bodies.

Du Roy picked up the lamp again: 'And now, bye-byes,' he said, with a meaningful look. She replied: 'You go first, master, since you are lighting the way.'

He did so, and she followed him into their room, tickling his neck between his collar and his hair with her fingertip, to make him go faster, for he dreaded that particular caress.

The article appeared under the signature of Georges du Roy de Cantel, and made a great impression. It caused quite a stir in the Chamber. Old Walter congratulated its author and made him political editor of *La Vie française*. The gossip column reverted to Boisrenard.

The newspaper then began a skilful, fierce campaign directed against the Ministry of Foreign Affairs. The attack, always adroit and well documented, ironic and serious in turn, occasionally amusing and occasionally vicious, struck home so unerringly and unremittingly that everyone was amazed. The other papers were always quoting *La Vie française*, borrowing whole passages from it, and those in power enquired about the possibility of muzzling this unknown and relentless enemy by bribing him with an administrative post.

Du Roy was becoming well known in political circles. He sensed his growing influence by the firmness of handshakes and the speed with which hats were raised. Furthermore he was filled with astonishment and admiration for his wife, for the ingenuity of her mind, the clever way she gathered information, and the number of people she knew.

When he came home he was forever encountering, in his drawing-room, a senator, a deputy, a magistrate, or a general, who treated Madeleine like an old friend, with respectful familiarity. Where had she met all these people? In society, she said. But how had she succeeded in gaining their trust and their affection? He couldn't understand it. She'd be a damned good diplomat, he reflected.

At meal times she would often come in late, out of breath, flushed, and excited and, even before removing her veil, would say: 'I've a special titbit today. Imagine, the Minister of Justice has just appointed two magistrates who were members of the bi-partisan commissions. We're going to give him a dressing-down he won't forget.'

And they would give the minister a dressing-down, and another the following day and a third the day after that. The deputy Laroche-Mathieu, who dined at the Rue Fontaine every Tuesday, after the Comte de Vaudrec who began the week, would vigorously shake the hands of both husband and wife, making an excessive show of his delight. He kept saying: 'What a campaign! How can we not succeed after this?'

In fact, he fully expected to succeed in landing the portfolio for Foreign Affairs, on which he had long since set his sights.

He was one of those political creatures of many faces, with no convictions, no great resources, no audacity, and no real attainments; a country lawyer, a handsome small-town gentleman, who maintained a crafty balance between the various political extremes, a sort of republican Jesuit and liberal champion of a dubious kind, such as spring up by the hundreds on the popular dunghill of universal suffrage.

Thanks to his village machiavellianism his colleagues—all those misfits and losers who are elected deputy—considered that he was very able. He was sufficiently well groomed and well mannered, sufficiently familiar and agreeable to get ahead. He met with success in society, in the mixed, unsettled, and undiscriminating society of the senior civil servants of the day.

People everywhere said of him: 'Laroche will be a minister,' and he too, with yet more conviction than everyone else, thought that Laroche would be a minister. He was one of the principal shareholders in old Walter's newspaper, and his ally and associate in a number of financial deals.

Du Roy supported him with confidence, and with vague expectations for the future. In any case, he was simply carrying on the work begun by Forestier, to whom Laroche-Mathieu had promised the

Cross of the Legion of Honour when the triumphal day arrived. The honour would decorate the chest of Madeleine's new husband, that was all. In a word, nothing had changed.

Everyone was so well aware that nothing had changed, that Du Roy's colleagues were constantly making a joke at his expense, which he was beginning to find annoying.

They never called him anything but Forestier.

As soon as he arrived at the paper someone would shout: 'By the way, Forestier.' He pretended not to hear, and looked in his pigeon-hole for letters. The voice called again, louder: 'Hey! Forestier!' There would be smothered laughter.

As Du Roy headed for the Director's office, he would be stopped by the man who had called to him: 'Oh! Excuse me, it's you I want to speak to. It's stupid, but I always confuse you with that poor Charles. It's because your articles are so damned similar to his. Everyone makes the same mistake.'

Du Roy made no reply, but raged inwardly, and secretly began to feel hatred for the dead man. Old Walter himself had declared, when they were all exclaiming over the glaring similarities of expression and thought between the new political editor's articles and those of his predecessor: 'Yes, it's like Forestier, but a meatier, terser, more virile Forestier.'

Another time, when Du Roy chanced to open the cupboard with the cup-and-ball collection, he had found those of his predecessor with a black band tied round the handle, while his own, the one he used when practising under the direction of Saint-Potin, bore a rose-pink ribbon. They had all been arranged, according to size, on the same shelf, and on a small card like those used in museums was written: 'Former collection of Forestier & Co., now property of his successor Forestier-Du Roy, certified SGDG.* Guaranteed never to wear out; suitable in all circumstances, including travel.'

He calmly shut the cupboard door again, saying, loudly enough to be heard: 'There are always jealous idiots everywhere.'

But his pride had been wounded, as well as his vanity, the writer's sensitive pride and vanity, which produces that irritable touchiness—always ready to take offence—typical of both the reporter and the poet of genius.

The word 'Forestier' grated on his ears; he was afraid of hearing it, and felt himself blush when he did so.

This name was, for him, a bitter taunt, worse than a taunt, almost an insult. It cried out to him: 'It's your wife who's doing your job just as she did the job of the other man. Without her you'd be nothing.' He readily admitted that Forestier would have been nothing without Madeleine, but as for himself, come on!

Then, when he was home again, the obsession persisted. Now it was the entire house that reminded him of the dead man, all the furniture, all the ornaments, everything he touched. In the beginning he had hardly thought about this; but the jokes played on him by his colleagues had created a kind of lesion in his soul, which countless trifles, hitherto unnoticed, were now infecting.

He could no longer pick up an object without immediately imagining Charles's hand on it. Everything he saw, everything he handled had formerly been used by him, was something he had bought, liked, and owned. And Georges was even beginning to be enraged by the thought of the former intimacies between his friend and his wife.

At times he was filled with astonishment by this emotional revolt, he did not understand it, and would ask himself: 'How the devil did this happen? I'm not jealous of Madeleine's friends. I never worry about what she's doing. She comes and goes as she chooses, and yet I'm infuriated by the memory of that boor, Charles!'

Mentally he would add: 'Basically, he was nothing but a moron; that must be what upsets me. I'm angry that Madeleine could have married such a fool.' And he wondered again and again: 'However did it happen that she could have been taken in for a single instant by an idiot like that!'

And every day his resentment grew, fed by a thousand insignificant details that stung like pinpricks, constantly reminding him of the other man, prompted by something said by Madeleine, or by the manservant, or the chambermaid.

One evening Du Roy, who had a sweet tooth, enquired: 'Why do we never have a sweet course? You never order them.'

The young woman replied cheerfully: 'That's right, I hadn't thought. It's because Charles loathed them...'

Unable to stop himself, he interrupted her with an impatient gesture: 'Oh! Really, that Charles is beginning to get to me. It's Charles here, Charles there, Charles liked this, Charles liked that. Charles has snuffed it, so let him rest in peace.'

Madeleine stared at her husband in stupefaction, unable to understand his sudden fury. Then, as she was a shrewd woman, she guessed something of what he was experiencing, this gradually corroding jealousy of the dead man, nourished at every turn by everything that recalled his existence. She may well have thought it childish, but she felt flattered, and did not reply.

He was annoyed with himself that he had not been able to hide his irritation. After dinner that evening, as they were working on an article for the following day, his feet got tangled up in the footmuff. Unable to right it, he kicked it to one side, asking with a laugh:

'So Charles's feet were always cold, were they?'

She laughed too, as she replied: 'Oh! He was terrified of catching cold; his chest wasn't strong.'

Du Roy went on in a savage tone: 'As he proved beyond a doubt.' Then he added politely: 'Fortunately for me.' And he kissed his wife's hand.

But as they were going to bed he again asked, still obsessed by the same idea: 'Did Charles wear a cotton nightcap to protect his ears from draughts?'

She joined in the joke and answered: 'No, a scarf tied round his forehead.'

Georges shrugged and declared in the scornful voice of a superior being: 'What a fool!'

From then on, Charles became, for him, a constant topic of conversation. He talked about him at every turn, invariably calling him 'that poor old Charles' with an air of infinite pity. And when he came home from the paper, where he had heard himself addressed, two or three times, by the name of Forestier, he took his revenge by heaping cruel jibes on the dead man even in his tomb. He recalled his faults, his silly habits, and his meannesses, enumerating them complacently, expatiating on them and exaggerating them, as though wanting to combat, in his wife's heart, the influence of a rival he feared.

He would say: 'Hey, Made, do you remember the day when that blockhead Forestier tried to prove that fat men are more vigorous than thin ones?'

Then he wanted to know a whole lot of intimate, very personal details about the dead man that the embarrassed young woman refused to relate.

But he pressed her, insisting. 'Come on, tell me. He must have been too funny for words, while he was at it?'

Barely moving her lips, she murmured: 'Oh, leave him alone, for heaven's sake.'

He went on: 'No, do tell! I bet the bastard was hopeless in bed!' And, invariably, he would conclude with: 'What an oaf he was!'

One night towards the end of June, as he was smoking a cigar at the window, the evening was so hot that he had the idea of going for a drive.

He asked: 'Made, my dear, would you like to go to the Bois?'

'Why yes, I would.'

They took an open cab, and drove down the Champs-Élysées, then the Avenue du Bois de Boulogne. The night was completely still, one of those scorching nights when the air of the overheated city feels, as it enters your lungs, like a blast from an oven. A huge number of amorous couples were being driven under the trees in an army of cabs. These cabs moved along one behind the other, never ending.

Georges and Madeleine enjoyed watching all the intertwined couples passing in their carriages, the women in pale dresses, the men sombrely clad. A vast river of lovers was flowing towards the Bois beneath a starry, burning sky. There wasn't a sound except for the muffled rumbling of wheels on the ground. Again and again they drove by, two creatures in every carriage, lying back silently on cushions and clasping one another tightly, lost in the delusion of their desire, trembling in anticipation of the approaching embrace. The warm darkness seemed full of kisses. A feeling of love hovering overhead, of ever-present animal desire, thickened the air, making it seem more stifling. All these couples intoxicated by the same thought, by the same passion, created a febrile aura around them. All these carriages heavy with love, over which caresses seemed to be hovering, gave off, as they passed by, a kind of sensual aroma, at once subtle and unsettling.

Georges and Madeleine found themselves affected by this contagious tenderness. Without speaking, they gently clasped hands, a little oppressed by the heavy atmosphere and by the emotion they were feeling. As they reached the turning after the fortifications, they kissed, and she, somewhat embarrassed, stammered: 'We're being just as childish as when we were on the way to Rouen.'

The great stream of carriages had divided up at the entrance to the woods. On the road by the lakes which the young people had taken, the carriages had spaced themselves out somewhat, but the dense darkness of the trees, the air freshened by the leaves and by the damp of the tiny creeks you could hear running under the boughs, a kind of coolness from the broad expanses of the star-studded night sky, gave the kisses of the passing couples a more intense charm, a more mysterious shadowiness.

Georges whispered: 'Oh! My little Made!' as he clasped her tight.

She said to him 'Do you remember the forest near your home, how sinister it was? To me it seemed full of terrifying beasts, and that it went on and on for ever. But this, now, this is lovely. You can feel the wind caressing you, and I know perfectly well that Sèvres* is just the other side.'

He replied: 'Oh! In the forest back home, there was nothing but stags, foxes, roebuck, and wild boar, and the odd hut belonging to a forester.'

That word* which his mouth had uttered, so like the dead man's name, surprised him as much as if someone had shouted it to him from deep in the woods, and abruptly he fell silent, gripped once more by this strange, persistent disquiet, by this jealous, gnawing, unconquerable anger which for some time now had been poisoning his life.

After a moment, he enquired: 'Did you ever come here with Charles, in the evening?'

She answered: 'Oh yes, often.'

And, suddenly, he felt a longing to return home, an agitated longing that struck him to the heart. But the image of Forestier had taken hold in his mind, possessing him, fastening upon him. He could think of nothing but him, talk of nothing but him.

He asked, his tone disagreeable: 'Tell me, Made?'

'What is it, dear?'

'Did you cheat on poor old Charles?'

She murmured scornfully: 'How silly you're being, the way you're forever harping on that.'

But he would not let it alone.

'Come on, dear, be honest, admit it! You made him a cuckold, didn't you! Admit you made him a cuckold!'

Shocked by this word, as are all women, she said nothing.

Obstinately, he went on: 'God, if ever anyone looked the part, then he did. Oh God, yes! Yes! It would make me split my sides to know old Forestier was a cuckold. Eh? Didn't he look the perfect sucker?'

He sensed that she was smiling, perhaps at some memory, and he repeated: 'Come on, say it. What does it matter? On the contrary, it would be ever so funny if you admitted that you'd cheated on him, if you admitted that, to me.'

And indeed he was quivering with the hope and wish that Charles, that hateful Charles, the dead man whom he detested, whom he execrated, might have been made a fool of in this shameful way. And yet... and yet, another, more ambiguous emotion was spurring on his urge to know. He said again: 'Made, my little Made, I beg you, say it. He deserved it if anyone did. You'd have been very wrong not to do that to him. Come on, Made, admit it.'

Perhaps she found his persistence amusing, now, for she was laughing, in short, staccato gasps. He had put his lips very close to his wife's ear. 'Come on... come on... admit it?'

Suddenly she moved away from him, and curtly declared: 'You really are silly. Questions like that don't deserve an answer.'

She had said this in such an odd tone of voice that her husband felt a cold shiver run through his veins, and, nonplussed and dismayed, he sat there a little out of breath, as if he had just suffered a nervous shock.

Now the cab was driving beside the lake, into which the sky seemed to have scattered its stars. Two swans were very slowly gliding past, their vague outlines barely visible in the shadows. Georges shouted to the driver: 'Turn back.' And the cab turned around, passing the others, which moved on at a walking pace, their big lanterns shining like eyes in the darkness of the Bois.

How strangely she had said that! 'Was that an admission?' Du Roy asked himself. And now this near-certainty that she had deceived her first husband made him seethe with rage. He felt like hitting her, strangling her, pulling out her hair!

Oh! If only she had answered him: 'But, darling, if I had wanted to deceive him, it would have been with you!' How he would have kissed her, held her tight, adored her!

He sat motionless, his arms crossed, gazing at the sky, his mind too agitated for further reflection. He could feel nothing but the ferment of that resentment and the growth of that fury smouldering in the heart of every male when faced with the capriciousness of female desire. For the first time, he knew the confused anguish of a suspicious husband. He was actually jealous, jealous on behalf of the dead man, on behalf of Forestier! Jealous in a strange and painful way, which included, all of a sudden, hatred of Madeleine. Since she had deceived the other one, how could he trust her himself?

Then, little by little, a kind of calm came over him, and, bracing himself to bear his pain, he thought: 'All women are whores, you have to use them, and not give them anything of yourself.'

The bitterness in his heart was bringing words of scorn and loathing to his lips. But he did not give them voice. He kept telling himself: 'The world is to the strong. I must be strong. I must rise above everything.'

The carriage was going faster. They passed the fortifications once again. Du Roy was gazing ahead at a reddish brightness in the sky, like the glow of a colossal forge; and he could hear an indistinct, immense, continuous humming, made up of countless different elements, a muffled sound that came both from near and far, a vague, tremendous throb of life, the sound of Paris breathing, on this summer night, like an exhausted colossus.

Georges was thinking: 'I'd be a real fool to get worked up over this. Everyone for himself. It's boldness that wins the day. There's nothing but selfishness. Selfishness in pursuit of ambition and money is better than selfishness over women and love.' At the entrance to the city the Arc de Triomphe of the Étoile loomed up, standing on its two monstrous legs, a kind of misshapen giant which seemed about to march off down the wide avenue that lay before it.

Once again Georges and Madeleine found themselves part of the procession of vehicles transporting the eternal couple, locked in a silent embrace, back to their home, to the long-desired bed. It was as if all of humanity was gliding along beside them, intoxicated with joy, pleasure, and happiness.

The young woman, who had certainly sensed something of what was going on in her husband's mind, asked in her gentle voice: 'What are you thinking about, Georges dear? You haven't said a word for the last half-hour.'

He replied with a nasty grin: 'I'm thinking about all those idiots kissing each other, and that really there's other things to do in life.'

She murmured: 'Yes... but sometimes it's nice.'

'It's nice... it's nice... when there's nothing better to do!'

Georges's thoughts, driven by a kind of malicious rage, were still bent on stripping life of its poetic dress. 'I'd be a real fool to put myself out, to do without anything I want, to get upset, and worry, and fret my heart out, the way I've been doing the last few weeks.' The image of Forestier came into his mind, without generating any anger. It seemed to him that they had just been reconciled, that they were friends again. He wanted to call out to him: 'Hallo, old man.'

Madeleine, disconcerted by his silence, asked: 'How about having an ice at Tortoni's,* before we go home?'

He gave her a sidelong glance. He saw her delicate fair profile by the brilliant illumination of a string of gas lights advertising a music-hall. He thought: 'She is pretty. Well! All the better. Tit for tat, my friend. But I'll be damned if anyone ever catches me upsetting myself over you again.' Then he replied: 'Of course, darling.'

And, so that she would not suspect anything, he kissed her.

It seemed to Madeleine that her husband's lips were icy cold. But as he helped her out of the cab in front of the café steps, he was smiling his usual smile.

CHAPTER 3

On arriving at the newspaper the following day, Du Roy went to look for Boisrenard. 'My dear fellow,' he said, 'I've a favour to ask of you. For some time now people have been finding it amusing to call me Forestier. I myself am beginning to think it's rather silly. Would you be so kind as to quietly inform our friends that I shall slap the face of the next one to take the liberty of making that joke. It's up to them to decide whether this nonsense is worth a duel. I'm asking you because you're a level headed man who can stop things going to unfortunate extremes, and also because you acted as my second in that other affair of mine.'

Boisrenard agreed to carry out this request. Du Roy departed on various errands, then came back an hour later. No one called him Forestier.

When he returned home, he heard women's voices in the drawing-room. 'Who's in there?' he enquired.

The servant said: 'Mme Walter and Mme de Marelle.'

His heart gave a little jump, then he told himself: 'Well now, let's see,' and opened the door.

Clotilde was by the fireplace, in a ray of sunlight from the window. It seemed to Georges that she turned a little pale on seeing him. After first greeting Mme Walter and her two daughters, who were sitting on either side of their mother like a pair of sentries, he turned towards his former mistress. She gave him her hand; he took it and pressed it in a meaningful way, as if to say: 'I still love you.' She responded to this pressure.

'It's ages since we last met. Have you been keeping well?'

She replied easily: 'Yes, indeed, and you, Bel-Ami?' Then, turning to Madeleine, she added: 'Have I your permission to go on calling him Bel-Ami?'

'Of course, my dear; you have my permission to do anything you like.' Perhaps there was a tinge of irony in this remark.

Mme Walter was talking about a party that Jacques Rival was going to throw in his bachelor apartments, a big fencing display which society ladies would be attending; she was saying: 'It will be so interesting. But I'm really disappointed, we've no one to escort us; my husband has to be away just then.'

Du Roy immediately offered his services. She accepted: 'We shall be most grateful, my daughters and I.'

He was looking at the younger of the Walter girls, and thinking: 'She's not at all bad, that little Suzanne, not at all bad.' She had the look of a delicate blond doll, too small, but dainty, with a slender waist, shapely hips and breasts, the face of a miniature painting, eyes of grey-blue enamel drawn with subtle brush-strokes by a meticulous, whimsical artist, flesh that was too white, too smooth, glossy, uniform, without texture or colour, and tousled curly hair, an artful, gossamer mass, a charming cloud, exactly like, indeed, the hair of those pretty luxury dolls you see in the arms of girls who are considerably smaller than their toy.

The older sister, Rose, was ugly, dull, insignificant, one of those girls you don't see, you don't speak to, and you don't talk about.

The mother rose, and turning towards Georges: 'So, I'm relying on you for next Thursday at two.' 'You can count on me, Madame.'

As soon as she had left, Mme de Marelle rose in her turn. 'Goodbye, Bel-Ami.'

It was she, now, who gave his hand a very tight, prolonged clasp, and, stirred by this silent admission, he suddenly felt a renewed desire for this good-natured little middle-class bohemian, who truly loved him, perhaps.

'I'll go and see her tomorrow,' he thought.

Once he and his wife were alone, Madeleine began laughing in an open, happy way and said, looking him straight in the face: 'I suppose you realize that Mme Walter's taken quite a shine to you?' He replied incredulously: 'Oh, come on!' 'Yes, really, she's spoken of you to me with the most extraordinary enthusiasm. It's so unlike her! She wants to find two husbands like you for her daughters!... Lucky that in her case these things have no significance.'

He did not understand what she was trying to say. 'What do you mean, no significance?' She answered with the conviction of a woman confident in her own judgment. 'Oh, Mme Walter is one of those women about whom there's never been any gossip; oh, in her case, never, never. She's beyond reproach in every way. Her husband, well you know him as well as I do. But, as for her, that's another matter. She's suffered quite a bit, moreover, from marrying a Jew, but she's remained faithful to him. She's a good woman.'

Du Roy was surprised. 'I thought she was Jewish too.'

'She? Not at all. She's lady patroness of all the charities run by the Madeleine. She was even married in church. I can't remember, now, whether there was some pretence of baptizing Walter, or whether the Church just closed its eyes.'

Georges muttered: 'Oh! So... she's... gone on me?'

'Definitely, and totally. If you weren't already taken, I'd advise you to ask for the hand of... Suzanne, I think, rather than Rose?'

Twirling his moustache, he replied: 'Hey! The mother's not half bad still.'

But Madeleine said impatiently: 'Well, my love, I wish you joy of the mother. But I'm not worried. You don't stray for the first time at her age. You have to start earlier.'

Georges was thinking: 'But what if it were true, that I could have married Suzanne?...'

Then he shrugged: 'Bah! It's crazy... Would the father ever have accepted me?' Nevertheless he told himself that from then on he would watch Mme Walter's behaviour towards him more closely, without, however, wondering whether he might ever profit from it in any way.

All evening, he was haunted by memories of his love-affair with Clotilde, memories both tender and sensual. He remembered the funny things she said, her sweet ways, their escapades. He kept telling himself: 'She's really very nice. Yes, I'll go and see her tomorrow.'

The next day, as soon as he had had lunch, he did go to the Rue de Verneuil. The same servant opened the door, and, in the familiar way of the servants of modest households, asked: 'Are you keeping well, Monsieur?'

He answered: 'Yes, fine, my dear.'

And he went into the drawing-room, where an unskilled hand was playing scales on the piano. It was Laurine. He expected her to fling her arms round his neck. She stood up solemnly, greeted him ceremoniously as an adult would have done, and departed in a stately fashion.

Her manner so closely resembled that of a slighted woman, that he was taken aback. Her mother came in. He grasped her hands and kissed them.

'I've thought of you so much!' he said.

'And I of you,' she said.

They sat down. They were smiling at one another, gazing into each other's eyes, longing to kiss one another's lips.

'My dear little Clo, I love you.'

'And I love you too.'

'So... so... you haven't been too angry with me?'

'Yes, and no... It hurt me, but then I understood your reasons, and I told myself: "Bah! He'll come back to me one of these fine days."'

'I didn't dare come back: I wondered how I would be received. I didn't dare, but I desperately wanted to. By the way, do tell me what's got into Laurine. She hardly said "hallo," and then off she went, looking furious.'

'I don't know. But, since you got married, one can't talk to her about you any more. I do believe she's jealous.'

'Oh, come on.'

'No, my dear, really. She no longer calls you Bel-Ami, she calls you M. Forestier.'

Du Roy blushed, then, going up to the young woman: 'Give me a kiss.'

She did so. 'Where can we see each other again?' he asked.

'In the Rue de Constantinople, of course.'

'Oh! So the flat hasn't been let?'

'No... I kept it.'

'You kept it?'

'Yes, I thought you'd come back there.'

A surge of joyful pride swelled his chest. So this woman loved him, with a love that was true, constant, and deep. He murmured: 'I adore you.' Then he asked: 'Your husband's well?'

'Yes, fine. He's just been here a month; he left the day before yesterday.'

Du Roy couldn't help laughing: 'How convenient!'

She replied ingenuously: 'Yes, very convenient. However, he's not a bother when he is here. Isn't that so?'

'Yes, that is so. Besides, he's a charming man.'

'How about you,' she said, 'how are you finding your new life?'

'Neither good nor bad. My wife's a friend, a partner.'

'Nothing more?' 'Nothing more... as regards my feelings...'

'Yes, I understand. Still, she's very nice.'

'Yes, but I don't find her exciting.' He went up to Clotilde, and whispered: 'When can we see each other?'

'Well... tomorrow... if you like.'

'Yes, tomorrow; two o'clock?'

'Two o'clock.'

He rose to leave, and then, a little embarrassed, stammered: 'You know, I plan to rent the Rue de Constantinople flat again on my own account. I want to. It wouldn't do at all for you to go on paying for it.'

It was she who kissed his hands adoringly, as she whispered: 'You do as you wish. I'm glad I kept it so we can meet there again.' And Du Roy, feeling very pleased with life, took his leave.

As he passed a photographer's shop-window, the portrait of a tall woman with large eyes reminded him of Mme Walter. 'All the same,' he thought, 'she's really not bad. How did I never happen to notice her? I'm looking forward to seeing how she behaves towards me on Thursday.'

He walked along rubbing his hands together, filled with a very private pleasure, pleasure at knowing success in all its forms, a selfish pleasure at being both clever and successful, and a subtle kind, made up of flattered vanity and satisfied sensuality, that comes from being loved by women.

On the Thursday, he said to Madeleine: 'Aren't you going to that fencing affair of Rival's?'

'Oh, no. It doesn't appeal to me at all; I'll go to the Chamber of Deputies.'

And he went to fetch Mme Walter in an open landau, for the weather was superb.

When he saw her he was surprised, she looked so beautiful and young. She was wearing a light-coloured outfit with rather a low-cut bodice, which, beneath the golden lace, hinted at generously rounded breasts. Never had she seemed so radiant. He found her truly desirable. Her manner was, as always, composed and well bred, with a certain air of maternal placidity that rendered her virtually invisible to a roving male eye. Furthermore, she rarely spoke, except to say reasonable things that were widely known and accepted, for her ideas were judicious, systematic, well organized, and free of all excess.

Her daughter Suzanne, all in pink, resembled a freshly varnished Watteau;* and her elder sister looked like the governess responsible for keeping this pretty little bauble of a girl company.

A row of carriages was standing in front of Rival's door. Du Roy offered Mme Walter his arm, and they went in. The fencing exhibition was being held to raise money for the orphans of the sixth *arrondissement* of the city, under the patronage of all the wives of those senators and deputies connected with *La Vie française*. Mme Walter had promised to come with her daughters, but had refused to be a patroness, for she only let her name be associated with charities run by the clergy, not because she was extremely devout, but because she believed that her marriage to an Israelite obliged her to maintain a certain standard of religious observance; and the affair organized by the journalist was taking on a kind of republican character that might be seen as anticlerical.

Over the last three weeks, people had read, in newspapers of every shade of opinion, the following announcement:

'Our distinguished colleague Jacques Rival has just come up with an idea as ingenious as it is generous: to organize, for the benefit of the orphans of the sixth *arrondissement*, a grand display of swordsmanship in the attractive fencing hall that adjoins his bachelor apartments.

'Invitations are being sent out by Mmes Laloigne, Remontel, and Rissolin, wives of those senators, and by Mmes Laroche-Mathieu, Percerol, and Firmin, whose husbands are well-known deputies.* A single collection will be taken during the intermission, and the sum collected will be immediately handed over to the mayor of the sixth *arrondissement*, or to his representative.'

The shrewd journalist had had the bright idea of this large-scale self-advertisement.

Jacques Rival was receiving the guests in the entrance-hall of his home, where refreshments had been laid out; their cost was to be deducted from the moneys received.

With a courteous gesture, he indicated the little staircase leading down to the cellar, where he had set up his fencing school and shooting gallery, saying: 'Downstairs, ladies, downstairs. The display will take place in the basement rooms.'

He hurried forward to greet his editor's wife, then, shaking Du Roy by the hand, said: 'Good afternoon, Bel-Ami.' Surprised, Du Roy asked: 'Who told you that...' Rival interrupted him: 'This very lady, Mme Walter herself, who thinks it a delightful nickname.'

Mme Walter blushed: 'Yes, I must admit that if I knew you better, I would do like little Laurine, I too would call you Bel-Ami. It suits you very well.'

Du Roy laughed: 'But please do so, Madame.'

Mme Walter had dropped her gaze. 'No, we don't know each other well enough.'

He murmured: 'May I hope that we shall become better acquainted?'

'Well, we shall have to see,' she said.

He stood aside at the entrance to the narrow stairway that was lit by a gas-burner; the sudden transition from daylight to this yellow glow had a dismal quality. A subterranean smell rose up from this spiral staircase, an odour of heated humidity and damp walls wiped dry for the occasion, together with gusts of aromatic scents evocative of religious services, and feminine perfumes of Lubin water, verbena, iris, and violet.

Out of this cavern arose a loud buzz of voices and the bustle of an excited crowd. The whole cellar was illuminated with strings of gas lights and Chinese lanterns hidden in the foliage which screened the walls of mould-encrusted stone. You could see nothing but greenery. The ceiling was decorated with ferns, the floor with leaves and flowers. People thought it all charming, delightfully imaginative. In the little cellar at the back, a stage for the fencers had been set up, between two rows of chairs for the judges. The entire cellar, on both sides, was filled with seating arranged in groups of ten, sufficient to accommodate about two hundred people. Four hundred had been invited.

In front of the stage, young men in fencing outfits—slender, long-legged, deep-chested, with curly moustaches—were already posing for the spectators. People were identifying them, pointing out the experts and the amateurs, all the well-known names of the Paris fencing world. Standing around them chatting were frock-coated gentlemen, both young and old, who bore a family resemblance to the swordsmen dressed in fencing gear. They too wished to be seen, recognized, and identified, for they were the princes of swordplay in mufti, the experts of the foil.

Ladies occupied almost every bench, creating a great stir of rustling skirts, a great buzz of voices. They were fanning themselves, as if in the theatre, for it was already as hot as an oven in that leafy grotto. From time to time some wit would bellow: 'Barley-water! Lemonade! Beer!'

Mme Walter and her daughters took the seats reserved for them in the front row. Du Roy, having installed them, was about to depart, murmuring: 'I'll have to leave you, the men can't take up these seats.'

But Mme Walter replied hesitatingly: 'I'm very tempted to keep you here all the same. You can tell me who the fencers are. Look, if you were to stand just at the end of this bench, you wouldn't be in anyone's way.' She was gazing at him with her large soft eyes. She insisted: 'Come, stay with us, Monsieur... Monsieur Bel-Ami. We need you.'

He replied: 'I shall obey... with pleasure, Madame.'

On every side people were repeating: 'This cellar is such fun, it's really nice.'

Georges knew this vaulted room only too well! He was remembering the morning he had spent there, the day before his duel, all alone, in front of a small white carton which stared at him, from the depths of the back cellar, like an enormous, menacing eye.

From the staircase Jacques Rival's voice rang out: 'Ladies, we're about to begin.'

And six gentlemen, their coats tightly buttoned so as to show off their chests to advantage, stepped onto the stage and took the seats placed there for the judges. Their names* spread through the crowd: General de Raynaldi, a little man with a big moustache, who was presiding; the painter Joséphin Roudet, a tall, bald man with a long beard; Matthéo de Ujar, Simon Ramoncel, Pierre de Carvin, three elegant young men, and Gaspard Merleron, a fencing master.

Two placards were displayed, one on either side of the cellar. The one on the right announced: M. Crèvecœur, the one on the left: M. Plumeau. These were two fencing masters, both of them good, though not in the top rank. They appeared; they were lean men of military bearing, who moved stiffly. Having saluted with the foils in a robot-like manner, they began to fight, reminiscent, in their costumes of canvas and white leather, of a pair of clowns pretending to be soldiers and fighting to raise a laugh.

From time to time you heard the word: 'Touché!' And the six judges would bend their heads forward to consult together in a knowing way. The audience saw nothing but two flesh-and-blood marionettes that moved around stretching out their arms; they did not understand anything, but were satisfied. They were reminded of those wooden puppets of wrestlers sold on the city streets on New Year's Day.

The first two competitors were replaced by M. Planton and M. Carapin, a civilian and a military fencing master. M. Planton was very small and M. Carapin very large. It looked as if the first touch of the foil would deflate that balloon like a blown-up toy elephant. People were laughing. M. Planton was leaping about like a monkey. M. Carapin moved only his arm, for the rest of his body was immobilized by fat, and every five minutes he lunged forward so heavily and with so great an effort that he seemed to be taking the most energetic step of his life. Afterwards, he would find it extremely difficult to straighten up again. The experts declared his style very steady and forceful. The audience, trusting to the experts, admired him.

Next came M. Porion and M. Lapalme, a fencing master and an amateur, who embarked on a frenzied display of gymnastics, dashing furiously at each other, forcing the judges to flee carrying their chairs, crossing and recrossing the stage from side to side, one advancing and the other retreating with vigorous, comic leaps. They would give little jumps backwards that made the ladies laugh, and great leaps forward that were actually quite thrilling. This display in double time was characterized by some kid or other who yelled: 'Why get in a sweat, they pay by the hour!' The audience, ruffled by this lack of taste, said: 'Shsh!' The experts' opinion did the rounds. The fencers had displayed a lot of vigour and an occasional want of propriety.

The first half came to a close with a very beautiful passage-at-arms between Jacques Rival and the famous Belgian Professor Lebègue. Rival was much admired by the ladies. He was a truly handsome man, well made, supple, agile, and more graceful than all who had preceded him. In his style of standing *en garde* and of lunging he showed a certain worldly elegance that appealed, and contrasted with the energetic but commonplace style of his adversary. 'You can tell he's a man of breeding,' people were saying. He was the winner. There was applause.

But for some time past a peculiar noise, coming from the floor above, had been bothering the spectators. There was a lot of trampling about, accompanied by loud laughter. The two hundred guests who had been unable to get into the cellar were, no doubt, amusing themselves in their own fashion. Some fifty men were crowded onto the little spiral staircase. The heat below was growing intolerable. There were shouts of: 'Give us air!' 'Water!' The same wit as before was yelling in a shrill tone which rose above the murmur of conversation: 'Barley-water! Lemonade! Beer!'

Rival appeared, very red, still wearing his fencing kit. 'I'll bring down some refreshments,' he said, hurrying towards the stairs. But all communication with the ground floor was cut off. It would have been easier to pierce a hole in the ceiling than to penetrate the human wall blocking the stairs. Rival shouted: 'Pass down some ices for the ladies!' Fifty voices repeated: 'Ices!' Finally, a tray appeared. But it bore nothing but empty glasses, as the refreshments had been consumed on the way down.

A loud voice bellowed: 'We're stifling in here, let's get it over with and go home.' Another voice called: 'The collection!' And the entire audience, gasping for air but still cheerful, repeated: 'The collection... the collection... the collection...' Then six ladies began doing the rounds of the benches; you could hear the faint clink of money dropping into bags.

Du Roy was identifying the well-known figures for Mme Walter. These were men-about-town, journalists from the great newspapers, the old newspapers, who looked down on *La Vie française* with a certain reserve born of experience. They had watched the disappearance of so many of these politico-financial periodicals, the fruits of questionable partnerships, that were destroyed by the fall of a ministry. Also to be seen there were painters and sculptors, who are often also sportsmen, a poet, a member of the Academy, whom people were pointing out to one another, two musicians and a number of aristocratic foreigners to whose names Du Roy attached the syllable 'Adv.' (adventurer) in imitation, he said, of the English, who put 'Esq.' on their visiting cards.

Someone shouted to him: 'Good afternoon, my dear fellow.' It was the Comte de Vaudrec. Du Roy excused himself to the ladies, and went to shake his hand. He declared when he returned: 'Vaudrec's so gracious. His breeding really shows.'

Mme Walter made no reply. She was a little tired, and her bosom, rising laboriously with every breath she took, attracted Du Roy's eyes. From time to time he would encounter the gaze of the

Director's wife, an uneasy, hesitant gaze, which would rest upon him
and then instantly move away. He was thinking: 'My... my... Can I
have made it with that one as well?'

The ladies passed by with the collecting bags, which were full of
gold and silver. A fresh placard was hung on the stage, announcing:
'A verrry big surprise.' The members of the panel returned to their
places. Everyone waited.

Two women appeared carrying foils and dressed in fencing outfits,
with dark tights, very short skirts reaching to mid-thigh, and a plas-
tron that ballooned out over the bust so that they were forced to hold
their heads high. They were pretty, and young. They smiled as they
bowed to the audience. They were applauded for a long time.

They took up their positions *en garde* to the accompaniment of
appreciative murmurings and whispered jokes. The judges, their lips
set in pleasant smiles, uttered little 'bravos' in approval of the sword
thrusts.

The audience loved this display and let the contestants know as
much; it excited desire in the men, and in the women aroused that
natural taste of Parisian audiences for faintly bawdy entertainment,
for rather smutty elegance, for what is pseudo-pretty and pseudo-
graceful, like *café-concert* singers and songs from operettas. Each
time one of the fencers lunged, a thrill of pleasure ran through the
audience. The fencer who turned her back—a nicely filled-out
back—to the hall would cause mouths to open and eyes to pop; it was
not the movements of her wrist that drew the most gazes.

They were wildly applauded.

A display using sabres followed, but no one looked at it, for the
audience's attention was entirely taken up with what was happening
up above. For several minutes they had been hearing a tremendous
noise of furniture being shifted about and dragged over the floor, as
though the apartment were being vacated. Then, all of a sudden,
the sound of a piano came through the ceiling, and they could clearly
hear the rhythmic thud of feet moving to the beat. The people
upstairs were treating themselves to a dance, to make up for not
being able to see anything.

At first a ripple of laughter ran through the audience in the fencing hall, then the ladies, feeling an urge to dance, stopped paying
attention to what was happening on the stage and began talking in
loud voices. The idea of this dance organized by the late-comers

struck them as funny. No, those people weren't having a bad time at all. It would have been really nice to be up there.

But two new contestants were saluting one another, and taking up their positions *en garde* with so much authority that every eye followed their movements. They lunged and recovered with such supple grace and restrained vigour, with such self-assured strength, such economy of movement, such flawlessness of bearing and control of swordplay, that the ignorant crowd was amazed and enchanted.

Their unruffled alertness, their judicious flexibility, their rapid movements, so studied as to appear slow, attracted and captivated the eye by the simple power of perfection. The audience felt that in them they were watching something beautiful and rare, that two great artists in their field were demonstrating the very best that could be seen, everything that two masters could possibly display of skill, of cunning, of technical knowledge, and physical dexterity. The audience was no longer talking, they were watching so intently. Then, when the two shook hands, after the final touch, cheers and hurrahs rang out. People were stamping and shouting. Everyone knew their names: Sergent and Ravignac.

Excited by all this, the audience was growing feisty. Men felt an impulse to pick a quarrel when they glanced at their neighbour. A duel might have been provoked by a smile. People who had never handled a foil sketched lunges and parries with their walking-sticks.

The crowd, however, was slowly making its way back up the little stairway. They were finally going to have something to drink. There was great indignation when they realized that the dancers had ransacked the buffet and had departed, declaring that it was rude to inconvenience two hundred people and then not show them anything.

Not a cake remained, not a drop of champagne, fruit cordial, or beer, not a sweetmeat, not a fruit, nothing, nothing whatsoever. They had pillaged, plundered, made a clean sweep. All these details were elicited from the servants, whose doleful expressions concealed their urge to laugh. The ladies were more desperate than the men, they declared, and had eaten and drunk enough to make them ill. You might have been listening to survivors describe the sacking and looting of a city during the Invasion.

So they all simply had to leave. Some of the men regretted having donated twenty francs to the collection; they were very annoyed that the people upstairs had gorged themselves without paying anything. The lady patronesses had collected more than three thousand francs. There remained, after all the expenses were paid, two hundred and twenty francs for the orphans of the sixth *arrondissement*.

Du Roy, who was escorting the Walter family, waited for his landau. Sitting opposite the Director's wife on the way back, he again met her tender, furtive gaze, which seemed troubled. He thought: 'My God! I do believe she's falling for me,' and he smiled, reflecting that he really was lucky with women, for Mme de Marelle, since their affair had begun again, seemed to be wildly in love with him.

He went home walking on air. Madeleine was waiting for him in the drawing-room.

'I've some news,' she said. 'The Morocco business is getting complicated. France might well send an expeditionary force there in a few months' time. In any event, that's going to be the excuse for overthrowing the government, and Laroche will take advantage of the chance to snap up Foreign Affairs.'

To tease his wife, Du Roy pretended not to believe her. They'd never be so crazy as to start the same idiotic thing that they did in Tunis. But she was shrugging her shoulders impatiently. 'I'm telling you they will! They will! You don't seem to grasp that for them there's a lot of money involved. These days, my dear, in politics, you shouldn't ask "who's the woman behind it," but "what's the money in it?"'

To annoy her, he muttered: 'nonsense!' in a scornful tone.

She was getting angry: 'Goodness, you're as green as Forestier.'

She meant to hurt him and expected an angry outburst. But he smiled, and replied: 'As that cuckold Forestier?'

Shocked, she murmured: 'Oh! Georges!'

With an insolent, mocking air he went on: 'Well, what? Didn't you confess to me, the other evening, that Forestier was a cuckold?' And he added: 'Poor devil!' in a tone of intense pity.

Madeleine turned her back to him, not deigning to reply; then, after a moment's silence, she continued: 'We're having guests on Tuesday: Mme Laroche-Mathieu will be coming to dinner with the Vicomtesse de Percemur. Will you ask Rival and Norbert de Varenne? Tomorrow I'll go and see Mme Walter and Mme de Marelle. We might have Mme Rissolin as well.'

For some time she had been building up a network of contacts, making use of her husband's political influence to attract to her home, by fair means or foul, the wives of senators or deputies who needed the support of *La Vie française*. Du Roy replied: 'Fine. I'll see to asking Rival and Norbert.'

Feeling pleased, he rubbed his hands, for he had discovered a perfect catchword to annoy his wife and satisfy the mysterious resentment, the obscure, corrosive jealousy that had been growing in him since their drive in the Bois. He would never mention Forestier again without calling him a cuckold. He was quite sure that this would, in the end, infuriate Madeleine. And ten times in the course of the evening he found a chance to utter, in tones of good-natured irony, the name of 'that cuckold Forestier.'

He no longer bore the dead man a grudge: he was avenging him.

His wife pretended not to hear and went on smiling at him, apparently unconcerned. The following morning, since she would be calling on Mme Walter to invite her, he decided to go there first, to catch his Director's wife alone and see if she really was attracted to him. He found this thought amusing and flattering. And then... why not... if it was possible?

Promptly at two o'clock he went to the Boulevard Malesherbes. He was shown into the drawing-room. He waited.

Mme Walter came in, offering him her hand with eager delight.

'What lucky chance brings you here?'

'No lucky chance, but a wish to see you. Something made me come to your house, I don't know why, I've nothing to say to you. I just came, and here I am! Will you forgive me for calling so early, and for this frank explanation?' He said this in a worldly, playful tone, with a smile on his lips and a serious note in his voice.

Astonished and rather pink, she stammered: 'But... really... I don't understand... you surprise me...'

He went on: 'This is a declaration in the light-hearted mode, so as not to alarm you.'

They had sat down side by side. She treated it as a joke.

'So this is a... serious declaration?'

'Of course! I've been wanting to make it for a long time, indeed for a very long time. But then I didn't dare. People say you're so strict, so unbending...'

She had regained her confidence. She answered: 'Why did you choose today?'

'I don't know.' Then, lowering his voice: 'Or, rather, because I've thought of nothing but you, since yesterday.'

Suddenly she turned white, and faltered: 'Come on, that's enough of this nonsense, let's talk of something else.'

But he had fallen to his knees, so abruptly that she was frightened. She tried to stand up; but he was holding her in her seat, his arms round her waist, and repeating in a passionate voice: 'Yes, it's true, I love you, madly, I've loved you for a long time. Don't answer me. I'm sorry, I'm losing my mind! I love you... Oh! if you only knew how much I love you!'

Gasping and panting, she tried to speak but could not utter a word. She was pushing him away with both hands, grabbing at his hair to prevent the approach of that mouth she could feel coming closer to her own. And, with rapid movements, she kept turning her head from right to left and from left to right, closing her eyes so she could no longer see him.

He was fondling her through her dress, running his hands over her body, pawing her; and she was almost fainting under this brutal, powerful caress. Suddenly he stood up and tried to embrace her, but she used her momentary freedom to move back and away, escaping, now, from chair to chair. Deciding that this pursuit was ridiculous, he let himself fall onto a chair, his face in his hands, and pretended to be racked by violent sobs.

Then, drawing himself up, he cried: 'Goodbye! Goodbye!' and fled.

In the entrance hall he calmly picked up his walking-stick and went out into the street, telling himself: 'Christ! I do believe it's in the bag.' And he went to the telegraph office to send Clotilde a wire, setting up a meeting for the next day.

On returning home at his usual time, he asked his wife: 'Well, did you get everybody for your dinner-party?'

She replied: 'Yes; there's only Mme Walter who's not sure she's free. She wavered; she said something about—oh, I don't know—an engagement, her conscience. I thought she seemed very odd. Anyway it doesn't matter, I hope she'll come just the same.'

He shrugged: 'Oh, Lord, yes; she'll come.'

He was not, however, certain of it, and felt uneasy right up to the day of the dinner.

On the morning itself Madeleine received a little note from the Director's wife: 'I've arranged, with considerable difficulty, to be free, and I shall be joining you. But my husband will not be able to accompany me.'

Du Roy thought: 'I was absolutely right not to go back there. She's calmed down. I must be careful.'

But he awaited her arrival with some anxiety. She appeared, very calm, rather cold, rather haughty. He made himself very meek, very circumspect and submissive.

Mme Laroche-Mathieu and Mme Rissolin accompanied their husbands. The Vicomtesse de Percemur talked about high society. Mme de Marelle was enchanting in a fantastic garment of black and yellow, a Spanish outfit that clung to her pretty waist, her breasts and her dimpled arms, and gave added sparkle to her tiny bird-like head.

Du Roy had seated Mme Walter on his right, and during the dinner spoke to her only about serious matters, with exaggerated respect. From time to time he glanced at Clotilde. 'She really is prettier, and fresher,' he thought. Then his eyes would come back to his wife; she wasn't bad either, although he still felt a repressed anger against her, a persistent, spiteful anger.

But it was precisely the difficulty of seducing the Director's wife which sexually excited him, as well as the novelty which men always want.

She wanted to leave early. 'I'll take you home,' he said.

She refused. He insisted. 'Why don't you want me to? You're going to hurt me very deeply. Don't let me think that you haven't forgiven me. You can see how calm I am.'

She replied: 'You can't abandon your guests like that.'

He smiled. 'Oh! I'll only be gone twenty minutes. They won't even notice. If you refuse, you'll cut me to the quick.'

She murmured: 'Very well, I accept.'

But as soon as they were in the carriage, he seized her hand, and, kissing it passionately: 'I love you, I love you. Let me tell you that. I won't touch you. I simply want to tell you again and again that I love you.'

She stammered: 'Oh... after what you promised... It's wrong, very wrong.'

He seemed to make a great effort, then, in a restrained voice, went on: 'There, see how I'm controlling myself. And yet... But allow me just to say this to you: I love you, and to tell you so every day... yes, let me go to your home and kneel a few minutes at your feet to utter those three words, while I gaze at your beloved face.'

She had surrendered her hand to him, and said, gasping for breath: 'No, I can't, I won't. Think what people would say, think of my servants, of my daughters. No, no, it's impossible...'

He continued: 'I can no longer live without seeing you. Whether it's in your home or somewhere else, I have to see you, were it only for one moment every day, I have to touch your hand, breathe the air stirred by your skirts, gaze at the shape of your body and at your beautiful big eyes that drive me demented.'

She was trembling as she listened to this banal music of love, and stammering: 'No... no... it's impossible. Be quiet!'

He was speaking very softly into her ear, realizing that with this one, this simple woman, he would have to ensnare her very gradually, persuade her to agree to meet him, first at a place she would choose, then, later, somewhere he chose: 'Listen... you must... I shall see you... I shall wait in front of your door like a beggar... If you don't come down, I shall go in to you... but I shall see you... I shall see you... tomorrow.'

She kept saying: 'No... no... don't come. I won't see you. Think of my daughters.'

'Then tell me where I can meet you... in the street, anywhere... whenever you wish... just as long as I see you... I shall bow, and say "I love you" and leave.'

She hesitated, uncertain what to do. And, as the vehicle was passing the door of her house, she said in a rapid whisper: 'Well, I'll go to the Holy Trinity,* tomorrow at three-thirty.' Getting out of the carriage, she said to her coachman: 'Take M. Du Roy home.'

On his return, his wife asked him: 'Where did you go?'

He replied in a low voice: 'To the telegraph office, to send an urgent wire.'

Mme de Marelle came up to them: 'You'll see me home, Bel-Ami, won't you? You know that's the only way I can come so far for dinner.' Then, turning to Madeleine, 'You're not jealous?'

Mme Du Roy slowly replied: 'No, not very.'

The guests were leaving. Mme Laroche-Mathieu looked like a little provincial housemaid. She was the daughter of a notary, and Laroche had married her when he was just a second-rate lawyer.

Mme Rissolin, elderly and pretentious, had the air of a former mid-wife whose education had been acquired in public reading-rooms. The Vicomtesse de Percemur looked down on both of them. Her 'white paw' disliked the touch of such vulgar fingers.

Clotilde, enveloped in lace, said to Madeleine as she went through the door onto the landing: 'Your dinner-party was perfect. In a little while you'll have the most influential political salon in Paris.'

As soon as she was alone with Georges, she clasped him in her arms. 'Ah! Bel-Ami, my darling, I love you more every day.'

The cab they were in was rocking like a ship. 'This isn't as good as our room,' she said. He replied: 'Oh, no!' But he was thinking of Mme Walter.

CHAPTER 4

The Place de la Trinité was almost deserted under a brilliant July sun. Paris lay sweltering in the oppressive heat, as if the air from the sky above, dense and scorching, had sunk down on to the city, viscous, burning air that hurt your lungs.

The fountain in front of the church flowed languidly. It seemed tired, equally weary and listless, and the water in the basin, upon which leaves and bits of paper were floating, looked faintly greenish, thick, and glaucous.

A dog that had jumped over the stone rim was soaking itself in this unappealing fluid. People on the benches in the small round garden in front of the church porch were eyeing the animal enviously.

Du Roy took out his watch. It was not yet three. He was thirty minutes early. He laughed as he thought about this meeting. 'She finds churches handy for everything,' he reflected. 'They comfort her for marrying a Jew, they provide her with a cause to champion in the political world, an irreproachable image in high society, and a safe place to meet her lovers. How nice, to be able to use religion like an umbrella-cum-sunshade. When it's fine, you've a walking-stick, when it's sunny, a parasol, when it rains an umbrella and, if you don't go out, you can leave it in the hall. And there are hundreds of women like that, who don't give a damn about God, but don't like anyone to speak ill of him, and who use him, if necessary, as a go-between. If you suggested meeting in a rented room, they'd be indignant, but it strikes them as perfectly normal to carry on an affair at the foot of an altar.'

He was walking slowly along the side of the basin; then he looked at the time again, by the church clock, which was two minutes faster than his watch. It said five past three.

Deciding that he would be more comfortable inside, he went in. He was met by a cellar-like coolness, which he breathed in with delight; then he strolled round the nave to familiarize himself with it.

From the depths of the vast building another regular footstep, which paused from time to time and then began again, echoed the sound of his own tread as it rose up sonorously under the high vaulted roof. Growing curious as to the identity of this other visitor, he looked for him. It was a stout, bald gentleman, who walked with his nose in the air, holding his hat behind his back.

Here and there, old women were kneeling at prayer, their faces in their hands. He was filled with a sense of solitude, of seclusion, of repose. The light, subtly tinged with colour by the stained glass, was gentle to the eye.

Du Roy thought it 'damned nice' in there.

He returned to the area by the door, and looked again at his watch. It was still only three-fifteen. He took a seat at the entrance to the main aisle, sorry that he could not light up a cigarette. The measured tread of the stout gentleman was still audible, near the choir, at the far end of the church.

Someone came in. Georges turned round sharply. It was a working-class woman in a woollen skirt, a poor woman who fell to her knees beside the first chair, and remained motionless, her fingers intertwined, her gaze directed upwards, lost in prayer. Du Roy watched her with interest, wondering what grief, or pain, or despair might be tormenting that humble heart. She was desperately poor, that was obvious. Perhaps she also had a husband who beat her mercilessly, or even a dying child.

He murmured to himself: 'Poor things. Some of them do suffer.' A wave of anger against implacable Mother Nature swept through him. Then he reflected that those wretches did at least believe that they mattered to someone up there, that the facts relating to their existence were inscribed in the heavenly register, along with the reckoning of their debits and their credits. Up there—but where?

And Du Roy, in whom the silence of the church had inspired vast conjectures, disposed of the Creation in a single thought, muttering: 'How stupid all that is.'

The rustle of a dress startled him. It was her.

He stood up, and moved rapidly towards her. She did not offer her hand, but whispered in a low voice: 'I've only got a few minutes. I must get home; kneel down near me, so that we shan't be noticed.'

And she went up the main aisle in search of a suitable, safe place, like a woman who knows every corner of a house. Her face was concealed by a thick veil, and she walked with a soft step that was barely audible. She had almost reached the choir when she turned round and mumbled in that mysterious tone that people affect in church: 'The side-aisles would be better. Round here we're too obvious.'

She bent her head low before the Tabernacle on the high altar, adding a slight bob; then, turning right, she moved back in the direction of the entrance, and, finally making up her mind, chose a prayer stool and knelt down.

Georges took the adjacent prayer stool and, as soon as they were kneeling as if at prayer: 'Thank you, thank you,' he said. 'I adore you. I would like to tell you so all the time, describe to you how I started to love you, how I was utterly captivated the first time I saw you... One day will you let me pour out my heart, and tell you all that I feel?'

She was listening to him in an attitude of deep meditation, as if she heard nothing. Between her fingers she replied: 'I'm mad to let you speak to me like this, mad to have come, mad to do what I'm doing, to allow you to believe that this... this intrigue can come to anything. Forget all this, you must, and never speak to me of it again.'

She waited. He searched for a reply, for decisive, passionate words, but being unable to translate words into action, he felt his will was paralysed. He answered: 'I expect nothing... I hope for nothing. I love you. No matter what you do, I shall repeat this to you so often, with so much force and passion, that in the end you will certainly understand. I want to fill you with my love, I want to pour it into your soul, word by word, hour by hour, day by day, so that you will eventually be permeated by it as if by a liquid falling drop by drop, so that it may disarm you, and soften you, and force you, one day, to tell me: "I love you too."'

He could sense, beside him, the quivering of her shoulders and the throbbing of her breast, as, very rapidly, she stammered: 'I love you too.'

He gave a start, as if he had been struck sharply on the head, and sighed: 'Oh! My God!'

She continued, in a breathless voice: 'Ought I to be telling you that? I feel guilty and despicable... I... who have two daughters... but I can't... I can't... I would never have believed... I would never have thought... I can't help it... I can't help it. Listen... listen... I've never loved... anyone but you... I swear to you. I've loved you for a year, secretly, in my secret heart. Oh, I've suffered, believe me, and struggled, I can't help it, I love you...'

She was weeping into the fingers that covered her face, and her whole body was trembling, shaken by the violence of her emotion.

Georges whispered: 'Give me your hand, let me touch it, let me press it...'

Slowly she took her hand from her face. He saw her cheek soaked with tears, and a drop of water on the edge of her lashes, just about to fall.

He had grasped her hand, he was squeezing it: 'Oh! How I would love to drink your tears!'

She said in a low, broken voice: 'Don't take advantage of me... I'm lost!'

He wanted to smile. How could he have taken advantage of her there? He put the hand he was holding on his heart, and asked: 'Can you feel how it's beating?' for he had run out of passionate phrases.

But, during the last few minutes, the regular step of the other visitor had been approaching. He had done the rounds of the altars and was now returning, for at least the second time, down the right side-aisle. When Mme Walter heard him very close to the pillar that concealed her, she pulled her fingers out of Georges's grasp and again covered her face.

And they both remained on their knees without moving, as if they were jointly addressing fervent prayers to heaven. The stout gentleman passed close beside them, casting them an indifferent glance, and moved off towards the rear of the church, still holding his hat behind his back.

Du Roy, intent on arranging a meeting somewhere other than in that church, whispered: 'Where shall I see you tomorrow?' She did not reply. She seemed lifeless, changed into a stone image of Prayer. He went on: 'Tomorrow, would you like to meet in the Parc Monceau?'

She turned her face to him, a ghastly face, convulsed by terrible suffering, and said in a shaky voice: 'Leave me, leave me now... go away... go away... just for five minutes... I suffer too much when I'm near you... I want to pray... I can't pray... go away... leave me to pray... for five minutes... I can't... let me beg God... to forgive me... to save me... leave me... five minutes.'

Her face was so distraught, so full of pain, that he rose without a word, and after hesitating asked: 'I'll come back in a little while?'

She gave a nod, meaning 'Yes, in a little while.' He walked off in the direction of the choir.

So then she tried to pray. She made a superhuman effort of invocation to reach God, as, shaking all over and full of torment, she cried out to heaven for mercy. Desperately she closed her eyes so that she could no longer see that man who had just left her. Banishing him from her thoughts, she struggled against him, but in place of the heavenly vision for which her anguished heart was yearning, what she still saw was the young man's curly moustache.

For a year now she had been struggling like this, day and night, against this growing obsession, against this image which haunted her dreams and her flesh and disturbed her sleep. She felt trapped like an animal in a net, bound, cast into the arms of this male who had overpowered and conquered her, simply by the hair on his lip and the colour of his eyes.

And now, in this church, very close to God, she felt herself weaker, more forsaken, more lost even than in her own home. She could no longer pray, she could think only of him. Already she was suffering because he had moved away. Nevertheless she fought like a desperate woman, defending herself, calling for help with all the power of her soul. She would have preferred to die, rather than fall like this, she who had never transgressed. She was whispering frantic words of supplication, but she was listening to the sound of Georges's footsteps dying away under the distant arches.

She realized that it was over, that struggling was useless. Nevertheless she did not want to surrender, and she was seized by one of those attacks of hysteria that fling women to the ground, quivering, howling, and writhing. She was trembling in every limb, certain that she was about to collapse and roll, shrieking, between the chairs.

Someone was approaching rapidly. She turned her head. It was a priest. So she stood up and, rushing over to him with clasped hands, stammered: 'Oh! Save me! Save me!'

He halted, surprised. 'What is it that you want, Madame?'

'I want you to save me. Have pity on me. Unless you help me, I am lost.'

He gazed at her, wondering if she might perhaps be crazy. He repeated: 'What can I do for you?'

He was a young man, tall and a trifle heavy, with full, pendulous jowls darkened by his scrupulously shaved beard, a handsome city priest for an affluent neighbourhood, accustomed to confessing wealthy women parishioners.

'Hear my confession,' she said, 'and counsel me, support me, tell me what to do!'

He replied: 'I hear confession every Saturday, from three until six.'

She had grabbed hold of his arm, and kept clutching at it as she insisted: 'No, no, no! Now, now! You must! He's here! In this church! He's waiting for me.'

The priest asked: 'Who's waiting for you?'

'A man... who'll be my downfall... who'll take me, if you don't save me... I can't escape him, I'm too weak... too weak... so weak... so weak!' She fell to her knees, sobbing: 'Oh, have pity on me, Father! Save me, in God's name save me!'

She was holding on to his black robe so that he could not get away from her; and he looked uneasily round, in case some spiteful or pious eye might see this woman lying at his feet. Realizing, finally, that he would not be able to get away from her: 'Stand up,' he said, 'it so happens I have the key to the confessional on me.' And, rummaging in his pocket, he produced a ring of keys, selected one, and then walked quickly over towards some little wooden booths, containers for the refuse of souls, into which believers empty out their sins.

He went in by the door in the centre which he closed behind him, and Mme Walter, who had flung herself into the narrow box on one side, stammered fervently, in an access of impassioned hope: 'Bless me, Father, for I have sinned.'

Du Roy, having walked round the chancel, turned down the left aisle. On reaching the centre he met the stout, bald gentleman, who was still calmly sauntering along, and he wondered: 'What in the world can this fellow be doing here?'

The other walker had also slowed his pace and was looking at Georges with an evident desire to speak to him. When he was close he bowed and said very politely: 'I beg your pardon, Monsieur, for troubling you, but could you tell me the date when this church was built?'

Du Roy replied: 'My word, I'm not quite sure, but I think twenty years ago, or twenty-five.* Actually, it's the first time I've been inside it.'

'Same for me. I'd never seen it.'

So then the journalist, who was growing curious, went on: 'You seem to be looking round it most attentively. You're studying all its details.'

The other told him, in a resigned tone: 'I'm not looking round it, Monsieur, I'm waiting for my wife who arranged to meet me here, and is extremely late.'

He fell silent, then said, after a few seconds: 'It's dreadfully hot, outside.'

Du Roy gazed at him, thinking he looked a bit of a fool, and suddenly it struck him that he resembled Forestier.

'You're from the provinces?' he asked.

'Yes, from Rennes.* And you, Monsieur, is it curiosity that brings you to this church?'

'No, I myself am waiting for a woman.' And, with a bow, the journalist walked away, a smile on his lips.

As he approached the main entrance, he again saw the beggar woman; she was still on her knees, praying. He thought: 'Good Lord! She's certainly persistent with her prayers.' He was no longer moved; he no longer felt sorry for her. He passed by her and began walking quietly up the right aisle to meet Mme Walter.

He examined, from far away, the spot where he had left her, and was astonished not to see her. Thinking that he must have mistaken the pillar, he went up to the end one, and then returned. So, she must have left! He was surprised and infuriated. Then he thought that she might be looking for him, and walked round the church again. Not having found her, he came back to the chair she had been occupying, hoping that she would join him there. He waited.

Before long a soft murmuring attracted his attention. He had seen no one in that part of the church. So where was this whispering coming from? Rising to his feet to investigate, he noticed, in the next chapel, the doors of the confessionals. The edge of a dress protruded from one of them, trailing over the flagstones. He went nearer and studied the woman. He recognized her. She was making her confession!...

He felt a violent urge to take her by the shoulders and drag her from the box. Then he thought: 'Who cares! Today it's the priest's turn, tomorrow it'll be mine.' And he sat calmly down opposite the confessional, biding his time, now laughing to himself derisively at how it had turned out.

He waited a long time. Finally, Mme Walter arose, turned round, saw him and came over to him. Her face was cold and severe: 'Monsieur,' she said, 'I must ask you not to accompany me, not to follow me, and not to come alone to my home. You will not be received. Goodbye!'

And away she walked, her manner stately.

He let her go, for it was one of his principles never to force matters. Then, as the priest was emerging somewhat uneasily from his lair, he went straight up to him, looked deep into his eyes, and growled into his face: 'If you weren't wearing skirts, what a punch I'd give you right on your ugly snout, wouldn't I just!'

Then he turned on his heels and left the church, whistling.

Tired of waiting, the stout gentleman was standing under the portal, his hat on his head and his hands behind his back, scrutinizing the vast square and all the streets that run into it. When Du Roy passed by him, they nodded to one another.

Finding himself at a loose end, the journalist walked down to *La Vie française*. As soon as he went in he saw, from the flurried manner of the employees, that something most unusual was going on, and he hurried to the Director's office.

Old man Walter was on his feet, excitedly dictating an article in disconnected sentences, and between paragraphs issuing orders to the reporters round him, giving Boisrenard advice, and opening letters.

When Du Roy came in, M. Walter cried delightedly: 'Oh! What luck, here's Bel-Ami!'

He stopped dead, a little embarrassed, and apologized: 'I beg your pardon for calling you that, I'm very flustered by what's happening. And then, I hear my wife and daughters calling you "Bel-Ami" all day long, and so I've picked up the habit myself. You're not annoyed with me?'

Georges laughed: 'Not in the least. I've no objection to that nickname.'

M. Walter went on: 'Fine, so I'll christen you Bel-Ami like everyone else. Well now! Some very important things are going on.* The ministry has fallen—the vote was 310 to 102. The recess has been postponed again, indefinitely, and today's the 28th of July. Spain is getting angry about Morocco, that's what brought down Durand de l'Aine and his followers. We're up to our necks in the mess. Marrot has agreed to form a new cabinet. He's giving the War Office to General Boutin d'Ancre and the Foreign Office to our friend Laroche-Mathieu. He himself will be Minister of the Interior and President of the Council. We're going to become an official news paper. I'm writing the leader, a simple declaration of principles, with suggestions on how the government should proceed.'

The old boy smiled, and added: 'I mean of course suggestions in keeping with their declared intentions. But we need something interesting on the Moroccan question, something current, sensational, an attention getter... oh I don't know... Give me something of that sort, Bel-Ami.'

Du Roy reflected for a moment, then replied: 'I've just the thing. I'll give you an analysis of the politics of all our African colonies, with Tunisia to the left, Algeria in the centre, and Morocco to the right, the history of the races that live in this vast territory, and an account of an excursion along the Moroccan frontier as far as the great oasis at Figuig,* where no European has ever set foot and which is the cause of the present conflict. Does that suit you?'

Old Walter exclaimed: 'Admirable! And the title? "From Tunis to Tangier!"'

'Excellent.'

And off Du Roy went, to hunt through the archives of *La Vie française* for his first article: 'Recollections of an African Cavalryman' which, retitled, reconfigured, and rewritten, was from start to finish precisely what was wanted, since it dealt with colonial politics, the Algerian population, and an expedition into the province of Oran.

In three-quarters of an hour the thing was redone, cobbled together, adapted, updated, with praises for the new cabinet tacked on.

After reading the article, the Director declared: 'It's perfect... perfect... perfect. You're absolutely invaluable. I do congratulate you.'

And Du Roy went home for dinner, delighted with his day, despite the setback at the Holy Trinity, for he was convinced that the game was his.

His wife was waiting for him in a fever of excitement. She

exclaimed on seeing him: 'You know that Laroche is Minister of Foreign Affairs?'

'Yes, in fact I've just been writing an article on Algeria in connection with that.'

'What do you mean?'

'You know the one, it's the first we wrote together: "Recollections of an African Cavalryman" revised and corrected for the occasion.'

She smiled: 'Ah yes, the very thing.'

Then after a few moments' thought: 'By the way, that sequel that you were going to write then, and that you... abandoned along the way. We can have a go at it now. It will give us a nice series that's just what's wanted.'

As he sat down to his soup he replied: 'Absolutely. There's no longer anything to stop us, now that that cuckold Forestier's dead.'

She said sharply, in a curt, injured tone: 'That joke is worse than uncalled for, and I beg you to give it a rest. It's been going on for too long.'

He was about to make a sarcastic retort when a message was brought to him containing just these words, with no signature: 'I lost my head. Forgive me, and come at four tomorrow to the Parc Monceau.'

He understood; suddenly his heart was filled with joy, and, slipping the blue sheet into his pocket, he said to his wife: 'I won't do it any more, my dear. It's silly. I admit it.'

And he began his dinner.

As he ate he kept repeating those few words to himself: 'I lost my head, forgive me, and come at four tomorrow to the Parc Monceau.' So she was surrendering. It meant: 'I give in, I am yours, wherever you want, whenever you want.'

He began to laugh. Madeleine asked: 'What is it?'

'Nothing much, I was thinking of a priest I met recently, who had a funny face.'

The next day, Du Roy arrived at the rendezvous exactly on time. All the park benches were occupied by Parisians overcome by the heat, and by listless servant-girls who seemed to be dreaming, while the children rolled about on the sandy paths.

He found Mme Walter in the small classical ruin where there is a spring of water. She was walking round the narrow ring of little columns, her air anxious and unhappy.

As soon as he had greeted her: 'What a lot of people there are in this park!' she said.

He snatched at the chance: 'Yes, that's right; would you like to go somewhere else?'

'But where?'

'Anywhere, in a cab, for instance. You can lower the blind on your side and you'll be quite safe.'

'Yes, I'd prefer that; I'm scared to death here.'

'All right, meet me in five minutes at the gate onto the outer boulevard. I'll come there with a cab.'

And off he went at a run.

As soon as she had got into the cab and had carefully screened the window on her side, she asked: 'Where did you tell the driver to take us?'

Georges replied: 'Don't worry about anything, he knows what to do.'

He had given the man the address of his flat in the Rue de Constantinople.

She went on: 'You can't imagine what I suffer because of you, what torment and agony I endure. Yesterday in the church I was cruel, but I wanted to get away from you at any price. I'm so frightened of being alone with you. Have you forgiven me?'

He was pressing her hands. 'Yes, yes. What wouldn't I forgive you for, loving you the way I do?'

She was gazing at him with an air of entreaty. 'Listen, you must promise to respect me... not to... not to... otherwise I couldn't see you any more.'

At first he did not reply; beneath his moustache he was smiling in the subtle way that women found so disturbing. Eventually he murmured: 'I am your slave.'

Then she started telling him how she had realized that she loved him when she learnt that he was going to marry Madeleine Forestier. She gave details, little details of dates and other very personal things.

Suddenly she fell silent. The cab had just halted. Du Roy opened the door.

'Where are we?' she enquired.

He replied: 'Get out and go into the house. We'll be less disturbed here.'

'But where are we?'

'At my place. It's my bachelor apartment that I've rented again... for a few days... to have somewhere where we could see each other.'

She had clutched hold of the back of the cab seat, appalled at the idea of such a tête-à-tête, and she stammered:

'No, no, I don't want to! I don't want to!'

He said very firmly: 'I swear to respect you. Come. You can see people are looking at us, soon they'll be crowding round us. Hurry... hurry... get out.' And he repeated: 'I swear to respect you.'

A barkeeper was standing at his door watching them in an inquisitive way. Overcome with terror, she fled into the house.

She started to climb the stairs. Holding her back by the arm, he said: 'It's here, on the ground floor.' And he pushed her into his flat.

The instant he closed the door, he pounced on her like a bird of prey. She struggled, fighting him off, stammering: 'Oh, my God! Oh, my God!'

He was passionately kissing her neck, her eyes, her lips, without her being able to avoid his savage caresses; and, even as she was pushing him away, and retreating from his mouth, she was, in spite of herself, returning his kisses.

Quite suddenly she stopped struggling; defeated and resigned, she let herself be undressed by him. Skilfully and speedily, with the light touch of a lady's maid, he removed her clothing item by item.

She had snatched her bodice from his hands to hide her face in, and she stood there, all white, surrounded by her garments that lay discarded at her feet.

Leaving her boots on, he carried her in his arms to the bed. Then, in a broken voice, she whispered in his ear: 'I swear to you... I swear... I've never had a lover...' just as a young girl might have said: 'I swear I'm a virgin.'

And he was thinking: 'As if I care!'

CHAPTER 5

It was autumn. The Du Roys had spent the entire summer in Paris, waging a vigorous campaign in *La Vie française* in support of the new cabinet, during the deputies' brief recess.

In spite of the fact that it was only the beginning of October, the two Chambers* were about to reconvene, for the Moroccan affair was becoming increasingly threatening.

Basically no one believed that an expeditionary force would be sent to Tangiers, although on the day Parliament was dissolved, a right-wing deputy, the Comte de Lambert-Sarrazin,* in an extremely witty speech that even the centrists had applauded, had offered to wager his moustache—and to hand it over as security just as a famous viceroy of India had once done in the past—against the side-whiskers of the President of the Council,* that the new cabinet would not be able to resist imitating the old one, and sending a force to Tangier to counterbalance the one in Tunis, out of love of symmetry, just as people put two vases above a fireplace.

He had added: 'Africa is in fact a fireplace for France, gentlemen, a fireplace that burns our best wood, a fireplace with a powerful draught, and which uses the paper of the Bank for kindling.

'You have allowed yourselves the artistic licence of decorating the left-hand corner with a Tunisian knick-knack which is costing you dear; and you'll see that M. Marrot will want to imitate his predecessor, and decorate the right-hand corner with a knick-knack from Morocco.'

This speech, which has gone down in history, provided Du Roy with a central theme for ten articles about the colony of Algeria, indeed for the whole series which had been stopped when he was first working for the paper, and he had strongly supported the idea of a military expedition, although he was convinced it would not materialize. He had harped on about patriotism and had blasted Spain with the entire arsenal of scornful arguments that people use against nations whose interests conflict with their own.

La Vie française had acquired considerable importance thanks to its known connections with those in power. It published items of political news ahead of the more serious papers, and revealed, through subtle hints, the plans of the ministers who were its friends; so that all the Parisian and provincial newspapers looked to it for their information. It was quoted, it was feared, it was beginning to be respected. It was no longer the suspect organ of a group of political speculators, but the acknowledged voice of the cabinet. Laroche-Mathieu was the soul of the paper and Du Roy his mouthpiece. Old man Walter, who as deputy never spoke, and as Director was invariably wary and skilled at self-effacement, remained in the background negotiating, it was said, an important deal involving some copper mines in Morocco.

Madeleine's drawing-room had become a centre of influence, for several members of the cabinet would meet there each week. The President of the Council had even dined twice at her table; and statesmen's wives, who in the past had hesitated to cross her threshold, now boasted of being her friends, and called on her more often than she on them.

The Foreign Secretary reigned over the household almost as if he were its master. He dropped in at all hours, bringing dispatches, reports, and information, which he would dictate to either husband or wife, as if they were his secretaries.

When the minister had departed and Du Roy was alone with his wife, he would lose his temper over the way that insignificant upstart behaved, and make insidious suggestions in a threatening tone.

But she, shrugging her shoulders disdainfully, would answer: 'Why don't you like him? Become a minister: then you can do as you like. Until then, keep quiet.'

Giving her a sidelong glance, he twirled his moustache. 'No one knows what I'm capable of,' he said. 'Maybe one day people will find out.'

She replied imperturbably: 'Time will tell.'

The morning when the Chambers reconvened, the young woman, still in bed, was showering her husband with advice while he dressed for a lunch engagement with M. Laroche-Mathieu at which he was to receive instructions, before the session, for the next day's political article in *La Vie française*; this article was to be a kind of semi-official announcement of the cabinet's real intentions.

Madeleine was saying: 'Be sure not to forget to ask him if General Belloncle* is being sent to Oran, as they were thinking of doing. That would be very significant.'

Georges replied edgily: 'I know as well as you what I have to do. Leave me alone! Stop harping on it all.'

Calmly she said: 'Georges dear, you always forget half the things I want you to ask the minister.'

He growled: 'Your minister gets on my nerves, he really does. He's an idiot.'

Madeleine's reply was cool: 'He's no more my minister than yours. He's more useful to you than to me.'

He turned a little towards her, curling his lip: 'I beg your pardon, but it's not me he's making up to.'

She said, slowly: 'Nor me, as a matter of fact; but it's because of him that we're doing so well.'

He fell silent, then, after a few moments: 'If I had to choose among your admirers, I'd prefer that old fogy Vaudrec. What's become of him, anyway? I haven't seen him for a week.'

She replied unemotionally: 'He's ill, he wrote me that he's actually in bed with an attack of gout. You ought to call and ask after him. You know he's very fond of you, and it would please him.'

Georges replied: 'Yes, certainly, I'll go round later on.'

He had finished dressing, and stood there, with his hat on, wondering if there was something he had forgotten. Not having thought of anything, he went up to the bed and kissed his wife on the forehead: 'See you later, sweetheart, I shan't be home before seven at the earliest.'

And off he went.

M. Laroche-Mathieu was expecting him, for he was lunching at ten that day, since the Council was due to meet at noon, before the start of the new Parliamentary session.

As soon as they were seated at table, alone except for the minister's private secretary, for Mme Laroche-Mathieu had not wanted to change her lunch hour, Du Roy talked about his article, describing its argument and referring to notes scribbled on visiting cards; then, when he had finished: 'Do you see anything you would like to change, my dear minister?'

'Very little, my good fellow. You may perhaps be a trifle too emphatic over the Morocco business. Talk about the military expedition as though it will take place, while making it clear that it isn't going to, and that you yourself don't even begin to believe in it.

Make sure the public can easily read between the lines that we're not
going to poke our nose into that affair.'

'Quite. I understand, and I'll make myself perfectly clear. On that
subject, my wife told me to ask you if General Belloncle would be
sent to Oran. In view of what you've just said, I assume not.'

The statesman replied: 'No.'

Then they chatted about the session that was about to open.
Laroche-Mathieu began making speeches, trying out the phrases
that he would be showering his colleagues with in a few hours' time.
He flapped his right hand about, waving in the air now a fork, now a
knife, now a chunk of bread, never looking at anyone but addressing
the invisible Assembly, his handsome well-groomed head spitting
out its gobs of sugary eloquence. On his lip, a tiny twirly moustache
poked up in two points like scorpion tails, and his brilliantined hair,
parted in the centre of his brow, was combed into two curls on his
temples, after the style of a provincial dandy. Despite his youth he
was a trifle overweight, a trifle puffy; his waistcoat stretched tightly
across his stomach. The private secretary sat calmly eating and
drinking, no doubt accustomed to these showers of loquacity; but
Du Roy, consumed with jealousy at Laroche-Mathieu's success, was
thinking: 'Oh, give it a rest, you half-wit; what morons these
politicos are!'

And, as he compared his own worth to the minister's garrulous
self-importance, he reflected: 'God! If I just had a hundred thousand
francs so I could stand as candidate for my fine native-city of Rouen,
and give all those worthy, wily Normandy yokels a dose of their own
cunning, what a statesman I'd make, compared with these
short-sighted rogues.'

M. Laroche-Mathieu talked until the coffee and then, seeing it
was late, rang for his carriage; offering the journalist his hand, he
said:

'Is that quite clear, my good fellow?'

'Certainly, my dear minister, rely on me.'

And Du Roy walked slowly off to the newspaper to begin his
article, for he had nothing to do until four o'clock. At four he was to
meet Mme de Marelle at the Rue de Constantinople; he saw her
there regularly twice a week, on Mondays and Fridays.

But, when he entered the office, he was handed a sealed message;
it was from Mme Walter and said: 'I absolutely must talk to you

today. It's very, very important. Expect me at the Rue de
Constantinople at two. I can do you a great service.
  'Eternally yours,
  'Virginie.'
  He swore: 'Christ Almighty! What a pest she is!' And, seized by a
fit of rage, he went straight out again, too annoyed to work.
  For six weeks now he had been trying to break with her, without
managing to weary her relentless devotion.
  After her seduction she had suffered a terrible attack of remorse,
and at three successive meetings had heaped reproaches and abuse
on her lover. Bored by these scenes, and already sated by this middle-
aged, over-dramatic woman, he had simply kept his distance, hoping
by this means to end the affair. But then she had attached herself to
him with desperation, throwing herself into this love-affair the way
people throw themselves into a river, with a stone tied round their
necks. He had let himself be caught again, out of weakness, and self-
indulgence, and politeness; and she had imprisoned him in a web of
frantic, exhausting passion, tormenting him with her affection.
  She kept trying to see him every day, summoning him by telegram
at all hours for brief meetings on a street corner, in a shop, in a public
park. Then, in a few sentences that never varied, she would tell him
that she adored him, that she idolized him, and would then leave,
assuring him that she was 'so very happy to have seen him'.
  She had turned out to be quite different from what he had
imagined, attempting to captivate him with a youthful winsomeness
and childish love-play that were ridiculous at her age. This virtuous
woman who had, until then, lived an entirely respectable life, a virgin
at heart, impervious to emotion and oblivious of sensuality, had suddenly found her tranquil middle age, which had been like a pallid
autumn following upon a chilly summer, transmuted into a kind of
faded spring, full of little half-open blossoms and aborted buds, a
strange flowering of adolescent love, passionate and artless, made up
of unexpected transports, of little girlish cries, of embarrassing
sweet-talk, of charms that had aged without ever being young. She
would write him ten letters in a day, foolish, demented letters, in
bizarre, ridiculously flowery language, embellished in the Indian
style, full of the names of animals and birds.
  As soon as they were alone she would kiss him with all the
awkward allurements of an overgrown girl, pouting her lips almost

grotesquely, and jumping about so that her heavy breasts made the fabric of her bodice jiggle.

Most of all he was sickened by hearing her say: 'my mouse', 'my pet', 'my kitten', 'my jewel', 'my sweetie-pie', 'my treasure', and by seeing how every time she gave herself to him, she went through a mini-comedy of childish modesty, with little fearful gestures that she imagined were pleasing, and little games suggestive of a depraved schoolgirl.

She would ask: 'Whose lips are these?' And, when he did not instantly reply, she would repeat insistently: 'They're mine,' until he turned white with exasperation.

She ought to have realized, he felt, that the most extreme tact, and skill, and circumspection, and appropriateness were necessary in love, that having surrendered to him, she, a mature woman with a family, with a position in society, ought to give herself with a certain gravity, with a kind of controlled passion, sternly, with tears perhaps, but the tears of Dido, not of Juliet.*

She was always saying to him: 'How I love you, my little pet! Tell me, my baby, do you love me as much?' He could no longer hear her say 'my little pet' or 'my baby' without wanting to call her 'my old girl'.

She would say to him: 'I was mad to give in to you. But I don't regret it. It's so wonderful to be in love!'

Georges found all this, coming from her mouth, irritating. She would murmur: 'It's so wonderful to be in love' just like an ingénue in a play.

Furthermore she exasperated him with the clumsiness of her love-making. Her sensuality having been suddenly kindled by the kisses of this handsome young man who had so fiercely aroused her passion, she brought to her embraces an awkward fervour and a heavy-handed concentration which struck Du Roy as comic, and reminded him of old men trying to learn to read.

And when she should have been crushing him in her arms, gazing ardently at him with that profound and terrible gaze of certain ageing women who are superb in their final love-affair, when she should have been biting him with her mute and quivering mouth as, exhausted yet insatiable, she pressed down upon him with her heavy, warm flesh, instead she would fidget about like a little girl and, thinking it would please, lisp: 'I love you so, sweetie-pie, I love you so. Give your little wifey a nice cuddle!'

Then he would feel a mad urge to swear, pick up his hat, and leave, slamming the door.

In the early days, they had often met at the Rue de Constantinople, but Du Roy, who feared an encounter with Mme de Marelle, now found a thousand excuses to avoid those meetings.

So then he had had to come to her house almost every day, sometimes to lunch, sometimes to dinner. She would squeeze his hand under the table, offer him her mouth behind the door. But what he most enjoyed was amusing himself with Suzanne, whose funny stories cheered him up. Her doll-like body contained a mind that was nimble and shrewd, unpredictable and sly, which sought constantly to entertain, like a puppet in a street-show. With mordant appositeness, she made fun of everything and everybody. Georges stimulated her lively wit, goading her into derision, and they got on wonderfully.

She was forever calling to him: 'Listen, Bel-Ami. Come here, Bel-Ami.' He would immediately leave the mother and hurry over to the daughter who would whisper some spiteful comment in his ear, and they would laugh heartily together.

Nevertheless, weary of the love of the mother, he came to feel an insurmountable aversion towards her; he could no longer see her, or hear her, or think of her without getting angry. So then he stopped going to her house, answering her letters, or responding to her pleas.

Finally she grasped that he did not love her any more, and this caused her terrible suffering. But she pursued him frantically, spying on him, following him, waiting for him in a cab with drawn blinds at the entrance to the newspaper, at the entrance to his home, in streets where she hoped he would pass by.

He wanted to hurt her, to swear at her, to hit her, to tell her outright: 'I've had enough, damn it, you're pestering me.' But he continued to treat her with circumspection, because of *La Vie française*; and he tried, by coldness concealed beneath good manners and even by occasional harsh words, to make her understand that this absolutely had to end.

She was especially determined in thinking up stratagems to lure him to the Rue de Constantinople, and he was always fearful that some day the two women would bump into each other at the door.

His affection for Mme de Marelle, by contrast, had increased over the course of the summer. He called her his 'little monkey', and there

was no question but that she pleased him. Their two natures had
similar quirks; both he and she indisputably belonged to that dare-
devil breed of high-society vagabonds who, without knowing it,
closely resemble the gypsies who travel the highways.

They had enjoyed a delightful summer of love, a summer of stu-
dents on a spree, escaping to lunch or dine at Argenteuil, at
Bougival, at Maisons,* at Poissy, spending hours in a boat, picking
flowers along the river banks. She adored fried fish from the Seine,
rabbit fricassees, and fish stews, eaten in tavern gardens, while listening to the cries of the boatmen. He loved setting off with her on a
bright day, sitting on the upper deck of a suburban train and chatting
nonsensically as they crossed the ugly Paris countryside, spotted
with hideous middle-class chalets.

And when he was obliged to return for dinner with Mme Walter,
he felt full of hatred for the old, persistent mistress, remembering
the young one he had just left, who had gathered the flower of his
desire and the harvest of his ardour in the grasses of the river bank.

He had thought that he was, at last, more or less free of the
Director's wife, to whom he had bluntly, almost brutally, expressed
his determination of making a break, when the telegram summoning
him at two o'clock to the Rue de Constantinople reached him at the
newspaper office.

He reread it while walking along: 'I absolutely must talk to
you today. It's very, very important. Expect me at the Rue de
Constantinople at two. I can do you a great service. Eternally yours,
Virginie.'

He was thinking: 'Whatever can the old witch want with me now?
I bet she's got nothing to say to me. She's going to tell me again that
she adores me. Still, I'd better see her. She mentions something very
important, a great service, perhaps it's true. And Clotilde's coming
at four. I'll have to get rid of her first, at three at the latest. Christ! As
long as they don't meet each other! What a pest women are!'

And he reflected that in fact his wife was the only woman who
never plagued him. She led her own life, and she seemed to love him
very much, at those times set aside for love, for she would not allow
anything to interfere with the unvarying order of her day's normal
occupations.

He was walking slowly towards his rendezvous, working himself
up into a fury against his boss's wife: 'Ah! I'll give her a fine welcome

if she has nothing to tell me! A trooper'll sound polite compared
with me! First, I'll tell her I'll never again set foot inside her door.'

And he went in to wait for Mme Walter.

She arrived almost immediately, and exclaimed, the moment she
saw him: 'Oh, you got my message! What luck!'

He said, with a nasty look: 'I certainly did; it came to the paper
just as I was leaving for the Chamber. Whatever is it now?'

Raising her little veil to kiss him, she approached him with the
timid, cowed look of a dog that is often beaten.

'How cruel you are to me... What hard things you say to me...
What is it that I've done? You can't imagine how I suffer because of
you!'

He growled: 'You're surely not going to start that again?'

She was standing close beside him, waiting for a smile, or a gesture, to fling herself into his arms.

She murmured: 'You should not have taken me just to treat me
like this, you should have left me the way I was, good, and happy. Do
you remember what you said to me in the church, and how you
forced me to come into this house? And now look at the way you
speak to me! The way you receive me! My God! My God! How
you hurt me!'

Stamping his foot, he said violently: 'Enough, damn it! That's
enough. The minute I see you it's the same old refrain. Really, anyone would think I had you when you were twelve and as innocent as
an angel. No, my dear, let's look at the facts, this wasn't a case of
seducing a minor. You gave yourself to me as a consenting adult.
Thank you very much, I'm infinitely grateful, but I'm under no
obligation to remain tied to your apron strings until death. You have
a husband and I have a wife. We're neither of us free. We indulged
ourselves in a passing fancy, and that's that, it's over.'

She said: 'Oh, what a brute you are, how coarse, how vile! No, I
wasn't a young girl any longer, but I'd never ever loved, never been
unfaithful...'

He cut her short: 'You've told me that over and over again, I know.
But you'd had two children... so I didn't deflower you...'

She recoiled: 'Oh, Georges, that's contemptible!'

And, with her hands on her breast, she began to gasp as sobs
choked her throat.

When he saw the tears start to flow, he took his hat from the end of the mantelpiece: 'Oh! You're going to cry! Then I'm off. Was this performance what you got me here for?'

She took a step so as to block his way and, quickly pulling a handkerchief from her pocket, wiped her eyes with a brusque gesture. In a voice that she made an effort to control, but which was still broken by an anguished quaver, she said:

'No, I came to give you some news... some political news... to give you the chance to make fifty thousand francs... or even more... if you want to.'

Suddenly appeased, he asked: 'How exactly? What do you mean?'

'Last night I happened to overhear something my husband and Laroche said. They didn't worry, anyway, about talking in front of me. But Walter was advising the minister not to let you into the secret because you'd reveal everything.'

Du Roy had put his hat down again on a chair. He waited, all ears. 'Well, what is it?'

'They're going to take Morocco!'

'Come on. I had lunch today with Laroche, who practically dictated the cabinet's plans to me.'

'No, darling, they've tricked you because they're afraid their scheme will get out.'

'Sit down,' said Georges.

And he himself sat down in an armchair. So then she pulled a little stool over and crouched on it, between Duroy's legs. She went on, in a wheedling tone: 'Because I'm always thinking of you, I pay attention, now, to all the whispering that goes on in my presence.'

And she quietly began describing to him how for quite a while now she had guessed that something was being planned from which he was being excluded, that although he was being used, they were afraid of including him.

She said: 'You know, being in love makes you crafty.'

At last, the night before, she had understood what was going on. It was an important affair, an extremely important affair that had been planned in secret. She was smiling now, pleased with her own cleverness; growing excited, she talked like the financier's wife she was, someone used to the engineering of stock exchange crashes, of changes in the value of shares, of sudden rises and falls that ruin, in a couple of hours of speculation, thousands of ordinary people, of small investors, who put their savings in the funds guaranteed by men with honoured and respected names, politicians or bankers.

She kept saying: 'Oh, what they've done is really something, really something. Actually it was Walter who managed it all, and he knows what he's doing. Really, it's quite remarkable.'

All this build-up was making him impatient.

'Come on, tell me.'

'Well, it's like this. The expeditionary force being sent to Tangiers was agreed upon between them from the very day Laroche took over at the Foreign Office; and, little by little, they've bought back the whole of the Moroccan loan, which had fallen to sixty-four or sixty-five francs.* They've bought it up very cleverly, using dubious, shady agents who didn't arouse any suspicion. They even hoodwinked the Rothschilds,* who were astonished that the Moroccan shares should be so much in demand. They were told the names of the agents, every one of them corrupt, every one of them penniless. That reassured all the great banks. And now the expedition is going to take place, and as soon as we're over there, the French government will underwrite the loan. Our friends will have made fifty or sixty million. So now that you know what's going on, you'll also understand how afraid they are of everyone, how afraid of the smallest indiscretion.'

She had leant her head against the young man's waistcoat, and with her arms resting on his legs she snuggled up and pressed against him, well aware that she had caught his interest now, ready to do anything, no matter what, for a caress or a smile.

'You're quite sure?'

She answered confidently: 'Oh, absolutely!'

He declared: 'Yes, it really is quite something. As for that bastard Laroche, I'll get him one day. Oh, what a wretch! He'd better watch out! He'd better watch out! I'll have his ministerial skin off him!'

Then, after a little reflection, he murmured: 'Still, this ought to be used to advantage.'

'You can still buy the debt,' she said. 'It's only at seventy-two.'

'Yes, but I've no spare cash.'

She looked up at him with eyes full of entreaty. 'I've thought of that, my pet, and if you were really nice, really really nice, if you loved me just a little, you'd let me lend you some.'

His reply was sharp, almost cold: 'As for that, no, certainly not.'

She whispered, in a beseeching voice: 'Listen, there is something you can do without borrowing money. I myself was going to buy ten thousand worth of this loan, to get myself a little nest egg. Well! I'll buy twenty thousand. You can be in for half. You understand, of course, that I'm not going to give Walter the cash. So there's nothing to pay at present. If it succeeds, you'll make seventy thousand francs. If it doesn't, you'll owe me ten thousand that you can pay me when it suits you.'

He said again: 'No, I don't like schemes of that kind.'

Then, to persuade him, she reasoned with him, proving that in reality he was pledging ten thousand on his word of honour, that he was running a risk, and that in consequence she wasn't advancing him anything, since the outgoings were the responsibility of the Walter Bank.

She also proved to him that it was he who, in *La Vie française*, had led the whole political campaign that made this affair possible, and that not to profit from it would be very simple-minded.

He still hesitated. She added: 'But, just think, in fact it's Walter who's lending you these ten thousand francs, and you've rendered him services that are worth more than that.'

'All right! Agreed. I'll go halves with you. If we lose, I'll repay you ten thousand francs.'

She was so pleased that she stood up, grasped his head in her two hands and began kissing him avidly.

At first he did not resist, then, as she grew bolder, hugging him and devouring him with kisses, he remembered that Clotilde would soon be arriving, and that if he weakened he would be wasting time, and exhausting, in the arms of the old woman, an ardour which it would be better to save for the young one.

So then he pushed her gently away: 'Come on, be good,' he said.

She looked at him with sorrowful eyes. 'Oh, Georges, I can't even kiss you any more.'

He replied: 'No, not today. I've a bit of a headache, and it hurts me.'

So then she sat down again obediently between his legs, and asked: 'Will you come and have dinner tomorrow at my house? It would make me so happy!'

He hesitated, but did not dare refuse. 'Yes, certainly.'

'Thank you, sweetheart.'

She was rubbing her cheek against the young man's chest in a slow, regular caress, and one of her long black hairs caught in his waistcoat. When she noticed this, a wild idea flashed into her mind, one of those superstitious notions that in women often take the place of reasoning. Very quietly, she began twisting this hair around the button. Then she attached another to the next button, and still another to the button lower down. To each button she affixed a hair.

In a moment, when he stood up, he would pull them out. He would hurt her, what happiness! And, without realizing it, he would carry away something of her, he would carry away a tiny lock of her hair, for which he had never asked. It was a bond by which she was attaching him, a secret, invisible link, a talisman she was leaving on him. Without wanting to, he would think of her, he would dream of her, he would love her a little better on the morrow.

Suddenly he said: 'I'm going to have to leave you, because I'm expected at the Chamber for the end of the session. I can't miss it today.'

'Oh! So soon' she sighed. Then, in a resigned tone: 'Off you go, darling, but come for dinner tomorrow.'

And she pulled away quickly. On her head she felt a brief, sharp pain as if her skin had been stuck with needles. Her heart was beating; she was happy to have suffered a little on his account.

'Goodbye!' she said. And, with a compassionate smile, he took her in his arms and coldly kissed her eyes. But, maddened by this contact, she murmured again: 'So soon!' Her beseeching gaze turned to the bedroom, where the door stood open. He pushed her away, saying hurriedly: 'I must be off, I'm going to be late.'

So she offered him her lips which he barely brushed with his, and, handing her her parasol which she would have left there, he continued: 'Come, come, we must hurry, it's after three.' She went out first, repeating: 'Tomorrow, seven o'clock,' and he replied: 'Tomorrow, seven o'clock.'

They separated. She turned to the right, he to the left.

Du Roy walked up as far as the outer boulevard. Then he turned back down the Boulevard Malesherbes, which he followed, walking slowly. Passing in front of a confectioners, he noticed some marrons glacés in a crystal bowl, and thought: 'I'll take a pound back for Clotilde.' He bought a bag of those sugared fruits which she absolutely adored.

By four he had returned and was waiting for his young mistress.

She came a little late because her husband had arrived for a week's stay. She asked: 'Can you come for dinner tomorrow? He'll be delighted to see you.'

'No, I'm having dinner with the Director. We've a lot of political and financial plans that we're working on.'

She had removed her hat. Now she took off her bodice; it was too tight. He indicated the bag on the mantelpiece: 'I've brought you some marrons glacés,' and she clapped her hands: 'Wonderful! You are sweet.' She took them and tasted one, declaring: 'They're delicious. I've a feeling I shan't leave a single one.' Then, gazing at Georges with playful sensuality: 'So, you pander to all my vices?'

She was slowly eating the chestnuts, glancing constantly into the bottom of the bag as if to see if there were still some left.

She said: 'Here, sit down in the armchair, I'll squat between your legs to nibble my bonbons. I'll be very comfortable.'

He smiled, sat down, and held her between his legs exactly as he had just held Mme Walter.

She raised her head to speak to him, and said, her mouth full: 'Can you imagine, sweetheart, I dreamt of you, I dreamt we were on a long journey, the two of us, on a camel. It had two humps, we were each riding on a hump and we were crossing the desert. We'd brought with us packets of sandwiches and a bottle of wine, and were having a picnic sitting on our humps. But I didn't like that because we couldn't do anything else; we were too far away from each other, and for my part, I wanted to get down.'

He replied: 'I want to get down too.'

He was laughing, amused by the story, and he egged her on to go on prattling away with her childish, tender nonsense in the way lovers do. This girlishness, which he found appealing in Mme de Marelle, would have exasperated him in Mme Walter.

Clotilde, too, called him 'my sweetheart, my little pet, my kitten'. These words sounded sweet and caressing to him. When the other woman had used them, a little while before, they had annoyed and sickened him. For the unchanging language of passion takes its flavour from the lips from which it comes.

But, while enjoying this nonsense, he was thinking about the seventy thousand francs he was going to make; and suddenly he gave a couple of little taps with his finger on his lover's head and stopped her flow of words: 'Listen, my kitten. I'm going to give you a message to pass on to your husband. Tell him, from me, to buy, tomorrow, ten thousand francs' worth of the Moroccan loan which is at seventy-two; I promise him he'll have made between sixty and eighty thousand francs before three months are up. Tell him not to breathe a word about this. Tell him, from me, that the military expedition to Tangiers is a certainty and that the French Government will underwrite the loan. But don't cut anyone else in. This is a state secret I'm passing on.'

She listened to him attentively, then said in a low voice: 'Thank you. I'll tell my husband this evening. You can trust him; he won't say anything. He's completely reliable. There's no danger.'

But she had eaten all the chestnuts. She squashed up the bag in her hands and threw it into the fireplace. Then she said: 'Let's go to bed.' And without getting up, she began unbuttoning Georges's waistcoat.

She stopped abruptly, and, drawing out a long hair from a buttonhole, began to laugh: 'Look, you've brought away a hair of Madeleine's. Now there's a faithful husband!'

Then, turning serious, she stared for a long time at her hand, at the almost invisible hair she had found; she murmured: 'This isn't Madeleine's, it's brown.'

He smiled: 'It's probably the chambermaid's.'

But she was inspecting his waistcoat as closely as a detective, and culled a second hair twisted round a button; then she saw a third, and, pale and trembling, exclaimed: 'Oh! You've slept with a woman who's put hairs round all your buttons.'

He stuttered in astonishment: 'No, no, you're mad...' Suddenly he remembered and understood; at first he was flustered, but then he denied the charge with a giggle, not really all that upset that she should suspect him of casual affairs.

She went on looking and went on finding hairs, which she rapidly unwound and then threw onto the carpet.

With her astute feminine instinct she had guessed, and, furiously angry, on the verge of tears, she stammered: 'She loves you, this one... and she wanted you to take away something of her... Oh, what a sod you are!' But then she gave a cry, a strident cry of nervous pleasure: 'Oh!... Oh!... she's old... here's a white hair... Ah yes, you go with old women now... Tell me, do they pay you... do they pay you... Ah! You've got old women... you don't need me any more... you keep her...'

She stood up, ran over to her bodice which she had thrown over a chair, and quickly put it on.

Full of shame, he tried to stop her, stuttering: 'No, no, Clo, you're being silly... I don't know what this is... listen... don't go... look, don't go...'

She was saying over and over again: 'Keep your old woman... keep her... get yourself a ring made with her hair, her white hair... You've enough of it for that..'

With sharp, rapid movements she had dressed, put on her hat and tied the veil; and when he tried to grab hold of her she gave him a tremendous slap on the face. While he was standing there in a daze she opened the door and fled.

As soon as he was alone, he was overcome with rage at that old bitch Mme Walter. Oh, he would tell her where to go, that one, and in no uncertain fashion.

He sponged his red cheek with water. Then he, in his turn, left, pondering his revenge. He wouldn't forgive her this time. No, definitely not!

He walked down as far as the boulevard, and, wandering along, stopped in front of a jeweller's to look at a watch which he had long coveted, and which cost eighteen hundred francs.

He suddenly thought, his heart jumping with joy: 'If I make my seventy thousand francs I'll be able to treat myself to it.' And he began dreaming of all the things he could do with those seventy thousand francs. First, he'd be elected a deputy. Then he would buy his watch, then he would gamble on the stock exchange, and then... and then...

He did not want to go to the newspaper, preferring to talk to Madeleine before seeing Walter again and writing his article; and so he set off for home.

He was nearing the Rue Drouot when he stopped dead; he had forgotten to enquire after the Comte de Vaudrec, who lived on the Chaussée-d'Antin.* So he turned round, and, still strolling slowly along, in a happy reverie, let his mind dwell on a host of things, on delightful things and good things, on his approaching wealth, but also on that scoundrel Laroche and that old shrew Mme Walter. He did not, however, worry about Clotilde's anger, knowing perfectly well that she would soon forgive him.

When he asked the concierge of the building where the Comte de Vaudrec lived: 'How is M. de Vaudrec? I understand he's been unwell these last few days,' the man replied: 'The count is very ill, Monsieur. They're afraid he won't last the night. The gout is affecting his heart.'

Du Roy felt so shocked that he couldn't think what to do. Vaudrec dying! A mass of confused ideas shot through his mind, disturbing ideas that he did not dare admit to himself. He stammered: 'Thank you... I'll be back...' without knowing what he was saying.

Then he jumped into a cab and had himself driven home.

His wife had returned. He rushed breathlessly into her room and immediately said to her: 'You haven't heard? Vaudrec's dying!'

She was sitting reading a letter. She looked up and repeated three times: 'Eh? What did you say?... What did you say?... What did you say?'

'I said that Vaudrec's dying, an attack of gout has affected his heart.' Then he added: 'What are you going to do?'

She had leapt to her feet, deathly pale, her cheeks trembling nervously, and began to sob in a heart-broken way, hiding her face in her hands. She went on standing there, shaken by sobs, rent by grief.

But, suddenly mastering her anguish, she wiped her eyes: 'I'm... I'm going there... don't worry about me... I don't know what time I'll be back... don't wait for me...'

He replied: 'All right, you go.'

They clasped hands, and she left so quickly that she forgot her gloves.

Georges, having dined alone, began writing his article. He did it exactly as the minister had wished, giving the reader the impression that the military expedition to Morocco would not take place. Then he took it to the newspaper, chatted for a few moments with the Director, and departed smoking a cigar and feeling cheerful, without knowing why.

His wife had not returned. He went to bed and slept.

Madeleine came back about midnight. Georges, awakening suddenly, sat up in bed. He asked: 'Well?'

He had never seen her so pale and upset. She murmured: 'He's dead.'

'Ah! And... he didn't speak to you?'

'No. He was unconscious when I arrived.'

Georges reflected. Questions came to his lips that he dared not voice.

'Come to bed,' he said.

She undressed quickly, and slipped in beside him.

He continued: 'Was any of his family at his deathbed?'

'Only a nephew.'

'Oh! Did he see this nephew often?'

'Never. They hadn't met for ten years.'

'Had he other relatives?'

'No, I don't think so.'

'So. . . it's this nephew who'll inherit?'

'I don't know.'

'Was he very rich, Vaudrec?'

'Very rich.'

'Do you know, more or less, what he had?'

'No, not really. One or two million, perhaps?'

He said nothing more. She blew out the candle. And they lay stretched out side by side in the night, not speaking, wide awake, thinking.

He no longer felt sleepy. The seventy thousand francs Mme Walter had promised now struck him as paltry. Suddenly he thought Madeleine was crying. He asked, to be certain:

'Are you asleep?'

'No.'

Her voice sounded tearful and tremulous. He went on: 'I forgot to tell you just now that your minister's cheated us.'

'What do you mean?'

And he described to her, in full, with all the details, the scheme thought up by Laroche and Walter.

When he had finished, she asked: 'How do you know this?'

He replied: 'You must allow me not to tell you. You have your methods of getting information that I don't enquire into. I have mine that I'd rather keep secret. In any event, I'm certain my information is correct.'

Then she murmured: 'Yes... it's possible... I suspected they were up to something without telling us.'

But Georges, who did not feel sleepy, had moved closer to his wife, and was gently kissing her ear. She pushed him away sharply: 'Please will you leave me alone? I'm not in the mood for fooling about.'

He turned over resignedly, closed his eyes and, eventually, fell asleep.

CHAPTER 6

The church was draped with black, and over the entrance a large coat of arms surmounted by a coronet informed the passers-by that this was the funeral of a man of noble birth.

The ceremony had just finished and the mourners were slowly departing, filing past the coffin and then past the Comte de Vaudrec's nephew, who was shaking their hands and returning their greetings.

Georges Du Roy and his wife left the church and set off together to walk home. They walked in silence, deep in thought. Eventually, as though talking to himself, Georges declared: 'Really, it's quite astonishing!'

'What is, my dear?' enquired Madeleine.

'That Vaudrec hasn't left us anything!'

She instantly turned pink, as though a rosy veil had suddenly been spread over her white skin from her breast to her face, and she said: 'Why should he have left us anything? He had no reason to.' Then, after a few moments of silence, she went on: 'There may perhaps be a will at his notary's. We wouldn't know anything yet.'

After some reflection, he murmured: 'Yes, it's likely, for after all he was our best friend, for both of us. He dined with us twice a week, and dropped in constantly. Our house was like home to him, just like home. He loved you like a father, and he'd no family, no children, no brothers or sisters, only a nephew, a distant nephew. Yes, there must be a will. I wouldn't want anything much, a memento, to show that he'd thought of us, that he loved us, that he recognized the affection we felt for him. He certainly owed us a token of friendship.'

She said, her manner thoughtful and unconcerned: 'Yes, it's entirely possible that there's a will.'

As they entered the house, the servant gave Madeleine a letter. She opened it, and then handed it to her husband.

Maître Lamaneur, Notary. 17, rue des Vosges.*

Madame:
I have the honour to request you to call at my office between two and four

o'clock on Tuesday, Wednesday or Thursday, regarding a matter which concerns you.

Believe me, etc.,

Lamaneur.

Georges, in his turn, had blushed. 'That must be it. It's funny that it's you he's sending for, and not me, who am the legal head of the household.'

She did not reply at first, then, after a moment's thought: 'Would you like us to go straight away?'

'Yes, I'd like that.'

They set off as soon as they had lunched.

When they entered Maître Lamaneur's office, the head clerk rose with great alacrity and ushered them into his employer's presence.

The notary was a little man, completely round, round in every part. His head looked like a ball nailed onto another ball, supported by two legs that were so tiny and so short that they also closely resembled balls.

He bowed, gestured to some chairs and said, turning towards Madeleine: 'Madame, I sent for you in order to apprise you of the Comte de Vaudrec's will, which concerns you.'

Georges could not resist muttering: 'Just as I thought.'

The notary added: 'I'm going to read the document to you, it's very short.'

He reached for a document from a box in front of him, and read: 'I the undersigned, Paul-Émile-Cyprien-Gontran, Comte de Vaudrec, being sound in body and mind, hereby state my final wishes.

'Since death may call us at any moment, I am taking the precaution, in anticipation of its summons, of writing my will, which I shall deposit in the office of Maître Lamaneur.

'Having no immediate heirs, I bequeath my entire fortune, composed of stock worth 600,000 francs, and real estate valued at approximately 500,000 francs, to Mme Claire-Madeleine Du Roy, free of all encumbrances. I beg her to accept this gift from a departed friend, in token of his devoted, profound and respectful affection.'

The notary added: 'That's all. This document is dated last August and replaced a similar document, in the name of Mme Claire-Madeleine Forestier. I have that first will which could prove, were the will to be contested by the family, that the intentions of M. le Comte de Vaudrec never varied.'

Madeleine, very pale, sat gazing at her feet. Georges was nervously twisting the ends of his moustache with his fingers. The notary went on, after a brief silence: 'It goes without saying, Monsieur, that Madame may not accept this legacy without your consent.'*

Du Roy rose, and said curtly: 'I need time to reflect.'

The notary, who was smiling, bowed, and said amiably: 'I understand the concern that makes you hesitate, Monsieur. I should add that M. de Vaudrec's nephew, who was informed this very morning of his uncle's last wishes, declares himself prepared to respect them if he is granted a sum of a hundred thousand francs. In my opinion, the will cannot be contested, but a lawsuit would cause a stir that you may perhaps prefer to avoid. The world is prone to malice. In any event, would you let me have your answer on every point before Saturday?'

Georges nodded: 'Yes, Monsieur.' Then he bowed ceremoniously, ushered out his wife who had still said nothing, and departed, his air so aloof that the notary was no longer smiling.

As soon as they were in their room, Du Roy quickly shut the door and, flinging his hat onto the bed, said: 'So you were Vaudrec's mistress?'

Madeleine, who was removing her veil, turned round sharply: 'Me? Oh, Georges!'

'Yes, you. People don't leave their entire fortune to a woman, unless...'

She had started trembling, and could not take out the pins that secured the transparent fabric.

After reflecting for a moment, she stammered, her voice agitated: 'Look... look... you're mad... you're... you're... Weren't you yourself, just now, weren't you hoping... that he'd leave you something?'

Georges was still standing close to her, observing all her reactions, like a magistrate bent on noting the tiniest slips a suspect might make. He declared, stressing every word:

'Yes... he could leave something to me... me, your husband... me, his friend... but not to you, a woman friend... you, my wife. The distinction is a vital one, an essential one, from the point of view of propriety, of public opinion.'

Madeleine in her turn stared at him steadily, straight into his eyes, in a profound, strange way, as if seeking to read something there, as if seeking to discover there that hidden part of a human being which can never be fathomed but may perhaps be glimpsed for a fleeting instant, in those moments of unguardedness or surrender or inattention, that are like doors left ajar onto the mysterious depths of the spirit. And she said slowly:

'Still, it seems to me that if... that people would have thought at least as strange a legacy of such significance from him... to you.'

He asked sharply: 'Why?'

She said: 'Because...' She hesitated, then continued: 'Because you're my husband... because, after all, you've only known him a short time... because I'm the one who's been his friend for a very long time... because the first will he made, while Forestier was still alive, was already in my favour.'

Georges had begun to stride up and down. He announced: 'You can't accept this.'

She replied with indifference: 'Fine; in that case, there's no point in waiting till Saturday; we can let M. Lamaneur know straight away.'

He stopped and faced her; and once again they stood for a few seconds, each gazing into the other's eyes, each striving to reach the impenetrable secret of the other's heart, to probe each other's thoughts to the quick. They tried, in a mute and passionate questioning, to see the other's conscience in its essential truth: the intimate struggle of two beings who, living side by side, never really know one another, who suspect and sniff round and spy on one another, but cannot plumb the miry depths of one another's soul.

And, suddenly, he whispered softly into her face: 'Come on, admit that you were Vaudrec's mistress.'

She shrugged her shoulders: 'You're being stupid... Vaudrec was very fond of me, very fond... but nothing more, ever.'

He stamped his foot: 'You're lying. It's not possible.' She calmly replied: 'Still, that's the truth.'

He began striding about again, then, stopping once more: 'So then explain to me why he's left you his entire fortune...'

She did so, her manner unconcerned, detached. 'It's very simple. As you were just saying, we were his only friends, or rather I was, because he knew me when I was a child. My mother was employed as companion by some relatives of his. He was always coming here, and as he had no natural heirs, he thought of me. He may have loved me a little, it's possible. But what woman has never been loved in that way? This hidden, secret affection may have guided his pen when he was thinking about making his will, well why not? He used to bring me flowers every Monday. You didn't find that at all surprising, and he didn't give you any, did he? Today he's giving me his fortune for the same reason, and because he had no one else to leave it to. It would, on the contrary, be extremely surprising if he had left it to you. Why should he? Who are you to him?'

She spoke so naturally and calmly that Georges hesitated.

He continued: 'All the same, we can't accept the inheritance under these conditions. It would make a terrible impression. Everyone would believe the worst, everyone would gossip about it and laugh at my expense. My colleagues are already only too inclined to envy me, to attack me. I, more than anyone, must be concerned about my honour and careful of my reputation. It's impossible for me to allow, to permit my wife to accept a legacy of this kind from a man who the grapevine already declares was her lover. Forestier, now, might perhaps have put up with it, but not me.'

She murmured gently: 'Oh well, my dear, don't let's accept, we'll be a million worse off, that's all.'

Still pacing up and down, he started thinking aloud, speaking to his wife without actually addressing her:

'Well, yes! A million... too bad... He didn't understand what a want of tact, what a disregard of convention he was displaying. He didn't see in what a false and ridiculous position he would put me. Life's entirely a matter of fine distinctions... He should have left me half, that would have solved everything.'

He sat down, crossed his legs, and began twisting the ends of his moustache, as was his habit in moments of boredom, anxiety, or perplexity.

Madeleine took up a piece of tapestry she worked on from time to time, and declared, as she picked out her wools:

'I'm not going to say anything. You must do the thinking.'

For a long time he made no reply, then said hesitantly: 'People will never accept either that Vaudrec picked you as his sole heir or that I myself agreed to it. To obtain this fortune in this manner would be tantamount to admitting... Admitting that there was, on your part, an illicit relationship, and on mine, a shameful acquiescence. Do you understand how our acceptance would be viewed? We must find some roundabout means, some clever way of justifying it. For example, we'd have to let it be known that he divided the legacy between us, leaving half to the husband and half to the wife.'

She asked: 'I don't understand how that could be done, since the will is quite specific.'

'Oh! It's perfectly simple. You could give me half of the legacy as a donation *inter vivos*. We've no children, so it's possible. In that way, we'd silence people's malicious tongues.'

She said, a trifle impatiently: 'I still don't see how that would silence malicious tongues, since the will is there, signed by Vaudrec.'

He replied angrily: 'Do we have to show it, to display it on our walls? You really are being stupid. We'll say that the Comte de Vaudrec left us each half his fortune... That's it... Now, you can't accept this legacy without my permission. I'll give you it, but only on condition that the legacy's divided, so I won't become a laughing-stock.'

She gave him another piercing look.

'As you wish. I agree.'

Then he stood up and started striding about again. He seemed to be hesitating once more, avoiding his wife's penetrating eye. He said: 'No... absolutely not... perhaps it would be better to refuse it outright... it's more dignified... more correct... more honourable... And yet, this way, there'd be no room for speculation, no room at all. Even the most scrupulous would have to accept it.'

He stopped in front of Madeleine. 'Well, if you like, sweetheart, I'll return on my own to Maître Lamaneur to ask his advice and explain everything to him. I'll tell him my concerns, and add that we've settled on the idea of sharing the legacy, for the sake of the proprieties, and so there won't be any talk. Obviously, from the moment I accept half this legacy, no one will be able to laugh at me. It's as if I declared: "My wife accepts because I accept, I, her husband, who am the judge of what she can do without compromising herself. Anything else would have been scandalous."'

Madeleine simply murmured: 'As you wish.'

Again he began talking volubly: 'Yes, it's all as clear as day with this arrangement of dividing it equally. We're inheriting from a friend who didn't want to treat us differently or make any distinction between us, who didn't want to seem to say: "I prefer one of them now I'm dead, just as I did when I was alive." He did prefer the wife, of course, but in leaving his fortune equally to them both he wished to show clearly that his preference was entirely platonic. You may be sure that, had he thought of it, it's what he would have done. He didn't reflect, he didn't foresee the consequences. As you so truly remarked just now, it's you to whom he gave flowers each week, it's you who occupied his final thoughts although he didn't realize...'

She interrupted him, a little irritated: 'It's agreed. I understand. There's no need for all these explanations. Go straight away to see the notary.'

Blushing, he stammered: 'You're right, I'll go.'

He picked up his hat and then, as he was leaving: 'I'll try to settle the difficulty with the nephew for fifty thousand francs, all right?'

Her reply was contemptuous: 'No. Give him the hundred thousand he's asking for. Take them from my share, if you want.'

Suddenly ashamed, he muttered: 'Oh, no, we'll share it. Leaving out fifty thousand each we'll still have a clear million.' Then he added: 'I won't be long, my pet.'

And off he went to explain the arrangement to the notary, claiming it was his wife who had thought of it.

The following day they signed a donation *inter vivos* of five hundred thousand francs that Madeleine Du Roy was turning over to her husband.

On leaving the office, as the weather was fine, Georges suggested walking down as far as the boulevards. He was making himself agreeable, being very attentive and considerate and affectionate. He was full of smiles, happy about everything, while her manner remained thoughtful and rather stiff.

It was a fairly chilly autumn day. The crowds seemed in a hurry, walking along briskly. Du Roy led his wife to the shop where he had so often admired the coveted watch.

'Would you like me to buy you a piece of jewellery?'

She murmured indifferently: 'If you want to.'

They went in. He enquired: 'What would you prefer, a necklace, a bracelet, or earrings?'

The sight of the golden baubles and the fine stones dispelled her studied impassivity, and she examined the jewel-filled showcases with an eager and searching eye. Suddenly, seeing something she fancied: 'That's a very pretty bracelet.'

It was a chain of a strange design, with a different stone set in every link.

Georges asked: 'How much is that bracelet?'

The jeweller replied: 'Three thousand francs, Monsieur.'

'If you let me have it for two-and-a-half thousand, it's a deal.'

The man hesitated then said: 'No, Monsieur, that's not possible.'

Du Roy went on: 'Look, throw in this watch for fifteen hundred francs, that makes four thousand, and I'll pay in cash. All right? If you don't want to, I'll go elsewhere.'

The jeweller, confused, finally agreed. 'Very well, Monsieur.'

And the journalist, after giving his address, added: 'Have the watch engraved with my initials, G.R.C., intertwined and surmounted by a baron's coronet.'

Surprised, Madeleine began to smile. When they left, she took his arm with a certain tenderness. She thought him really clever, really capable. Now that he had a private income, he needed a title, it was only right.

The jeweller bowed them out: 'You can count on me, it will be ready Thursday, Monsieur le Baron.'

They passed the Vaudeville theatre. It was showing a new play. 'If you like,' he said, 'we can go to the theatre this evening, let's try to get a box.'

There was a box, which they took. He added: 'Shall we dine at a restaurant?' 'Oh, yes, I'd like that.'

He felt as happy as a king, and thought about what else they might do.

'How about seeing if Mme de Marelle can spend the evening with us? Her husband's home, someone told me. I'd be so pleased to see him.'

They went there. Georges, who felt a little apprehensive about meeting his mistress again, was not sorry that his wife's presence made any explanation impossible. But Clotilde appeared not to remember anything, and even forced her husband to accept the invitation.

The dinner was lively and the evening delightful.

Georges and Madeleine returned home late. The gas lights were out. To light the stairs, the journalist struck a wax vesta every now and again.

When they reached the first-floor landing, the match suddenly flared up as it was being struck, illuminating their two faces as they loomed out of the mirror amid the shadows of the stairwell.

They looked like ghosts that had materialized and were about to vanish into the night.

Du Roy lifted his hand to light up their images properly, and said, with a triumphant laugh: 'There go a couple of millionaires.'

CHAPTER 7

Two months had passed since the conquest of Morocco had been completed. France, mistress of Tangiers, controlled the entire Mediterranean coast of Africa as far as the Regency of Tripoli, and had underwritten the debt of the newly annexed country.

According to rumour, two ministers had pocketed some twenty million in this affair, the name of Laroche-Mathieu being mentioned almost openly.

As for Walter, everybody in Paris knew that he had won twice over, collecting between thirty and forty million on the debt, and between eight and ten million on the copper and iron ore mines, as well as on vast tracts of land bought up for a song before the conquest, and resold on the day after the French occupation to companies that dealt in colonial property exploitation.

In a few days he had become one of the masters of the world, one of those omnipotent financiers more powerful than kings, in whose presence heads bow low, tongues are loosened and all the basest, most envy-ridden, and cowardly qualities of the human heart rise to the surface.

No longer was he 'Walter the Jew', head of a shady bank, editor of a questionable newspaper, a deputy suspected of dubious dealings. He was M. Walter, the wealthy Israelite.

This he intended to prove.

Learning of the financial straits of the Prince de Carlsbourg, who owned one of the finest mansions in the Rue du Faubourg-Saint-Honoré,* with a garden giving onto the Champs-Élysées, that very same day he made him an offer for the house, complete with all its furnishings, exactly as it stood. He offered three million for it. Tempted by the sum, the Prince accepted.

The following day, Walter moved into his new home.

Then he had another idea, an idea worthy of a conqueror bent on subjugating Paris, an idea worthy of a Bonaparte.

The entire city, at that time, was flocking to see a vast canvas by the Hungarian painter Karl Marcowitch,* which was on exhibition in the salon of the art connoisseur Jacques Lenoble,* and depicted Christ walking on the water. The art critics, wildly enthusiastic, declared this picture the most magnificent masterpiece of the century.

Walter bought it for five hundred thousand francs and took it home, thereby suspending, from one day to the next, the established flow of public curiosity, and forcing the whole of Paris to talk about him in terms of envy, blame, or approval.

Then he made an announcement in the newspapers, inviting all the well-known figures of Paris society to come to his home one evening and view the masterpiece by this great foreign painter, so that nobody could say that he had hidden away a work of art.

His home would be open to all. Whoever wished to, might come. All you had to do was show the announcement at the door. This was worded as follows: 'Monsieur and Madame Walter request the honour of your presence at their home on the 30th of December, between nine p.m. and midnight, to view, by electric light,* the painting by Karl Marcowitch entitled *Jesus Walking on the Water.*' Then, as a postscript, in very small letters, it said: 'Dancing from midnight.'

Consequently, those who wanted to stay would do so, and from among that group the Walters would recruit their future acquaintances. The others would gaze at the picture, at the house, and at its owners, with worldly, insolent, or indifferent curiosity, then would leave as they had come. And old man Walter knew perfectly well that they would be back, later, just as they had gone to the homes of his brother Israelites who, like him, had become wealthy.

First of all it was essential that all those titled down-and-outs whose names appear in the newspapers should come to his house; and come they would, to see the face of a man who had made fifty million in six weeks; they would also come to observe and take note of who else might be there; and they would come, furthermore, because he had had the good taste and good judgement to summon them to admire a Christian painting in his, an Israelite's, home.

He seemed to be telling them: 'Look, I've paid five hundred thousand francs for Marcowitch's religious masterpiece, *Jesus Walking on the Water.* And this masterpiece will remain in my house, where I can see it, for ever; in the house of Walter the Jew.'

In high society, in the world of duchesses and members of the Jockey Club,* this invitation, which after all did not commit one to anything, was much discussed. One would go there just as one went to look at watercolours, at M. Petit's. The Walters owned a master-piece; they were opening their doors one evening so that everyone might admire it. Nothing could be nicer.

Every day for the past fortnight *La Vie française* had included a titbit about this reception on the 30th of December in an effort to whet the public's curiosity.

Du Roy was enraged by the Director's triumph. He had thought himself wealthy with the five hundred thousand francs extorted from his wife, and now he believed himself poor, dreadfully poor, when he compared his paltry fortune to the deluge of millions pouring down around him, without his having been able to pick up any part of it.

Every day his jealous rage grew greater. He felt angry with every-one, with the Walters whom he no longer visited at home, with his wife who, deceived by Laroche, had advised him against buying into the Moroccan debt, and, above all, he was angry with the minister who had tricked him, who had used him, and who dined at his table twice a week. Georges served as his secretary, his agent, his fac-totum, and when he wrote under his dictation, he felt a mad urge to strangle that triumphant fop. As minister, Laroche was only moder-ately successful, and to protect his position he never let it be sus-pected that he was overflowing with gold. But Du Roy was conscious of it, conscious of that gold, in the parvenu lawyer's haughtier tones, more arrogant gestures, bolder statements, and absolute self-confidence.

Laroche ruled the roost, now, in Du Roy's home; he had taken over both the Comte de Vaudrec's role and his 'days', and he spoke to the servants like a second master.

Trembling, Georges endured his presence, like a dog longing to bite without daring to. But he was often hard and rough with Madeleine, who would shrug, and treat him as a clumsy child. But she was amazed by his perpetual ill humour, and kept saying: 'I don't understand you. You're forever complaining. Yet you're in a splendid position.'

He would turn his back on her, without replying.

At first, he had declared that he would not go to his Director's party, and that he wished never again to set foot in the home of that dirty Jew.

For the past two months Mme Walter had written to him every day, begging him to come, or to meet her anywhere he chose, so that she could give him, she said, the seventy thousand francs she had made on his behalf. He did not reply, and threw these desperate letters into the fire. Not that he had forsworn taking his share of their winnings, but he wanted to drive her mad, to treat her with contempt, to trample her underfoot. She was too rich! He wanted to show he had pride.

The very day when the painting was to be displayed, as Madeleine was pointing out to him that he was making a big mistake in deciding not to go, he replied: 'Shut up. I'm staying at home.'

Then, after dinner, he suddenly announced: 'Still, we'd better do our duty. Hurry up, get dressed.'

She had expected as much. 'I'll be ready in a quarter of an hour,' she said.

He grumbled while dressing, and was still railing bitterly in the cab.

The main courtyard of the Hôtel de Carlsbourg was lit up by four electric lights, like little bluish moons, in the four corners. A magnificent carpet covered the tall flight of steps, and on each step stood a man in livery, as rigid as a statue.

Du Roy muttered: 'Talk about showing off!' He shrugged, jealousy clutching at his heart.

His wife said to him: 'So keep quiet and do what he's done.'

They went in, and handed their heavy outdoor garments to the footmen who advanced to take them.

A number of women, accompanied by their husbands, were similarly removing their furs. There were murmurs of 'How very beautiful! How beautiful!'

The enormous entrance hall was hung with tapestries depicting the story of Mars and Venus. To the right and left the two branches of a monumental staircase wound up, meeting again on the first floor. The banisters were a miracle of wrought iron, whose old, faded gilding gleamed softly all the way up the pink marble steps.

At the entrance to the drawing-rooms, two little girls dressed as jesters, one in pink, the other in blue, handed bouquets to the ladies. People thought this a charming idea.

The drawing-rooms were already crowded. Most of the ladies were wearing town clothes, to indicate clearly that they had come there in the same way that they went to any private exhibition. Those that expected to stay on for the ball had bare arms and necks.

Mme Walter, surrounded by friends, stood in the second drawing-room, acknowledging the greetings of the guests. Many did not know her, and walked about as if in a museum, paying no attention to the masters of the house.

On catching sight of Du Roy, she turned a ghastly white, and moved as if to go up to him. But instead she stood still, and waited for him. He made her a formal bow, while Madeleine showered her with affectionate compliments. So then Georges left his wife with the Director's wife and disappeared into the crowd, to listen to the nasty remarks that people would undoubtedly be passing.

There were five successive reception rooms, decorated with precious fabrics, Italian tapestries, or Oriental carpets in different shades and styles, and bearing on their walls paintings by old masters. In particular, people stopped to admire a small Louis XVI room, a kind of boudoir whose walls were entirely hung in silk printed with pink bouquets on a pale blue background. The low pieces of furniture, of gilded wood, upholstered in a fabric matching that of the walls, were exquisitely delicate.

Georges recognized some famous people,* the Duchesse de Ferracine, the Comte and Comtesse de Ravenel, General the Prince d'Andremont, the very beautiful Marquise des Dunes, as well as all the men and women who frequent opening nights.

His arm was seized and a young voice, a happy voice whispered in his ear: 'Ah, here you are at last, you naughty Bel-Ami. Why do we never see you these days?' It was Suzanne Walter, looking at him with her eyes of delicate enamel, from under her cloud of unruly blond curls.

He was delighted to see her again and heartily shook her hand. Then, apologetically: 'I haven't been able to. I've had so much to do, the last two months, that I haven't been out.'

She went on, her manner serious: 'It's bad, very bad, very bad. You've really upset us, Mama and me, because we both adore you. For my part, I can't do without you. If you're not there I'm bored to death. As you see, I'm telling you this frankly, so that you'll no longer be able to disappear like that. Give me your arm, I myself am going to show you *Jesus Walking on the Water*, it's at the back, behind the conservatory. Papa put it over there so that people would have to walk all the way through. It's amazing, the way Papa's showing off, with this house.'

They made their way slowly through the crowd. People turned round to look at this handsome man and this ravishingly pretty doll of a girl. A well-known painter remarked: 'My word! What a handsome couple. Quite delightful!'

Georges was thinking: 'If I'd really been clever, this is the one I'd have married. And yet it was a possibility. Why didn't I think of it? However did I let myself take the other one? What stupidity! One always acts too hastily, one never reflects enough.' Envy, bitter envy, was permeating his soul drop by drop, like a poison that tainted all his pleasures and made his life hateful.

Suzanne was saying: 'Oh, do come often, Bel-Ami, we'll have such fun now that Papa's so rich. We'll do the craziest things.'

He replied, still pursuing his idea: 'Oh, you'll be getting married now. You'll marry some handsome prince, a bit strapped for money, and we'll hardly ever see you again.'

She exclaimed quite candidly: 'Oh no, not yet, I want someone that I like, that I like very much, that I really, really like. I'm rich enough for two.'

He smiled an ironic, proud smile and began naming the people who were passing by, people of noble birth who had sold their rusty titles to financier's daughters like herself, and now lived either with their wives, or apart from them, but were free, shameless, well known, and respected.

He concluded: 'I don't give you six months before you let yourself fall into that trap. You'll be Madame la Marquise, or Madame la Duchesse, or Madame la Princesse, and you'll look down on me from very high up, mademoiselle.'

Growing indignant, she tapped him on the arm with her fan, swearing she'd marry only to suit her heart.

His tone was mocking: 'Well, we'll see, you're too wealthy.'

She said to him: 'But what about you, you've had a legacy.'

'Oh yes indeed, a real fortune,' he replied in a pathetic voice. 'Barely twenty thousand in income. That's not much, these days.'

'But your wife has inherited as well.'

'Yes, a million between us. An income of forty thousand. We can't even keep our own carriage, with that.'

They were approaching the final drawing-room; ahead lay the entrance to the conservatory. This was a big winter garden filled with large tropical trees, that sheltered beds of rare flowers. As they entered this shadowy greenery where the light glided like ripples of silver, they breathed in the warm fresh smell of the damp earth, and the heavily perfumed air. It was a strange sensation of sweet and delightful corruption, at once artificial, enervating, and yielding. They walked on carpets that were just like moss, between two dense plantings of shrubs. Suddenly, Du Roy noticed on his left, beneath a broad dome of palm trees, an enormous white marble pool, big enough to bathe in, on whose rim four large delftware swans gushed water from their half-open beaks.

The bottom of the pool was sprinkled with gold dust, and in it some enormous red fish were swimming, weird Chinese monsters with bulging eyes and scales edged in blue, kinds of mandarins of the waves, recalling, as they floated haphazardly about over the golden bottom, the strange tapestries of that far-off land.

The journalist, his heart beating fast, came to a halt. He was thinking: 'This is luxury, real luxury. These are the houses one should live in. Others have managed it. Why shouldn't I?' He considered possible means but could not immediately think of any, and grew angry at his own impotence.

His companion, rapt in thought, was no longer talking. He gave her a sidelong glance and once more reflected: 'Yet all I had to do was marry this little puppet of flesh-and-blood.' But all of a sudden, Suzanne appeared to wake up. 'Come on,' she said. She pushed Georges through a group that blocked their way, and made him turn sharply to the right.

In the centre of a group of strange plants that thrust into the air their trembling leaves, which opened like hands with slender fingers, you could see a man standing, motionless, on the sea.

The effect was astonishing. The painting, its sides hidden by the moving greenery, looked like a black hole surrounded by a fantastic, stunning background.

You had to look closely, in order to understand. The frame cut across the middle of the boat where the apostles sat, faintly lit by the slanting rays of a lantern held by one of them who, seated on the boat's edge, was directing all the light onto Jesus as he approached.

Christ was setting his foot on a wave that you could see rising, obedient, smooth, and caressing, beneath the divine step pressing upon it. Everything surrounding the Son of God was in darkness. Only the stars shone in the sky.

The faces of the apostles, by the uncertain light of the lantern the man was holding so that it shone on the Lord, seemed overcome with astonishment.

Powerful and unexpected, indisputably the achievement of a master, it was one of those works that turn your ideas upside down, and linger in the mind for years.

At first those who looked at it said nothing, but went away deep in thought, and then had nothing to say except to comment on the value of the painting.

Du Roy, after gazing at it for some time, declared: 'Nice to be able to treat yourself to baubles like that.'

But, as people were jostling and pushing in order to see, he moved off, still keeping on his arm Suzanne's tiny hand, which he pressed slightly.

She asked him: 'Would you like a glass of champagne? Let's go to the buffet. We'll find Papa there.'

And once again they passed slowly through all the reception rooms, where the crowd, larger now, lively, elegant, and quite at ease, was behaving as if it were at some public festivity.

Suddenly, Georges thought he heard a voice say: 'There's Laroche and Mme Du Roy.' These words brushed past his ear like distant sounds carried on the wind. Where had they come from?

He looked all round, and did indeed see his wife walk past on the arm of the minister. They were chatting softly in an intimate manner, gazing into each other's eyes and smiling.

He imagined that he noticed people whispering as they looked at them, and he felt in himself a brutal, stupid urge to leap on the two of them and beat them with his fists.

She was making him look ridiculous. He thought of Forestier. Perhaps people were saying: 'That cuckold Du Roy.' Who was she? Just a little upstart, fairly shrewd, but in actual fact without any remarkable gifts. People came to his home because they feared him and realized that he was a force to be reckoned with, but no doubt they showed scant respect when discussing this insignificant journalist couple. Never would he go far with this woman who would always make his home appear suspect, who was always compromising herself, whose manner proclaimed her a schemer. She would be a millstone round his neck, now. Ah! Had he only guessed, had he only known! How much greater would have been the stakes he played for!

What a lovely hand he would have won with that little Suzanne as the prize. How could he have been so blind as not to understand that?

They were approaching the dining-room, an immense room with marble columns, its walls hung with Gobelin tapestries.

Walter noticed his reporter and rushed forward to shake his hand. He was drunk with happiness. 'Have you seen everything? Tell me, Suzanne, have you shown him everything? What a crowd, eh, Bel-Ami? Did you see the Prince de Guerche? He was here a moment ago, having a glass of punch.'

Then he hurried over to Senator Rissolin, who was hauling along his bewildered lady, all hung about with finery.

A gentleman was bowing to Suzanne, a tall, thin young man with blond sidewhiskers, a trifle bald, and with that unmistakable air of someone who moves in the best circles. Georges heard his name: the Marquis de Cazolles, and suddenly felt jealous of this man. How long had he known her? No doubt since she had become an heiress? He sensed this was a suitor.

His arm was taken. It was Norbert de Varenne. The old poet wore his lank hair and tired-looking suit with an indifferent, exhausted air.

'This is what's called enjoying yourself,' he said. 'Soon there'll be dancing, and then everyone will go to bed, and all the little girls will be happy. Have some champagne, it's excellent.' He had a glass filled and, with a bow to Du Roy who had taken another: 'I drink to the revenge of wit over wealth.' Then he added, in a gentle voice: 'Not that it bothers me in others or that I wish them ill on that account. But I'm protesting on principle.'

Georges was no longer listening to him. He was looking for Suzanne, who had disappeared with the Marquis de Cazolles, and, hastily abandoning Norbert de Varenne, he set off in pursuit of the young girl. A dense throng in search of something to drink stopped him. When, eventually, he pushed his way through, he found himself face to face with the Marelles. He was still seeing the wife, but it was a long time since he had met the husband, who seized both his hands: 'I do so thank you, my friend, for the advice you sent me via Clotilde. I made almost a hundred thousand francs over the Moroccan loan. It's all due to you. You are indeed a wonderful friend.'

Men were turning round to look at this elegant, pretty brunette.

Du Roy replied: 'In exchange for that service, my dear fellow, I'll take your wife, or rather I'll offer her my arm. One should always separate husband and wife.'

M. de Marelle bowed. 'Fair enough. If I lose you, we'll meet again here in an hour.'

'Certainly.'

And the two young people disappeared into the crowd, followed by the husband. Clotilde was saying: 'Those Walters are lucky devils. What a difference it makes to have a good head for business.'

Georges answered: 'Nonsense! Strong men always succeed, if not by one means, then by another.'

She went on: 'Those two girls will have between twenty and thirty million each. Added to which, Suzanne's pretty.'

He said nothing. His own thoughts in someone else's mouth annoyed him.

She had not yet seen *Jesus Walking on the Water*. He suggested taking her there. They entertained themselves passing malicious remarks about people and poking fun at those they did not recognize. Saint-Potin walked past close by them, wearing numerous decorations on the lapels of his coat, which they thought highly amusing. A former ambassador, behind him, displayed a more modest collection.

Du Roy exclaimed: 'What a bunch!'

Boisrenard, who shook him by the hand, had also decorated his buttonhole with the green and yellow ribbon he had produced the day of the duel.

The Vicomtesse de Percemur, huge and over-dressed, was chatting to a duke in the small Louis XVI boudoir.

Georges murmured: 'An assignation.' But as they passed through the conservatory, he again saw his wife, sitting close to Laroche-Mathieu, both of them almost hidden behind a clump of plants. They seemed to be saying: 'We planned on meeting here, in public. Because we don't care what people think.'

Mme de Marelle acknowledged that this Jesus of Karl Marcowitch's was quite amazing; and they made their way back. They had lost the husband.

He asked: 'And Laurine, is she still annoyed with me?'

'Oh yes, still just as annoyed. She refuses to see you and always disappears when we talk about you.'

He made no reply. He was upset and troubled by the little girl's sudden hostility.

Suzanne caught them as they turned through a doorway, crying: 'Ah! Here you are! Well, Bel-Ami, you're going to be left on your own. I'm stealing the lovely Clotilde to show her my room.'

And away went the two women, walking fast, slipping through the throng with that sinuous, serpentine movement that they know how to use in crowds.

Almost at the same moment, a voice murmured: 'Georges.' It was Mme Walter. She continued, very softly: 'Oh, how horribly cruel you are! How you make me suffer needlessly. I told Suzanne to take your companion away, so that I could speak to you. Listen... I must... I must speak to you this evening... or else... or else... you don't know what I'll do. Go into the conservatory. There's a door on the left, it will take you into the garden. Follow the path you see opposite. You'll find an arbour at the end. Wait for me there in ten minutes; if you won't, I swear I'll make a scene, here, right now!'

He replied, haughtily: 'Very well. I'll be there, where you say, in ten minutes.'

And they parted. But Jacques Rival almost made him late. He had grasped him by the arm, and was telling him all sorts of things, his manner overexcited. He must have been patronizing the buffet. Finally Du Roy left him in the hands of M. de Marelle, whom he had run into again for a moment, and fled. He still had to take care not to be seen by his wife and Laroche. In this he was successful, for they appeared very involved with one another, and he found himself in the garden.

The cold air gripped him like an icy bath. He thought: 'God, I'll catch a chill,' and tied his handkerchief round his neck like a cravat. Then he made his way slowly along the path, because he could not see clearly after the bright lights of the drawing-rooms.

To his right and left he could make out leafless shrubs with slender, quivering boughs. Greyish lights played on these branches, lights from the windows of the house. He saw something white in the middle of the path, ahead of him, and Mme Walter, wearing a short-sleeved, low-cut dress, stammered in a quavering voice:

'Ah! Is it you? Do you want to kill me?'

He replied calmly: 'I beg you, let's not have a scene, all right? Or else I'm off, straight away.'

She had grabbed him round the neck, and, with her lips very close to his, was saying: 'But what have I done to you? You're treating me horribly. What have I done to you?'

He was trying to push her away: 'You twisted your hair round all my buttons the last time I saw you, and that nearly caused a break-up between my wife and me.'

She seemed surprised and said, shaking her head: 'Oh! As if your wife cared! It must have been one of your mistresses who made a scene.'

'I haven't any mistresses.'

'Be quiet! Why don't you even come and see me any more? Why won't you have dinner at my house even just once a week? Oh, I'm going through such agonies; I love you so much that I can no longer think of anything but you, I can no longer look at anything without seeing you before my eyes, I no longer dare say anything, for fear of uttering your name! You can have no idea, Georges, what it's like. I feel as if I've fallen into someone's clutches, that I'm tied up in a sack, oh I don't know. The memory of you is always with me, seizing me by the throat, tearing at something here, in my bosom, beneath my breast, making me so weak that I no longer have the strength to walk. And I just sit on a chair all day, like a half-wit, thinking of you.'

He stared at her in astonishment. This was no longer the clumsy, giddy girl he had known, but a frantic, desperate woman, capable of anything.

However a vague plan was taking shape in his mind. He replied: 'My dear, love isn't eternal. People come together, and then they part. But when it lasts, as it has with us, it becomes a terrible bore. I've had enough. That's the truth. Still, if you can behave sensibly, receive me and treat me like a friend, I'll come again, the way I used to. Do you think you can do that?'

Putting her bare arms on Georges's black coat she murmured: 'I can do anything, if it means seeing you.'

'Then it's agreed,' he said, 'we're friends, nothing more.'

She stammered: 'It's agreed.' Then, raising up her lips to his: 'One more kiss... the last.'

Gently, he refused: 'No. We must stick to our agreement.'

She turned, wiping away two tears, then, pulling out from the neck of her dress a packet of papers tied with a pink silk ribbon, she offered it to Du Roy: 'Here. It's your share of the profit from the

Morocco venture. I was so happy to have made that for you. Here, go on, take it...'

He tried to refuse: 'No, I won't take that money!'

At that she protested: 'Ah! You can't do that to me, now! It belongs to you, no one else. If you don't take it, I'll throw it into a drain. You're not going to do that to me, are you, Georges?'

He accepted the tiny packet and slipped it into his pocket. 'We'd better go in,' he said, 'you'll catch your death of cold.'

She murmured: 'All the better! If I could die...'

She took his hand and kissed it passionately, fiercely, despairingly, then fled into the house.

He returned slowly; he was thinking. Then, with head held high and a smile on his lips, he went back into the conservatory.

His wife and Laroche were no longer there. The crowd had thinned. It was obvious that people would not be staying for the ball. He saw Suzanne, who was arm in arm with her sister. They both came up to him to ask him to dance the first quadrille with the Comte de Latour-Yvelin.

'Whoever's that?' he asked in astonishment.

Suzanne replied maliciously: 'A new friend of my sister's.'

Blushing, Rose murmured: 'You are naughty, Suzette, that gentleman's no more my friend than yours.'

The other said with a smile: 'I know what I know.'

Rose turned her back on them, annoyed, and moved away.

Grasping, in a familiar way, the elbow of the young girl who was still standing at his side, Du Roy said in a fond voice: 'Listen, my dear little creature, do you believe that I'm really and truly your friend?'

'Yes, I do, Bel-Ami.'

'Do you trust me?'

'Completely.'

'Do you remember what I was saying to you just now?'

'About what?'

'About your marriage, or rather about the man you'll marry.'

'Yes.'

'Well! Will you promise me something?'

'Yes, what?'

'To consult me every time someone asks for your hand, and not to accept anyone without having heard my advice.'

'Yes, certainly.'

'And it's a secret of ours. Not a word about it to your father or your mother.'

'Not a word.'

'You swear?'

'I swear.'

Rival bustled up to them: 'Mademoiselle, your father needs you for the ball.'

She said: 'Come along, Bel-Ami.'

But he refused, deciding to leave immediately, for he wanted to be alone in order to think. Too many new things had come into his mind, and he began to look for his wife. After a while he caught sight of her, drinking chocolate at the buffet with two men he did not know. She introduced her husband to them, without telling him their names.

He waited a moment or two then enquired: 'Shall we leave?'

'Whenever you wish.'

She took his arm and they walked back through the drawing-rooms, which were rapidly emptying.

She asked: 'Where's our hostess? I'd like to say goodbye.'

'There's no point. She'd try to make us stay for the ball and I've had enough.'

'That's true, you're right.'

The whole way home they kept silent. But as soon as they were in their room, Madeleine, without even removing her veil, said to him with a smile:

'There's something you don't know, I've a surprise for you.'

He grunted crossly: 'What?'

'Guess.'

'I can't be bothered.'

'Well! It's the 1st of January the day after tomorrow.'

'Yes.'

'The time for presents.'

'Yes.'

'This is yours, which Laroche gave me just now.'

She handed him a small black box, like a jewel case.

He opened it unconcernedly, and saw the cross of the Legion of Honour. Turning a little pale, he smiled and said: 'I would rather have had ten million. This doesn't cost him much.'

She had expected him to be overjoyed, and was annoyed by this coolness. 'You really are incredible. Nothing satisfies you now.'

He replied calmly: 'That man's only paying his debt. And he owes me a lot more.'

Astonished at his tone, she went on: 'But it's still wonderful, at your age.'

He declared: 'Everything's relative. I could have had more, today.'

He had picked up the case, and placed it, wide open, on the mantelpiece, gazing for a few seconds at the brilliant star that lay inside. Then he closed it again, and, shrugging his shoulders, got into bed.

Sure enough, *L'Officiel** of the 1st of January carried the announcement that M. Prosper-Georges Du Roy, journalist, had been nominated a Chevalier of the Legion of Honour, in recognition of exceptional services.

The name was written in two words, which gave Georges greater pleasure than the decoration itself.

An hour after reading this news which was now public property, he received a note from Mme Walter begging him to come for dinner that very evening, with his wife, to celebrate this honour. He hesitated for a few moments, then, tossing the note, which was ambiguously worded, into the fire, he said to Madeleine: 'Tonight we're dining at the Walters'.'

She was astonished: 'Goodness! But I thought you didn't want to set foot there ever again?'

He simply said: 'I've changed my mind.'

When they arrived, the Director's wife was alone in the small Louis XVI sitting-room which she preferred for intimate little parties. Dressed in black, she had powdered her hair, which gave her a charming appearance. From a distance she looked old, from close up she looked young, and when you studied her closely, she looked like a pretty snare for the eye.

'Are you in mourning?' enquired Madeleine.

She replied sadly: 'Yes and no. I haven't lost any member of my family. But I've reached the age where one is in mourning for one's life. I'm wearing black today, as a beginning. In future I shall wear it in my heart.'

Du Roy wondered: 'Will that resolution last?'

The dinner was somewhat gloomy. Only Suzanne chattered

incessantly. Rose seemed preoccupied. The journalist was much congratulated.

In the evening they wandered, chatting, through the drawing-rooms and the conservatory. When Du Roy was walking at the rear, beside his hostess, she took his arm and held him back.

'Listen,' she said in a low voice, 'I'll never again say anything to you. But come and see me, Georges. You can see that I'm no longer addressing you in an intimate way. It's impossible for me to live without you, impossible. It's unimaginable torture. I feel you, I keep you in my eyes, in my heart, in my flesh all day and all night long. It's as if you'd made me drink a poison that was eating me away, inside. I can't, no, I can't. I'm willing to be simply an old woman, for you. I made my hair white to show you that, but come, come now and again, as a friend.'

She had taken his hand and was squeezing it, crushing it, digging her nails into his flesh.

He answered calmly: 'Very well. There's no need to speak of this again. As you can see, I came today, straight away, when I got your letter.'

Walter, who had gone ahead with his two daughters and Madeleine, was waiting for Du Roy beside *Jesus Walking on the Water*. 'Just imagine,' he said laughingly, 'yesterday I found my wife kneeling in front of this picture as though she were in a chapel. She was saying her prayers. I did laugh!'

Mme Walter replied in a firm voice, in a voice that thrilled with secret exaltation: 'It's this Christ who will save my soul. He gives me courage and strength every time I look at him.'

And, halting in front of the God who was standing on the sea, she said softly: 'How beautiful he is! How frightened these men are, and how they love him! Just look at his head, at his eyes, how he seems both simple and supernatural at the same time!'

Suzanne exclaimed: 'But he looks like you, Bel-Ami. I'm positive he looks like you. If you had side-whiskers, or else if he were clean-shaven, you'd look just the same, the pair of you. Oh, but it's quite striking!'

She made him stand beside the painting; and everybody agreed that the two faces were indeed alike!

They were all amazed. Walter thought it a most remarkable thing. Madeleine declared with a smile that Jesus had a more virile appearance. Mme Walter stood motionless, gazing fixedly at the face of her lover beside the face of Christ; she had turned as white as her white hair.

CHAPTER 8

During the remainder of the winter, the Du Roys visited the Walters often. Georges even dined there frequently on his own, when Madeleine said she was tired and would rather stay at home.

He had taken over Friday as his regular day, and the Director's wife never invited anyone else that evening; it belonged to Bel-Ami, to him alone. After dinner they would play cards, or feed the Chinese fish, relaxing and entertaining themselves as a family. Several times, behind a door or a clump of shrubs in the conservatory, or in a dark corner, Mme Walter had suddenly seized the young man in her arms and, clasping him to her bosom with all her strength, had gasped into his ear: 'I love you... I love you... I'm dying of love for you!...' But he had always repulsed her coldly, his tone curt as he answered: 'If you begin again, I won't come here any more.'

Suddenly, towards the end of March, there was talk of marriage for both sisters. It was rumoured that Rose was to marry the Comte de Latour-Yvelin, and Suzanne the Marquis de Cazolles. These two men had become regular visitors to the house, visitors of the kind that are accorded special favours and obvious privileges.

Georges and Suzanne lived in a sort of fraternal, free intimacy, chatting for hours, making fun of everyone and apparently greatly enjoying each other's company. They had never spoken again of the young girl's possible marriage, nor of the suitors that were presenting themselves.

One day, when the Director had brought Du Roy home with him for lunch, Mme Walter was called away after the meal to deal with a tradesman. Georges said to Suzanne: 'Let's go and give the goldfish some bread.'

They each took a big chunk of soft bread from the table and went into the conservatory.

All round the alabaster basin, cushions lay on the ground for people to kneel on, so as to be nearer the fish as they swam. The young people each took a cushion and, leaning side by side over the water, began throwing in little pellets that they had rolled between their fingers. The second they caught sight of them, the fish came over, swishing their tails, flapping their fins, rolling their huge protruding eyes, spinning round, diving to snatch their spherical quarry as it sank and instantly coming back up to demand another one.

They did comic things with their mouths, they gave sudden, rapid leaps, they had a strange appearance, like miniature monsters; and they stood out, fiery red against the golden sand of the bottom, as they passed like flames through the transparent water or displayed, the instant they stopped, the strip of blue that edged their scales.

Georges and Suzanne could see their own faces upside down in the water, and they smiled at their reflections.

Suddenly, he said in a low voice: 'It isn't nice to hide things from me, Suzanne.'

She asked: 'What things, Bel-Ami?'

'Don't you remember what you promised me, on this very spot, the evening of the party?'

'No, I don't.'

'To consult me every time anyone asked for your hand.'

'Well?'

'Well, someone's asked for it.'

'Who?'

'You know perfectly well.'

'No. I swear I don't.'

'Yes, you do. That smug creature the Marquis de Cazolles.'

'He's not smug, for one thing.'

'Perhaps not, but he is stupid, he's been ruined by gambling and worn out by fast living. He really is a fine match for you, so pretty, so fresh, so intelligent.'

She asked with a smile: 'What have you got against him?'

'Me? Nothing.'

'But there's something. He's not all that you say.'

'Oh come on! He's a fool and a schemer.'

She turned a little, no longer looking at the water: 'Tell me, what's the matter?'

He said, as if a secret was being wrenched from the bottom of his heart: 'It's... it's... it's that I'm jealous of him.'

She was somewhat surprised: 'You?'

'Yes, me!'

'Goodness, why's that?'

'Because I'm in love with you, as you perfectly well know, you naughty creature!'

At that she said, her tone severe: 'You must be crazy, Bel-Ami!'

He went on: 'I'm well aware that I'm crazy. Ought I to admit this to you, I, a married man, to you, a young girl? I'm worse than crazy, I'm culpable, almost despicable. I've no possible hope, and I'm going out of my mind thinking about it. And when I hear it said that you're going to be married, I'm overcome with rage, to the point where I could kill someone. You must forgive me for this, Suzanne!' He fell silent. The fish, at which no more bread was being thrown, remained motionless, lined up almost perfectly like English soldiers, staring at the faces of those two people who, bending over the water, were no longer paying them any attention.

The young girl murmured, half sadly, half cheerfully: 'It's a pity you're married. But there we are. There's nothing to be done. That's that!'

He turned abruptly towards her and said, his face very close to hers: 'If I were free, would you marry me?'

She replied in a sincere tone: 'Yes, Bel-Ami, I would marry you, because I like you much better than all the others.'

He stood up, stammering: 'Thank you... thank you... I beg you, don't say "yes" to anyone. Wait a little longer. I beg you! Will you promise me that?'

Feeling a little upset, and not understanding what he wanted, she said softly: 'I promise.'

Du Roy flung into the water the big chunk of bread he still held in his hands, and fled like someone who had taken leave of his senses, without saying goodbye.

The fish all pounced avidly on the mass of crumbs which, not having been kneaded into a ball, was still floating, and tore at it with their voracious mouths. They dragged it to the other end of the pool, moving feverishly beneath it, then forming into a mobile cluster, a kind of animated, whirling flower, a living flower that had fallen head first into the water.

Suzanne, astounded and uneasy, stood up, and went slowly back. The journalist had left.

He returned home very calmly and, as Madeleine was writing letters, he asked her: 'Will you be dining on Friday at the Walters'? I'm going.'

She hesitated. 'No. I'm not feeling very well. I'd rather stay here.'

He replied: 'Just as you wish. No one's forcing you.'

Then he picked up his hat again and promptly departed.

He had been spying on her for some time, watching her and following her, aware of everything she did. The moment he had been waiting for had finally arrived. He was not deceived by the tone in which she had answered: 'I'd rather stay here.'

He was charming to her during the days that followed. He even appeared cheerful, which was unusual for him. She kept telling him: 'You've become nice once again.'

He dressed early on the Friday, in order, he said, to do a few errands before visiting the Walters. Then at about six, after kissing his wife, he left, and went to find a cab in the Place Notre-Dame-de-Lorette.

He said to the cab driver: 'Stop in front of number 17, rue Fontaine, and remain there until I give you the order to leave. Then you can take me to the Restaurant du Coq-Faisan, in the Rue Lafayette.'

The cab lumbered off at the horse's slow pace, and Du Roy lowered the blinds. From the moment he was opposite his door, he kept his eyes fixed upon it. After a ten minute wait, he saw Madeleine emerge and walk in the direction of the outer boulevards.

As soon as she was some distance away, he stuck his head out of the window and cried: 'Off you go.'

The cab set off again, and deposited him in front of Le Coq-Faisan, a popular middle-class restaurant in the area. Georges went into the main dining-room and ate in a leisurely way, occasionally checking the time on his watch. At seven-thirty, having drunk his coffee, enjoyed two glasses of excellent champagne, and slowly smoked a good cigar, he left, hailed another cab that was empty, and had himself driven to the Rue La Rochefoucauld.

Without consulting the concierge he climbed up to the third floor of the house he had asked for, and said, when a servant opened a door: 'M. Guilbert de Lorme is at home, isn't he?'

'Yes, Monsieur.'

He was shown into the drawing-room, where he waited for a few moments. Then a tall, military-looking man wearing decorations came in; his hair was grey although he was still young.

Du Roy bowed, then said: 'Just as I foresaw, Monsieur le Commissaire de Police, my wife is dining with her lover in the furnished rooms they have taken in the Rue des Martyrs.'*

The superintendent bowed: 'I am at your service, Monsieur.'

Georges continued: 'You have until nine, do you not? After that hour, you may no longer enter a private residence to substantiate an adultery.'

'Correct, Monsieur, seven o'clock in winter, nine o'clock after the 31st of March. Today's the 5th of April, so we have until nine.'

'Well, Monsieur le Commissaire, I've a cab down in the street, we can pick up the constables you'll take with you, and then we can wait for a while at the door. The later we arrive, the better chance we have of catching them in the act.'

'As you wish, Monsieur.'

The superintendent left the room, then returned wearing an overcoat that concealed his tricoloured sash. He stood aside to let Du Roy pass. But the journalist, his thoughts elsewhere, refused to go first, saying: 'After you... after you.' The policeman declared: 'After you, Monsieur, I'm in my own home.' The other, bowing, walked out of the door.

They went first to the police station to pick up three constables in civilian dress who were waiting, for Georges had sent word, during the day, that the surprise visit would take place that very evening. One of the men climbed onto the front seat, beside the driver. The other two got inside the cab, which then drove to the Rue des Martyrs.

Du Roy said: 'I have the plan of the apartment. It's on the second floor. First there's a little vestibule, then a dining-room, then the bedroom. The three rooms are connected. There's no exit they can use to get away. There's a locksmith a little further down the road. He's prepared to have his services requisitioned.'

When they had reached the house in question it was only eight-fifteen, and they waited in silence for more than twenty minutes. But when he saw that a quarter to nine was about to strike, Georges said: 'We'll go now.' They climbed the stairs without troubling the porter, who in any case did not see them. One of the policemen remained in the street to guard the exit.

The four men halted at the second floor, and first Du Roy placed his ear against the door, and then his eye to the keyhole. He heard nothing and saw nothing. He rang.

The superintendent said to his men: 'You're to stay here, ready in case we call.'

And they waited. After two or three minutes Georges rang the bell again, several times in a row. They heard a noise at the rear of the flat, and then a light step approaching. Someone was coming to check. Then the journalist rapped sharply with his knuckles on the wooden panels.

A voice, a woman's voice, that someone was trying to disguise, asked: 'Who's there?'

The superintendent replied: 'Open, in the name of the law.'

The voice repeated: 'Who are you?'

'I'm the Superintendent of Police. Open the door, or I'll break it in.'

The voice went on: 'What do you want?'

And Du Roy said: 'It's me. It's useless to try to escape us.'

The light step, the step of feet that were bare, withdrew, then returned after a few seconds.

Georges said: 'If you won't open, we'll break down the door.' He was gripping the brass door-handle and pushing slowly with one shoulder. As there was no reply, he suddenly gave such a violent, powerful shove that the old lock of this furnished apartment house gave way. The screws pulled right out of the wood and the young man almost fell onto Madeleine, who was standing in the vestibule dressed in a bodice and petticoat, her hair down, her legs bare, holding a candle in her hand.

He exclaimed: 'That's her, we've got them.' And he shot into the apartment. The superintendent, who had removed his hat, followed him. The frightened young woman came behind, lighting their way.

They passed through a dining-room with a table still laden with the remains of a meal: empty champagne bottles, an opened terrine of *foie gras*, a chicken carcass and some half-eaten pieces of bread. Two plates lying on the dresser bore piles of oyster shells.

The bedroom looked as if it had been wrecked in a fight. A dress covered a chair, a pair of men's trousers straddled the arm of an easy chair. Four boots, two small and two large, lay on their sides at the foot of the bed.

It was one of those bedrooms typical of furnished flats, with inferior furniture and that horrible stale smell of hotel rooms, a smell that comes from the curtains, the mattresses, the walls, and the chairs, the smell of all the individuals who have slept or lived, for a single day or for six months, in this public lodging, leaving there something of their scent, of that human scent which, added to that of their predecessors, eventually becomes a mixed, sweet, intolerable stench, the same in all such places.

A plate of cakes, a bottle of Chartreuse, and two little glasses— still half-full—stood on the mantelpiece. The ornament decorating the bronze clock was hidden by a man's large hat.

The superintendent turned sharply and, looking Madeleine straight in the eye: 'You are indeed Mme Claire-Madeleine Du Roy, the lawful wife of M. Prosper-Georges Du Roy, journalist, here present?' She said in a hoarse voice: 'Yes, Monsieur.'

'What are you doing here?'

She made no reply. The official asked again: 'What are you doing here? I find you away from your home, half-dressed, in a furnished room. What did you come here for?'

He waited for a few moments. Then, as she still kept silent: 'Since you refuse to admit anything, Madame, I shall be obliged to establish the facts.'

In the bed, the outline of a body could be seen, hidden by the sheet.

The superintendent approached and called: 'Monsieur?'

The man in the bed did not move. He seemed to have turned his back, and buried his head under a pillow.

The official touched what appeared to be his shoulder, and repeated: 'Monsieur, do not oblige me, I beg you, to resort to force.' But the veiled form remained as motionless as if it were dead.

Du Roy, who had quickly moved forward, grabbed the coverlet, pulled it off, and, snatching up the pillow, revealed the dreadfully white face of M. Laroche-Mathieu. He bent over him and, trembling with the desire to grab him by the neck and strangle him, said between clenched teeth:

'At least have the courage to admit your infamy.'

The official asked again: 'Who are you?'

As the terrified lover made no answer, he went on: 'I am a Superintendent of Police and I require you to tell me your name!'

Georges, trembling with savage fury, cried: 'Answer him, you coward, or I myself will name you.'

At that, the man in the bed stammered: 'Monsieur le Commissaire, you should not allow me to be insulted by this individual. Am I dealing with him or with you? Am I answerable to you or to him?'

He appeared to have no more saliva left in his mouth.

The official replied: 'To me, Monsieur, to me alone. I am asking who you are?'

The other said nothing. He was holding the sheet tightly round his neck and rolling his eyes in fright. His little curly moustache looked dead black against his white face.

The superintendent continued: 'You don't wish to reply? Then I shall be forced to arrest you. In any case, get up. I shall question you when you are dressed.'

The body moved restlessly in the bed, and the head muttered: 'But I can't, in front of you.'

The policeman asked: 'Why not?'

The other stammered: 'Because I'm... because I'm... I'm completely naked.'

Du Roy gave a nasty laugh and, picking up a shirt that had fallen on the floor, he threw it on to the bed, crying: 'Come on... get up... Since you undressed in front of my wife, you can perfectly well dress in front of me.'

Then he turned his back, and walked towards the fireplace.

Madeleine had recovered her composure and, seeing that all was lost, was ready to dare anything. Her eyes gleamed in brazen defiance as she twisted a scrap of paper and lit, as if for a party, the ten candles in the ugly candelabra that stood on the ends of the mantelpiece. Then she leaned her back against the marble and holding one of her bare feet to the dying fire—thereby raising up the back of her petticoat which barely covered her hips—she took a cigarette from a pink paper packet, lit it, and began to smoke.

The superintendent had returned to her, while waiting for her accomplice to get up.

She asked insolently: 'Do you do this work often, Monsieur?'

He replied gravely: 'As little as possible, Madame.'

She smiled at him defiantly: 'I congratulate you, it's a dirty job.'

She made a show of not looking at, not seeing, her husband.

But the gentleman in the bed was getting dressed. He had put on his trousers and his boots, and walked over, slipping on his waistcoat.

The police official turned towards him: 'Now, Monsieur, will you tell me who you are?' There was no reply. The superintendent declared: 'I find myself forced to arrest you.'

Then the man suddenly exclaimed: 'Don't touch me, I am immune from the law!'*

Du Roy leapt at him, as if to knock him down, and growled into his face: 'It's a case of *flagrante delicto... flagrante delicto*. I can have you arrested, if I want to... yes, I can.'

Then, in ringing tones: 'This man's name is Laroche-Mathieu; he's the Minister for Foreign Affairs.'

The police superintendent stepped back in astonishment, stammering: 'For the last time, Monsieur, will you tell me who you are?'

The man made up his mind, and said forcefully: 'For once, the bastard didn't lie. I am indeed Laroche-Mathieu, the minister.'

Then, reaching out to point at Georges's chest, where a little red dot gleamed like a tiny light, he added: 'And this scoundrel's wearing on his coat the Legion of Honour I gave him.'

Du Roy had gone dreadfully pale. With a rapid movement he snatched the small flame-coloured ribbon from his button-hole and, throwing it into the fireplace: 'Here's what a decoration that comes from swine like you is worth.'

Face to face they stood there, jaw to jaw, enraged, their fists clenched, one thin, his moustache flowing, the other fat, his moustache curling up.

The superintendent moved quickly between the two of them, and, separating them with his hands: 'Gentlemen, you forget yourselves, this is beneath you!' In silence, they turned on their heels. Madeleine stood motionless, still smoking, smiling.

The policeman continued: 'Minister, I found you alone with Mme Du Roy here present, you in bed, with her almost naked. Since your clothes were lying in disorder about the room, this constitutes a case of adultery *in flagrante delicto*. You cannot deny the evidence. What have you to say?'

Laroche-Mathieu murmured: 'I've nothing to say, do your duty.'

The superintendent addressed himself to Madeleine: 'Do you admit, Madame, that this gentleman is your lover?'

She declared brazenly: 'I don't deny it, he is my lover!'

'That is sufficient.'

Then the policeman made some notes on the condition and the arrangement of the flat. As he was completing these notes, the minister, who had finished dressing and was waiting with his overcoat on his arm and his hat in his hand, asked:

'Do you still need me, Monsieur? What should I do? May I go?'

Du Roy turned towards him, smiling insolently. 'Why go? We've finished. You may get back into bed, Monsieur, we're going to leave you alone.'

And, putting his hand on the superintendent's arm: 'Let us leave, Monsieur le Commissaire, we've no further business here.'

Somewhat taken aback, the official followed him; but on the threshold of the bedroom Georges halted to let him go first. The other politely refused. Du Roy insisted: 'After you, Monsieur.' The policeman said: 'After you.' At that the journalist bowed, and declared in a tone of ironic courtesy: 'It's your turn, Monsieur le Commissaire. I am almost in my own home, here.' Then, discreetly, he gently closed the door behind him.

An hour later, Georges Du Roy walked into the offices of *La Vie française*.

M. Walter was there already, for he continued vigilantly to direct and oversee his newspaper, which had grown enormously, and which was very valuable to the ever-increasing business of his bank.

The Director raised his head and enquired: 'Goodness, you here? You look ever so strange. Why didn't you come to the house for dinner? Where have you been?'

The young man, certain of the effect, declared, emphasizing every word: 'I've just brought down the Minister for Foreign Affairs.'

The other thought he was joking. 'Brought down. . . what did you say?'

'I'm going to change the cabinet. That's all! It's high time we got rid of that filthy skunk.'

Stupefied, the old man believed his reporter must be drunk. He muttered: 'Come on, you're raving.'

'Not at all. I've just caught M. Laroche-Mathieu *in flagrante delicto* with my wife. The Commissaire de Police has proof of the affair. The minister's done for.'

Walter, bewildered, pushed his glasses right up on his forehead and asked: 'You're not having me on?'

'By no means. I'm even going to write a paragraph for the gossip column about it.'

'But what is it you want, then?'

'To disgrace that rogue, that wretch, that public menace!' Georges put his hat on an armchair, then added: 'Woe betide anyone who gets in my way. I never forgive.'

The Director was still not sure he understood. He murmured: 'But... your wife?'

'I'm going to file for divorce* first thing in the morning. I'm giving her back to the late lamented M. Forestier.'

'You mean to divorce?'

'I most certainly do! I was a ridiculous figure. But I had to act stupid in order to catch them. I've done it. I've got the upper hand.'

M. Walter could not take it in; and he gazed at Du Roy in bewilderment, thinking: 'God! Here's a fellow one should handle with kid gloves.'

Georges continued: 'I' m free now... I've a little money. I'll stand for election at the October polls, back home, where I'm very well known. I couldn't establish myself as a man of good standing, a man to be respected, with that wife whom everybody mistrusted. Like an idiot I was taken in by her, she conned me and she caught me. But since I discovered what she was up to, I've kept my eye on the bitch.'

He began to laugh and added: 'It was that poor Forestier who was a cuckold... a cuckold without ever suspecting, a trusting, untroubled cuckold. Now I'm rid of the shrew he left me. My hands are no longer tied. I'll go far.'

And old Walter went on staring at him, his eyes still unprotected by his glasses which remained up on his forehead, as he said to himself: 'Oh yes, he'll go far, the bastard.'

Georges stood up: 'I'm going to write the piece for the gossip column. It must be done carefully. As you know, it will be a terrible thing for the minister. He's done for. Nothing can save him. *La Vie française* has no incentive to spare him.'

The old man hesitated for a few moments, then made up his mind: 'Go ahead,' he said, 'too bad for people who land themselves in that kind of mess.'

CHAPTER 9

Three months had passed. Du Roy's divorce had just been made final. His wife had gone back to calling herself Forestier. As the Walters were leaving on the 15th of July for Trouville,* they resolved to spend a day in the country before going their separate ways.

They chose a Thursday, and set off at nine in the morning in a large touring landau, a six-seater drawn by four horses. They intended to lunch at Saint-Germain,* in the Pavillon Henri IV. Bel-Ami had asked that he be the only man of the party, for he could stand neither the presence, nor the appearance, of the Marquis de Cazolles. But, at the last moment, it was decided to pick up the Comte de Latour-Yvelin as soon as he was up. They had sent him word the preceding evening.

The carriage went up the Champs-Élysées at a brisk trot, then drove through the Bois de Boulogne.

It was a beautiful summer day, not too hot. Across the blue of the sky, the swallows were tracing broad arcs which still seemed to be visible even after the birds had gone.

The three women sat in the back of the landau, the mother between the two girls; the three men sat facing them, Walter between the two guests.

They crossed the Seine, skirted the Mont-Valérien,* then, after reaching Bougival, followed the river as far as Le Pecq.*

The not-so-young Comte de Latour-Yvelin had long, feathery side-whiskers whose ends fluttered in the slightest breeze; this had prompted Du Roy to remark: 'The wind does pretty things with his beard.' The Comte was gazing tenderly at Rose. They had been engaged for a month.

Georges, very pale, looked often at Suzanne, who was also pale. Their eyes would meet, seem to consult together, reach an understanding, exchange a secret thought, then dart away. Mme Walter sat quiet and content.

The lunch lasted a long time. Before returning to Paris, Georges proposed that they take a walk along the terrace.

First they stopped to admire the view. They all stood in a row along the wall, and went into raptures over the broad sweep of the horizon. The Seine, lying like a gigantic snake in the greenery at the base of a long hill, flowed towards Maisons-Laffitte. To the right, on the summit of the hill, the Marly* aqueduct, like a caterpillar with large feet, displayed its enormous silhouette against the sky, while below it Marly disappeared into a dense cluster of trees.

Here and there, on the immense plain stretching before them, they could see a village. The lakes of Vésinet appeared as distinct, neat patches in the scanty greenery of the little forest. On the left, in the far distance, you could see the pointed belfry of Sartrouville.*

Walter declared: 'You won't find a view like this anywhere in the world. Not even in Switzerland.'

Then, slowly, they set off to enjoy this view for a little while.

Georges and Suzanne hung back. As soon as the others were a few steps ahead, he said to her in a low, controlled voice: 'Suzanne, I adore you. I'm head-over-heels in love with you!'

She murmured: 'Me too, Bel-Ami.'

He went on: 'If I can't have you for my wife, I'll leave Paris, and this country.'

She answered: 'Then try asking Papa for my hand. Perhaps he'll agree.'

With a tiny gesture of impatience he said: 'No, for the tenth time, I tell you it's useless. I'll never be able to come to your house again; I'll be thrown out of the newspaper, and we won't even be able to see each other any more. That'll be the splendid result I'm sure to achieve if I make a formal request for your hand. You've been promised to the Marquis de Cazolles. They're hoping that in the end you'll say "yes". They're waiting.'

She asked: 'So what should we do?'

He hesitated, glancing sideways at her: 'Do you love me enough to do something insane?'

She replied firmly: 'Yes.'

'Completely insane?'

'Yes.'

'The most insane thing imaginable?'

'Yes.'

'Would you be brave enough to defy your father and your mother?'

'Yes.'

'You're sure?'

'Yes.'

'Well now! There is a way, only one! It will have to come from you, not from me. You're a spoilt child; they let you say anything you like, so they won't be too astonished if you say something else outrageous. So listen. This evening, when you get home, first go and find your mother, just your mother by herself. And confess to her that you want to marry me. She will be terribly shocked and terribly angry...'

Suzanne interrupted him: 'Oh! Mama will be very pleased...'

He went on sharply: 'No. You don't know her. She'll be more upset and more furious than your father. You'll see how she'll refuse. But you'll be firm, you won't give way, you'll keep saying that you want to marry me, only me, no one but me. Will you do that?'

'I will.'

'And when you've been to see your mother, then you'll go and say the same thing to your father, in a very earnest, very decided manner.'

'Yes, yes. And then?'

'That's when it gets serious. If you're determined, really determined, really, really, really determined to be my wife, my dear, dear little Suzanne... We'll... We'll elope.'

She gave a great jump of joy and almost clapped her hands. 'Oh! How wonderful! We'll elope! When, oh when can we do that?'

All the old romances of nocturnal abductions, post-chaises, and inns, all the charming adventures in books flew simultaneously into her head like some enchanting dream about to come true. She said again: 'When, when can we elope?'

He replied very softly: 'Well... this evening... tonight.'

Trembling, she asked: 'Where will we go?'

'That's my secret. Think carefully about what you're doing. Remember that after this elopement you'll have no choice but to be my wife. It's the only way, but it's... it's very dangerous... for you.'

She declared: 'I've made up my mind... where shall I meet you?'

'Can you get out of the house, on your own?'

'Yes. I know how to open the little door.'

'Fine! When the concierge has gone to bed, about midnight, come and meet me in the Place de la Concorde. You'll find me in a cab waiting in front of the Admiralty building.'

'I'll come.'

'Really and truly?'

'Really and truly.'

He took her hand and pressed it. 'Oh, how I love you! How good you are, how brave! So, you don't want to marry M. de Cazolles.'

'Oh, no!'

'Was your father very annoyed when you refused?'

'He certainly was, he wanted to send me back to the convent.'

'You can see we've got to do something decisive.'

'I shall.'

She gazed at the broad horizon, her head full of this idea of elopement. She would be going further away than those distant places... with him! She was to be abducted! This made her proud. She gave no thought to her reputation, to the shameful dishonour to which she might be exposing herself. Did she even know about this? Had she the slightest notion of it?

Mme Walter, turning round, called: 'Come along, my pet. What are you doing with Bel-Ami?'

They caught up with the others, who were talking about sea-bathing at the coast, where they would soon be going. Then they drove back via Chatou, so as not to repeat the same route.

Georges sat in silence. He was thinking: so, if this little creature had just a tiny bit of courage, he was finally going to succeed! For the past three months he had enveloped her in the irresistible cocoon of his affection. He had led her on, captivated her, engineered her surrender. He had made her fall in love with him, as he was used to doing with women. This light-weight and immature doll had barely offered any resistance.

First of all, he had persuaded her to refuse M. de Cazolles. Now, he had just persuaded her to run away with him. For there was no other way.

He was well aware that Mme Walter would never consent to give him her daughter. She still loved him, she would always love him, violently and uncompromisingly. He restrained her with his calculated coldness, but he sensed that she was ravaged by a frustrated, voracious passion. Never would he be able to bring her round. Never would she agree to his having Suzanne.

But once he had the girl far away, he could negotiate with the father, as one powerful man to another.

Absorbed in these thoughts, he gave disjointed replies to the remarks addressed to him, which he barely listened to. When they drove into Paris, he seemed to pull himself together.

Suzanne, too, was deep in thought; and in her head the harness bells of the four horses were ringing, filling her imagination with never-ending highways bathed in eternal moonlight, dark forests traversed, roadside inns, and ostlers hurrying to bring fresh horses, for everyone would guess that they were being pursued.

When the landau reached the courtyard of the mansion, Georges was pressed to stay for dinner. He refused, and returned home.

After having something to eat, he organized his papers as if he were setting off on a long journey. He burned some compromising letters and hid some others, then he wrote to a few friends.

From time to time he would glance at the clock and think: 'Things'll be warming up over there.' Anxiety gnawed at his heart. What if he failed? But what had he to fear? He could always find a way out! Still, this time, it was a very powerful opponent he was taking on!

He left again towards eleven, wandered about for a while, then hailed a cab and ordered it to stop in the Place de la Concorde, alongside the arcades of the Admiralty building.

Now and again he lit a match to look at the time by his watch. When he saw that midnight was approaching, he became feverish with impatience. He kept poking his head out of the window to look.

A distant clock struck twelve times, then another, closer by, then two together, then a final one, very far away. When that one stopped chiming, he thought: 'It's over. It hasn't worked. She isn't going to come.'

He was, however, determined to remain there until daybreak. In these matters you had to be patient. Again he heard the quarter strike, then the half-hour, then the three-quarters; and all the clocks repeated one o'clock, exactly as they had announced midnight.

No longer waiting, he went on sitting there, racking his brains to guess what might have happened. All of a sudden a woman's head appeared through the window and asked: 'Is that you, Bel-Ami?'

He gave a start, and gasped. 'Suzanne?'

'Yes, it's me.'

He couldn't turn the handle fast enough, and kept saying: 'Ah! It's you... it's you... get in.'

She got in and collapsed against him. He shouted to the cab driver: 'Drive on!' and the cab set off.

She was panting, and said nothing.

He asked: 'Well? What happened?'

So then, almost fainting, she whispered: 'Oh, it was terrible, especially with Mama.'

Trembling with apprehension, he said: 'Your Mama? What did she say? Tell me.'

'Oh, it was ghastly. I went in to her room and recited my little piece, I'd prepared it very carefully. Then she turned white, and shouted: "Never! never!" As for me, I cried, I got angry, I swore I'd marry no one but you. I thought she was going to hit me. She seemed to go crazy; she said she'd send me back to the convent, tomorrow. I'd never seen her like that, never! Then, hearing her gabbling all this nonsense, Papa came in. He didn't get as angry as her, but he declared that you weren't a good enough match.

'As they'd made me angry too, I shouted louder than them. And Papa told me to leave the room in a dramatic way that didn't suit him in the least. That's what made me decide to run away with you. Here I am, where are we going?'

He had put his arm gently round her waist; and he was listening avidly, his heart pounding and a feeling of bitter hatred for these people welling up in him. But he had her, their daughter. Now they would see.

He replied: 'It's too late to catch the train, so this cab's going to take us to Sèvres, where we'll spend the night. Then tomorrow we'll set off for La Roche-Guyon. It's a pretty village on the Seine, between Mantes and Bonnières.'

She murmured: 'It's just that I haven't any things. I haven't anything.'

He smiled unconcernedly. 'Bah! We'll see to that when we're there.'

The cab drove along the streets. Georges took one of the young girl's hands and began kissing it, slowly, respectfully. He did not know what to say to her, being quite unaccustomed to platonic endearments. But, suddenly, he thought he could see that she was crying.

Terrified, he asked: 'Whatever's the matter, my little sweetheart?'

She answered in a very tearful voice: 'It's my poor Mama, who at this moment won't be able to sleep, if she's discovered I've gone.'

Her mother, indeed, was not asleep.

When Suzanne had walked out of her room, Mme Walter was left with her husband. Bewildered and horror-stricken, she asked: 'My God! Whatever does this mean?'

Walter shouted furiously: 'It means that that schemer has got round her. He's the one who got her to refuse Cazolles. He likes the look of her dowry, God help us!'

He began striding angrily round the room, and continued: 'And as for you, you were forever enticing him here, flattering him, stroking his vanity; you thought nothing was too good for him. It was Bel-Ami here, Bel-Ami there, morning, noon, and night. Well, it serves you right.'

She had gone white, and whispered: 'Me? I enticed him here?'

He bellowed into her face: 'Yes, you! You're all crazy about him, the Marelle woman, Suzanne, and the others. Do you imagine I didn't see that you couldn't let two days pass without inviting him here?'

She drew herself up, full of tragic dignity. 'I will not allow you to speak to me like that. You forget that, unlike you, I was not brought up in a shop.'

At first he stood rooted to the spot in stupefaction, then, uttering an enraged 'God Almighty!', he left, slamming the door.

As soon as she was alone she went instinctively to the mirror, as if to see whether she herself looked any different, so impossible, so monstrous did everything that was happening to her seem. Suzanne in love with Bel-Ami! And Bel-Ami wanting to marry Suzanne! No, she was mistaken, it wasn't true. Naturally enough, the girl had taken a violent fancy to this handsome young man, she'd hoped they'd let her have him for a husband, she'd had her little moment of madness! But what about him? Surely he couldn't be party to this! She mulled it over, deeply perturbed as people are when faced with great disasters. No, surely Bel-Ami couldn't know anything about what Suzanne had in mind.

And for a long time she thought about the possible treachery or innocence of this man. What a scoundrel, if he had planned this!

And what would happen? She could foresee so many dangers, so much anguish!

If he knew nothing, everything could still turn out all right. They would take Suzanne on a trip for six months, and that would be the end of it. But how could she herself see him again, afterwards? For she still loved him. This passion had entered into her like one of those arrowheads that can never be removed.

It was impossible to live without him. She might as well die.

In the agony of her uncertainty, she did not know what to think. Her head began to ache, her thoughts were becoming laboured, confused, painful. She grew agitated as she sought for answers, and angry at not knowing for certain. Looking at the clock, she saw it was past one, and thought: 'I can't go on like this, I'm losing my mind. I must know. I'll wake Suzanne up, to ask her.'

And, candle in hand, she set off, her feet bare so as to make no noise, to her daughter's room. She opened the door very softly, went in, and looked at the bed. It had not been slept in. At first she did not understand, and supposed that the girl was still talking to her father. But, instantly, a dreadful suspicion suggested itself; she raced to her husband's bedroom and burst in, white-faced and panting. He was in bed, still reading.

He looked startled: 'Well, what is it? What's the matter with you?'

She stammered: 'Have you seen Suzanne?'

'Me? No. Why?'

'She's... she's... gone. She's not in... in her room.'

He leapt down onto the rug, put on his slippers and, bare-legged, his nightshirt flying, rushed in his turn to his daughter's room.

The moment he saw it, he realized the truth. She had run away.

He sank into an armchair, setting his lamp down on the floor in front of him.

His wife had joined him. She said falteringly: 'Well?'

He did not have the strength to reply; he was no longer even angry; he moaned: 'It's over, he's got her. We're done for.'

She didn't understand: 'What do you mean, done for?'

'Oh, Lord, yes. He'll have to marry her now.'

She gave a kind of animal cry: 'Him! Never! Are you mad?'

He answered sadly: 'It's no use screaming. He's abducted her, he's dishonoured her. The best thing is to give her to him. If we go about it right, no one will know about this business.'

Overcome by an appalling feeling, she repeated: 'Never! He'll never have Suzanne! I'll never consent!'

Walter muttered despondently: 'But he's got her. It's done. And he'll keep her and hide her for as long as we refuse to give in. So, to avoid scandal, we must give in immediately.'

His wife, tortured by a pain she could not acknowledge, said again: 'No, no, I'll never consent!'

Losing patience, he continued: 'But there's nothing to discuss. We must agree. Ah, the rogue, how he deceived us!... All the same, he's strong. We could have found someone of much better social standing, but nobody more intelligent or with better prospects. He's a man with a future. He'll be a deputy, and a minister.'

Mme Walter declared, with a wild determination: 'I'll never let him marry Suzanne... Do you hear me... never!'

In the end he grew angry, and being a practical man, began to defend Bel-Ami.

'Oh, do be quiet... I keep telling you we must, we absolutely must. And who knows? Perhaps we won't regret it. With people of that kind, you never know what may happen. You saw how he destroyed that idiot Laroche-Mathieu with three articles, and how he did it in a dignified way, which, given his position as husband, was horribly difficult. Well, we'll see. The fact remains we're caught. We can't get out of it.'

She wanted to scream, to roll about on the ground, to tear out her hair. She declared once more, in a furious voice: 'He won't get her... I... won't... have... it!'

Walter rose, picked up his lamp, and continued: 'Goodness me, you are stupid, like all women. You never act unless it's out of passion. You don't know how to yield to circumstances... you're all stupid! I'm telling you that he'll marry her... he must.'

He went out, shuffling along in his slippers. A comic ghost in a nightshirt, he crossed the broad corridor of the vast mansion and noiselessly returned to his bedroom

Mme Walter remained standing, torn apart by an unendurable pain. Moreover she did not yet fully understand. She was simply suffering. Then it seemed to her that she could not stay where she was, motionless, until daybreak. She felt in herself a violent need to escape, to run, to get away, to seek aid, to be helped.

She tried to think whom she could turn to for help. Who was

there? She could think of no one! A priest! Yes, a priest! She would throw herself at his feet, tell him everything, confess her sin and her despair. He would understand that that wretch could not marry Suzanne, and he would prevent it.

She needed a priest, straight away! But where could she find one? Where could she go? Yet she could not remain like this. Then, like a vision, the serene image of Jesus walking on the waves appeared before her eyes. She saw him just the way she saw him when she looked at the painting. So, he was summoning her. He was telling her: 'Come to me. Come and kneel at my feet. I will comfort you, and I will reveal to you what you should do.'

Taking her candle, she left, and went down to the conservatory. The painting of Christ was at the far end, in a small room closed off by a glass-panelled door, so that the humidity of the soil would not damage the picture. It made a kind of chapel, in a forest of strange trees.

When Mme Walter walked into the winter garden, which she had never seen other than full of light, she was startled by its total darkness. The atmosphere was heavy with the oppressive breath of the massive plants from tropical countries. And, since the doors were no longer open, the air in that strange grove, enclosed within its dome of glass, was hard to breathe, making her feel dizzy and a little drunk, causing pleasure and pain, and producing in her body a vague sensation of enervating voluptuousness, and of death.

The poor woman walked softly, disturbed by the shadows in which, by her candle's wavering light, could be seen outrageous plants shaped like monsters or weirdly deformed human beings.

Suddenly, she caught sight of the figure of Christ. Opening the door that separated him from her, she fell to her knees.

At first she prayed to him frantically, stammering out words of love, ardent, desperate appeals. Then, when her passionate outburst subsided, she raised her eyes to him, and was overwhelmed with anguish. By the flickering light of the single candle illuminating him dimly from below, he looked so very like Bel-Ami that it was no longer God, but her lover who was gazing at her. Those were his eyes, his forehead, the expression on his face, his cold, proud air!

She stammered: 'Jesus!... Jesus!... Jesus!' And the word 'Georges' came to her lips. Suddenly, she thought that at this very moment, perhaps, Georges was making love to her daughter. He was alone with her somewhere, in a bedroom. Georges, with Suzanne!

She kept saying: 'Jesus!... Jesus!' But she was thinking of them... of her daughter and her lover! They were alone, in a bedroom... and it was nighttime. She could see them. She could see them so clearly that they appeared before her, instead of the painting. They were smiling at one another, they were kissing. The room was dark, the bed turned back. She rose to approach them, to take her daughter by the hair and tear her from this embrace. She was going to seize her by the throat and strangle her, her daughter whom she loathed, her daughter who was giving herself to this man. She was touching her... and her hands encountered the painting. She was clutching at the feet of Christ.

She gave a great cry, and fell on her back. Her candle overturned, and went out.

What happened after that? She dreamt for a long time of strange, frightening things. Georges and Suzanne passed constantly before her eyes, entwined with Jesus, who was blessing their odious love.

She was vaguely aware that she was not in her own room. She wanted to get to her feet and leave, but could not. She was overcome by a kind of inertia which fettered her limbs and left only her mind alert, although this was haunted and tormented by frightful, unreal, fanciful images, lost in a noxious dream, the strange, sometimes deadly dream produced in the human brain by the soporific plants of hot climates, with their bizarre shapes and heavy perfumes.

In the morning Mme Walter was found lying unconscious, almost suffocating, in front of *Jesus Walking on the Water*. She was so ill that they feared for her life. Not until the following day did she regain the full use of her faculties. Then she began to weep.

To explain Suzanne's disappearance, the servants were told that she had been sent, at very short notice, to a convent. And M. Walter replied to a long letter from Du Roy, granting him the hand of his daughter.

Bel-Ami had posted this letter just as he was leaving Paris, for he had prepared it in advance the evening of his departure. In it he stated, in respectful terms, that he had loved the young girl for a long time, that this had never been planned, but that when she came to him of her own free will to say: 'I will be your wife,' he considered himself justified in keeping her, even in hiding her, until he had received a reply from her parents, whose legal agreement was of less importance to him than the wishes of his fiancée. He asked M. Walter to reply poste restante, since a friend would forward the letter to him.

When he had obtained what he wanted, he brought Suzanne back to Paris and returned her to her parents' home, refraining from appearing there himself for some time.

They had spent six days on the banks of the Seine, at La Roche-Guyon.*

Never had the young girl enjoyed herself so much. She'd played at being a country maid. Since he was passing her off as his sister, they lived in an intimacy that was free and chaste, a kind of amorous comradeship. He judged it wise not to take advantage of her. The morning after their arrival, she bought a peasant girl's linen and clothing, and settled down to fishing with rod and line, her head covered by an enormous straw hat decorated with wild flowers. She thought the area delightful. There was an old tower, and an old castle where some splendid tapestries were on display.

Georges, wearing a smock he bought ready-made at a local store, took Suzanne out, either for walks on the river banks, or in a boat. Trembling, they kissed one another all the time, she innocently, he on the point of succumbing. But he knew how to control himself; and when he said to her: 'Tomorrow we're returning to Paris, your father's granted me your hand...' she murmured naïvely: 'So soon? I was so enjoying being your wife!'

CHAPTER 10

The small apartment in the Rue de Constantinople was in darkness, for Georges Du Roy and Clotilde de Marelle, after meeting at the door, had entered immediately and she had said to him, without giving him time to open the shutters:

'So, you're marrying Suzanne Walter?'

He quietly admitted it, and added:

'Didn't you know that?'

Standing before him, furious, indignant, she went on: 'You're marrying Suzanne Walter! It's too much! Too much! For the last three months you've been stringing me along so I wouldn't find out. Everybody knows, except me. It was my husband who told me!'

Du Roy began to grin, but he was, all the same, somewhat embarrassed; he put his hat on a corner of the mantelpiece and sat down in an armchair.

She looked him straight in the face and said, in a low, angry voice: 'You've been working on this ever since you left your wife, and you very kindly kept me on as your mistress, to tide you over? What a bastard you are!'

He asked: 'Why so? I had a wife who was deceiving me. I caught her at it, I've obtained a divorce, and I'm marrying someone else. What could be simpler?'

Trembling, she murmured: 'Oh, how cunning you are, how dangerous!'

He began smiling again: 'What of it? Half-wits and fools are invariably taken in!'

But, still following her train of thought, she said: 'I really ought to have guessed what you were up to right at the start. But no, I couldn't believe you'd be such a shit as that.'

With an air of dignity, he said: 'Please be more careful of your language.'

His righteous indignation infuriated her: 'What! Now you want me to watch my language when I speak to you! You've treated me vilely ever since I've known you, and you expect me not to tell you so? You deceive everyone, you exploit everyone, you take your

pleasure and pick up your money anywhere, and you want me to
treat you like a gentleman?'

He stood up, and said with trembling lips: 'Shut up, or I'll throw
you out.'

She stuttered: 'Throw me out... throw me out... You'd throw me
out of here... you... you?'

She could no longer speak, so choked was she with anger, and
suddenly, as though the floodgates of her rage had been breached,
she exploded:

'Throw me out? So you've forgotten that I'm the one who's been
paying for it, this flat, ever since the beginning! Oh, yes, you did take
it on from time to time. But who was it that rented it?... Me... Who
was it that kept it?... Me... And now you want to throw me out of
here... So just shut up, you good-for-nothing! D'you think I don't
know that you robbed Madeleine of half Vaudrec's legacy? D'you
think I don't know that you slept with Suzanne so as to force her to
marry you...'

Seizing her by the shoulders, he was shaking her with both his
hands: 'Don't say a word about her! I forbid you to!'

She cried: 'You slept with her, I know you did.'

He would have tolerated just about anything, but this lie was too
much. The home truths that she had screamed into his face just now
had sent shivers of rage right through him, but this lie about the
young girl who was to be his wife aroused, in the palm of his hand, a
desperate craving to hit Clotilde.

He said again: 'Shut up... be careful... shut up...' And he was
shaking her the way you shake a branch to make the fruit fall off.

Her hair dishevelled, her mouth gaping open, her eyes demented,
she bawled: 'You slept with her...'

Letting go of her, he gave her such a slap in the face that she fell
against the wall. But she turned towards him and, raising herself up
on her wrists, shouted once again: 'You slept with her!'

He threw himself upon her and, holding her beneath him, hit her
as if he were striking a man.

She suddenly fell silent, then began moaning under the blows.
She was no longer moving. She had hidden her face in the corner
between the floor and the wall, and kept uttering plaintive cries.

He stopped hitting her, and stood up. Then, after walking round
the room a bit to regain his equanimity, he had an idea, went into the

bedroom, filled the basin with cold water, and dipped his head into it. Next he washed his hands, and, while carefully drying his fingers, came back to see what she was doing.

She had not moved. She was lying stretched out on the floor, crying quietly.

He asked: 'How much longer are you going to go on snivelling?'

She did not reply. So then he remained standing in the middle of the room, a little embarrassed, a little ashamed, in the presence of this body lying there in front of him.

Abruptly making up his mind, he took his hat from the mantelpiece: 'Goodbye. Give the key to the concierge when you're ready. I'm not going to wait about at your convenience.'

He walked out, closed the door, went into the porter's office and said to him: 'Madame is still here. She'll be leaving soon. Tell the proprietor that I'm giving notice for the 1st of October. Today's the 16th of August, so I'm within my rights.'

And off he went at a great pace, for he had urgent business to complete in connection with the final purchases for the bride's wedding gift.

The wedding was fixed for the 20th of October,* after the start of the new parliamentary session. It was to be solemnized in the Church of the Madeleine. There had been a lot of gossip about it without anyone knowing the precise truth. All sorts of stories were going around. It was rumoured that an abduction had taken place, but nothing was known for certain.

According to the servants, Mme Walter, who no longer spoke to her future son-in-law, had made herself ill with rage the evening this marriage had been decided upon, after having had her daughter taken to a convent, at midnight.

She had been at death's door when she was found. She would certainly never recover her health. She looked like an old woman now; her hair was turning completely grey; and she had thrown herself into religion, taking communion every Sunday.

Early in September, *La Vie française* announced that the Baron Du Roy de Cantel was to be its chief editor, with M. Walter keeping the title of Director. A host of well-known reporters, gossip writers, political correspondents, and art and drama critics, were then appointed, lured away by money from the great newspapers, the powerful, established papers.

Veteran journalists, sober, respectable journalists, no longer shrugged their shoulders when they spoke of *La Vie française*. Its rapid and complete success had wiped out the disdain which serious writers had felt for this newspaper when it began.

The marriage of its chief editor was what you could call a Parisian event, for Georges Du Roy and the Walters had excited considerable curiosity for some time. All those whose names featured in the gossip columns were determined to be present.

This event took place on a bright autumn day.

By eight in the morning, all the workmen of the Madeleine were busy laying a broad red carpet on the steps leading down from the entrance to this church which overlooks the Rue Royale. Their activity brought passers-by to a halt, and proclaimed to the inhabitants of the city that an important ceremony was about to occur.

Clerks on their way to the office, little working girls, delivery boys, all stopped, gazed and thought vaguely about rich people who spent so much money in order to mate.

By about ten, sightseers began to collect. They would stand about for a few moments, hoping that perhaps something would begin immediately, and then leave.

At eleven, some detachments of police arrived, and almost immediately began to move the crowd on, for bystanders were gathering into groups all the time.

Soon the first guests appeared, those who wanted to be well placed so that they could see everything. They took the aisle seats, along the central nave.

Little by little others came, women who moved with a rustling of fabric, a rustling of silk, and stern-looking men, almost all of them bald, who, in that setting, walked with a worldly decorum even more than usually solemn.

The church was slowly filling up. A stream of sunlight, entering through the immense open door, lit up the front rows of guests. In the choir, which was rather dark, the altar, covered in candles, glowed with a yellow light that seemed humble and wan by contrast with the patch of radiance of the great door.

People were spotting one another, and beckoning to one another, and gathering into groups. The literary fraternity, less respectful than the society figures, conversed in audible voices. They were studying the women.

Norbert de Varenne, on the look-out for a friend, caught sight of Jacques Rival near the middle of the rows of chairs, and joined him.

'Well!' he said. 'It's the devil that wins the day!'

The other, who was not envious, replied: 'Good luck to him. He's made for life.' And they began identifying the faces they could see.

Rival enquired: 'Do you know what's become of his wife?'

The poet smiled: 'Yes and no. She's living very quietly, I've been told, in Montmartre. But... and there is a but... for some time I've been reading, in *La Plume*, political articles that are terribly similar to those of Forestier and Du Roy. They're by a Jean Le Dol, a young man, good-looking, intelligent, who's of the same breed as our friend Georges, and who has made the acquaintance of his former wife. From which I've deduced that she likes beginners, and will always like them. Incidentally, she's rich. It wasn't for nothing that Vaudrec and Laroche-Mathieu were regular visitors to the house.'

Rival declared: 'She's not bad, that little Madeleine. Very shrewd, very cunning! Between the sheets, she must be charming. But, tell me, how can Du Roy be getting married in church after being divorced?'

Norbert de Varenne replied: 'He's getting married in church because as far as the church is concerned, he wasn't married, the first time.'

'How so?'

'Our friend Bel-Ami, either out of indifference or out of economy, thought the town hall adequate when he married Madeleine Forestier. He therefore did without an ecclesiastical blessing, which, in the eyes of our Holy Mother the Church, constitutes a simple state of concubinage. As a result, he can present himself to the church today as a bachelor, and she is giving him the benefit of all her ceremonial, which will cost old man Walter a pretty penny.'

Beneath the vaulted roof the noise of the assembled crowd was growing louder. You could hear voices speaking in almost normal tones. Guests were pointing out famous people to one another, individuals who, delighted to be on show, were posing, sedulously preserving their public image, accustomed to displaying themselves at every big social event for which they provided, they believed, essential ornamentation and artistic decoration.

Rival went on: 'You often visit the Director, my dear fellow, so do tell me, is it true that Mme Walter and Du Roy never speak to one another now?'

'Never. She didn't want to give him the girl. But he had a hold over the father, it seems, connected with the Moroccan affair. So he threatened the old boy with dreadful revelations. Walter remembered what had happened to Laroche-Mathieu, and gave in immediately. But the mother, who like all women is stubborn, has sworn never to speak to her son-in-law again. They're damn funny when they're together. She looks like a statue, the statue of Revenge, and he's very ill-at-ease, although he carries it off well, because he knows how to handle himself, if anyone does!'

Colleagues came over to shake them by the hand. Snippets of political talk could be heard. And, muffled like the sound of a distant sea, the rumbling of the crowd gathered in front of the church came in through the door with the sunlight, rising up into the vault, above the more discreet excitement of the select assembly collected inside the temple.

Suddenly, the verger knocked three times on the flagstones with the shaft of his staff. The entire congregation turned round, accompanied by much rustling of skirts and shifting of chairs. And the young woman appeared, on the arm of her father, in the bright light of the portal.

She still looked like a doll, a delicious white doll crowned with orange-blossom.

She stood for a few moments on the threshold, then when she took her first step down the nave, the organ gave a mighty shout, announcing the entrance of the bride with its great metallic voice.

She walked in with bent head, but not timidly: she seemed rather moved, sweet, charming, a miniature bride. Women smiled and murmured as they watched her go by. Men whispered: 'Exquisite, adorable.' M. Walter walked with exaggerated dignity, a little pale, his glasses firmly on his nose.

Behind them, four bridesmaids, all four of them wearing pink and all four of them pretty, were the court attendants to this jewel of a queen. The pages, carefully chosen to look the part, walked at a pace that might have been regulated by a ballet-master.

Mme Walter followed, on the arm of the seventy-two-year-old Marquis de Latour-Yvelin, the father of her other son-in-law. She was not walking, but dragging herself forward, almost fainting each time she took a step. You could sense that her feet were sticking to the flagstones, that her legs were refusing to move on, that her heart was beating in her chest like that of an animal making a dash for freedom.

She had grown thin. Her white hair made her face look even paler and more hollow-cheeked. She gazed straight ahead so as not to see anyone, so as not to think, perhaps, of anything except what was torturing her.

Then Georges Du Roy appeared, with an unknown elderly lady.

Walking with upright head, he too kept his gaze forward, his eyes intent, hard, beneath slightly contracted brows. His moustache flamed on his lip. People thought him a very handsome man. His bearing was proud, his waist slender, his leg straight. He looked well in his coat, on which the tiny red ribbon of the Legion of Honour made a spot like a drop of blood.

The family came next, Rose with Sénateur Rissolin. She had been married for six weeks. The Comte de Latour-Yvelin escorted the Vicomtesse de Percemur.

Finally a bizarre procession of Du Roy's connections or friends appeared, people whom he had introduced to his new family, well-known figures on the fringe of Paris society who instantly become the close friends or, if appropriate, the distant cousins of wealthy upstarts: noblemen who have come down in the world, or lost their money, or have a bad reputation, or sometimes a wife, which is worse. These were M. de Belvigne, the Marquis de Banjolin, the Comte and Comtesse de Ravenel, the Duc de Ramorano, the Prince Kravalow, and the Chevalier Valreali; then came the Walters' guests, the Prince de Guerche, the Duc and Duchesse de Ferracine, the beautiful Marquise des Dunes. Some of Mme Walters' relatives still retained, in the middle of this procession, their air of provincial respectability.

And the organ went on singing, spreading throughout the vast building the throbbing, rhythmical notes of its shining throat, which proclaim to the heavens the joy or suffering of men. The great doors of the entrance were closed again, and suddenly it was dark, as if the sun had been shut out.

Now Georges was kneeling beside his bride in the choir, facing the illuminated altar. The newly appointed bishop of Tangiers,* his crozier in his hand and his mitre on his head, appeared from the sacristy, to unite them in the name of the Lord.

He asked the customary questions, exchanged the rings, pro-
nounced the words that bind like chains, and addressed a Christian
homily to the newly weds. He spoke at length, in pompous language,
of fidelity. He was a heavy man of good stature, one of those
handsome prelates whose belly has majesty.

A sound of sobbing made some heads turn. Mme Walter was
weeping, her face in her hands.

She had had to give in. What could she have done? But since the
day when, upon her daughter's return, Mme Walter had ordered her
out of her bedroom, refusing to embrace her, since the day when she
had said, her voice very low, to Du Roy, in response to his ceremonious greeting when he reappeared before her: 'You are the vilest
creature I know, never speak to me again, for I shall not answer
you!'—ever since then she had been suffering an intolerable and
unbearable torture. She hated Suzanne with a bitter hatred, made up
of exacerbated passion and agonizing jealousy, the strange jealousy
of a mother and a mistress, unacknowledgeable, fierce, burning like
an open wound.

And now a bishop was marrying them, her daughter and her lover,
in a church, in the presence of two thousand people, and in front of
her! And she could say nothing? She could not prevent this? She
could not shout: 'But he's mine, that man, he's my lover. This union
that you are blessing is infamous.'

Several women murmured sympathetically: 'How affected the
poor mother is.'

The bishop was declaiming: 'You are among the blessed of this
earth, among the richest and the most respected. You, Monsieur,
whose talent raises you above others, you who write, and teach, and
advise, you who guide the common people, you have a fine mission to
carry out, a fine example to set...'

Du Roy listened, drunk with pride. A prelate of the Roman Catholic Church was speaking to him like this, to him. And he was
conscious, behind his back, of a crowd, a distinguished crowd that
was here because of him. He felt as if a power was thrusting him
forward, raising him up. He was becoming one of the masters of the
earth, he, the son of two poor peasants of Canteleu.

Suddenly he saw them, in their humble tavern at the top of the
hill, up above the great valley of Rouen, his father and his mother,
serving drinks to the local countryfolk. He had sent them five

thousand francs on receiving the legacy from the Comte de Vaudrec. Now he was going to send them fifty thousand, and they would buy a small property. They would be pleased, happy.

The bishop had completed his homily. A priest dressed in a golden stole climbed up to the altar. And once again the organ began proclaiming the glory of the newly wed couple.

Sometimes it gave long-drawn-out, tremendous shouts that swelled like waves, so resonant and so powerful that it seemed they must raise the roof and shatter it, spreading out into the blue sky. Their vibrant sound filled the whole church, sending shivers through body and soul. Then, abruptly, they quietened; and delicate, sprightly notes ran through the air, brushing the ear like soft breath: charming, slight, frisky little tunes that hopped about like birds; then suddenly this charming little tune was amplified afresh, again inspiring fear with its power and volume, as if a grain of sand was transforming itself into a world.

Next, human voices rose up, passing above the bowed heads. Vauri and Landeck, of the Opéra, were singing. A delicate fragrance of incense was filling the church and, on the altar, the divine sacrifice was being celebrated; the Son of God, at the summons of his priest, was descending to earth to consecrate the triumph of the Baron Georges Du Roy.

Bel-Ami, kneeling at Suzanne's side, had bent his head. At that moment, he felt himself almost a believer, almost religious, full of gratitude for the divinity that had thus blessed him, that was favouring him in this way.

As soon as the service was over, he stood up and, with his wife on his arm, passed into the vestry. Then, in an unending stream, members of the congregation appeared. Wild with joy, Georges felt like a king being acclaimed by his people. He shook people's hands, stammered out meaningless words, bowed, said in response to compliments: 'You're most kind.'

Unexpectedly, he caught sight of Mme de Marelle; and the memory of all the kisses that he had given her, that she had given him in return, the memory of all their caresses, of her charming ways, of the sound of her voice, of the taste of her lips, kindled in his blood a sudden desire to get her back. She was pretty, elegant, with her impish air and bright eyes. Georges thought: 'After all, she really is a delightful mistress!'

She came up, a little diffident, a little uneasy, and offered him her hand. He took it in his, and kept it. Then, he felt the discreet signal of her womanly fingers, the soft pressure of forgiveness and promise. And he gripped it, this tiny hand, as if to say: 'I still love you, I belong to you!'

Their eyes met, smiling, sparkling, full of love. She murmured in her pleasant voice: 'Goodbye for now, Monsieur.'

He replied cheerfully: 'Goodbye for now, Madame.' And she moved away.

Other people were pushing forward. Like a river, the crowd flowed along before him. Eventually, it thinned. The last guests left.

Once more Georges took Suzanne's arm, to go back down through the church. It was full of people, for every one had resumed his or her place, in order to watch them pass by together. He walked slowly, his pace steady, his head held high and his eyes fixed on the great sunlit opening of the door. He could feel faint shivers running over his skin, those cold shivers that come with great happiness. He noticed no one. He was thinking only of himself.

When he reached the threshold, he saw the crowd that had gathered, a dark, buzzing crowd that had gathered there for him, for him, Georges Du Roy. The people of Paris were gazing at him and envying him.

Then, raising his eyes, he saw in the distance, behind the Place de la Concorde, the Chamber of Deputies. And it seemed to him that he was about to make one leap from the portico of the Madeleine, to the portico of the Palais-Bourbon.

He walked slowly down the long flight of steps, between the two rows of spectators. But he did not see them; his thoughts now were of the past, and before his eyes, which were dazzled by the brilliant sunshine, there floated the image of Mme de Marelle in front of the mirror, tidying the little curls on her temples, which were always undone when she got out of bed.

EXPLANATORY NOTES

3 *five-franc piece*: monetary denominations are notoriously difficult to translate into modern values. They make more sense in relative terms. In 1860, for example, the average male wage in Paris was about five francs per day. By 1900 the annual salary of a civil servant was 1,490 francs, which was little better than that of a labourer. Duroy's subsequent calculation here of his daily budget gives an indication of the cost of living during this period.

former NCO: while it covers the same non-commissioned ranks between sergeant and officer cadet, the original French here, *sous-officier*, ironically underlines the contradiction between Duroy's pretentious pose and the subaltern status of one whose ambitions had been to become 'an officer, a colonel or a general' (p. 31).

28th of June: the novel supposedly begins in 1880 (see Introduction, p. ix).

twenty-two sous: the expression has outlived the actual coin, worth five centimes.

boulevard: i.e. the Boulevard des Italiens, so well-known as the hub of metropolitan life that it could be referred to in this abbreviated form (see Introduction, p. xxvii).

Rue Notre-Dame-de-Lorette: in the ninth *arrondissement*, but it is not by chance that Duroy takes this particular street to make his way down from working-class Montmartre to the centre of the city. A *lorette* signified a young woman of easy virtue.

hussars: light cavalry.

cocky air: the original French term here, *chic*, had specific military connotations, derived as it was from the exemplary elegance associated with the contemporary German officer-corps.

4 *sixty-franc outfit*: the French here, a *complet*, included not only a silk-lined cape, trousers, jacket, and satin waistcoat, but also a silk hat. In 1885 a mere thirty-five francs would have bought a top-quality outfit. Duroy goes to extravagant lengths to impress.

the 'ne'er-do-well' of popular novels: exemplified by the work of Georges Ohnet (*Le Maître de forges*, 1882) and Xavier de Montépin (*La Porteuse de pain*, 1884), in whose sentimental fictions the villain likely to seduce the innocent daughter of the house is characterized by a roguish charm.

Madeleine: i.e. the church of the Madeleine (built between 1764 and 1842, facing—down the Rue Royale—the Place de la Concorde) situated at the far end of the boulevard along which Duroy is making his way as he ventures further into the city (see Introduction, p. xxxvi).

5 *L'Américain*: i.e. the fashionable Café Américain, at 4 boulevard des Capucines (across the Place de l'Opéra from the Boulevard des Italiens).

gold and silver: there were gold coins worth 5, 10, 20, 50, and 100 francs; denominations between 20 centimes and 5 francs were silver; small change (1, 2, 5, and 10 centimes pieces) was bronze.

in the South: i.e. in the southern part of Algeria. See Introduction, p. x.

an escapade which had cost three Ouled-Alane tribesmen their lives: real-life incident exploited by Maupassant as the basis for his short story, *Mohammed-Fripouille*, published in *Le Gaulois* on 20 September 1884, while he was writing *Bel-Ami*. The Ouleds were the dominant nomadic tribe of southern Algeria.

6 *the Vaudeville*: i.e. the Théâtre du Vaudeville, reopened in 1869 at the corner of the Rue de la Chaussée d'Antin and the Boulevard des Capucines, specializing in light comedy known, precisely, as *le boulevard*. It closed down in 1925.

7 *Bougival*: hamlet on the Seine (just to the west of Paris), the site of many of Maupassant's boating stories and often pictured by the Impressionists.

La Vie française . . . Le Salut . . . La Planète: see Introduction, p. xi.

a paltry fifteen hundred francs a year: exactly Maupassant's own starting salary, in 1873, when he worked as a a clerk in the Admiralty.

8 *Pellerin riding-school*: there were half a dozen such schools in Paris at the time, none of them of this name. This is a further example of Maupassant's caution in his transposition of identifiable realities; see Introduction, p. xvii.

baccalauréat: secondary education terminal certificate giving those successful the right to pursue university studies; the subsequent ironic reference to the knowledge of Cicero and Tiberius thereby acquired reflects the nineteenth-century reality of the many careers spectacularly made without prior scholarly certification.

Menton: on the French Riviera, near the Italian border. Those Mediterranean climes were already so populated by the elderly and the convalescent that Maupassant elsewhere scathingly refers to it as a paradise for pharmacists ('la Californie des pharmaciens').

9 *Boulevard Poissonnière*: located east of the Boulevard des Italiens. Duroy, having met Forestier, is thus retracing his steps.

10 *thirty thousand francs a year . . . for two articles a week*: precisely Maupassant's own income for the same number of contributions to *Le Gaulois* and the *Gil Blas*.

the Napolitain: i.e. the Café Napolitain, on the Boulevard des Capucines.

11 *louis*: a twenty-franc piece.

Rue Fontaine: in the ninth *arrondissement*, which becomes the Rue Notre-Dame-de-Lorette down which Duroy walked at the beginning of the novel (cf. note to p. 3).

the Bois: i.e. the Bois de Boulogne, the park developed for the specific enjoyment of the leisured classes.

café-concert: place of entertainment where spectators could drink, smoke and walk around during the performance of singers, acrobats and other kinds of popular artists.

Parc Monceau: in the wealthy eighth *arrondissement* and fashionable since the Second Empire (1852–70). It had been purchased by the state in 1852 and subsequently developed as a public space within Haussmann's rebuilding of Paris.

at Musard's: Philippe Musard (1792–1859) had organized public concerts, in the summer evenings, off the Champs-Élysées; in 1860 entry was one franc and ladies had to be accompanied. By the period in which *Bel-Ami* is set, the original establishment had been replaced by *Le Jardin de Paris*, but nostalgic Parisians still spoke of going to 'Musard's'.

the Folies-Bergère: as well as having a magnificent garden, the Théâtre des Folies-Bergère offered an astonishing diversity of entertainment, from trapeze-artists to trick-cyclists. This music-hall was also known, however, as one of the capital's major centres of prostitution. See Introduction, p. xxix.

13 *Italians*: i.e. the Théâtre Italien, once situated near the present-day Opera, and so called because it was sited where troupes of Italian singers and actors had made it their destination from the seventeenth century onwards. It closed in 1878, but there were attempts to reopen it only during the 1883–4 season; so here the novel's chronology is slightly at odds with reality.

14 *Saint-Lazare or Lourcine*: originally for lepers in medieval times, the Saint-Lazare remained a women's prison from the Revolution until 1935, a large section of which was reserved for prostitutes and with a hospital annexe for the treatment of venereal diseases. Located at 97–107 rue du Faubourg Saint-Denis, it was destroyed in 1942. The Lourcine hospital, in the former Rue de Lourcine (now the Rue Broca, in the fifth *arrondissement*, thus explaining why it changed its name to the Hôpital Broca in 1893) was originally for beggars but, since 1836, had also specialized in medical treatment for prostitutes. Both were as well-known as the meaning of a *station hygiénique* there (as the original French puts it).

17 *Third floor*: in nineteenth-century Paris, the higher the floor one lived on, the higher one's social standing.

Louvre: i.e. the Magasin du Louvre, on the Rue de Rivoli, one of the great department-stores of the era, founded in 1855. Shirts were far cheaper there than at a high-class shirtmaker (like the Grande Maison de Blanc in the Boulevard des Capucines), and this is the point being made here.

20 *Midi*: the South of France.

21 *colonization of Algeria*: see Introduction, pp. ix–xi.

22 *Corton or Château Larose*: respectively, a very famous red burgundy from
the commune of Aloxe-Corton in the Côte d'Or and a Saint-Émilion
from the right bank of the valley of the Dordogne.

23 *three provinces*: those of Oran, Algiers, and Constantine.

the Mzab: in the Algerian Sahara, with its main oasis town of Ghardaïa
some 500 km. due south of Algiers. It had ceased to be an autonomous
'little Arab republic' in 1853, the year in which the French occupied
Ghardaïa.

24 *a Johannisberg*: a fine white wine from the Moselle.

25 *Paris Métro*: initiated in 1855, it was only in 1877 that plans were elaborated to bring the encircling lines to a central point within the city. In 1898
the present-day métro became part of the capital's public transport system, with the first line (Porte de Vincennes–Porte Maillot) opening for
the 1900 Universal Exhibition.

omnibuses: forerunners of the modern bus, but of course horse-drawn at
this time.

29 *Rue Boursault*: off the Boulevard des Batignolles, in the distinctly
unfashionable and materially deprived seventeenth *arrondissement*.

immense cutting of the Western Railway: where the lines out of the Gare
Saint-Lazare converge.

tunnel by the Batignolles station: the present-day Pont–Cardinet station, at
the intersection of the Rue de Rome and the Rue Cardinet and adjacent
to the Square des Batignolles. The tunnel used to reach as far as Rue de la
Condamine, before the line was opened to the sky in 1921.

Asnières: then still a village on the left bank of the Seine, now part of the
western suburbs (cf. note to p. 104).

30 *the terrible year*: the original French here, *l'année terrible*, is shorthand
(made familiar by Victor Hugo's 1872 volume of poetry with this title)
for 1870–1, marked by France's catastrophic defeat in the Franco-
Prussian War and by the civil war of the Commune.

31 *to the sea*: the Western Railway (the 'Chemin de fer de l'Ouest') goes from
Paris (via Rouen, 123 km. north-west of the capital) to the port of Le
Havre.

Canteleu: village 6 km. to the west of, and overlooking, Rouen.

33 *Argenteuil, the Sannois hills, and the mills of Orgemont*: a view to the west
only possible because the area beyond the Rue de Rome had not yet been
fully developed during this period.

reached the Parc Monceau: about a kilometre from Duroy's address in the
Rue Boursault (cf. note to *Parc Monceau*, p. 11); Duroy takes the 'outer
boulevard' following the line of the old city wall demolished just prior to
1860 (when the number of *arrondissements* was increased from twelve to
the present twenty).

37 *Doctor Ipecac*: ipecac is the name of a drug which induces vomiting.

38 *Saïda*: some 135 km. south-east of Oran.

esparto factory at Aïn-el-Hadjar: village south of Lake Sebkra (in the province of Oran and over 1,200 km. from the Mediterranean) known for its colonialist (especially Spanish) exploitation of this crop.

40 *a Duval restaurant*: the 'Bouillons Duval', named after their founder (a butcher by trade, 1811–70) were the first example of what we now think of as a restaurant 'chain'. They became popular after his death, developing their menus beyond the original bouillon and beef while remaining cheap and gastronomically mediocre.

41 *cup-and-ball*: a game that was all the rage in 1880s Paris, particularly in newspaper offices (see Introduction, p. xii).

42 *game of écarté*: card-game for two players, so called because each (with the other's agreement) can lay aside (*écarter*) cards and substitute new ones for them.

43 *Budget Commission*: rather like a parliamentary select committee, i.e. a group of deputies charged to scrutinize (in this case) government spending plans.

48 *the Chinese General . . . at the Continental, and the Rajah . . . at the Hotel Bristol*: the two hotels were amongst the finest in the city, the Bristol in the Place Vendôme and the Continental, hardly a stone's throw away, in the Rue de Castiglione; while the names of the personages are invented, since 1881 the French had been negotiating with China in order to reinforce her influence in the Gulf of Tonkin. It has been noted that a certain Rajah of Abusahib Koanderao died on the Normandy coast during the summer of 1884, providing Maupassant with the opportunity to describe the incongruity of an Indian funeral-pyre in his native resort of Étretat (in 'Le Bûcher', *Le Figaro*, 7 September 1884).

49 *Orléanist*: i.e. of the party supporting the branch of the Bourbon monarchy represented by Louis-Philippe, Duc d'Orléans (1773–1850), the last French king (1830–48). During a period marked by the politics of restoring the monarchy, the Orléanists were opposed by the Legitimists who supported the heirs of Charles X, deposed in 1830.

50 *Fervacques*: see Introduction, p. xvii.

51 *gossip column*: better captured by the original French term, the *échos* (on the front page immediately below the leading article) consisted of a column and a half of snippets, and often second-hand at that: rumours and scandal; trivial anecdotes; sightings of prominent figures; political, financial, and literary information; and even items picked up from other newspapers. For the kind of paper exemplified by *La Vie française*, there was no more influential section than this, a measure of its penetration into the social and commercial world of the French capital, and thereby guaranteeing the column's continuing reverberations in Parisian conversations.

self-publicity: a trick of the trade (to which Maupassant was not averse) was to insert within this often anonymously written column an admiring reference to one's own publishing and other activities.

54 *a club*: in the original French, *du cercle*, i.e. (generically) one of the numerous private gambling clubs; of none of which, of course, would Duroy have been a member, given his lack of means and status.

56 *a Château-Margaux from an Argenteuil*: i.e. between one of France's finest vintages (from the Bordeaux wine area) and a local *vin ordinaire*.

58 *Rue de Verneuil*: in the seventh *arrondissement*, in the stolidly upper bourgeoisie Saint-Germain area. Critics of *Bel-Ami* have pointed out that this is an unlikely address for Mme de Marelle, given her character and lifestyle, let alone for 'the inspector in the Northern Railway' (p. 39) to whom she is married.

61 *Café Riche*: at 16 boulevard des Italiens and the corner of the Rue Le Peletier, one of the most famous of contemporary restaurants. Named after its founder in 1847 and surviving until 1916, it had a wine-cellar of 200,000 bottles and a gastronomic reputation to match.

62 *private dining-room*: the so-called *cabinet particulier* was a nineteenth-century institution which provided both the illusion of domesticity and a service so discreet that it was the perfect location (with the appropriate furniture!) for amorous encounters.

70 *'Ah! Bel-Ami!'*: for a discussion of the name 'Bel-Ami', see Introduction, p. xxxv.

72 *an "express"*: a *petit bleu* (in the original French), so-called because of the blue colour of the form on which one copied the message to be telegraphed.

rue de Constantinople: in the eighth *arrondissement*.

73 *Lubin water*: an *eau-de-toilette* popularized by a perfume manufacturer by the name of Lubin.

74 *Père Lathuile's*: high-profile restaurant (founded 1793) on the Boulevard de Clichy, immortalized in Manet's 1879 painting, *Chez le Père Lathuile* (Tournai, Musée des Beaux-Arts).

75 *bare-headed girls*: not to wear a hat was contemporarily synonymous with lower-class.

the Café Anglais: one of the finest restaurants in Paris, at 13 boulevard des Italiens, almost opposite the Café Riche (cf. note to p. 61).

La Reine Blanche: the Bal de la Reine-Blanche, famous since the Romantic period and until its demise in 1889, was on the Boulevard de Clichy on the site of the present-day Moulin-Rouge. Such dance halls were notorious for the vulgarity of their entertainment and clientele.

77 *rhinestones*: i.e. crystal of various colours, used for costume jewellery.

79 *Luxembourg*: i.e. the Luxembourg Gardens, suitably embellished in 1867 to make it a fashionable place for an evening stroll.

86 *Batignolles*: the emphasis implies the base origins from which he comes (cf. note to *Rue Boursault*, p. 29).

91 *Boulevard Malesherbes*: opened in 1840, this wide avenue traversing the wealthy eighth *arrondissement* was soon lined with the great homes of the newly rich.

92 *the Moroccan question . . . the war in the East . . . problems England was encountering in the southernmost tip of Africa*: these references speak of a somewhat muddled chronology. While the 'Tunisian question' has to be substituted for the first of these (see Introduction, pp. ix–xi), the novel's own time-scale situates this conversation before 1881 when Italy began to challenge French sovereignty there. The 'war' in the East barely fits the localized uprisings (and Franco-British diplomatic protests) in Egypt at the end of 1881; it is more likely that it refers to the conflict with China in 1884 (i.e. at the very moment Maupassant was writing *Bel-Ami*). The final reference to England can only relate to events leading to the Boer War at the end of 1881.

Academy: i.e. the Académie Française, established in 1795 and with a membership of forty as the self-appointed electoral college to fill vacancies as they arise. The names of the candidates mentioned here are both inventions; the second is hardly innocent, given the meaning of *cabanon* as a hut in which madmen were incarcerated, and *le bas* signifying his unworthiness. Maupassant was never less than scathing about the institution itself, as is also evident from the subsequent demystification of the so-called 'Immortals' in Duroy's allusion to the 'game of death and the forty old men' (p. 93).

Don Quixote: such a verse adaptation of Cervantes's novel (1605) is almost certainly another authorial invention on Maupassant's part, intended to underline the 'quixotic' criteria determining the preferences of the Academy.

the Odéon: i.e. the Théâtre de l'Odéon, one of the capital's most traditional theatres; founded in 1797, rebuilt and re-established in 1819, and ultimately annexed by the venerable Comédie-Française in 1946.

93 *Lope de Vega*: Spanish dramatist (1562–1635).

94 *head of the gossip column*: (cf. note to *gossip column*, p. 51). To be appointed 'chef des Échos' was to take responsibility for the paper's topical interface with its Parisian public and therefore puts Duroy in a key social and political position.

96 *'Domino Rose' and 'Patte Blanche'*: virtually untranslatable; the half-mask worn at a masquerade to conceal the wearer's identity is obviously appropriate for a pseudonym; the 'white glove', on the other hand, suggests a *passe-partout* ability to open any door.

97 *Antilles*: the Caribbean.

Rue de Londres: crossing the dividing-line of the eighth and ninth *arrondissements*, just north of the Gare Saint-Lazare, which would take Duroy from work back towards his lodgings in the Rue Boursault.

99   *M. Laroche-Mathieu*: there has been speculation that this figure is based
on the real-life deputy, Laroche-Joubert (1820–83), famous for his political *volte-faces*. (see Introduction, p. xviii). But he may also be partly
modelled on Léon Renault (born 1839), the deputy for Grasse from 1882
and head of the centre-left grouping in the Assemblée Nationale.

landscapes: by, successively, Antoine Guillemet (1842–1918), Henri Harpignies (1819–1916), Gustave Guillaumet (1840–87). None of the details
of the individual paintings are sufficiently precise to allow one to identify
them.

100   *Major paintings*: what is called (in the original French, and following the
classic taxonomy) *la grande peinture*. Henri Gervex (1852–1929) was a
close friend of Maupassant's; the picture mentioned here at least evokes
his *L'Autopsie à l'Hôtel-Dieu* (1876) (now lost, but reproduced in the
Catalogue of the 1992–3 Gervex retrospective, p. 98), but also his *Le
Bureau de bienfaisance* (1883) which incongruously decorates the 'salle
des mariages' in the Mairie of the nineteenth *arrondissement*. Jules
Bastien-Lepage (1848–84) was once famous for his paintings of rural life.
William-Adolphe Bouguereau (1825–1905), now often dismissed as a
mere 'academic painter', had an exceptionally successful career: his work
was so avidly collected in America that attempts, in 1878, to assemble an
exhibition in France were abandoned; he commanded high prices from
the moment he distinguished himself in the 1848 Prix de Rome; and the
widely known huge cost of a Bouguereau added greatly to the prestige of
the purchaser. Jean-Paul Laurens (1838–1921) was much admired as a
history painter, though the picture described here is not identifiable.

Vendée: appropriately, given the long counter-revolutionary history of
this area of western France (in the Loire-Inférieure and Maine-et-Loire);
between 1793 and 1799–1800 half a million of its inhabitants were killed
resisting 'the French Republican Army'.

lighter works: in the original French, *les fantaisistes*. Jean Béraud (1849–
1936), much liked by Maupassant himself, was one of the foremost painters of Parisian life, specializing in street-scenes. Eugène Lambert (1825–
1900) was nicknamed 'Lambert des chats', so often did he paint them.
Édouard Detaille (1848–1912) made his reputation by depicting scenes
from the Franco-Prussian War. The anecdotal scene here bears no
resemblance to his epic and history paintings. Maurice Leloir (1853–
1940) was another friend of Maupassant's, but was principally an illustra-
tor and stage-designer; he is probably being confused here with his
brother, Louis (1843–84), known for his watercolours.

101   *Salon Carré*: it was in this room in the Louvre, otherwise known as the
Grand Salon, that an annual art exhibition (thus called the Salon) was
held between 1725 and 1848. In 1852 it was reorganized, on the model of
the Tribune in the Uffizi, in order to accommodate the most prestigious
works in the Louvre's collections.

102   *Vicomtesse de Percemur*: probably based on Jeanne-Thilda (on the staff of

the *Gil Blas*), and on 'Daniel Darc', the pseudonym of another such journalist, Marie Serrur.

104 *the Seine at Asnières*: it was here that the sewers of the capital emptied their contents. The river was so polluted at this point that the many Impressionist pictures of it are as deceptive as the subsequent evocation of it, in *Bel-Ami* itself (p. 156), described as 'thronged with boats, anglers, and people rowing'.

107 *Palais-Bourbon*: housing the National Assembly, i.e. the French parliament, immediately across the river from the Place de la Concorde.

Rue de Bourgogne: just behind the National Assembly, in the seventh *arrondissement*.

113 *La Plume*: see Introduction, p. xvii.

Duroy enjoys himself: the original French here is *Duroy s'amuse*, quite possibly a wickedly topical reference to Paul Bonnetain's notorious novel about onanism (*Charlot s'amuse*), published in 1883, the year before Maupassant started writing *Bel-Ami*. The other title Maupassant mischievously evokes here is that of Victor Hugo's 1832 play, *Le Roi s'amuse*.

118 *Bois du Vésinet*: Le Vésinet is just to the west of Paris, in the bend of the Seine.

123 *Gastine Renette*: famous gun-maker with a shooting range on the Allée d'Antin (which is now the Avenue Franklin-Roosevelt), frequented by Maupassant himself.

130 *from Le Cannet to Golfe Juan*: to the north-east of Cannes.

132 *the Îles de Lérins*: the Île Sainte-Marguerite and the smaller Île Saint-Honorat, the former barely 1 km. offshore.

the Esterel: i.e. the Massif de L'Esterel, the range of hills south-west of Cannes towards Saint-Raphael, culminating in Mont Vinaigre (618 m.). Given the latter's distance from the sea, the 'pyramid-shaped mountain' in question here is probably the Pic de l'Ours.

133 *Le Voltaire*: see Introduction, p. xvii.

136 *Comte de Paris*: still, today, the title assumed by the pretender to the French throne. The very rich Orléanist descendant referred to here, born in 1838, had been allowed back into France in 1872, claiming the title of Philippe VII from 1883 until his death in 1894.

Bazaine: Marshal Achille Bazaine (1811–88) had commanded the army of the Lorraine during the Franco-Prussian War. His surrender at Metz, with 170,000 officers and men, had been such a military catastrophe that in 1873 he was condemned to death before the sentence was commuted to twenty years' imprisonment. But he managed to escape from the Île Sainte-Marguerite, spending the rest of his life in Madrid.

Le Colbert' . . . *'La Dévastation*: a mixture of real and imaginary names. See Introduction, p. xviii.

151 *May the 10th, which is a Saturday*: it has been pointed out that this was

only the case in 1879. The chronology of the novel places Duroy's marriage in May 1882, Forestier having died the previous spring.

156 *fortifications*: built 1840–4, creating a new fortified boundary just outside the line of the present-day *boulevard périphérique*; beyond it was a (military) zone on which no building was officially allowed.

157 *Chatou*: another of Maupassant's riverside haunts, 2 km. to the east of Le Vésinet (see note to p. 118).

forest of Saint-Germain: filling the curve of the Seine north of Saint-Germain-en-Laye, some 20 km. west of Paris.

158 *Poissy*: 5 km. north-west of Saint-Germain-en-Laye.

160 *Mantes*: i.e. Mantes-la-Jolie, approx. 60 km. north-west of Paris; from there to Rouen, the railway more or less follows the Seine.

163 *Cheops pyramid*: the Great Pyramid of Cheops (built in 2600 BC) is nearly 140 m. high. A 51m. fretted ironwork spire (described here as 'ugly' by the same Maupassant who would later develop a particularly ferocious loathing for the Eiffel Tower) was added to Rouen cathedral in the nineteenth century, thereby doubling its height.

La Foudre: literally 'The Thunderbolt'. This was a powerful steam-engine supplying Rouen with water, with a 136m. high chimney. The reference to the 'smoky horde of factories' reminds us that Rouen was France's fifth largest city in the nineteenth century, and a major industrial centre (notably for ship-building and metallurgy). Most of this Saint-Sever sector, on the south side (i.e. the left bank) of the Seine, was destroyed during the Second World War.

165 *Paul and Virginie*: the idealized young lovers in Bernadin de Saint-Pierre's classic novel, *Paul et Virginie* (1787). Both its subject and its exotic location (Mauritius) form an ironic contrast to the setting and context of this scene.

Napoleon I on a yellow horse: yellow because of the faded image itself; as for the evocation of a heroic national past, such imperial nostalgia was often prevalent in conservative rural France.

167 *Saint-Denis*: formerly a village just outside Paris, now part of its northern suburbs.

raspail: a liqueur, popular at the time, invented by François-Vincent Raspail (1794–1878) who combined a career in chemistry and revolutionary politics.

168 *one of the biggest in France*: the forest of Roumare, in the bend of the Seine west of Rouen. The *Michelin Guide* proposes a 36-km. and two-hour round trip by car.

175 *SGDG*: it has been suggested that this acronym stands for 'Sans Garantie Du Gouvernement' (i.e. no government liability). A possibly wittier alternative is the 'Syndicat Général de la Direction Générale' (i.e. the management union).

179 *Sèvres*: across the river, south of the Bois de Boulogne.

   that word: i.e. *forestier*, the French for 'forester'.

182 *Tortoni's*: famous café at the corner of the Boulevard des Italiens (no. 22) and the Rue Taitbout. Established by Velloni at the very end of the eighteenth century, it had been taken over by another Italian who gave it his name. As early as 1840 it was known for its ices (more like sorbet than ice-cream) and remained fashionable in spite of its humble décor. It was one of Flaubert's favourite haunts. It closed down in 1894.

187 *Watteau*: the painter Antoine Watteau (1684–1721), whose *fêtes galantes* and *fêtes champêtres* are filled with young women of porcelain beauty.

188 *senators . . . deputies*: the names appear to have been invented by Maupassant who almost certainly enjoyed doing so, given the punning possibilities contained in them ('Remontel' has sexual connotations, 'Rissolin' culinary ones, etc.).

190 *names*: also probably invented (see previous note). At one point in his drafting, Maupassant called Crèvecœur 'Percecote', as appropriate a name for a man with a rapier as Carvin.

199 *Holy Trinity*: the Église de la Trinité, in the ninth *arrondissement*; and situated on what is later called the 'vast square and all the streets that run into it' (p. 208), i.e. the Place d'Estienne-d'Orve (so named in 1860 but incorrectly called in the novel (p. 201) the '*Place* de la Trinité', though the church does open out onto a small terrace—with the fountain to which Maupassant refers—which has always been known as the 'Square de la Trinité'). It should be noted that, in having her choose this particular rendezvous (Maupassant had orginally planned for it to be at the church of Saint-Augustin, at the end of her street), Mme Walter goes a symbolically considerable distance away from her own conjugal home and towards Duroy's stamping ground. This had been precisely his strategy: 'first at a place she would choose, then, later, somewhere he chose'

207 *twenty years ago, or twenty-five*: it was completed, in fact, in November 1867, fifteen years before. 'All its details' included decorations for which a number of Maupassant's artist friends had been responsible. In drawing attention to this church, the novel mimes the advertising mechanisms of the *échos* (see notes to p. 51).

   Rennes: in Brittany.

208 *Some very important things are going on*: the whole of this paragraph more or less transposes events leading to the downfall of Jules Ferry's government over the Tunisian crisis. See Introduction, pp. ix–xi.

209 *Figuig*: in the Moroccan Sahara, on the border with Algeria.

213 *two Chambers*: the Chamber of Deputies and the Senate.

   Comte de Lambert-Sarrazin: the speech of this imagined figure bears more than a passing resemblance to the one by the Duc de Broglie (1821–1901) in the same summer of 1882 as in the novel.

213 *President of the Council*: the official term for the head of the government, the equivalent of prime minister. The 'side-whiskers' in question belong to Jules Ferry. See Introduction, p. ix.

214 *General Belloncle*: the model for this figure is General Saussier, sent to command French troops in Tunisia on 10 October 1881.

218 *tears of Dido, not of Juliet*: the contrast here is between the way these two tragic heroines gave themselves tearfully to their lovers: Dido (in Virgil's *Aeneid*) because she did not want to be unfaithful to the memory of her dead husband; Juliet because Romeo had killed her cousin and was about to go into exile.

220 *Maisons*: i.e. Maisons-Lafitte, another riverside hamlet (north of Saint-Germain-en-Laye).

223 *fallen to sixty-four or sixty-five francs*: the scam is based on fact: in 1879, the value of these bonds had fallen to 203 francs; by 1884 thay had shot up to 506 francs.

   Rothschilds: at the time, the most powerful of all the Jewish banking families in France, collectively known as the 'Haute Banque'. The phenomenally rapid rise of Alphonse de Rothschild (1827–1905) resulted from the enormous profits his extended family made from state loans after the battle of Waterloo.

228 *Rue Drouot . . . Chaussée d'Antin*: Duroy is in the ninth *arrondissement*. The Rue Drouot is only two blocks from the offices of *La Vie française* (on the Boulevard Poissonnière). By turning left up it, he can get back up the Rue Notre-Dame-de-Lorette to his marital address in the Rue Fontaine. To reach the Rue de la Chaussée d'Antin, he has to retrace his steps along the Boulevard Montmartre.

232 *rue des Vosges*: now part of the Rue des Amiraux, in the heart of the working-class eighteenth *arrondissement*, and a somewhat unlikely address for the Comte de Vaudrec's lawyer.

234 *consent*: French law at the time held women to be 'legally incapable', thus requiring the agreement of their closest male relative in order to inherit.

241 *Rue du Faubourg-Saint-Honoré*: the premier Parisian address, instantly recognizable as a marker of wealth and power.

   a vast canvas by the Hungarian painter Karl Marcowitch: identifiable as Mihály Munkácsy (1844–1900), living in France since 1870 and best known for his religious and history paintings. The picture in question evokes his gigantic *Christ devant Pilate*, rejected by the Salon but put on show in June 1881 at the Hôtel Sedelmeyer, 6 rue La Rochefoucauld. It was sold to an American collector in 1887 for a price rumoured to be between 150,000 and 600,000 francs.

   Jacques Lenoble: revealingly, Maupassant first wrote here 'Jacques Legrand', too easily identifiable as (an inversion of) Georges Petit who owned a gallery at 8 rue de Sèze where he promoted modern painting. Petit is himself referred to on p. 243.

242 *electric light*: invented as recently as 1880 and thus a sign of luxury.

   Jockey Club: the most élitist of the Parisian gambling-clubs, founded in 1833 (cf. note to p. 54), and situated during this period at the corner of the Boulevard des Capucines and the Rue Scribe.

245 *famous people*: more authorial inventions.

255 *L'Officiel*: i.e. the *Journal Officiel*, the government newspaper in which honours and awards were gazetted.

261 *Rue des Martyrs*: also in the ninth *arrondissement*, not very far from the Duroys' own address.

266 *immune from the law*: a privilege enjoyed by deputies since 1875, *except* in cases of *in flagrante delicto*.

268 *divorce*: not in fact restored until the 1884 Loi Naquet. This scene in the novel takes place in 1883, at a time when the whole question of divorce was a matter of vigorous public debate.

269 *Trouville*: popular summer resort on the Normandy coast.

   Saint-Germain: i.e. Saint-Germain-en-Laye.

   Mont-Valérien: fortress on the western outskirts of the capital, just across the river from the Bois de Boulogne.

   Le Pecq: at that time still a village, on the river itself, just outside Saint-Germain-en-Laye.

270 *Marly*: i.e. Marly-le-Roi, due south from where they stand.

   Sartrouville: across the Seine (i.e. on the right bank) towards Argenteuil.

280 *La Roche-Guyon*, east of Vernon which is some 80 km. from Paris.

283 *20th of October*: of 1883. The novel thus lasts just over three years (cf. note to *28th of June*, p. 3).

287 *bishop of Tangiers*: the final transposition of the Moroccan affair (see Introduction, p. ix–xi). The establishment of the Tunisian protectorate had resulted in the creation of an archdiocese of Carthage under the aegis of Algiers under Cardinal Lavigerie (1825–92). There were also bishops of Oran and Constantine, such spiritual direction being inseparable from colonial domination. Lavigerie himself moved to Tunisia and built a cathedral on the site of the citadel of Carthage. His order of White Fathers effectively extended French influence throughout central Africa.

JANE AUSTEN

Catharine and Other Writings
Emma
Mansfield Park
Northanger Abbey, Lady Susan, The
   Watsons, and Sanditon
Persuasion
Pride and Prejudice
Sense and Sensibility

ANNE BRONTË

Agnes Grey
The Tenant of Wildfell Hall

CHARLOTTE BRONTË

Jane Eyre
The Professor
Shirley
Villette

EMILY BRONTË

Wuthering Heights

WILKIE COLLINS

The Moonstone
No Name
The Woman in White

CHARLES DARWIN

The Origin of Species

CHARLES DICKENS

The Adventures of Oliver Twist
Bleak House
David Copperfield
Great Expectations
Hard Times
Little Dorrit
Martin Chuzzlewit
Nicholas Nickleby
The Old Curiosity Shop
Our Mutual Friend
The Pickwick Papers
A Tale of Two Cities

GEORGE ELIOT	Adam Bede
	Daniel Deronda
	Middlemarch
	The Mill on the Floss
	Silas Marner
ELIZABETH GASKELL	Cranford
	The Life of Charlotte Brontë
	Mary Barton
	North and South
	Wives and Daughters
THOMAS HARDY	Far from the Madding Crowd
	Jude the Obscure
	The Mayor of Casterbridge
	A Pair of Blue Eyes
	The Return of the Native
	Tess of the d'Urbervilles
	The Woodlanders
WALTER SCOTT	Ivanhoe
	Rob Roy
	Waverley
MARY SHELLEY	Frankenstein
	The Last Man
ROBERT LOUIS STEVENSON	Kidnapped and Catriona
	The Strange Case of Dr Jekyll and Mr Hyde and Weir of Hermiston
	Treasure Island
BRAM STOKER	Dracula
WILLIAM MAKEPEACE THACKERAY	Barry Lyndon
	Vanity Fair
OSCAR WILDE	Complete Shorter Fiction
	The Picture of Dorian Gray

The Oxford World's Classics Website

www.worldsclassics.co.uk

- Information about new titles
- Explore the full range of Oxford World's Classics
- Links to other literary sites and the main OUP webpage
- Imaginative competitions, with bookish prizes
- Peruse *Compass*, the Oxford World's Classics magazine
- Articles by editors
- Extracts from Introductions
- A forum for discussion and feedback on the series
- Special information for teachers and lecturers

www.worldsclassics.co.uk

American Literature

British and Irish Literature

Children's Literature

Classics and Ancient Literature

Colonial Literature

Eastern Literature

European Literature

History

Medieval Literature

Oxford English Drama

Poetry

Philosophy

Politics

Religion

The Oxford Shakespeare

A complete list of Oxford Paperbacks, including Oxford World's Classics, OPUS, Past Masters, Oxford Authors, Oxford Shakespeare, Oxford Drama, and Oxford Paperback Reference, is available in the UK from the Academic Division Publicity Department, Oxford University Press, Great Clarendon Street, Oxford OX2 6DP.

In the USA, complete lists are available from the Paperbacks Marketing Manager, Oxford University Press, 198 Madison Avenue, New York, NY 10016.

Oxford Paperbacks are available from all good bookshops. In case of difficulty, customers in the UK can order direct from Oxford University Press Bookshop, Freepost, 116 High Street, Oxford OX1 4BR, enclosing full payment. Please add 10 per cent of published price for postage and packing.